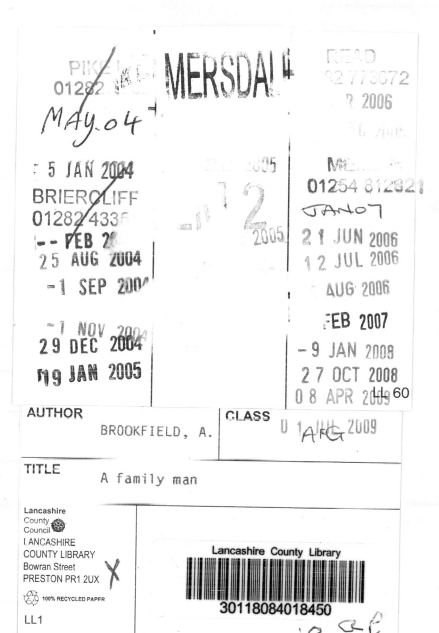

PIKE
01282

MAY.04

5 JAN 2004
BRIERCLIFF
01282 4335

-- FEB 2

25 AUG 2004
-1 SEP 200

-1 NOV 200
29 DEC 2004
19 JAN 2005

MERSDAL

2005

2

2005

READ
92 773072
R 2006

ME
01254 812821
JAN 07
2 1 JUN 2006
1 2 JUL 2006
AUG 2006
FEB 2007
-9 JAN 2008
27 OCT 2008
08 APR 2009 LL 60

U 1 JUL 2009

AUTHOR	CLASS
BROOKFIELD, A.	AFG

TITLE	
	A family man

Lancashire
County
Council
LANCASHIRE
COUNTY LIBRARY
Bowran Street
PRESTON PR1 2UX

100% RECYCLED PAPER

LL1

Lancashire County Library

30118084018450

LL1

D0410956

A FAMILY MAN

Also by Amanda Brookfield

ALICE ALONE

A CAST OF SMILES

WALLS OF GLASS

A SUMMER AFFAIR

THE GODMOTHER

MARRIAGE GAMES

SINGLE LIVES

THE LOVER

A FAMILY MAN

Amanda Brookfield

Hodder & Stoughton

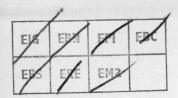

08401845

Copyright © 2001 by Amanda Brookfield

First published in Great Britain in 2001
by Hodder and Stoughton
A division of Hodder Headline

The right of Amanda Brookfield to be identified as the Author of
the Work has been asserted by her in accordance with the
Copyright, Designs and Patents Act 1988.

10 9 8 7 6 5 4 3 2 1

All right reserved. No part of this publication may be
reproduced, stored in a retrieval system, or transmitted,
in any form or by any means without the prior written
permission of the publisher, nor be otherwise circulated
in any form of binding or cover other than that in which
it is published and without a similar condition being
imposed on the subsequent purchaser.

All characters in this publication are fictitious
and any resemblance to real persons, living or dead
is purely coincidental.

A CIP catalogue record for this title
is available from the British Library

ISBN 0 340 77009 0

Typeset by Hewer Text Ltd, Edinburgh
Printed and bound in Great Britain by
Mackays of Chatham plc, Chatham, Kent

Hodder and Stoughton
A division of Hodder Headline
338 Euston Road
London NW1 3BH

For John and Sue

Chapter One

Released from the nose-to-tail traffic which had persisted since the Isle of Dogs, the taxi accelerated noisily across Tower Bridge. Matt sank farther into the beaten leather seat, tightening his grip round the edges of his briefcase. Although it was only 2.30, the afternoon had already been sucked of light, surrendering to the drabness of a January dusk. Through the smeary window there was nothing to see but a canvas of greys, an almost seamless sweep embracing the band of river water, city buildings and the thick umbrella of cloud overhead. Against such a backdrop, the huge steely wings of the bridge looked faintly unreal, like cardboard cut-outs stuck on for dramatic effect.

Glancing at his watch, Matt swore quietly. 'It's quicker if you cut left at these lights,' he called, sliding his briefcase on to the seat beside him and leaning forward with both elbows pressed to his knees.

The taxi turned off the Kennington Road with a lurch, flinging its passenger sideways and causing the briefcase to shoot on to the floor.

'Just here will do fine,' said Matt a minute later, judging from the traffic that it would be quicker to walk the last few hundred yards. He handed over seventeen pounds, tapping his fingers impatiently while the driver wrote out a receipt. By the time he turned down the cul-de-sac that housed the red-bricked horror of a Gothic church in which his son attended nursery school, it was spitting with rain.

On the church steps, next to the billboard saying, 'Bright Sparks Montessori', a couple of mothers were chatting while their children played tag on the steps. Relieved not to have missed the collection process entirely, Matt increased his stride to a trot, the tails of his long dark overcoat flapping round his shins. Joshua was standing in the doorway, his hand slotted firmly in that of the school's head teacher, Miss Harris. She was talking earnestly to a woman with a baby in a sling, her billowing flowery skirt exposing thick tights and wide knees. Joshua's new blue anorak was buttoned up to his chin, its too-large hood pulled so thoroughly over his head that all Matt could make out of his face was the lower part of his nose and his mouth.

'Josh,' Matt called, all his irritation at having the Friday school pick-up so suddenly thrust upon him dissolving at the sight of his four-year-old son, so small beside the wide woman and the vast spires of the church looming behind. 'Josh,' he called again, more urgently, feeling a knot at the back of his throat at the realisation that the brown eyes peering from under the blue hood were looking for Kath and had yet made no connection to the man in the overcoat jogging towards the church gates.

Miss Harris spotted him first. 'Ah, Mr Webster, here we are at last.'

'Sorry I'm late.' Matt bent to scoop Josh and a creation of egg-box and yoghurt cartons into his arms. 'And how are you, young man?'

'I made a ship.'

'A ship? Marvellous.'

'Where's Mummy?'

'At the supermarket, I think. She asked me to get you for once. Let's go.'

'Oh, and Mr Webster' . . . Miss Harris had almost closed the door when her ruddy-cheeked face appeared back round the side of it. 'The parents meeting is now at eleven next Friday, not ten, as I told Mrs Webster. I hope that's still convenient.'

'Oh, I'm sure it is – I'll tell Kath.' Having got to the bottom of the steps, Matt set Joshua down on the ground.

'Come on, then.' He held out his hand.

'Where's the car?'

'It's at home, or maybe with Mummy. So Daddy and Josh have to walk.'

'Car,' Josh wailed, hurling the word from the back of his throat with all the volume and energy which had made parenthood – the first twelve months in particular – enough of an ordeal for neither Matt nor Kath yet to feel tempted to repeat the experience. 'Want Mummy,' he sobbed. With theatrically perfect timing the specking rain chose that moment not only to transform itself into fat wet dollops, but also to adjust the angle of its fall from a gentle vertical trickle to a slanting barrage of what felt like vindictive ferocity.

Matt opened his mouth to say 'Fucking hell' only to remember that his son had reached an age where mimicry of adults was a prime pastime. 'Come on, let's run,' he suggested instead, squatting in as friendly a manner as he could manage, given the inclemency of the weather, his rising ill temper and the already visibly drooping egg-boxes in his arms. 'Please, Josh,' he begged, inwardly cursing Kath for the unprecedented act of commanding him south of the river on a Friday afternoon, when he had planned to catch up on his paperwork and go straight to the theatre from the office.

The child paused, merely, as it turned out, to summon extra breath before raising the pitch of his protest to new heights. Matt cast an anxious glance up at the church, fearful that Miss Harris or one of her band of pretty young assistants might be judging this spectacle of failing parental control through a slit in the door.

'Now calm down,' he commanded, exasperation making it impossible to sound calm himself. 'Okay, then, Dad will run.' He crammed the artwork into his briefcase, hoiked his son back up into his arms and set off at a gallop for home, gritting his teeth against the awkwardness of his load. Only at the sight of their three-bedroomed terraced home, set in the middle of a long line of Georgian houses in various states of repair and dilapidation, did Matt slow his pace. By which time his eyes were so full of rain he could hardly see and Joshua was jigging round his hips with all the glee of a jockey approaching a finishing post.

'There now, not so bad, was it?' Breathing heavily, Matt leaned against the door to recover while Joshua shouted through the letterbox. When there was no response, Matt found his own keys and let them in.

Given their dripping state, it seemed a reasonable idea to have a bath. Josh, used to having to wait until after tea for this most precious time of day, was so excited at the news that he rushed upstairs still in his coat and muddy shoes. Dropping his keys on to the hall table, Matt slung his coat over one of the two laden pegs wedged behind the door, frowning absently at the amount of clobber apparently required by a family of three. He felt a familiar stab of longing for the early echo of emptiness when he and Kath had moved in five years before, when their possessions were too few to fill every room, when the paint smelt fresh and the stripped floorboards gleamed with varnish. Coming from a cramped flat in Shepherd's Bush, the Kennington house had felt huge, full of possibilities, a wonderful blank sheet waiting to have its identity splashed upon it. That such an identity was to include a child had come as something of a surprise. Only four months after moving in, Kath, who hadn't had periods since an anorexic phase in her teens, and who had feared that recent bouts of exhaustion and nausea might be heralding the onset of ME, discovered instead that she was twelve weeks pregnant. The clutter had started then, with the investment in Moses baskets, breast pumps and prams – a mere taster for the paraphernalia of toddlerhood and all the more sophisticated gadgets of the fully mobile child. Matt had waved gleeful farewells at stair gates and baby walkers only to find them replaced by trikes, trucks and large items of plastic weaponry.

Finding nothing of interest among the morning's post, Matt dropped the envelopes back on to the hall table next to a vase of weary-looking flowers. He stretched and yawned deeply, running both hands back through his wet hair. Momentarily forgetting his excursion to the barber's that morning, he was surprised to feel how little there was to get hold of, and stooped to reassure himself of his appearance in the hall mirror. Kath would like it, he was sure. She had a thing about short hair on men, particularly men with slightly receding hairlines and not as much to boast about on top as they would have liked. It made him look older, but more sophisticated too, more modern even, he decided, flexing his eyebrows and noting with mild surprise that the brightness of his eyes betrayed none of the exhaustion he felt inside. Before turning away, he cast a scowl of dissatisfaction at the rest of his reflection, thinking, as he always did, that being in proportion was at least some consolation for never having quite reached the magic milestone of six foot. Kath in heels was easily as tall as him. But then Kath was a particularly tall lady, eyes level with his chin even in her bare feet.

Upstairs, promising tap noises had been superseded by an ominous silence. Arriving out of breath at the bathroom door, Matt was relieved to find his son neither imperilled nor visibly wetter than before, but sitting on the white-tiled bathroom floor tugging crossly at the zipper on his coat. Next to him the bath was full but by no means overflowing.

'Good boy, well done.' Matt knelt down and tried to intervene with the zip, which had caught a wedge of material in its teeth.

'Josh do it.'

'But Daddy can—'

'Josh do it.'

'Fine. Josh do it.' Matt sighed and began peeling off his own clothes, dropping them into a heap behind the door and then crossing to the loo to pee.

'Daddy's willy,' remarked his son, pointing.

'Yes, which, like Daddy, is getting in the bath. But not Josh because he won't let Daddy help with his clothes.' Seeing this observation induce a distinct tremble in the lower lip, Matt executed a comical jumping entry into the water by way of encouragement and diversion. A moment later he was back out again, skidding on the wet tiles and emitting a string of unfatherly profanities. Joshua, who assumed such eccentric behaviour to be all part of the afternoon's entertainment, clapped in appreciation.

'It's cold, Josh . . . cold . . . bloody icy . . . bloody hell.'

'Mummy says only touch the green one.'

'Yes, well . . . quite right. Mummy is quite right, of course.' Matt put the toilet seat down and sat with a towel round his shoulders, gloomily contemplating the mercurial challenge of seeing to the needs of a small child. Tiny slugs of mud had worked their way out of the ridges in the soles of Joshua's desert boots, converting the white-tiled floor to a sea of smeary brown. Having successfully removed the anorak, his son was grappling with the double knots on his shoes, his breathing heavy with concentration. Taking in the scene, Matt felt a rush of longing for Kath, for her power to impose domestic order, for permission to be released back into the infinitely more manageable world of his career. His appointment that evening was with Noël Coward's *Private Lives*, a star-studded revival which promised to be as pleasurable to watch as it would be to write about. The theatre's press representative, an American called Beth Durant, had agreed to meet him in the bar before the start with a view to discussing a feature interview with the actress playing the part of Amanda. If it came off it would be Matt's first brush with true celebrity, a real feather in the cap, both for the paper and his own career. The actress, a twenty-eight-year-old RADA-trained Hollywood success story called Andrea Beauchamp, was blessed not only with considerable talent but also with the kind of private life to set the heart of any journalist ticking with expectation.

Seeing Joshua now beginning to sob with impatience over his footwear, Matt dangled his wristwatch – a much-prized toy – by way of a diversionary peace offering. 'You do this, Dad does your clothes, okay? And we'll have bubbles,' he added, turning the hot tap on full and tipping in several capfuls of the green slimy substance in which Kath liked to soak herself.

Half an hour later Matt took some satisfaction in propping a somewhat perfumed but pleasingly spruce child among the sofa cushions, together with a bag of crisps and the console for the video. Joshua pounced on it with his usual dexterity, eighteen months of nursery school having done little to encourage similar proficiency with anything in a pencil case. Particularly favoured was the rewind button, used to watch favourite scenes, sometimes four or five times on the trot. While mildly disturbed by the habit, Kath and Matt had long since given up trying to put a stop to it, not only to avoid tantrums, but because it converted a measly twenty-minute cartoon into an entertainment of feature-length proportions.

Upstairs Matt made a desultory attempt to clean up the mess in the bathroom, wiping his already damp chinos and shirt across the smeared floor before stuffing them into the laundry basket for Kath to deal with the following day. Pulling on the cleanish set of clothes draped over his bedroom chair, he headed down to the kitchen, where he made a cup of coffee and reached for the phone.

'Gemma, it's me. The message from Kath – she didn't happen to say when she would be home, did she?'

'No, don't think so. Just for you to pick up Josh because she was going out.'

'Going out?'

'That's what she said.'

'Right. Thanks.'

'Is there a problem?'

'No, not at all. She's probably on a foray to Safeway's and got snarled up in rush-hour traffic. See you Monday. Have a good weekend.' Matt put the phone down with a grunt of irritation. If this was Kath's idea of a wind-up, he was not amused. He wallowed in annoyance for a few minutes before wondering if perhaps he should be worried instead. What if she had been in a crash? Or been mugged in the supermarket carpark? Stuff like that happened, especially in the areas fringing their own grid of respectable streets, areas like Elephant and Castle and the Old Kent Road, where some of the estates had become such ghettoes that the police were rumoured only to venture into them in broad daylight with several panda cars' worth of back-up. An image of Kath lying knifed in a gutter flickered and died. More likely she was with Louise, he decided angrily, reaching for the address book to look up the number of Kath's oldest friend, who was married to a consultant and lived in Camberwell.

'Hello?' The voice sounded hesitant and rather young.

'Is Louise there, please?'

'She out. Au pair is speaking.'

'Do you know where she has gone?' Matt delivered the question with exaggerated slowness, all the while drumming his fingers on the wall with impatience.

'Is drink with friend.'

'Ah. Which friend? Do you know which friend?'

'Which friend.'

'The friend is called Kath?'

'Yes. It is.'

'Thank you very much. Sorry to have troubled you.' Matt dropped the receiver back into place, muttering to himself about what some people were prepared to put up with in the name of childcare. Checking the kitchen clock, reassured to see that there was still a good hour to go before he need think about getting himself back across the river into town, he returned to the sitting room to keep his son company through the repeating travails of his favourite fireman.

Chapter Two

Seated in the Aldwych a couple of hours later, Matt was reminded of why he had allowed his once broad journalistic interests to be streamlined into the narrow field of theatre criticism. The production was even better than he had dared to expect, the set subtly inventive, the actors skilfully directed to inject fresh layers of modern nuances into even the most familiar lines. While not as outrageously beautiful as her publicity photographs suggested, Andrea Beauchamp was undeniably compelling, showing an impeccable precision in her timing and quite unafraid to use the silence between the words as much as the words themselves. The unmistakable aura of sexual confidence shadowed every gesture, every arch of the slim neck, every blink of the large kohl-rimmed eyes. Pitifully unprofessional though it was, the thought of talking in person to such a creature made his heart pound.

Leaning forward slightly, he cast a glance at the strong profile of the press agent, Beth Durant, seated a few yards to his right, a forty-something blonde with big hair and a soft voice. While producing no concrete results, their talk before the start of the play had gone well.

'Andrea likes to limit her media exposure to a minimum, as I'm sure you are aware,' she had said, eyeing him steadily over the rim of her glass of mineral water, the unhurried drawl of her

West Coast accent adding to the impression of a woman in no rush to compromise.

'Of course. But I gather that she is keen to help promote the success of the play, and also to remind us all of her formidable abilities as an actress – not that I would want to put down any of her achievements at the box-office.'

Beth laughed. 'No, you wouldn't want to do that, Mr Webster. Nor will she be willing to comment on the recent events in her private life in any depth – the split with her partner, her children, all that stuff.'

'If there are any no-go areas, obviously I would respect them absolutely.'

When she bumped into him again after the play, Beth suggested dinner. 'Or will you be rushing to file? I know what you guys are like, scribbling to get your pieces on to breakfast tables.'

Matt was tempted. He didn't have to file his review until the morning. But the invitation reminded him that he had a home to return to, a home about which he suddenly felt an involuntary spasm of guilt. He had left before Kath's return, his departure made possible by the unexpected materialisation of a teenager called Clare, waving a five-pound note.

'I owe you this, remember? You only had twenty and I said I'd drop by with the change. I've been meaning to for ages. And now I'm going away – to start a hotel management course in Bristol – so I won't be able to sit any more. Sorry it's taken so long—'

'You're not free now, are you?' blurted Matt, who had forgotten completely about the unpaid debt. 'Just to cover for an hour or so? Until Kath gets back. She's out with a friend. She knows I'm working tonight but I forgot to tell her I've got to be at the theatre earlier than usual. What with the traffic being what it is, the sooner I set off the better.'

'I suppose so.' She looked uncertain.

'You could keep the fiver as a bonus.'

'I guess.'

Matt had rushed out of the house a few minutes later, primed both by a genuine sense of anticipation about the evening and an ignoble reluctance to be involved in the laborious, noisy rituals of persuading his son into bed.

'Thanks.' He smiled at Beth Durant. 'But I'd better not.'

'Other commitments?'

'A wife and small son, counting every second till my return.'

'How sweet. I love that. I'll call you next week, then, just as soon as I've gotten a response from Andrea.'

Matt strode off in search of his third taxi of the day, wondering whether he had imagined the innuendo in Beth Durant's dinner invitation. The flutter of regret at being in no position to explore the matter further had, he knew, little to do with desire and everything to do with being thirty-one years old and half a decade into a marriage with one demanding child. Before Josh, Kath would often come to the theatre with him, making use of the perk of free tickets that went with the job. Now she usually chose to baby-sit and was often asleep when he got in. It was of considerable regret to Matt that their sex life had suffered accordingly, a state of affairs made no easier by the fact that their son had celebrated the transition from cot to the freedom of an uncaged mattress by acquiring the habit of wandering into his parents' bedroom at all times of the night. With the result that on the rare occasions they did make love, Matt often caught himself pinning one feverish eye on the door handle, or resisting turning the light on when he would have liked to, for fear of glancing up to find the pale elfin face of his only child watching them from the doorway. His suggestion that they put a lock on the bedroom door had been rejected out of hand. It wouldn't be right, Kath said, to close Joshua's only avenue of comfort, to make him feel unwanted on any level.

He was imagining things, Matt told himself, his thoughts returning to the press agent. Apart from anything else she was clearly several years older than him and rather too heavy-featured for his tastes. He went for willowy, dark-eyed women, with cropped haircuts and high cheekbones. Reminded thus of his wife, he walked with a fresh sense of purpose towards a street less likely to be in demand with a post-theatre crowd. He would make love to Kath that very night, he decided, wake her if necessary, tease her till she was begging for it, clawing his back like she used to in the squeaky lopsided bed in Shepherd's Bush.

By the time he put the key in the door it was almost 11.30. The hall was dark, lit at the far end by a slice of buttery light coming from the sitting room.

'It's me, returned from another night at the coalface.' Matt slung his coat over the banisters and kicked off his shoes. 'Are you full of white wine and loving thoughts . . . ?' He was stopped short by the appearance of the girl Clare, rubbing her knuckles in her eyes and yawning deeply. Her face was pasty pale and there were purple smudges under her eyes.

'Sorry, I fell asleep on the sofa.' She stretched, revealing a section of flat white midriff and a gold loop stapled through her tummy button.

'Is Kath upstairs, then?'

'No . . . at least, I don't think so.'

'So she's not back yet?'

'No, I guess not.'

'No phone calls?'

The girl shook her head.

'Right. Thanks.' Matt spoke briskly, trying not to show his irritation at the girl's sulkiness. He reached into his back pocket for his wallet and handed over a twenty-pound note. 'Sorry you ended up doing the whole night. You'd better keep all of that this time.'

'And the fiver?'

'And the fiver.' Matt wanted her to be gone, so he could stop pretending to be polite and give way to his anger instead. Not even to call was unforgivable. He poured himself a large glass of wine and took it up to the bedroom. Flicking on the small television positioned on top of the chest of drawers opposite the bed, he reached for his bedside pad and began making a few notes for his review, which would need filing by eleven o'clock the next morning. He would not look at the time, he told himself, nonetheless glancing at his wristwatch and wondering how Louise's husband, Anthony, was faring as the victim of similar abandonment in Camberwell.

A few minutes later he cast aside his notepad with a sigh. Kath put up with a lot, he reminded himself. With his job he was out late three or four nights every week. How could he begrudge her one small impromptu outing with her oldest friend?

At midnight he made a final sortie to the kitchen to refill his wineglass and make a note of the Bryants' phone number. Anthony wouldn't mind him phoning, he was sure. According to Kath, he was always up late, fielding hospital emergencies or working on one of his endless research papers.

Anthony's voice came on the line after only the second ring.

'I hope they've got money for a taxi.'

'I beg your pardon? Who *is* this?'

All Matt's vague hopes of a dose of male solidarity faded in an instant. Instead he remembered in a rush the extent to which he did not like Anthony, with all his medical pomposity and studied air of academic gravitas. 'Anthony, sorry, I know it's fiendishly late – it's me, Matthew Webster. I was just ringing to ask if you'd had any news of our errant wives. Kath hasn't got a mobile so I—'

He was prevented from continuing by a burst of puzzled laughter. 'Have you been on the bottle or seen a disturbing show? Louise is fast asleep upstairs.'

It was Matt's turn to laugh, but with diminishing conviction. 'Louise and Kath went out together – if Louise is back then Kath presumably is—'

'Hold your horses. Louise had a bridge evening round the corner. She got back hours ago.'

'But your au pair said she was with Kath.'

13

'Which confirms that the girl's a Slovakian imbecile with the language skills of a five-year-old. I'm furious with Louise for hiring her. There was a much better Spanish one for half the price. No, my dear fellow, whatever party Kath is at I can assure you it does not involve my wife. I'm only up because I'm working on a paper for a conference in Boston . . . Hello? Are you still there? Matt?'

'Yes – sorry to have bothered you, Anthony. I think I can hear the front door now. Goodnight.'

Moving in slow motion, Matt returned the telephone to his bedside table, his eyes fixed, as they had been for the preceding two minutes, on the small white envelope propped against a vase on the mantelpiece over the fireplace; a fake hole of a fireplace, which they had kept for the sake of the pretty surround – imitation Delft with a rich blue border that just happened to match the blue in the only pair of curtains they had bothered to bring from the flat. Which in turn matched the uplighters over the bed. Everything fitting and perfect and full of hope. The diamonds on the vase blurred under Matt's gaze. It had been a wedding present from his friend Graham, heavy lead crystal with such a narrow base that Kath complained she could never get enough stems in it to make a decent bunch.

She had written his name in full across the middle of the envelope, her tiny tidy writing looking small and lost in the middle of all the whiteness. *Matthew.* Seeing the formality of it, Matt knew at once that there could be nothing good inside, that he was standing on the precipice of catastrophe. He slid his finger under the flap and took out the single folded sheet inside.

I am leaving you. It is the hardest thing I have ever done. I have been living a death. Kath.

Matt stared at the torn envelope, marvelling at how long it had sat there, how he had managed not to see it or sense its presence. He had come in and out of the bedroom numerous times during the course of the afternoon – after the bath, pulling on his clothes from the chair, crawling under the bed for his smart shoes. And each time he had failed to notice it. Just as he had failed to notice that his wife was *living a death*. Matt looked again at the sentence. That they had rowed, compromised and not made love enough had always struck him as the general run of things, no different from any other self-respecting young parents trying to lead decent lives. Kath had expressed frustration sometimes, reluctant to return to the seesaw of euphoria and depression that had gone with being an actress, yet wanting something beyond domesticity and motherhood to fill her time. But *living a death*. Matt screwed the paper into a ball, snorting in an attempt at disbelief.

It wasn't until he got up and opened the wardrobe doors and saw the half-emptiness inside that he experienced the first rush of anger, so strong that he could taste it, a thick, gagging, metallic taste that made it hard to breathe. *Living a death*. How dare she wipe out six years with one such outrageous sentence? Without giving him the chance to argue his part, to sort it out. He kicked the wardrobe door shut with his bare foot. So hard that it swung open again, while the score of empty metal coat hangers chimed in protest. Numbed by shock, it was a little while before he thought of Josh. Then he was across the landing in three strides, a part of him fully expecting to find the small wooden bed unoccupied. On seeing the skinny frame of his son, spread-eagled peacefully on his back, one leg thrust out of his duvet, his pyjama top rucked up round his ribcage, Matt froze in the doorway, suffused with a terrible confusion of tenderness and terror.

He was breathing heavily, one thick clump of hair plastered across his forehead. Stroking the hair away, Matt bent over and softly kissed the patch of skin underneath. Standing upright again, he felt momentarily reassured. Not taking Josh meant she would come back. Of course she would come back. Then he remembered the empty coat hangers and felt less sure. Back out on the landing he became aware of a strange groaning noise. It took a few seconds to register that it was pushing up from somewhere inside his own chest. He lurched back into his bedroom and quietly pressed the door shut before daring to open his mouth and release the sound. Turning out the light, he groped for the bed and lay flat on his back, his throat pumping, the tears spilling down the side of his face, cold in the warm crevices of his ears.

Chapter Three

Some plays are like old friends, loved as much for their innate qualities as their sheer predictability. We expect to be pleased but not surprised, entertained, but not shaken. Taking my seat at the Aldwych in such a frame of mind for the latest revival of Noel Coward's Private Lives, *it was therefore thrilling to find that the erstwhile* enfant terrible *of the West End theatre, twenty-six-year-old director David Travis, has somehow pushed both the packaging and subtext of this national treasure to new heights . . .*

Matt broke off and rubbed his eyes till a palette of vivid yellows and pinks filled his vision. The terror that had descended in the doorway of his son's bedroom was with him still, bulldozing through his concentration, stilting his usually fluid style, making the target of five hundred respectable words even harder than usual. He would have to talk to his boss, Oliver Parkin, he realised, tell him what had happened, beg for some time off. His heart galloped. If Kath did not come back he would need help, childcare on a regular basis, for hours every day, evenings too.

It was half past five on Saturday morning. He had slept for one hour, maybe two, his mind in a wretched state of vigilance over both the mayhem of his own reactions and any creak suggestive of a key turning in a door. Mothers did not leave their children. Kath would relent, he was sure. She was punishing him, making him see what it was like to be alone all day with a child, teaching him a lesson. A lesson which, through his hurt and anger, Matt knew he would be able to forgive, in part out of sheer desperation and in part because he had the grace to recognise an element of justification to the reasoning behind it. The bounce of relief with which he kissed his wife and son goodbye in the mornings, the latter splashing through breakfast cereal, already bellowing and demanding, was not something of which he was proud. Early zeal to share bottle and nappy-changing duties had quickly waned. He never seemed to manage it as well as Kath anyway, all fingers and thumbs. Besides which, as Kath herself agreed, working in an office all day and out so many evenings, he needed his sleep.

Through the window next to his desk, dawn was breaking over south-east London, an insipid light seeping through the thick cloud like the dim glow of a lamp in fog. Below lay the twenty-foot square of muddied grass which passed for a garden, surrounded on all three sides by other similar squares, each marked by a rough assortment of walls and fences in varying states of disrepair. In the distance were treetops and a greenish bulge that was the dome of the Imperial War Museum, once a common destination for their Sunday walks with the pram, not because of an interest in military memorabilia so much as the need to have something to aim for, some purpose other than the gruelling challenge of persuading their son to sleep.

Matt blinked, wresting his attention back to the words on the screen in front of him.

. . . Andrea Beauchamp as Amanda is a revelation, capturing both the flirtatious scheming and the beguiling vulnerability of the character in a way that highlights the ultimately tragic push-and-pull of the plot. We hate what we have and long for what we have not . . .

What had Kath longed for? And who with? The possibility that his wife had deserted him for another man was a scenario that Matt still found hard to consider head-on, even in the private turmoil of his own mind. He could not shake the belief that he would have had an inkling of such a truth, or at least be able to look back with grim hindsight and pinpoint the signs. But as Kath herself had joked once or twice, mothers of young children simply did not have enough time to conduct affairs. It was only Fridays that Josh did a full day at the nursery; for the rest of the week it was just three hours each morning. Three or four nights out of seven Kath baby-sat while Matt went to the theatre. The other evenings they spent together. If ever his reviewing took him out of town for a night, she was invariably there when he called home. For the two-week stint in Edinburgh the previous summer she had come with him, seeming to enjoy the frenetic atmosphere and even finding a local baby-sitter so that they could attend some of the evening events hand in hand.

The more Matt thought about it the more it seemed likely that Kath had actually gone a little mad, turned a corner of sanity inside her own head. He imagined her holed up in some drab motel, sobbing into grey sheets and resisting the urge to pick up the phone. Attention-seeking maybe. She had been an actress, after all, and an over-sensitive one at that, Matt reminded himself, recalling the fragile state of his wife's confidence during their first year together, when she seemed to be in a perpetual state of dread, either at having to go on-stage or at not being required to do so. Once over the shock of the pregnancy Kath seemed to relish the diversion it offered, the legitimate pretext for putting away her grease paints for a far worthier long-term alternative.

'Is it the morning?'

'Hey, Josh, come here.' Matt patted his knees, aware that his entire body was trembling.

His son remained standing in the doorway, the picture of sleepy indecision. His hair was fuzzed and matted at the crown; one leg of his Disney pyjamas was up above his knee, the other looped over the back of his heel. Under his arm was a large acrylic green seal which Matt had won during an excursion to a funfair the previous summer. 'I'm hungry.'

'So am I. Shall we have breakfast together?'

'I want Frosties.'

'Me too. Masses of them.'

Josh looked at him so curiously that Matt blushed, ashamed of the false heartiness of his tone. The lump that had been blocking his throat for some moments began to ache from the effort of containment. He felt a terrible urge to bury his face in the Mickey Mouse print, to confess that the linchpin of both their lives had left and he didn't have a clue what to do about it.

'I'm afraid Mum has had to go away for a little while.' The words came out in a clumsy rush, triggered by the realisation that Josh, unconvinced by the Frosties diversion, was about to go in search of her.

'But I want Mummy,' he replied stoutly, as if the very fact of this requirement was enough to ensure its fulfilment.

'I want Mummy too,' said Matt, his mouth so dry he could feel his gums sticking together, 'but she has had to go away for a special holiday. Mummies do that sometimes, you know.'

'Why?'

'Because they need to rest.'

'I'm going to feed Spotty,' Josh shouted suddenly, rushing from the room. 'Spotty likes Frosties.'

Matt listened to the tiny feet pounding down the stairs with a heavy heart, grateful for the small reprieve. Spotty was a hamster, given as a fourth birthday present by Matt's father, and so lovingly manhandled that every day of its survival seemed a minor miracle. 'Not too much – it's bad for him, remember?' he called weakly, clinging to the banisters as he descended the stairs.

A couple of hours later the review was somehow complete and filed. Since it was only 8.30, still too early on a Saturday to embark on the grisly task of communicating his stricken state to the outside world, Matt began a desultory check for unread e-mails. His postbox was empty apart from a circular of a message from his old friend Graham Hyde, a successful City trader and

Net addict who had recently rented out his two-bedroomed flat in Borough and moved to New York.

Colleague taking bets on the Superbowl — Giants or Redskins — serious money to be made. Any takers?

Matt stared at the screen for a while, contemplating the possibility of a reply that encompassed both a refusal of the offer and the mention of the fact that he appeared to have been deserted by his wife. Graham and Kath had never got on very well, Graham being too much of the man's man, beer-drinking breed for her tastes. By the time Matt introduced them Graham already had one failed marriage behind him and was back in full swing as a well-heeled bachelor, betraying few signs either of emotional damage or of the inclination to repeat the experiment with another woman. While Kath obstinately refused to acknowledge them, Matt had always been vividly aware of Graham's multifarious charms. A successful product of a classic English public school, he possessed an enviable self-confidence, an infectious conviction that no obstacle in life was ever insurmountable. He was also good-looking, with a naturally elegant physique, a sweep of strawberry-blond hair and a smile to trigger caution in the hearts of alert females. Balance in the friendship had always been provided by Matt being by far the cleverer, an attribute for which Graham showed open respect and over which Matt knew he concealed his own private well of envy. With Kath's antipathy and the fact that Graham was never with one woman long enough for serious cross-couple relationships to be established, Matt had long since given up trying to integrate him into the web of his married life. Instead, Graham had gradually replaced Kath as an irregular but excellent theatre companion, lighting up many an evening when Matt might otherwise have felt lonely or uninspired. Recalling his departure to New York two months before, lured across the Atlantic by the kind of salary increase of which theatre critics could only dream, Matt experienced a fresh sense of loss. He could have done with some of Graham's humour now, some of that steely self-belief with which he rode out his own personal crises.

By nine o'clock, the telephone could no longer be deferred. Josh, full of cereal and propped among the pillows in front of his parents' television, had committed the unprecedented act of falling asleep again, the green seal tucked up under the duvet on Kath's side of the bed.

'Oliver, sorry to interrupt your weekend.' In the background Matt could hear sounds of crockery clashing and general merriment.

'No worries. How was last night?' His boss sounded as if he had a mouth full of food. 'Hang on, I'm walking into my study. The thirteen-year-old had four friends to stay the night – birthday treat – better than a disco, Pat assures me, but the house is like a zoo.'

'Last night was fine – excellent in fact – I've already filed. I'm ringing about something quite different . . . because . . . well, the fact is it looks as if Kath has left me.'

There was a moment's silence. 'Left you? You mean, just walked out?'

'That's exactly what I mean. And Josh – she's left Josh.' Matt had to fight to stop his voice breaking. 'Gone. Don't know where. Some silly note saying nothing. The thing is, it could just be a . . . you know, bad patch sort of thing . . . it's hard to be sure because, to be frank, this has come right out of the blue. What I'm trying to say, Oliver, is that it looks as if I might need a little time off – to sort things out – if I could perhaps take a week – even if Kath does get in touch—'

'Take two weeks, for God's sake, Matt. Take three, if you need to. I'll square it with Stephen. January is dead, as you know. You never take what's owing to you anyway. All that matters is that you sort things out. And if there is anything Pat or I can do, anything at all—'

'That's very kind,' murmured Matt, feeling a surge not only of gratitude but of envy for his employer, who lived in a splendid detached Edwardian house in Hampstead with a loving wife and four teenaged children. Two decades older, he was bear-like life-and-soul-of-the-party type, who wore shocking coloured bow ties and was universally admired for his sparkling, florid prose. Ten years previously he had written a controversial biography of an American playwright which had earned him international critical acclaim and many thousands of pounds. Hearing his voice, the background hubbub of the sort of normal family life to which he himself had once aspired, Matt felt a fresh wave of desolation.

'Things will work out, of that I'm sure. Keep me posted, won't you?'

'Of course.'

Phoning his father was harder. Matt clenched the receiver as he delivered his news, knowing there would be no pussy-footing around, that his father would cut to the heart of things in that brusque, unsentimental way he had of dealing with life's pitfalls.

'What do you mean, she's gone?'

'Just that. A note, no explanation.'

'Bloody hell. Kath could be flaky but . . . has she got someone else, then?'

'I don't know, she doesn't say. I don't even know where she is.'

'Well, what does she say?'

Matt hesitated, unable quite to bring himself to quote the phrase at the heart of the note. 'Just that she was unhappy.'

'Well, we're all bloody unhappy, aren't we? That's the human condition. But it doesn't give us the right to go marching out on each other without so much as a by your leave.' As always when he was in a state of high excitement, his father's Yorkshire accent, which thirty years of working in the South as a research engineer in the aviation industry had almost drummed out of him, grew much more pronounced. 'You poor sod, Matt, I'm so sorry. Do you think she means it? I mean, have things been that bad between the pair of you?'

'I don't know . . . I mean, no, things had not been that bad, at least not as far as I was aware.'

'Don't tell me you don't know if your own wife was unhappy.'

'If she was she didn't tell me . . . Christ, Dad, I don't know. I thought we were okay. Up and down, maybe, but okay.'

'And how does she think you're going to manage, that's what I'd like to know.'

'Oliver Parkin – my boss – has been very kind. Says I can have three weeks off if I need it. Hopefully Kath will get in touch long before then and we'll sort something out.'

'I'm sure she will. Because of Josh if nothing else.'

'Because of Josh,' Matt echoed, gritting his teeth at the thought of the implications of the situation for his son. 'She's got this friend Louise. I'm going to phone her next, see what I can find out. She's bound to know the whole story.' He bit his lip, so hard he tasted blood. 'To be honest I'm still a bit . . . I just can't believe that she would—' He broke off, unable to complete the sentence.

'Of course you can't. It's bloody shocking. Do you want me down there? I could come and help out for a bit.'

'Thanks, Dad, but no. I'll be all right for now.' Matt put the receiver down wishing that he was thirteen instead of thirty-one, with no responsibilities beyond the chore of homework and avoiding trivial humiliations in the playground. Life had known no shadows until the death of his mother from cancer in his late teens, a process so drawn out, so pitted with hospital visits and stages of fragile remission, that some edge of shock had been removed from her actual loss. Putting the experience behind him had been greatly aided by the fact that Dennis Webster had always been one of the rare breed of fathers who managed to involve himself in the woof of his only son's daily life; swimming galas, trips to museums and castles, afternoon concerts and sporting fixtures – no childhood event was without the image of Dennis's moustachioed, stalwart figure in the background, often silent but unrelenting in his support. Having for years taken such attentions for granted, seeing them as his God-given right, Matt had found the early odyssey of his own fatherhood something of a shock; particularly the realisation that such a sense of commitment did not always come naturally, that resentment and love could be so confusingly intertwined.

As if to remind him of such difficult truths, Josh chose that moment to surface from among his parents' bedclothes, hollering with rage at the temporary misplacement of his favourite toy and the vague recollection of some deprivation connected to the unfathomable order of the adult world. Matt hurriedly left the study, calling nonsense comforts that he did not feel, sick at heart for what the future might hold.

Chapter Four

Louise stroked the mascara brush through her upper lashes, watching with some satisfaction as they thickened and separated, bringing an added lustre to her greeny-blue eyes. Her hair, freshly washed that morning, had blossomed under the recent attentions of her heated hairbrush, its honey-blond making a striking contrast to her new mohair polo neck. Instead of the old padded jacket usually reserved for excursions to the park, she would wear the sheepskin coat Anthony had given her for Christmas, she decided, together with her new brown suede boots, bought on a sales shopping spree with her mother the week before. It felt important to look good, to present an attractive front in the face of the crisis. Outer composure helped the threat of inner turmoil. Like breathing regularly through contractions. It gave one something to focus on, some rhythm for the chaos of pain.

Before getting up from her dressing-table stool, Louise gave several quick squirts of perfume to her wrists and neck. Beneath the shock and the very real desire to be of whatever help she could to poor Matt and little Joshua, she was aware of the tremor of other, less selfless emotions. Like the distinct sense of personal injury that Kath could carry out such a disappearing act without telling her oldest friend. Fifteen years of friendship and shared intimacies and not one measly hint as to her intentions.

On the other hand, a small ugly part of her was enthralled. It was not every day that one's closest friend deserted a husband and child, let alone without notifying a soul – not even her own parents, according to Matt – of where she was going, with whom, or why. Such wickedness, such audacity. From Kath of all people. Kath, who lived in perpetual terror of what the outside world thought of her; who had spent most of their schooldays and the decade since moaning to Louise about dissatisfactions without ever giving the remotest hint that she was capable of committing a visible rebellion against anything.

Louise closed her eyes, trying in vain to imagine a desperation large enough to encompass abandoning her own offspring – a boy and girl of six and eight – to fend for themselves with their father and a string of nannies. As it happened Anthony had a happy knack of being endearing when it mattered, like whisking her off to Prague when she'd been so depressed about her thirtieth and needing no persuading – as some of her friends' husbands did – as to why a non-working mother should require paid help to look after children. A choice not open to the cash-strapped Websters, Louise reminded herself, bending down to pull on her boots, and sighing at the recollection of Kath's occasional complaints on the subject.

She arrived in the park with both children in tow almost twenty minutes early. Though sunless and grey, the air had none of the icy dampness which had made many similar excursions so gruelling since the start of the new year. Thankful that her offspring had reached an age where playgrounds required super-vision but not much manual assistance, Louise sat on a bench and scanned the various tarmac paths circling the recreation area. Behind her a couple of teenagers on rollerblades were chasing pigeons into the trees; while on the stretch of muddied grass next to the playground some hefty men were kicking a ball to each other, cigarettes wedged into their mouths, the change jangling in their pockets. Louise shrank farther inside her new coat, feeling suddenly vulnerable and conspicuous, wishing they could have met in the infinitely cosier park near her own home, where there were no graffiti on the fences and the people coming in and out of the loo huts did not look like potential paedophiles. They had to meet somewhere within walking distance of his front door, Matt had explained, sounding desperate, because Joshua needed fresh air and Kath had taken the car. Which was really rubbing salt in it, mused Louise, switching her attention from her surroundings to her boots, one of which had acquired an unsightly scuff mark across the toe.

'Thanks for coming.'

'Oh, Matt, there you are . . . poor you.' Louise flung her arms round his neck, wanting suddenly to cry at the sight of him, looking so pale and hollow-eyed, the collar of his coat up round his ears. 'Poor, poor you,' she said again, sucking in her cheeks as Josh trotted over to join her own two on the slide. 'What on earth have you told him?'

'That mummies need holidays,' replied Matt grimly, thrusting both hands into his coat pockets and slumping down on the bench next to her. 'I'm hoping you can give me some answers, Louise, because I'm fucked if I know what's going on.'

In spite of having had all of Saturday and half that morning to consider the drama – she had thought of little else, throughout their dinner party the night before and the ritual of helping Anthony pack for Boston that morning – Louise found herself at a momentary loss for words. The feelings of the man next to her were so raw, the suffering etched so visibly and deeply into his usually amiable face, that she felt quite unequal to the occasion.

'She said she was living a death, Louise, those were her exact words – God knows, there were few enough of them – so what I would most like to know is whether this state of abject misery was something she confided in you, as women do, I believe, tell each other any number of things that they would not dream of telling their partners, because she sure as hell did not confide in me, and if, as I suppose, inevitably, there is, as they say, Someone Else – a third party in this little sordid domestic malfunction – I would be most grateful if you could give me some history of the relationship's beginnings and likely progression, and maybe even an indication of her possible long-term plans with regard to our son.' He stopped and turned to look at her, with an expression of such glazed desperation that Louise immediately felt guilty for looking so parcelled and pretty, for having had the luxury of giving even a single second thought to her appearance.

'I wish I did know something, but as I said on the phone—'

'I don't believe you,' Matt said flatly, squinting in the direction of Joshua, who had lost interest in the slide and was now moving towards a set of bedraggled rope ladders, slung round four sides of a large metal frame. Louise, following the line of his gaze and experiencing some concern at the thought of Joshua's small limbs grappling with so advanced a piece of apparatus, caught herself wondering about Matt's competence as a single parent. He hadn't exactly been the hands-on type, at least not when Kath was around, which was the only time she ever saw him.

'I don't believe you,' he said again, pressing his lips together.

'Honestly, Matt, you've got to. I'm as baffled as you are.'

Joshua had reached the lowest rung of one set of ladders and was swinging on it. Several feet above him a group of sullen teenage girls were sitting in puffa jackets and short skirts, their bare knees and thighs bruised with cold.

'So she wasn't having an affair.'

'If she was she didn't tell me. The only thing that I—'

'Yes?'

Louise hesitated, fearful of his eagerness. 'I was just going to say that if I really think about it I knew she wasn't happy, not really. But then Kath never was, not deep down. Even when we were a lot younger . . . well, I'm sure you know she never exactly got on with her parents. They hated her acting, wanted her to be a lawyer or something respectable. And though I think she was good enough to have made it as an actress, somewhere deep inside herself she did not have the self-belief. And I know she found the whole baby thing hard – feeling so sick right through her pregnancy, being in labour for two days solid and then having all that trouble with Joshua not sleeping. All that took its toll. But then you would know that as well as anyone,' she added, watching Matt carefully.

Matt swallowed. 'Yes, I did, but then . . . perhaps not enough. I mean, you don't always when you're up close against something, do you? You don't see the big picture. I know I wasn't always around as much as she would have liked, but with my line of work it's not exactly easy . . . But I had no idea – not until you just put it all together – that she was clinically depressed.'

'Hang on a minute, I never said—'

'But don't you see it all fits? It's what a part of me has suspected all along – that something inside her snapped, something she had been bottling up – that she's gone away to sort it out.'

'Yes, that could be it,' murmured Louise, not wholly convinced but recognising that for Matt it helped to have a version of events that made sense.

'Otherwise she would never have left Josh. I mean, leaving me was understandable.' He managed a bitter laugh. 'But Josh . . . she loved him so.'

'Yes, she did.'

They both looked in the direction of the climbing ropes. Joshua was still only on the first rung. Above him, the largest of the teenage girls was reaching from her perch and pressing the sole of her foot – a big leather-booted foot – on the flat of his head. Puzzled at what was halting his ascent, Joshua was just beginning to whimper. Louise had barely registered the situation when Matt was on his feet. He sprang across the playground in three strides, shaking his fist and roaring in anger. Joshua, more alarmed by this stampeding, noisy version of his father than by the foot on his crown, which had caused no pain, began to cry loudly.

'You bloody great bullies. Get down here. You're too old anyway to be in this playground. Look at the notice – under the age of eleven, it says. Get down here – I want your names.' The girls, exchanging looks and giggles, were scrambling down the ropes as fast as they could. Louise seized hold of Joshua and hurriedly bore him off to safety, uncomfortably aware of the stares of other parents and children, their expressions communicating more a sense of entertainment than shared outrage. That Matt had overreacted badly was painfully clear. But then who could blame him, in his current fragile state? she thought sadly, sliding Joshua into a wide swing with high boxed sides and waving at her own children to come and join her. Matt, meanwhile, had managed to catch one of the girls by the arm, a tall, thin one with spindly white legs and a head of frizzy red curls. A few moments later she ran off and he came marching over, a look of grim satisfaction on his face.

'I got a name and an address anyway.' He waved a scrap of paper. 'It just won't do, the way these kids behave. Someone's got to make a stand. I will follow this up, you know,' he added fiercely, seeing the look on Louise's face. 'I bloody well will.'

'I think perhaps you need a cup of tea,' she said quietly. 'I've parked over there.' Detecting hesitation, she added, 'I'm more than happy to drop you back afterwards. Anthony is away but Gloria's around to mind my two.'

Matt took a deep breath and slid the piece of paper into his coat pocket. 'Thank you, Louise, I'd like that. But we won't need a lift in either direction. Turns out Kath hasn't taken the car after all. It was parked round the corner – our road is so full we sometimes have to do that.'

'Well, that's something anyway.'

'Yes . . . yes, I suppose it is,' he murmured, slipping his hands under his son's armpits to pull him out of the swing. Not sharing any enthusiasm for the idea, Joshua went rigid in protest. A noisy tug-of-war ensued, the child screaming, the father struggling to be gentle, tight-lipped with angry frustration. Louise, watching the spectacle helplessly, clenched her fists among the loose bits of new fluff in her pockets, pity tearing at her heart.

Chapter Five

The Bryants lived in a double-fronted six-bedroomed Victorian house in Camberwell, to which they had moved shortly after Anthony's appointment at Guy's. Since Matt's previous and only visit the year before, the gated space at the front, once full of skips and piles of sand, had been transformed into a crescent-shaped drive. In the centre was a small but perfect circle of brilliant green grass and a huge stone urn, cascading with vigorous foliage. Matt edged carefully past it, rolling to a stop a few inches behind Louise's Espace. Thanks to Kath, who had given him frequent and often irritating updates on the progress of the Bryants' fine new home, the immaculate state of the exterior came as no surprise. The urn, he recalled suddenly, had cost eight hundred pounds, more than Joshua's nursery school fees for an entire year.

'Let Josh choose a video,' instructed Louise, once they were all inside the hall, which was beautifully lit by two rows of crystal wall lights and furnished only with a huge gilt-framed mirror. 'We put the playroom upstairs,' she explained, as the children thundered up the wide carpeted staircase, 'so we didn't have to do any more tripping over trucks and Barbie dolls. Though they find their way down here anyway,' she added ruefully, leading the way into the kitchen, which was a gleaming gallery of stainless steel and painted green wood.

'Earl Grey or Tetley's?' She smiled apologetically, as if to indicate her awareness of the fact that in the face of Matt's current circumstances the question suggested priorities of the tritest kind.

'Actually, I'd prefer coffee, if you don't mind. Need a pick-me-up — I'm a bit short on sleep.'

'Yes, of course you are . . . Oh, Matt, this is so awful, I just wish there was something I could do. I still can't believe that Kath would behave so badly, however miserable she might have been inside — I mean, it's just so unfair, so hateful, for you and for poor Josh. Jesus,' she added in a whisper, 'what was she thinking of. What *is* she thinking of.'

'Coming to her senses, with any luck. On her way home even.'

'And would you have her back?' She set a mug of coffee on a coaster in front of him and pushed the sugar bowl and a teaspoon across the table.

'Yes . . . yes, of course I would. I want her back more than anything, to get back to where we were, but better—' Matt broke off, his face twisted with emotion. 'Louise, if you hear anything, anything at all, you will let me know, won't you?'

She reached out and pressed her hand over his. 'Of course. In the meantime, I've been thinking that perhaps you should talk to some of the mums at Bright Sparks. On a day-to-day basis she saw far more of them than me.' She hesitated. 'What Kath's done is very wrong. Nobody has the right to vanish. You deserve an explanation. And I'm sure you will get one, eventually.' She took a slow sip of her tea. 'Until things sort themselves out I'm more than happy to help out with Joshua where I can. As you probably know, I've got an insane school run to Clapham, but because of Gloria I can be pretty flexible — the only really difficult day is Thursday when she has her English course and I do my bit for charity, but I'm sure that—'

'I'll be fine,' Matt interrupted, so curtly that an expression of hurt flickered across her face. 'I've already been told I can have up to three weeks off work. If nothing is resolved during that time I'll sort out some childcare arrangements, maybe rework my contract so that I can spend more time at home. Cut out the subbing and just do the reviews. My boss, Oliver Parkin, only goes into the office for one weekly meeting with the arts editor – the rest of his time is his own. Okay, I'd need to take a bit of a cut in salary, but at least then I could be around for Josh. All I'd need would be a baby-sitter for the evenings.'

'Sounds good,' murmured Louise, secretly thinking that it would be a lot harder than Matt imagined, but not wanting to burst the small bubble of conviction buoying him along. The warmth of the house and the hot coffee had brought some colour to his face and a bit of life back into his eyes – beautiful dark-lashed brown eyes set attractively far apart and hooded by dark, tidy eyebrows. Anthony's eyebrows, she'd noticed recently, were showing premature signs of unruliness, curling out at the edges in a way that suggested an even more professorial look for his later years. Vague unease about this development had been overridden by the fact that it was the professor aspect of him which had drawn her in the first place; not just that he was ten years older and innately wiser, but that as a doctor specialising in heart surgery and research, his strong, hairy hands had to be so deft with the most delicate of things. As a young medical secretary she had fantasised about those hands on her skin, probing her with their strong, knowing touch, long before the Christmas party when the first of such dreams had actually begun to materialise.

Whereas Anthony knew full well that his chiselled features and towering figure were impressive, one of the other endearing things about Matt Webster, Louise mused, fishing out a tin of biscuits from her walk-in larder and offering them across the table, was that he seemed to have very little idea of his own attraction. Even in less harrowing circumstances there was a shadow of uncertainty hovering round the edges of his big smile, and flashes of anxiety in his dark eyes, as if he were constantly

AMANDA BROOKFIELD

gauging the reactions of those around him, checking himself for
mistakes. That so unsure a creature was in fact in possession of a
fine brain, and – as she had discovered on the occasional joint
family excursion to indoor swimming pools – a fine body, had
always struck her as a rather appealing paradox.

And the new haircut was good too, she mused, studying Matt
approvingly through the steam of her second cup of tea, and
thinking that if Kath really had gone for good he would have
little trouble finding a replacement.

'I'd better go.'

'But I've been no use at all.' Louise wrung her hands, blushing
at the shameful way her thoughts had strayed and trying to deter
him with offers of more coffee and biscuits.

'You've been great. Just talking is a big help. I'll let you know
of any developments.'

Glimpsing the look of pained concern on Louise's face in his
rear-view mirror as he drove away, Matt was struck by the
unhappy thought that Kath's desertion had transformed him into
an object of pity. He had felt it a bit at the kitchen table too,
with all her watery-eyed looks and offers of help. Well intentioned though such reactions clearly were, they made him want
to melt with shame, not only on his own account, but for Joshua
as well. How on earth did a child live down being abandoned by
his own mother? he wondered bitterly, checking over his
shoulder and sighing with relief to see that the object of his
concern had fallen asleep, one cheek pressed in what looked like
an impossibly uncomfortable position up against the window
lock.

That Kath clearly had not confided in Louise or anyone else
was the only small straw of comfort that Matt could draw from
the situation. It meant that her betrayal, desperation, whatever it
was, was all-embracing, non-selective, that she hadn't just walked
out on her family but on everything else as well.

It took a while for Matt to register that he was driving very
slowly, distracted not just by the treadmill of his own thoughts,

36

but also by an irresistible urge to scan the pavement walkers for signs of Kath. At four o'clock on a cold, grey January Sunday, the number of people about was rapidly decreasing; the few shops that had opened for trading were closing their shutters, while car and streetlights flickered in response to the thickening gloom. She would be in her black jacket, he decided, with her red scarf wrapped up to her chin and her black hair bunched over the top of it. Her face would be pale, scrubbed of make-up as usual, apart from the heavy black line she traced every morning across the upper lids of her eyes. The image hovered before him, tantalisingly real, before blurring and merging with the figure of a tall dark-haired woman in a black jacket stepping out in front of the car. Having failed to notice the zebra crossing, Matt lurched to a halt, his pulse racing, his palms sliding on the steering wheel. The woman, who was not Kath, glared at him as she walked across the road, acknowledging Matt's tentative head-nod of apology by jabbing her index finger at the monochrome sky.

As he moved off, checking with trembling, exaggerated care for any more hovering pedestrians, his eye was caught by the name of a road immediately to his left. Recognising it as the street he had scribbled on the scrap of paper in the playground, and pursuing some dim urge to salvage something worthwhile from a dreadful day, he edged the car round the bend and began screening the doors for numbers. It was a scruffy street of narrow terraced houses, with chipped, flaky windowsills and unkempt front gardens housing dustbins and motorbikes. Reaching the number the girl had given him, Matt pulled into a space directly outside it and eased the now crumpled piece of paper from his coat pocket. *Josie, 36 Denver Street.* Compared to its neighbours, the house looked relatively well cared for. Although the front garden comprised squares of cracked and heaving concrete, the front door had a handsome coat of black paint, to one side of which sat a large flowerpot sprouting with cyclamen and miniature firs. Undecided how or whether to proceed, and because the car was beginning to steam up, Matt wound down his window. At precisely the same moment the front door opened and the girl herself spilled out of it, laughing and eager, her squiggly red hair flying. A few steps behind her emerged a woman with a head of looser long dark curls, wearing a brown trench coat and flat-heeled boots. Strung like a satchel across her chest was a large black leather bag.

'Hang on,' the woman called, turning to double-lock the door.

But the girl had already stopped, arrested by the sight of Matt's face framed in the open window of his car.

'Bloody hell, it's him.' She began to back away.

'What's up?'

Seeing there was nothing for it, and not wanting to disturb Joshua, who was still asleep in the back, Matt got out of the car. 'Yes, it's me. Is this your mother?'

'What is all this?' The brown-haired woman pushed her way forward, past the girl. 'What do you want?' It was now clear that she was too young to be the girl's parent. Apart from the sheen of copper in the hair, there was no physical resemblance either. As she spoke to Matt, she took a step closer, her hazel eyes blazing, her broad mouth stretched thin with hostility.

'I'm sorry, I was actually looking for Josie's mother. She was part of a gang that bullied my four-year-old son in the playground this afternoon. I think it's disgraceful. I . . .' Matt dried up, aware of sounding both pompous and futile. 'It's just that there is a perfectly clear sign up saying that the playground facilities are for children under the age of eleven.'

'Josie? Is this true?' The woman sounded incredulous.

Josie was leaning up against the low wall that ran along the front of all the houses, her arms crossed and her mouth working furiously on a piece of gum. She was still in her short skirt; her legs were so thin that Matt could see the web of blue veins near the surface of the skin. Her hair was a brilliant orange, a cruel colour, Matt thought, for anyone, let alone a gawky adolescent with a flat plain face and the figure of a starved orphan.

'Look, please, all I wanted was a quiet word with her parents.' Matt glanced uncertainly at the house, realising from what had been said that it was not in fact the girl's home.

'Josie, is it true?' repeated the woman, not looking at him.

The girl shrugged. 'Of course not. I wouldn't hurt a kid, would I? I was with Tilda and that lot. I didn't do anything. I didn't even see what they did. They ran off, but he asked my name and where I lived and I said I lived here 'cos I didn't want him going to my place. I didn't do anything.'

'No, she didn't,' put in Matt, 'as a matter of fact. All I—'

'Well, in that case I'm not quite sure why you are here,' interjected the woman, swinging her bag farther round her hip and giving an impatient toss of her head. 'If there was any trouble I am of course extremely sorry. Clearly none of them should have been in the playground. I am not, as you have probably gathered, related to Josie, but I see a lot of her and will do my best to ensure that it does not happen again.'

'Thanks.' Matt stared at her bleakly, the weight of his other troubles suddenly resurfacing in his mind.

'Come on, Josie, we're late already.'

Matt watched them walk down the street before throwing himself back into the car with the distinct feeling that he had compounded his misery by making a fool of himself. Joshua, stirring in the back, began to cry softly.

'Easy, little man, easy.' Matt reached behind his seat to stroke the ruffled head. His hand was grasped at once by small sleepy fingers looking for comfort. The whimpering stopped in the same instant, replaced by the more regular huffing breaths of sleep. With the engine off, the car began to grow noticeably cold. Underneath the palm of his hand, twisted awkwardly behind him, Matt could feel the pulse of his son's heart, fast and fragile, a tiny trapped bird of a thing. He remembered suddenly the grainy black-and-white screen showing Joshua inside Kath's womb, a blurred, pulsing, nodular shadow that had meant little at the time. So little he had had to fake some enthusiasm to fill the guilty void inside.

It was a long time before Matt eased his arm back into his lap and started the engine. He drove home in a trance, aware only of the aching stiffness across his left shoulder, a part of him relishing the diversionary relief it offered, pain in the body instead of the heart.

Chapter Six

The chair was so small, its seat no more than a foot off the
ground, that it was impossible to know how to sit, whether to
sprawl with both legs straight out in front, or to bend them,
bringing both knees absurdly close to his chin. Miss Harris, in
spite of her bulk, looked perfectly poised on her own identical
perch, like a large queen on a tiny throne, her big blue corduroy
skirt trailing on the ground in a way that masked all four legs of
the chair. On the walls around them was a merry collage of eggs,
chicks and rabbits in various stages of development and recog-
nisability. On Miss Harris's wide lap were a pile of papers
relating to Joshua's progress in the classroom.

'He's very good with the beads.'

'Beads?'

The teacher reached to a set of low shelves next to her and
extracted what looked like a small bread basket containing scores
of plastic baubles of different colours and sizes. 'We sort them,' she
explained, beginning – quite unnecessarily, Matt felt – to demonstrate on the low table positioned next to her chair. 'Large, medium
and small. Like that. And when the children have finished they
learn to put the activity away before choosing a new one. Joshua is
wonderfully co-operative in that way – such a tidy-minded child.
It's the more creative activities that he finds hard, the ones where
there's mess and noise and no obvious pattern to follow.'

Matt clenched his face in a show of understanding. With all that had happened, the thought of Joshua clinging to microscopic patterns of order in an otherwise disordered and terrifying world seemed suddenly unbearably poignant.

He had only remembered the parents' meeting at the last minute, the recollection of the time and date somehow filtering through the maelstrom of confusion and unhappiness which had reigned during the week since Kath's disappearance. Knowing that some explanation for her absence would be called for, he had approached the encounter with a dread that bore little relation to concerns about his son's education.

'I'm afraid my wife cannot be here,' he had stammered the moment he was across the wide threshold of the church. Behind Miss Harris he caught a glimpse of Joshua, whom he had deposited an hour before, lost among a stream of children heading towards a side door. 'In fact, I'm afraid to say we have — for the time being at least — decided to separate.'

The head teacher had pressed her hands together as if in prayer, only the arching of her gingery eyebrows suggesting reactions of a more tumultuous kind. 'Oh dear, Mr Webster, I am very sorry to hear that. We will of course be extra vigilant regarding Joshua's needs at such a difficult time.'

'Thank you. Yes, indeed . . . it is extremely hard for him, of course. For all of us . . .' Matt had broken off, inwardly despising the cowardly way he had labelled his situation, packaging it as something manageable and preconceived. 'My wife has gone away for a short while, but we're managing very well so far,' he continued brightly. 'Things will no doubt sort themselves out in the end, as things do. I just thought you ought to know.'

'Oh yes, absolutely. Family situations are always very important.' She had turned and led the way to an empty classroom, indicating for him to sit on one of the tiny seats. Talk about bead-arranging was followed by a rigorous analysis of paint-splattered pages and Joshua's loopy renditions of the alphabet.

'His pencil technique still needs a lot of work.'

'Pencil technique. Right.'

'Joshua's tendency, like many children his age, boys in particular' – she picked out a pencil from a cluster in a pot on the table – 'is to use all four fingers, like this, instead of the thumb, third and index, like this. As I have said many times to your wife, anything you can do to discourage this habit at home will be most beneficial. Though I'm the last person to worry about pressurising the children, the more basic skills he can master now, the easier he will find his first term at primary level in September. Have you decided finally on where he is going? Your wife said it was between St Leonard's and Broadlands – a really excellent state school given the constraints under which they work. But then St Leonard's is tempting, a real example of what the private system has to offer. Quite tough to get into, of course, but then I have every confidence that Joshua will sail through the assessments. Next month, I believe. Have you been notified of a date yet?'

'Not yet,' murmured Matt, unwilling to reveal the shameful inadequacies of his knowledge on the subject. Like most aspects of family life, it was something Kath had been dealing with. He knew that she had looked at and registered Joshua at both the schools Miss Harris had mentioned, but had not progressed his own research beyond the vague notion that a free institution with a solid reputation had to be better than one that subjected four-year-olds to exams for the subsequent privilege of hoovering up the entire contents of his savings account.

'If the St Leonard's assessment means missing a morning of nursery then a little prior warning is all I need. I run a very relaxed ship, as I'm sure you know.'

Matt nodded, inwardly cringing at the sugary spoon-feeding tone, wondering if it was specially for him or something ingrained into her speech, acquired perhaps through years of persuading infants to arrange beads into orderly piles.

As he was leaving the church, he heard patchy treble voices

43

launching into the familiar strains of 'All Things Bright and Beautiful'. A lump swelled in his throat, triggered by the innocent tunelessness of the music, but deriving, Matt knew, from deeper concerns. The silence from Kath, still absolute after a week, was worse than her absence. Not knowing where she was, what she was going through, what she was thinking, left him feeling like a mourner without a corpse, oscillating crazily between hope and angry despair. That he had managed any sort of self-control at all was due solely to the existence of his son, the need to fill him with food and package him in a manner suitable for delivery to Miss Harris. Apart from a few brief tearful episodes, Joshua himself had been remarkably accepting of their new circumstances, even when Matt confessed to being unsure as to when Kath would return. The awful truth was that he trusted him, Matt realised despairingly; that when a father said everything would be all right, a four-year-old had no reason to think otherwise.

Back home, the emptiness of the house was so crushing that it was all Matt could do to drag himself to the kitchen and plug in the kettle. One and a half hours remained until he needed to make the return journey to the nursery school, so small a slit of time that it hardly seemed worth doing anything. He dropped a heaped teaspoon of coffee granules into the brown-stained mug he had used the night before and twice already that morning, and splashed boiling water over the top. A small shower of muddy droplets sprayed over the wall. He reached for a cloth to wipe it clean but then dropped it back into the sink. The kitchen was in such a mess anyway there didn't seem any point. Every room in the house was in a state of mounting chaos; miniature pieces from Lego and Playmobil sets were strewn across most of the ground floor, while upstairs the landing and bedrooms were awash with large toys, books and soiled items of laundry that had failed to make it into the brimming basket behind the bathroom door. Looking about him now, Matt was aware that the mess went far beyond a reluctance to work the washing machine or the time-consuming distractions of caring for a young child, but related instead to a fundamental refusal to accept his new state of solitude.

When the phone rang a moment later he almost punched the air with gratitude. Here she was at last, penitent, tremulous, loving, needing him. Resisting the urge to lunge for the receiver, he took several slow deep breaths. There might be negotiating games to play, and he had no desire to open proceedings sounding like the disadvantaged desperado. But it wasn't Kath, it was a woman called Maria Schofield inviting Joshua to a birthday tea.

'I meant to catch Kath this morning but my eldest was sick and we had to rush to the doctor's. It's only going to be a small party – more than a handful under the age of five and I find my stress levels shoot off the scale. Three o'clock next Friday. We're at sixteen Avril Close – within walking distance from you, I think.'

'Three o'clock Friday. I'll make sure he's there.'

'And all parents are invited to stay as well.'

'Thank you very much,' said Matt, his heart sinking.

'We should be through by six o'clock – that is if the entertainer lasts that long.' There was a whoop of merriment before she hung up the phone.

Matt looked at the kitchen clock. An hour left. Time for a good trawl round Mr Patel's tiny aisles with a mini-trolley. The freezer as well as the fridge were shamefully bare, especially of the breadcrumbed microwaveable nursery food on which both he and Joshua had been surviving all week. The last few of a packet of twenty fish-fingers had done for tea the previous night, together with the farting remains of a large plastic bottle of ketchup. Seeking the wherewithal to make a list, Matt went to the large pad Kath kept for such purposes, pinned out of obvious sight by the back door, above the ledge that housed the hamster cage. Reaching for a page, he saw that a list had already been composed, in the tidy alien hand that had penned his name on the letter of farewell. It was a sizable list too — including not only ketchup and fish-fingers but details about dry-cleaning items and milk bills. Matt scanned it several times, suspicion rising that this organised, precise composition had been intended as a prescriptive list for himself, left not by a person in the throes of emotional despair, but by someone most lucidly acquainted with the impulses of her own brain.

He had been expecting her to return, he realised, staggering against the wall as a wave of panic broke inside. Every minute, every hour, he was expecting her to return. Now, for the first time, it dawned on him that she might not. Because all the imperfections he had imagined to be normal ingredients of a married life had not in fact been normal at all. They had been signs that he had either missed or misread. Signs of someone *living a death*.

Matt slammed his hand against the pad, knocking it off its hook. It fell awkwardly, catching the edge of the hamster cage with one corner and knocking everything into the pile of muddied shoes and wellington boots below. Matt lifted his foot to punish the pad harder, wanting to kick the pages into non-existence. As he did so he noticed that the pet cage had not only been knocked off its perch but that its small brown occupant had somehow been catapulted out of the wire door and was lying motionless next to the door mat.

'I need a hamster.' He tried to smile, tried to keep the panic out of his voice. The woman behind the counter, who had thick-lensed spectacles that magnified her eyes to the size of small saucers, and who had kept Matt waiting for almost ten minutes by discussing the merits of cat flaps with another customer, sighed deeply.

'Do you, now?'

'And it has to be brown.'

'Well, I don't think we've got any pink ones, love.'

'I've been looking – I couldn't see that you had any at all, unless I just didn't—'

'We've got these little ones, came in last week.' She tapped a cage Matt had already scrutinised. 'Only a few weeks old.'

'No, it needs to be fully grown, sort of this size.' He cupped his hands to demonstrate.

'Does it, now?' She eyed Matt with a look of amusement and suspicion to which he felt too wretched to respond. Not having a clue as to the whereabouts of a vet, and seriously doubting the prognosis of a creature who had failed to stir in spite of the tenderest encouragement and repeated heart massage with the balls of his thumbs, Matt had screeched round Kennington's disparate shop parades in search of a replacement. He had finished up in Camberwell High Street with only half an hour until Joshua required picking up from school. Outside, his car was parked on a double yellow line, hazard lights flashing in the vague hope of eliciting sympathy from any prowling traffic wardens.

'Hang on a minute. I'll just see out the back.' The woman disappeared through a doorway of brightly coloured tassels. Standing there, alone among cages of scrabbling creatures and tanks of Technicolored fish, Matt became aware that he was praying, delivering a heartfelt inner monologue to an omniscient presence in whom he did not believe.

'You're in luck, mister.' The woman reappeared through the curtains holding up a small wire cage, her smile revealing the hitherto concealed presence of two massive overlapping front teeth. 'A brown male, six months old – we're selling it on for a friend.'

'Oh God, thank you – thank you so much. You've no idea how . . . I . . . How much is it?' He fumbled for his wallet, aware that in his desperation he would have paid almost anything for so sweet a prize.

'Thirty, including the cage. Cheeky-looking fella, isn't he?' She made a clucking noise at the wire bars.

Matt hurriedly handed over the notes. Though it was extravagant, buying the cage made the thing easier to transport. He drove at speed, feeling like a criminal as his mind raced over the logistics of transferring the new hamster into the old cage, disposing of Spotty's body and getting to Bright Sparks in time to avoid glowering looks from Miss Harris. It wasn't until halted by some traffic lights that he turned to check on the welfare of his purchase, wedged on to the seat beside him. It dawned on him in the same instant that without being able to pinpoint exactly why, the creature did not look anything like the pet he was attempting to replace. Joshua, who knew every twitch of Spotty's whiskers, every smudge of grey on his tail, would be not be fooled for long, if at all. There was nothing for it but the truth, he realised bleakly, gripping the steering wheel at the impossible prospect of finding a painless way in which to deliver it.

Chapter Seven

At 8.30 that night the doorbell rang. Matt, lying on the floor with a cushion under his head, next to an intricate Lego creation which had not only kept Joshua happy for two hours but also successfully absorbed every one of the tiny pieces that had been littering the carpet, felt little inclination to answer it. He rolled his head sideways, casting a sleepy eye at his son, who was conducting an intense fight between two members of what he had decided was an intergalactic space station. The only two members, as it happened, since their colleagues had already been lost to the far side of the room during the course of earlier, more violent bouts of warfare.

When the doorbell sounded a second time, Joshua sat up and looked enquiringly at his father. 'Is that Mummy?'

'I doubt it, little man. More likely to be one of those men with trays selling gardening gloves.' Matt struggled to his feet, seizing the corner of the sofa to counteract the dizzying effects of three glasses of wine on an empty stomach.

'Do we want some gloves?'

'No, we certainly don't. Let's go and tell him, shall we? And then it's time for bed. Daddy's very naughty for letting you stay up so late.' He caught Joshua in his arms before he could scuttle out of reach, tickling him to ensure co-operation and whispering, 'No gloves, no gloves, no gloves.' Joshua took up the chant, with such enthusiasm that by the time they reached the front door Louise, alarmed first by the delay and then by the noise, took a step backwards to check she was on the right doorstep.

'Louise, my dear, what a pleasant surprise.'

Louise hovered uncertainly in the doorway. She could see at a glance that Matt was somewhat the worse for wear. There was an unnatural pink flush to his face and a gleam in his eye that suggested alcohol-assisted merriment. He was wearing a crumpled white shirt, three-quarters untucked, the panels hanging almost to the knees of his jeans. His feet were bare and looked faintly grubby. When he turned round, gesturing at her to follow him into the house, she saw that the hair on the back of his head was flattened and sticking out at the sides, like that of a child who has slept all night on his back. Joshua, in contrast, looked healthily pink and spruce, with his hair plastered flat across his forehead from a recent bath. Louise was faintly impressed to note that he was clad not only in pyjamas but a dressing gown and slippers as well.

'Come in,' called Matt breezily, 'I was just putting Josh to bed. Say goodnight, Josh.'

Instead of complying, Josh wriggled round until he was facing Louise over Matt's shoulder. The large brown eyes blinked at her slowly. 'Is my Mummy at your house?'

Matt, who had reached the foot of the staircase, stopped and stiffened.

'No, my sweet, she isn't.'

'Where's her holiday, then?'

'Daddy's not sure,' interjected Matt in a muffled voice, his head still facing up the stairs. 'Remember I told you we're waiting for Mummy to tell us exactly where she has gone on holiday.'

'I want Mummy.' He started to sob, softly at first and then louder, arching his back in protest at his father's efforts to calm him down. Flailing with both arms his face now puce and screwed up with rage, he managed to hit Matt several times across the chest and once across the face. Matt flinched visibly at the pain. Louise, watching, took a step towards them before hurrying into the kitchen, shaking her head in despair.

It was quite some while before Matt joined her. Time enough for Louise to note the lamentable dishevelment of the house. Toys, books and newspapers lay everywhere; in front of the television was a heap of videos, most divorced from their cases. Two of the sofa cushions were on the carpet next to a glass of red wine and a half-empty bottle. A crisp packet had spilled its crumbling remains next to a big square Lego contraption, sporting curious arched sides and precarious wings. Stepping carefully over it, Louise found a space for her bags on the kitchen table, next to a fruit bowl containing one black-speckled banana and a pile of old letters. Wanting, in however small a way, to be helpful, she began emptying the stack of crockery piled on to the drainer and exploring cupboards for likely places in which to stow everything away. At the sound of Matt's footsteps on the stairs, however, she stopped, fearful suddenly that such efforts at assistance might be interpreted as criticism.

'I hope you don't mind my dropping round. I brought you some supper, a chicken salad – keep it for later if you've eaten.' She delved into one of her bags and pulled out a plastic tub. 'I haven't put the dressing on yet.' Producing a jar of home-made vinaigrette, she gave it a vigorous shake. 'So it will still be all right tomorrow. I just thought that you might have been too busy to do much cooking . . .' She faltered, deterred by the look on Matt's face, unsure whether she had overstepped the bound-aries of neighbourliness into some dark forbidden territory of male pride. 'Anthony's not back until tomorrow and Gloria's boyfriend has given her the heave-ho so she's mooching in front of her television every night, so I just thought I—'

'This is extremely kind, Louise. Extremely.' Matt ran his hands over his face and through his hair.

'How are you coping?'

He managed a tired grin. 'Badly. Today's triumph was

concussing the hamster. I rushed out and spent an extortionate sum on a replacement, only to find that the original had not died after all, but was merely sleeping off a sore head. Ergo, we now have two hamsters. Both males, thank God. Joshua was delighted, which was good. I opened a bottle of wine, which was not so good.' He smiled ruefully. 'I would love some real food. Supper so far has been . . . let me see now . . .' He frowned in a show of deep thought, 'one Jaffa cake and one – no, I lie – two packets of prawn cocktail crisps.' He grimaced. 'I don't even like the fucking things, they were Kath's favourite flavour – more of a cheese and onion man myself.' He took the lid off the tub and peered at the salad approvingly. 'Looks wonderful. I hope you're going to join me?'

'I've had a sandwich. I wasn't going to stay––'

'Whyever not? Have a drink. I'll never eat all of this alone.'

A few minutes later they were sitting at right angles to each other down one end of the kitchen table, their plates wedged into a small space Matt had swept free of clutter. Louise noted that he ate fast and methodically, clearly out of a compulsion that bore little relation to pleasure. Though she wanted to talk about Kath, it seemed right to wait to let him raise the subject, which he did quite quickly.

'I just wish I knew what had happened, what to think. One minute I'm convincing myself she'd been coldly planning her getaway for months, and the next I imagine her banged up in some decrepit motel having some kind of breakdown, without the courage or will to pick up the phone––' He broke off and plunged another forkful of salad into his mouth. 'The weird thing is she doesn't have any money. Nothing has been taken from our joint account and the small stash we've got in the Halifax is untouched – I found the pass-book and phoned them to check. So what the hell she is living on I cannot imagine.'

'Matt.' Louise put down her knife and fork. 'There is something you should know.'

He stopped eating at once, alerted by her tone.

'I've had a letter.'

'From Kath?'

'From Kath.'

'Where is it? Let me see it.'

'Just listen a minute.' Louise pushed her knife and fork together and folded her arms. She could feel the pounding of her heart through the fine cashmere of her cardigan. Even now, on the very edge of revelation, she was not sure she was doing the right thing. The letter had only come that morning. Its arrival had made her feel relieved and curiously pleased, both because Kath was clearly okay and because the confidences within it pulled her at last towards the knot at the heart of the drama. The question of how much to reveal to Matt had throbbed inside her all day, gathering intensity until seeing Matt himself seemed the only way to cope with it, to find a pretext for planting herself in front of him and then to let her instincts direct the rest. She unfolded her hands and pressed her palms on the tops of her thighs. 'It's not good, Matt. It's . . . I wasn't sure even whether to tell you about it . . . She's . . .' Louise curled the tips of her fingers until all ten nails were digging so deeply into the thin wool of her tights that she could feel the ridges in her skin. 'Turns out there is someone else. Though she doesn't say who. The postmark was too smudged to read. She's gone, Matt, I really think she's gone.'

'Let me see,' he repeated, his voice hoarse.

Louise reached down into her bag and handed the letter across the table; one side of one sheet, folded up small, as if shy of itself. Like one of the secret missives passed round desks in a classroom, she thought, watching as Matt pressed out the folds of the paper and read of greater cruelty than Louise had ever expected to meet in her lifetime. Civilised cruelty, though, phrased and packaged in the language of emotional reasoning.

. . . I don't know when, if ever, we shall meet again. I am far away now with someone else, someone whom I love more than words can say. My only regret, of course, is Joshua. Even writing his name hurts more than perhaps even

you can imagine. If there was any way I could have taken him with me I would. I know Matt will treat him well. Matt is kind. If he hadn't been I would never have stayed with him so long. If you see him, tell him to get on with his life and not look back. Tell him I had to do it in the way I did or I would have chickened out. As it is, I know I have done the right thing. I am happy. At last I have seized life instead of waiting for it to seize me.

'Matt, I'm so sorry.'

'Pretty definitive, isn't it?' He picked up his wine, made as if to drink it but then set the glass down again, gripping the stem so roughly that Louise feared it might snap.

'Do you want to talk or do you want me to go?'

He ignored her question and slapped the letter with the back of his free hand. 'Not much room for manoeuvre, is there? She can't bring herself to write to me because I'm the living-death merchant, good enough to bring up her son apparently – or rather, *kind* enough – but not worthy of a direct explanation, an apology, for fuck's sake—'

'I think she felt that if—'

'Don't tell me what she fucking felt,' he cut in, his voice low and hard. 'It's quite clear that neither of us knew what the fuck Kath felt about anything.' He pushed his chair back and stood up, searching for the pockets of his trousers and finding only the flaps of his shirt. 'Humans do not really touch each other, you know, Louise. They don't *know* anything about each other. I mean, take Anthony. What can you be sure of other than the fact that he is the father of your children? He could be bed-hopping his way down the East Coast for all you know; and if he isn't perhaps he's wishing he is. But he's not going to tell you, is he? Because it would be inconvenient, unhelpful, irrelevant to his requirements as far as you are concerned . . .' He broke off, appalled at himself. 'Sorry, Louise, I'm not thinking straight.'

Louise had gone very pale. 'I know. It's okay. I'm going now. You can keep the letter if you want to.'

'No, you have it. I don't want it.'

There was a small squirl of lettuce stuck to the bottom of the paper, she noticed, glued with dressing like a piece of green phlegm. She stared it at hard, saying, 'What Kath has done is the most terrible, selfish, unbelievable . . .'

'But men leave their wives and families all the time, don't they?' He laughed bitterly. 'No big deal. Who am I to complain? It's high time the trend went the other way. The fact that I happen to be a useless father—'

'You're not useless, you're—'

'Who is he, Louise? Who's she with?'

'I don't know.' She held his gaze, noting the bloodshot fatigue of his eyes, the way the fine lines under his lower lashes looked so deep and delicate suddenly, as if carved into being by the tip of a sharp knife. 'I really don't know. I'd better go.' She turned and slowly made her way to the front door. 'Call me any time. And if you ever need help in the evenings I'm sure Gloria wouldn't mind, now she's got some free time again. You've only to ask.'

He reached round her and opened the door, bracing visibly at the gust of cold air that surged in from outside.

'Thanks. If things get desperate I might need to take you up on that. In the meantime I've decided to put a notice up in Mr Patel's window – regular baby-sitter required, that sort of thing. See what turns up. We had a really nice girl called Clare who came from time to time, but she's left. Gone to learn how to manage hotels in Bristol or something.' He stepped outside and turned to face the wind, which beat at his cheeks and stung his eyes with tears. 'Next Friday I'm meeting some of the parents from Josh's school. A birthday party. You never know, it might throw up some answers.' He made a face, hugging his elbows against the cold.

Louise pulled the lapel of her coat across her chest and fastened it under her chin. 'Night, then.'

'Where's your car?'

'Round the corner.'

'I'll walk you if you like.'

'No need.' She was in a hurry suddenly to be gone, away from his dejection and her helplessness in the face of it. The thought of her own home, her own life, swelled inside her mind like light. She pictured her two children wrapped under their bright duvets with their mobiles stirring gently on the slight currents of warmed air, their night-lights casting pretty shadows across the bookshelves and tidy huddles of soft toys. She would put on her pyjamas, brew herself some cocoa and curl up with the phone; tell Anthony how she cherished him, how much she longed for him to come home.

Chapter Eight

After the grime and shambles of London, Matt always entered the Yorkshire village to which his father had retired six years before with a distinct sense of unreality, marvelling at the trimmed hedges, the litter-free pavements and gleaming paint-work. Even the ducks, invariably bobbing on the pond next to the main green, were inclined to look somehow coiffeured and orderly, as if programmed to behave in a manner befitting an environment so masterfully under the thumb of its residents. Sometimes he had to remind himself that the wildness of the moors was only a mile away, sanitised in part by footpaths and signposts, but still sufficiently sweeping and magnificent to remind onlookers that habitats like Rushton were tiny tri-umphs of orderliness among a beauty of vast and superior strength; that only the briefest of spells without lawnmowers and residential societies would see the place engulfed by its natural surroundings once more, crushed like a pebble beneath a boulder.

Dennis Webster's home was the last in a line of converted almshouses, each with pocket-sized gardens back and front, and small, brightly painted front doors, set deep into the dark stone, like open mouths in a line of startled faces. Opposite them, across a stretch of green that played host to a memorial cross to the Great War, was Rushton's main public house, an imposing

57

building of grey brickwork fronted by tyres full of flowers and several decorative cartwheels.

By the time Matt turned the final bend of the main street and caught the cross in his car headlights, a ghostly shadow in the dark, his head ached with fatigue. Thanks to the birthday tea at Maria Schofield's, it had taken an unprecedented two hours to reach the M1, an exhausting stop-start process in the gridlock of the Friday night rush hour. Instead of falling into a proper sleep, Joshua had dozed and woken in rhythm with the faltering progress of the traffic, making demands that added to the stress of the journey and quietening only when Matt traded UB40 for the taped ordeals of Bob the Builder.

The week since Louise's evening visit had passed in a blur of continuing to go through the motions with Josh, interspersed by long patches of indolence and hopeless retrospection. Though he posted an advert for a childminder in the grocer's window, Matt could muster nothing beyond resigned despondency when no one responded to it. When Dennis had suggested a weekend break in the country, he leaped at the idea, promising to drive up after the ordeal of the birthday party and secretly pinning his hopes on the journey as a reason to leave early.

In the event, they stayed rather late. Partly because of Joshua's evident enjoyment of the occasion and partly because Matt himself, much to his surprise, had had something of a good time; or had at least sensed that he might one day rediscover a state of mind where having a good time could become a real possibility. As well as heaped plates of enticing children's party food, there was beer and wine for the adults. While the entertainer earned his fee in the sitting room, Matt and the other parents had hung around in the kitchen, picking at leftovers and the half-consumed birthday cake, an impressive home-made replica of a cartoon monster with yellow fruit pastilles for eyes and a shaggy coiffure of red liquorice tendrils. Charged with glucose and two bottles of beer, Matt had found some of his initial unease dissolve. Having steeled himself for enquiries about Kath, it had been something of a relief to find himself welcomed into the group with no probing questions at all. They knew, he had realised suddenly, looking round the room at his companions, all of them female apart from a starved, intense-looking man called Desmond, who spent most of the time with his ear glued to a mobile phone. Grateful that some version of his stricken circumstances should have become public knowledge without any effort on his part, Matt slipped easily in and out of their faintly riotous conversations about the vile habits of four-year-olds and whether being a party entertainer was a career pursued out of love or insanity. When a reference to Kath finally came, from an earnest grey-eyed woman called Heather, it was proffered so timorously and with such obvious concern for his feelings that Matt felt nothing but gratitude.

'I just want to say that we all know you're going through something of a hard time at the moment,' she murmured, catching him when no one else was within easy earshot. She paused to sip her wine, eyeing him uncertainly. 'None of us knew Kath that well. She kept very much to herself. We had no idea . . . but if there's anything we can do, anything at all . . .'

'Mary Poppins would be a big help, if anyone's got her phone number,' said Matt wryly.

She smiled. 'I can't manage that, but I do know a good au pair agency.'

'Thanks, but I don't really feel up to sharing the house with anyone else at the moment, though I may have to resort to that in the end.'

'Well, any time Josh wants to come and play with Lucy we'd be delighted to have him.'

Matt was prevented from responding to this kindness by Desmond, who – perhaps out of some delayed primeval reaction to being so outnumbered – chose that moment to intervene with a monologue on Arsenal's chances in the Premiership. Matt, who had always related more easily to rugby than to football, found himself glancing back enviously at the knot of women huddled round the debris of paper plates and crumbs on the kitchen table. He had enjoyed Heather's expression of support and wanted more of it, he realised. That these women should turn out not to know Kath very well after all only enhanced the appeal of talking to them. Louise was too close to home — too close to Kath.

He managed to shake off Desmond at last, but not until the doors of the sitting room burst open, heralding the conclusion of the entertainer's routine and the resumption of normal parental duties. Joshua was one of the first to rush out, waving a creation of twisted balloons, his face pink with overexcitement and heat, his T-shirt plastered with smeary brown remnants of his tea. Across the room, Heather caught Matt's eye and smiled.

'A few of us meet on Tuesday afternoons,' she called, her voice barely audible above the hubbub. 'Next week it's at my house. Laycock Avenue. Number eighty-two. Three o'clock. Do join us if you would like to, if you've got the time.'

'Thanks, I might just do that.'

And then again he might not, thought Matt, turning into the road that ran past the last of the cottages, some of the appeal of being welcomed into such a group waning from having had five hours in which to ponder the matter. As he turned off the engine, his father emerged from a side door waving a torch and shouting, his Jack Russell, Hoppit, springing round his ankles.

'I'd half given you up.'

Matt eased himself out of the car and stretched, curling his fingers at the sky, which was a velveteen black and prinked with more stars then ever seemed to penetrate the murk of London. 'Sorry. I would have called. Battery on my mobile's dead and I didn't want to waste more time by stopping. Christ, the traffic. Unbelievable.'

'What can I carry?'

'The bags, if you can manage them. I'll do Josh.'

Though small, the cottage boasted three bedrooms. The largest was on the right side of the central staircase, next to the bathroom, while the other two were on the left, linked to each other through a low-beamed door. The farthest and smallest of these was where Joshua slept, in a narrow divan bed which Matt himself had used as a small boy.

Having successfully eased his son under the sheets without eliciting more than a sleepy murmur, Matt sat down on the edge of his own bed. Dropping his face into his hands, he rubbed his eye sockets till pink and yellow fuzz filled his vision. It was weird to make the journey on his own, to be there with Joshua tucked up next door and no Kath at his side. His father had moved to the cottage around the time they first met. He had rarely been there without her. Never, in fact, Matt realised, frowning at the effort of remembering the past, seeing the pair of them suddenly like characters in the story of someone else's life.

Downstairs he could hear his father clumping in through the back door with the bags, grunting and muttering to himself as he always did when imagining he was out of earshot. A strong smell was coming from the kitchen, something meaty. Though he should have been hungry, Matt felt suddenly faintly sick. As time passed, the confusion of missing Kath – of how to miss her – had got worse. To want someone who had committed such a gross act of betrayal was too desperate, too pathetic, to accept. To be angry was far easier, but unsustainable. A part of him wished that she had simply had a breakdown after all, as he had tried to believe in the beginning. Breakdowns weren't anybody's fault. They did not involve failure or the conscious decision to cause pain.

In spite of the temperature of the bedroom, Matt shivered. For a moment nothing more than to crawl into bed; not to have to face the effort of communication that awaited him downstairs. He had spent much of the previous night clawing his way through drawers and cupboards out of a sudden frenzied need for clues as to the identity of Kath's lover. For the first time since her departure, he stripped the sheets off their bed, filled with a sudden revulsion at the thought of what might have taken place between them. An image of Kath naked astride another man, her back arched, her head thrown back in the throes of a pleasure so acutely familiar to him, blocked his mind as he grappled with the bedding, struggling to stuff it into the laundry basket. Before tugging off the pillowcases he pressed each one to his face, breathing in the musty smell of unwashed cotton, too distraught to know whether it was the scent of his rival or some sweet lingering perfume of his wife that he hoped to find. His only meagre discovery had been a slim brown envelope of black-and-white photos, slipped under the paper lining of a drawer. They were the kind done for portfolios and auditions, showing Kath in glamorous mode, her lips dark with lipstick, her eyes wide and adoring.

Matt was jolted back to the present by the sound of Dennis's gravelly voice, loud and slightly indignant, bellowing up the stairs. 'Matt? Are you coming down or what?'

They ate steak and kidney pie, of the sort bought ready made and steamed in a tin, with thick gravy and suety pastry that stuck round the ridges of Matt's teeth. By way of accompaniment there was a generous pile of packet mixed vegetables and two cans of Boddington's. Sitting opposite his father at the small square kitchen table, Matt was transported back to the latter part of his teens, when the death of his mother had led to the first of many such meals, in another, larger kitchen, when the silence had been filled with sorrow of a different kind.

'Have you heard from her?' grunted Dennis at length. He put his cutlery down to await the reply, working his tongue at a piece of gristle lodged between two back molars.

'Louise, her friend, got a letter. She's met someone else, broken off all contact.'

Dennis whistled quietly, shaking his head. 'You poor bugger, Matt, I'm sorry. And Josh too.' He shook his head again, more gravely.

'I just wish she had told me that she was so unhappy. Then we might have . . .'

'Your mother didn't tell me she was ill for ages, almost a year in fact.'

'Are you saying unhappiness and illness are the same thing?'

'Not the same, but similar maybe, yes. That is, they both eat away at you, and can make their victims selfish.'

'Well, Kath has certainly been that,' muttered Matt. He pushed his knife and fork together on his empty plate, lining up the faded bone handles until they were perfectly parallel. Once he had started eating he had been surprisingly hungry, even for the soft, tasteless vegetables.

'A little more?'

'Yes, thanks.' He watched in silence as his father scooped out the remains of the pie from the metal dish. 'You could almost say history is repeating itself. Father and son left to their own devices—'

'No you couldn't.' Dennis paused, gravy dripping off the spoon, the light of something like belligerence inflaming his usually placid face. 'Your mother left involuntarily; and managed to do so at an age when the main things required to keep you in line were shouting at from touchlines and a bollocking for failing exams. Whereas Joshua is barely out of nappies and your dear wife has buggered off to have a good time. The two situations hardly warrant comparison.' He swung the spoonful of pie over Matt's plate, shaking it hard to disengage the pastry.

'Thanks, Dad, nicely put.' Matt pushed his chair back and stood up. 'I don't think I want any more after all.'

'Look, Matt, I didn't mean to—'

'Don't worry about it,' Matt interrupted quickly, too weary to point out that it was his father who had raised the comparison between the two situations in the first place. 'You're right. It's all very different. Except now, for the first time, I'm beginning to appreciate some of what you went through – coping alone, cooking all those meals.' He managed a smile. 'Josh is going to turn into a fish-finger if I'm not careful.'

Dennis laughed, a shade too heartily, Matt sensed, clearly accepting the bid to lighten the mood rather than truly feeling it. 'Hoppit will certainly enjoy this,' was all he said, whistling for his dog and setting Matt's plate down on the quarry-tiled floor. 'You get your head down. I'll clear up.'

Back upstairs, Matt undressed and checked on Joshua before returning to his own room. As he climbed into bed the old springs sank and squeaked under his weight. Minimising such noises had proved a considerable challenge when making love, he remembered, feeling a well of fondness at the memory and then quickly checking himself. It was hard to be sure about anything any more, what he and Kath had ever felt for each other, whether even the good times had been a sham.

Before turning out the light he reached into his bag for the brown envelope of photos. Kath, the actress, her hair sweeping low across one eye, the chin tilted down, coy but inviting. They were more recent than he had first supposed, he realised, holding the images up to the bulb above his head for a closer look. Maybe only a year old. Kath's hair was in a longer style, but she was always doing different things with her hair. Matt scowled, bristling with fresh curiosity, wondering whether he was staring at a vital clue in the puzzle of her betrayal.

'Daddy?'

Matt slipped the envelope back into his bag and hurried over to where Joshua was standing, dazed with sleepiness, in the doorway separating their two rooms. 'Do you want to come into Daddy's bed tonight?'

Joshua nodded, rubbing his eyes against the glare of the light.

'Come on, then, as a treat.'

Though Joshua fell asleep in seconds, Matt lay awake in the dark for a long while, hugging the small frame next to him with guilty love, knowing full well that such a gesture of fatherly comfort derived as much from his own needs as the compulsion to offer solace to his son.

Chapter Nine

Hurrying downstairs the next morning at the shamefully late hour of half past eleven, Matt found the ground floor of the cottage empty. Propped between the kettle and a box of cornflakes was a note, saying, 'Gone to feed ducks'. He smiled to himself as he filled the kettle, luxuriating in this small let-up in an otherwise brutal two weeks, the first sense that, in terms of caring for his son at least, he was not facing his ordeal entirely alone.

Faced with no immediate demands on his time, the grogginess induced by twelve hours of uninterrupted sleep redoubled. He spooned cereal into his mouth like an automaton, feeling quite hungover with fatigue. Half an hour later, revived a little by food and caffeine, he fetched his telephone, which he had left charging overnight, and dialled the code that accessed any messages on his machine at home. There was only one, from Oliver Parkin, delivered in the usual abrupt style that communicated his distrust of technology of any kind.

Wondering how things are going. Stephen says taking next week as well is fine. Give me a call anyway – I'd like to meet for lunch on Monday if possible. Oh, and that woman Beth Durant has been trying to get hold of you.

After hanging up, Matt stood staring into space for a few minutes, aware that in his other, previous existence, such a message – the latter half at least – might have prompted something akin to excitement. Whereas now, Beth Durant, the challenge of interviewing celebrities, all the loves and ambitions of his career, hovered as uncertainly as the memories of his marriage. Given the sea change in his circumstances, a total of three weeks in which to reassemble his life felt like the blink of an eye. The thought of even broaching the subject of revising the terms of his contract filled him with dread, as did the prospect of a life that involved juggling the role of full-time parent with the need to pay bills. The early surge of conviction at how he would cope, expressed to Louise two weeks and a lifetime before, had faded fast, pounded out of being by the realisation of the enormity of such a task, the sheer relentlessness of being solely responsible for a small child. Not even a sudden upturn in his finances would solve anything, Matt realised grimly, slipping out of the side of the house and slamming the door behind him. For even if he could have afforded the services of a full-time nanny it was already unthinkable that he should compound Joshua's loss by reverting to being as absent as he had in the past, slotting some stranger in place of Kath.

Matt walked along the main street of the village, his hands deep in the pockets of his jacket, the collar pulled up to keep the worst of the chill off his neck. Although the day was clear and bright, the sky fired with a brave gold button of a sun, a bitter wind was cutting down from some northern hinterland, whipping the empty black boughs of the trees into a frenzy. He headed left towards the pond, keeping his head bent so that all his eyes had to contend with was the unexacting challenge of the smooth tarmac pavement, a subconscious part of him searching for a similar blankness with which to line his mind.

They were standing with their backs to him, at the very edge of the water. Seeing them side by side like that, with Joshua barely reaching his grandfather's knee, each in wellingtons, one pair tiny and bright yellow, the other large and black, Matt was struck by the poignancy of the companionship of so young a life and one that spanned almost seven decades. The silvery tufts of his father's hair,

roughly edged round the bald pinkness in the middle, were sticking
up in the breeze, while Joshua's unruly mop was being blasted all
over the place, flying in his eyes and mouth as he turned and offered
up some comment about ducks or life in general.

'Hey, there.' Matt broke into a run, taking his hands out of
his pockets to wave. He had to shout twice before they turned.
At which point he noticed that his father's good sense with
regard to footwear did not extend to the rest of their attire.
Dennis was wearing only his cardigan while Joshua, looking
pinched, his lips violet with cold, had on nothing but a sweat-
shirt, a grubby, almost too-small old favourite he had worn to
the party the day before. 'Jesus, Dad, didn't you think to put a
coat on him? It's bloody freezing.'

'And good morning to you too. Don't fuss, he's fine, aren't
you, lad?'

'We had some bread but it's gone,' explained Joshua solemnly, extending two empty palms to emphasise the point.

'Mostly in here,' chuckled Dennis, giving his grandson a
friendly poke in the stomach. 'I told him it was stale and horrible
but he wouldn't listen.'

'Thanks for looking after him,' said Matt, a little sheepishly,
unsettled by the realisation that he would never have thought to
utter the rebuke about coats had Kath had been around; that
when it came to the tedious basics of their son's welfare he had
relied on her completely. In fact, he mused, offering his hand to
Josh for the walk back, he would have been far more likely to
have taken the line his father had, to have waited for Kath's
predictable scolding and then told her not to fuss. Parenting
wasn't about hormones at all, he reflected bitterly, squeezing
Josh's small hand in his in the hope of pressing out some of the
icy cold, it was about who was there to take the flak of
responsibility, to suffer all the push and pull of wonder and
worry that went alongside. With Kath around he had been a
part-time father, he realised, not just doing the job in spurts, but
feeling it in spurts too.

They ate lunch in a local pub, not the big dark-beamed hostelry opposite the memorial cross, but in a much smaller thatched cottage of a place behind the church, where – as Dennis was fond of pointing out – a pork pie and a pint could be enjoyed without rubbing elbows with day-trippers and eager Americans on the trawl for nuggets of Local Colour. Joshua, who did not like pork pies, was given a basket of chips and a glass of orange juice. He sat perched high on a bar stool, looking nervous and thrilled in equal measure, clinging on to the edge of the bar-top, but beating off every attempt of Matt's to offer an arm of support. Hoppit, meanwhile, clearly at home in his surroundings and exhausted from a long forage among the undergrowth at the farther end of the pond, sat curled up in the corner of the bar next to the spitting log fire.

Shortly after they got home Dennis fell asleep, stretched out in his favourite leather armchair with his arms folded across his chest, his mouth slack and gormless, his head tipped to one side. Matt, who had been contemplating the awesome possibility of inviting his father to help him out in London for a few weeks, decided that a flexible young teenager with some common sense and a penchant for chewing gum as opposed to real ale was still a better prospect after all. Taking a packet of biscuits for emergencies and leaving a note of his own, scribbled over the morning's communiqué about ducks, he bundled dog and boy into the car and drove out of the village and into the moors.

Alone he would have been more adventurous. He was in the mood to walk for miles, to strike out into the wilderness, to be drenched by rain, hijacked by snowdrifts and lost till dawn. But if Matt had learned anything in the last four years it was to set his recreational sights on targets that could be achieved without the calamity of a miserable child. With this in mind, and deliberately avoiding a favourite spot where he had walked many times with Kath, he pulled into a large lay-by advertising the start of a footpath. Even so, it was not the easiest of excursions. Hoppit strayed badly and had to be put on the lead, while Joshua, after a promising start of galloping sprints and war cries with an imaginary sword, began to complain so vociferously that Matt swung him on to his shoulders to postpone the necessity of turning back. With his energies thus rapidly depleted, it was barely half an hour before he collapsed gratefully on to a capsized tree trunk, sliding Joshua down alongside. He produced the biscuits, to the considerable appreciation of both his companions, particularly the dog, who got most of Joshua's share as well. By the time the packet was empty, it was getting dark. Re-energised by the food, Joshua insisted on taking sole charge of Hoppit's lead for the walk back, even when the animal's exuberance was in danger of dragging him on his stomach along the ground. Rather respecting his determination in the matter, Matt kept a close watch behind, narrowing his stride to match his son's and resisting the urge to yell warnings at every tug and stumble. Instead, he began to look about him properly for the first time, noting with a swell of pleasure that the drama of early evening was in full swing, transforming the vivid greens and browns of daylight to black and silvery grey. A small bird of prey, with spiky tips to its wings and a hook of a beak, swooped and hovered barely twenty feet above the path, sizing up some invisible target before jetting off, its silhouette quickly merging into the darkness overhead.

'Eagle,' said Joshua breathlessly, pointing after it and yanking the lead so hard that Hoppit was forced into startled submission.

'Yes, an eagle,' replied Matt, believing suddenly that it could have been, that the walk for all its tameness had been an adventure of sorts after all.

Supper that night – shepherd's pie out of tinfoil basins and two green mountains of frozen peas – was easier, partly because the day had wrought a sense of companionship and partly because instead of facing each other at the table they ate in front of the television, with their plates balanced on their laps. The conversation was consequently more drawn out and punctuated by the gentle comic relief of a Morecambe and Wise classic.

'So who've you got that's any help in all this?' ventured Dennis, pressing peas into the prongs of his fork. 'Graham, I suppose.'

'Graham's moved to New York. We're on e-mail terms only. In fact, I haven't told him yet.'

There was a pause, while Angela Rippon and her two hosts performed a routine in top hats.

'So who's helping you out?'

'The parents I met yesterday afternoon were very kind – and there's Louise, of course, Kath's friend – she's very keen to be supportive.'

Matt tried to sound positive while inside he was confronted by a fresh sense of his own isolation. In latter years he had never really spoken properly to anyone except Kath. The thought prompted the recollection of a distant hazy era when life had seemed an endless merry-go-round of doing things with other people, of multiple friendships and shared escapades. When had it all stopped? he wondered miserably, raising a heaped forkful of food to his mouth before setting it down again uneaten.

On the TV Eric and Ernie were side by side in bed, wearing loud checked pyjamas and sparring like a couple of old queens. In the chair next to him his father chuckled quietly, nodding his head in appreciation. His job was to blame, Matt decided wretchedly, knowing deep down that it was almost certainly more than that, that somewhere along the line he appeared to have stopped noticing things, started backing out of life instead of participating in it.

'What about Kath's parents?' barked Dennis suddenly. 'Have they been any help?'

'No more than usual.' It had never been any secret that his in-laws were of the insufferable variety, a view fortunately held by Kath as much as by Matt himself. 'Gillian's phoned a couple of times, worried sick, she claims, suddenly full of concern for her dear daughter when she's spent the best part of the last twenty years criticising everything she's ever done. Pretending to be anxious about Josh when they only ever saw him as a bother before. It's bloody obvious they think it's all my fault, which it probably is,' he concluded darkly, shovelling in the last of his mash and using a large swig of beer to wash it down.

Dennis left his chair and began gathering up their plates and empty cans. Behind him the closing credits of Morecambe and Wise were followed by the cheery crumpled face of Michael Parkinson, promising a programme of old favourites. How wonderful to be able to live off work completed years before, thought Matt enviously, feeling a fresh bout of panic at having to pick up the reins of his own career – the treadmill of deadlines, of being only as good as the most recent set of words on a page.

'I'll have none of that talk,' retorted Dennis, handing him the plates and ushering him into the kitchen. 'For one thing it gets you nowhere. And for another it's not true. None of these situations is ever one person's fault. It's bloody, the whole business, and you're dealing with it as best you can. Now, then.' He rubbed his hands together as if to dismiss the subject. 'I'm having tea and a Mars bar. Do you want the same?'

'I certainly do.' Matt dropped the plates into the cracked sink and quickly set about the washing up, using brisk circular motions with a brush bereft of all but a small cluster of bristles. He still had a week in which to sort himself out, he reminded himself. He would manage somehow. He turned, wanting to say as much to his father, to express some gratitude for his support. But Dennis was already half out of the kitchen, a mug in each hand and bars of confectionery sticking out of the saggy side pockets of his cardigan.

Chapter Ten

'In my experience few things are irretrievable,' said Oliver Parkin, peering over the top of his spectacles at the wine menu. 'Molly and I have had the most terrible rifts, World War Three stuff, I can tell you, but we always relent in the end. It gets so tiring apart from anything else, maintaining a stand about something when it's so much easier – so much nicer all round – to kiss and make up. How long had you and Katherine been together? Eight years? Nine?'

'Just six actually,' Matt corrected him before sitting back and allowing the torrent of well-intentioned assurances to continue. They were wedged at a table in one of Oliver's favourite eating haunts in Soho, surrounded by packed tables of business executives and West End shoppers. He had agreed to the lunch with some reluctance, in truth wanting no such intrusions into his final week of leave, but recognising that it would be an opportunity to mention his hopes of an altered contract, an arrangement that he knew would have no hope of success without his boss's full backing.

'Well, that's heaps,' gushed Oliver, 'enough of an investment on both your parts to give the thing another whirl, especially with the little one to consider. Though I'm well aware I need hardly remind you of that aspect of the situation, given the couple of weeks you must have had,' he added hastily, pushing his glasses up to the bridge of his nose, where they promptly slipped back down again. 'All I'm trying to say is that from what I've seen of these matters, even the more serious marital misdemeanours usually turn out to be red herrings when it comes to reasons to separate for good. I can't tell you the number of acquaintances who have expressed mid-life crises of one variety or another by rushing into the arms of unlikely people, only to find that it's all been a big mistake.' He broke off to postpone the attentions of a hovering waiter. 'A few months on and there's nothing they'd rather do than come crawling back to the marital nest.'

Matt made a conscious effort to relax, wondering all the while whether his boss's evident failure to grasp the full dimensions of his situation could be attributed to his own cowardly explaining of its essentials or to some deep strand of emotional obtuseness on Oliver's part. That he meant well was not in doubt. Ever since rescuing Matt from a meandering career with one of the less prestigious tabloids five years before, he had always adopted an overtly avuncular tone, behaving like some master with an apprentice to a craft. From anyone else Matt might have found such an attitude patronising, but with Oliver there was too much exuberance, too much genuine human warmth, to take offence. His writing style harnessed a similarly infectious energy, capable of teasing out a reader's interest for even the most improbable productions.

'I recommend the steak *au poivre*, which means I'll be on the red stuff. What about you?'

Matt, who wasn't particularly hungry, made a show of studying the menu before choosing the same for himself.

'And I've decided I want you to do New York next month,' Oliver declared, once their order had been taken. 'I hog it to myself each year – and by God, it's not as if you aren't ready for Broadway. I'll cover *She Stoops* at Chichester and the new David Hare back here. What do you say?'

Matt slowly wiped a crust of bread round the dribble of oil

left in the saucer between them. His employer, he knew, was trying to be kind. Jetting across the Atlantic was a treat indeed, the jewel in the proverbial crown, a far cry from hacking down to the Sussex coast for the evening to see a mediocre line-up tackle Goldsmith. 'Oliver, that's more than generous – I'd love to, you know I would. But the fact is – you must understand – there really seems no possibility of Kath coming back. I don't even know where she is – she's broken off all contact – started again with someone else.' Oliver tried to interrupt but Matt persisted. 'Which means my life is going to be a little more complicated. That is to say, I can't just take off and leave Josh – nor would I want to, he's been through enough as it is. So what I've decided – if you would be good enough to back me up – is to try and alter my contract so that I can work from home, still cover as much, but cut out all the subbing. That way I can be something of a father – at least, not go down the full-time nanny route, which I couldn't afford anyway. I'm going to get a regular baby-sitter so I can still go out in the evenings. I know it's not going to be easy. I could only manage today because Louise – she's a friend of Kath's – agreed to collect Josh from nursery school. You see, he's still only on four half-days and one full – that's on Friday – but in September he'll be starting primary school – I don't quite know where yet – but that will mean I'll have six uninterrupted hours every day in which to work . . .' Matt knew he was ranting, making the mistake he had vowed not to, of appearing frantic and close to the edge, sounding like a man unworthy of any employment at all, let alone a flexible deal as a freelance theatre critic. But once he had started he couldn't stop, partly out of a desperate urge to set the picture as regards Kath straight, and partly because Oliver, uncharacteristically, was looking some-what at a loss for words. 'So New York, tempting though it is, almost certainly will not work,' he ended lamely, 'because it would be several nights away and therefore beyond my current organisational capabilities.'

'And what the devil are grandparents for, may I ask?'

countered Oliver, thrusting out his lower jaw as he did when feeling particularly determined. 'Surely they could man the fort while you went to the States for a few days. You've had a rough time, Matt. Dare I say, it would even do you good to get away for a bit.'

Matt smiled, touched by his persistence. 'Kath's parents are . . . let us say, difficult. And my dad is . . . well, he's getting on a bit.' He hesitated, weakening in spite of himself at the prospect of so appealing a respite. 'Though I suppose I could sound him out on the matter.'

'Do it,' exclaimed Oliver, slamming the table with the palm of his hand, so hard that all the crockery rattled. 'And, as to your contract, I'll have a word with Phillip, explain the situation and see how the land lies. I'm sure we'll be able to work out something that suits us all in the end.' He paused to clear his throat, turning aside from his plate of half-eaten food and coughing into his fist. 'The more pressing question is, are you going to be able to manage for the next week or so?'

'Oh yes,' Matt reassured him wildly, though he still had no clue as to how he was going to manage anything.

'Marvellous.' Oliver picked up the wine bottle and topped up both their glasses with a flourish of celebration. 'And Beth Durant, what's going on there? Will the divine Andrea Beauchamp bare her soul, that's the question.' He chuckled, popping a final neat triangle of steak into his mouth and washing it down with a generous swig of wine. 'Sadly, even if these creatures agree to talk they rarely *say* anything except to spout about their next projects. And for God's sake make sure the tape recorder's running. Any misquote and she's bound to sue – she's just the type.'

'I haven't even got the interview yet. I'm meeting with Beth Durant to discuss it this Friday. Though, to be honest, I don't hold out much hope. She's been prevaricating for so long and the woman's so bloody famous she hardly needs the publicity. The Aldwych is selling out every night.'

'Ah, but the other thing about such creatures is they want publicity none the less,' interjected Oliver, raising his finger like a schoolmaster. 'They feed off it. It makes them feel alive and loved. It *defines* them.'

While the rest of us are left to define ourselves, Matt thought, but did not say because all in all the lunch had gone very well and he had no wish to cast doubt upon Oliver's confidence in him by revealing any more of his gloomy state of mind than necessary. They parted a few minutes later, agreeing to meet in the office early on the following Monday for the weekly assessment and allocation of assignments.

'Meantime you enjoy the rest of your break,' commanded Oliver. 'Never say die,' he added, by way of a rallying parting shot, 'particularly not on the question of the fairer sex.'

Although Matt had intended to rush straight round to Louise's to collect Joshua, he changed his mind and went home first. The possibility of a trip across the Atlantic reminded him that he had still to inform Graham of the downturn in his personal life. Unhappiness brought the most terrible indolence, he had discovered, even over matters containing the possibility of a grain or two of comfort.

Dear Graham, he wrote, punching each key slowly with his index fingers, his mind groping for the right words, wondering whether to aim for a tone of bravado or be as bleak as he felt inside. Graham wasn't a great one for bleakness. He was a getter-on-with-life, a man who, more than most males, preferred to keep his emotional depths uncharted, who responded to life's knocks by punching back and moving on. When his own marriage collapsed, he had been the first to make humorous quips about the situation. Within weeks he had signed up with some headhunters and moved to an even better paid job. Leaving the marital home to his wife by way of a settlement, he acquired the flat in Borough, a silver sports car and a string of new lady friends — all of which had confirmed Kath's worst opinions, but not fooled Matt for a second. During the course of their regular evenings at the theatre, which started around the same time, he had had plenty of time to observe a real sense of personal failure, the flashes of self-doubt behind the merry façade.

Bad news from my neck of the woods, I'm afraid. There's no easy way to say it. Kath has left me. Me and Josh to be exact. Done a runner with someone else. Don't know who he is or where they've gone. So life is a bit sticky at the moment, as you might imagine. I've taken three weeks off to be a full-time father and am trying to renegotiate my contract so that I can work from home and be around for Josh. I know you never got on that well with Kath, but I also know that you'll understand this has hit me pretty hard. Her parents are being the usual nightmare, but my Dad has been great . . .

Matt paused, frowning as he reread what he had written, resisting the urge to edit it as he would one of his articles.

On a more cheery note, Oliver Parkin seems determined to get me over to New York to cover a couple of Broadway openings in February. I need to sort out the logistics but obviously if it comes off it would be good to meet up. I could do with you being around, you bastard. Matt.

He pressed the send button and then waited for a few minutes before checking for a reply. Graham, who spent most of his working life in front of a computer screen, did not disappoint.

Really sorry to hear about you and Kath. Must be bloody hard managing on your own. Would be great to see you if you can wangle a trip this way. Only possible problem is skiing — I've signed up with a big group going to the Rockies. Off-piste and snowboarding, so should be fun. Let me know your dates and we'll see if we can work something out.

Cheers — hang on in there—

Graham

Cheered immensely, Matt closed down his computer and set off to retrieve Joshua from Camberwell. He would do his very best to make the New York trip happen, he decided, slamming the steering wheel in frustration at the already clogged afternoon traffic. Electronic mail was all very well, but it was the actual physical presence of his friend that he longed for most, his infectious ability to be funny and energised in the face of misfortune.

Louise took some time to answer the door, looking, so Matt could not help observing, a little frayed. Behind her, all three children, dressed in an assortment of plastic helmets and breastplates, were charging up and down the stairs, wielding shields and swords and emitting bloodcurdling cries of enthusiastic hostility.

'King Arthur,' she said weakly. 'I got the video and it's been like this ever since.'

'Thank you so much for having him.'

'No problem. Would you like some tea?' During the course of this last sentence her youngest careered into the back of her legs, almost knocking her over. 'George, I've told you,' she shouted, turning and trying to grab the child, who skidded away, back towards the stairs, sliding the last few yards on his socks. 'Jesus, I—'

'Are you all right?'

'Fine, I'm fine,' replied Louise tightly, pushing her normally tidy hair out of her eyes and brushing imaginary specks from her jumper. 'My fault. I couldn't face the park, and they've gone a bit stir-crazy. Gloria asked for the day off — she says it's flu but I haven't heard one sneeze. I'm sure she's just moping for the boyfriend, a horrible creature with rings in his eyebrows — she's well rid of him but of course can't see it that way. God, these au pairs, worse than bloody teenagers. Anthony's in Brussels; he was supposed to be coming home tonight but there was some problem with the plane—' She broke off, and took a deep breath. 'Sorry. Burdening you with my woes when you've got quite enough of your own.'

'Don't be silly . . . and thank you so much — not just for today but for everything. Joshua and I had a wonderfully relaxing weekend with my father and I've started negotiating new terms for my work. Everything is beginning to sort itself out.'

'Did you want that tea?' She turned to lead the way into the kitchen.

'No thanks, we'd better be getting back. You've done quite

enough for one day. Though something to bribe my Arthurian knight out of his armour might be a big help – confectionery of some kind. Otherwise I can see I'm going to be chasing him round the furniture all afternoon.' He followed her into the kitchen and watched as she burrowed in a cupboard and came out with a packet of Rolos.

'These do the trick?'

'Perfect. Thank you.' He grinned and took the sweets, planting a kiss of gratitude on her cheek.

Chapter Eleven

The following afternoon Matt, clutching Joshua's hand rather more tightly than Joshua himself required, set off for their tea engagement in Laycock Road. Although the sky was grey, the air felt warmer than it had for a while, containing at least a hint of a spring breeze as opposed to the cutting winds that had prevailed through most of January. Matt walked slowly, much to the dismay of his son, who bounced impatiently on the end of his arm. He was having tea with three women for the sake of his son's social life, Matt told himself, confused by the extent of his anxiety, unsure whether it was because he wanted to be grilled about his feelings or because he didn't. He tried to focus on the Heather woman's kindness the week before, the way he had wanted to open up to her, wondering if he would feel similarly inclined over a cup of tea as opposed to two bottles of French lager.

'I'm so glad you've come,' she exclaimed at once, managing to communicate both genuine pleasure and a reassuring hint that she had some notion of his reservations. 'There's only three of us this week – Maria, whom you know, and Ambreen Seldon, whose little girl Jessica is in the same class as Joshua.'

Ten minutes later, slotted between Heather and Maria in the middle of a deep, comfortable sofa, Matt found himself responding to a few gentle prompts by pouring out the whole sorry story, for the first time fully articulating the horror of his abandonment, the slow, sickening realisation that Kath had found someone else and disappeared for good. The women listened patiently, crooning with a brand of sympathy he hadn't come across before, one that felt remarkably close to admiration. Kath's desertion had cast him in a heroic light, he realised for the first time, not necessarily as a husband but as a father to a half-orphaned four-year-old child. His battered ego warmed to the discovery like a plant starved of light. He even found himself embellishing certain bits, adding touches of drama and a few heart-rending details about Josh, which in a less guarded moment he might have seen fit to keep to himself.

'How could she? That's what I want to know,' murmured Maria, hugging a toddler who had wandered in from the group entertaining themselves in the garden. 'I mean, to leave one's own child voluntarily, it's . . . unthinkable.'

'She must be mad,' agreed Heather, shaking her trim fair hair in wonderment as she passed round a second plate of home-made biscuits, still warm from the oven. 'And not to give you any warning of her state of mind.'

'I really did think the two of us were all right,' admitted Matt ruefully. 'Like I said, my job kept me rather too busy on occasions, but I was there as much as I could and we seemed to be getting on fine – usual ups and downs.'

The assembled trio exchanged knowing nods, each performing rapid mental assessments of the compromises and disappointments of their own domestic situations.

'When Derek was on nights we'd pass each other in the hall like strangers,' confessed Ambreen, the quietest of the three, with smooth café au lait skin and a long curtain of jet-blue hair. A baby with tufts of similar silky black sprouting haphazardly from its scalp was asleep in a car seat next to her chair. 'If it wasn't for Sunday nights – his one night off a week – we wouldn't have managed to produce Jessie at all.' She waved through the window at one of the children charging round the garden with Joshua. All three women burst out laughing. Matt, a shade less confident, joined in halfway through. 'But things got better,' Ambreen went on, warming to her theme. 'He doesn't work any night shifts now. Making Thomas here wasn't nearly such a problem.'

They all laughed again, Matt with even less confidence, preoccupied suddenly by the fact that it was weeks since he had had sex and that unless his circumstances underwent a radical transformation many more months of enforced celibacy stretched ahead. It wasn't a state of affairs he was used to. Sex had been in more or less regular supply for as long as he could remember. Before Kath there had been Janie, a journalist plodding the same provincial footpath as himself, but who had subsequently given it all up for a career in television. Rather successfully, as it turned out. He would stop and stare at her face on billboards sometimes, trying to merge the glossy pouting image with the rather insecure, flighty creature who had shared his bed. Before that there had been a messy few years of stop-start relationships, sometimes with prolonged gaps between each one, but fuelled by the natural momentum of an era when the emergence of new, eligible sexual prospects was taken as much for granted as the belief that wages and life in general were on single-track routes towards improvement.

Once sex had entered Matt's head there was no getting rid of it. To make matters worse, Ambreen, in a flattering demonstration of the extent of his acceptance into their hallowed female circle, began unbuttoning her shirt in order to deliver a liquid snack to the baby at her feet. Trying not to look – trying to look as if he wasn't trying not to look – Matt made much of sipping the last dregs of his cold tea, while his mind flipped back to the last occasion on which he and Kath had made love. A week before she left, or had it been more? He tensed from the effort of remembering, wishing he could recall every detail, wanting in retrospect to wring out some sense of the deception of which he had been so pitifully oblivious at the time. She had come once, hadn't she? Or had she faked it? Had she always faked it? Matt frowned at the sludge of tea leaves in the bottom of his mug, wondering what grim unreadable secrets they might hold.

'Have you decided where Josh will be going next term?'

It was Ambreen talking, one huge milky breast now fully exposed. The baby had quickly fallen asleep on the job, the bulbous nipple hanging out of its open mouth like a half-eaten cherry.

'Not yet sorted on that front, no.' Matt drilled his gaze into hers, careful not to let his eyes flick below her neckline. 'We're registered with the obvious places, St Leonard's and Broadlands, but I've yet to visit them myself. The whole business seems rather a minefield.'

'Oh, it is,' they all cooed, launching into a string of anecdotes about south London primary schools. Made bold by the distraction, Matt let his glance slip to Ambreen's chest, feeling some curious primeval stirrings at the way the baby had once again started chomping on the nipple, so unashamedly greedy and uncaring. Ambreen's insouciance was attractive too, he mused, crossing his legs in case his erection was more detectable than it felt and giving an earnest nod to a comment he hadn't heard. His thoughts slipped back to Kath, for whom breast-feeding had been a constant trial, pursued only because of pressure from peers and visiting nurses smugly implying that resorting to formula milk would be tantamount to murder.

Ambreen's baby had fallen asleep again, leaving a perfect pearl-drop of milk hanging off the tip of the nipple. For one heady moment Matt pictured his own tongue licking it clean, until the image fizzled out in a blush of shame. He was the faker, he thought wretchedly, seeking now to avoid the earnest expressions of the women, realising that he could never be truly integrated among them; that no matter how much he pretended or tried, a female would always trigger some degree of sexual response. Little did they know that he had already assessed how attractive the three of them were, half run through in his mind their potential as sexual partners: Heather with her kind eyes and wide waistline was the least obviously attractive, but had none the less an intensity about her which was appealing; Maria was the primmest and prettiest, with the kind of alert, intelligent expression that Matt had always found attractive; while Ambreen had a sultriness that the other two lacked, something to do with her coffee-cream skin and the languid way she moved.

'Matt, what do you think — would you like to?'

'Like to what? Sorry, I lost it there for a moment. I'm afraid I have trouble focusing these days — a lot on my plate and so forth.'

There was a round of exchanged glances and sympathetic murmurs.

'I was just saying that if you hadn't yet looked round St Leonard's we could go together,' repeated Maria. 'I've only been once and was planning to go back. It's almost certainly our preferred choice, if Harry gets in, of course, but I'd still be curious to take a peek at Broadlands as well. We could do both in the same morning. Only if you want to,' she added, the lack of response from Matt making her suddenly uncertain.

'Absolutely. Yes, please. Much nicer to look with someone — to share opinions and so on. Help me — help Josh and I — come to some sort of decision. Thanks, Maria, I'd like that very much. Though it will have to be a Saturday, I'm afraid, as I go back to work next week.'

The party was broken up by a set-to in the garden. Joshua and Ambreen's little girl came hurtling into the sitting room in tears, howling conflicting accounts as to what had happened. Ambreen began at once to try to engineer a reconciliation, but Matt, who had caught a glimpse of the girl pulling Josh's hair, could not bring himself to do likewise. While it was clear that his adversary was suffering from little more than hurt feelings, Josh had a livid purple bruise on his forehead and what looked suspiciously like bite marks on his forearm.

'I just hate them to go without saying sorry,' wailed Ambreen, as Matt embarked on his farewells, bearing his still-sobbing son towards the door.

'Perhaps next time, when they've calmed down,' he replied, uttering the reassurance through gritted teeth, suddenly seeing Ambreen as not so much sultry as fawning and complacent, thinking that if she fished her breast out again he would stare all he liked and not feel a thing.

Turning into his street some ten minutes later, Matt was disheartened to see Kath's mother leaping out of a lime-green Saab parked outside their front door.

'At last – I'd almost given up. I suppose I should have called, but I was in the area and decided to chance it. Remembered you were taking time off. Joshy, darling, come to Nan.' She bent down and pressed her grandson into her arms, undeterred by the stiffness of his response. 'And what's this, you poor darling? Matthew, what on earth has happened to his face?'

'A collision with a particularly hard-headed playmate – don't worry, he's fine. But this is such a surprise, Gillian, how good of you to drop by,' he added, determined for Joshua's sake at least to be as civil as he could. His mother-in-law, true to her usual defiance of the passing years, was attired in a skirt suit of brilliant raspberry pink, a colour that sat rather questionably with the gingery tint she gave her hair. Her legs, as long as Kath's and undeniably shapely for a pair that had been kicking around the planet for well over sixty years, were handsomely displayed in stiletto heels and seamed stockings, the dark straight line drawing attention to the daring hemline of the skirt.

'I've been having lunch with an old and very dear friend, and thought it would be mad not to drop by,' she explained, starting to stroke and rearrange Joshua's hair. 'But how are you, Matthew? How are you coping?'

'As well as can be expected,' he replied dryly, reaching out a hand to rescue Josh, who was cringing under the fiddling fingers messing with his scalp. 'Though I'm sure you too must be upset,' he added, leading the way up the steps to the front door. Even during the least troubled times, maintaining a spirit of generosity towards his wife's parents had been hard. By Kath's own, frequent admission, they were snobs of the worst kind. Having escaped from Hounslow to Ascot thanks to the timely sale of a chain of launderettes, the pair of them had transferred their relentless aspirations to their only child. The way Kath defied them was something Matt had always admired, especially when that defiance had encompassed agreeing to marry him instead of somebody blessed with rather more obvious prospects of success.

'I can't believe we've still not heard one word from her,' complained Gillian now, pushing her way into the house after Matt, 'and after all we've done over the years. Really, I could weep. Every chance, every opportunity, and this is the gratitude she shows. The shame of it . . . God in heaven, that a daughter of mine should abandon her own *child.*' As she talked, she flopped down on to the sofa, eased off her shoes with a sigh, and began massaging the balls of her feet.

'Can I get you anything? Tea or coffee?'

'Tea would be heaven.' Seeing Josh hovering in the doorway, she patted the seat on the sofa next to her. 'Come and sit next to Nan and tell her all about school.' Josh, eyeing her suspiciously, stayed where he was. With the intermittent state of hostility that had reigned between Kath and her mother throughout his brief life, he had passed very little time in the company of his grandmother. What moments they had spent together had, for Joshua at least, been marked by a baffling seesaw of gushing affection and coldness, coupled with a mysterious concern over both the state of his appearance and the mode by which he addressed her. Not Grandma, not Granny, not Gran, not even Nanny. But Nan. Reprimands over this issue in particular had alerted Joshua at a very tender age to the confusing possibility of Being Wrong. Musing upon this very possibility now, he gingerly approached the sofa.

'That's it, come on, Nan doesn't bite.'

When Matt appeared with the tea the pair of them were

sitting side by side, Josh propped stiffly under the crook of his grandmother's arm, his bottom wedged so far into the back of the sofa that his little legs were aligned with her skinny stockinged thighs. Sneaking a wink at his son, Matt distributed drinks, followed by biscuits.

'Do you have a plate, Matthew?' asked Gillian, easing herself free of her grandson, who was blithely spraying crumbs on to her lap. 'He's very subdued, isn't he?' she remarked, taking the plate Matt offered her, a pitying frown creasing her face. 'But then that's hardly surprising.'

Matt, who had managed in all the various discussions of his circumstances to make no disparaging or thoughtless remarks either about Kath or Josh's reactions to her absence in the presence of Josh himself, gripped the handle of his mug in a bid to control himself. There was a big chip on the rim of his mother-in-law's mug, he noticed, drawing deep and unreasonable satisfaction from the observation, particularly when he noticed the raspberry-red lips' surreptitious efforts to avoid it.

'Thank you, Matthew, dear. Just the right amount of milk too.' She sipped again, imprinting a smudgy pink crescent of a stain on the china. 'I've come, as I said, to see how you are and because – as you can probably imagine – Lionel and I have done a lot of thinking and talking. God, how we have talked.' She sighed, pressing one palm to her chest. 'Wondering what more we could have done, where we went wrong. Kath has always been such a . . .' She tutted, searching for the right word. '. . . a worry. And now this.' She sighed again, more deeply. Josh, seeing his chance, slithered off the sofa and disappeared into the kitchen, where Matt heard what sounded suspiciously like the rustling of a fresh packet of biscuits. 'Which brings me to my point. Lionel and I are both quite clear on it.'

'Clear on what?' interrupted Matt impatiently, all efforts to accept the unattractive behaviour of his mother-in-law as being everything he might have predicted making it no less easier to tolerate.

'That we should take Joshua to live with us.'

Matt opened his mouth but no words came out.

'We can give him everything. A good solid home, the best schools, the best prospects. I know I'm not in my first flush and that the onus of it all will no doubt fall upon my shoulders because Lionel will, as per usual, spend every waking moment on the golf course and expect me to cope. But I am still full of energy. All my friends remark upon it. And besides which, the way Katherine has behaved, it's the least we can do. She is, after all, our responsibility,' she added, shaking her gingery ringlets mournfully.

'No, Gillian, Kath is not your responsibility. She is her own responsibility. She is thirty-one years old.'

'That's a sweet, generous view to take, Matthew, but the fact remains, I know my duty. It's not exactly how I had planned to spend my twilight years, but rest assured I will do a good – dare I say the best – job. Obviously you can see him whenever you like, and if Kath returns . . . well, in that case we shall all have to do our best to forgive and forget.'

Matt, still struggling for the right words, sought temporary refuge in an explosion of disdainful laughter, not at the thought of forgiving his wife, as Gillian assumed, but at the notion of surrendering his son to the chilly polished rooms of the Trumans' mock-Tudor residence in Ascot.

'Really, Matthew, we've all got to be grown-ups about this. I hardly think—'

'And I think you should leave now, Gillian.' He dropped to his knees, picked up her shoes and handed them to her. 'Touched as I am by your and Lionel's astounding generosity, I would not dream of accepting.'

Gillian stared at him, her purple-lidded eyes fluttering with doubt, unsure what to make of him at her knees with her shoes, behaving like a gallant prince but sounding suspiciously sarcastic. 'But you are not coping,' she burst out at length, taking the shoes and throwing up her arms.

'Who says?'

'This place, for a start. Look at it.'

Matt looked. He saw his home and all the props that made it so. 'What?'

'It's a pigsty, that's what it is,' she retorted, spitting the words, little specks of white saliva gathering in the corners of her mouth.

'Pigs are clean,' murmured Matt, getting to his feet, not wanting to flatter her with an attempt at an intelligent response. 'Joshua, given the circumstances, is fine.' He clenched his fists, feeling a protective lump block his throat. 'I love him. He loves me. We're going to get through this together.'

'How very touching,' she replied icily, sweeping out of the room.

'Of course, if you ever want to see him—' Matt began, but the front door slammed before he could finish the sentence. He stood staring at it for a few minutes, trying to summon some guilt for almost certainly having deprived his son of an entire wing of his rightful family. It was a while before he became aware that he was shaking, so badly that he leaned against the wall and closed his eyes.

When he opened them again it was to see Joshua sitting halfway up the stairs, his face streaked with sticky brown. Open on his lap was a box of chocolate fingers. Clearly bored of simply eating the biscuits, he was pushing them through the banisters and watching with mild interest as they broke on the hard floor below.

'Joshua – for God's sake, stop that. Where did you get those?'

Joshua hurled the remaining biscuits, box and all, down the stairs. He then turned and began to slither up towards the landing.

'Come here. I said, come here.' Matt took the stairs two at a time, crushing several biscuits underfoot before successfully seizing his son. 'You made that mess so you're going to help Daddy clean it up.'

'No!' The word began as a shout but ended up as a prolonged howl. Pinned in Matt's arms, the child wrestled furiously. 'Mummy! I want Mummy!'

Matt relaxed his grip at once. He had been holding him too tightly, he realised, hurting him. Joshua went limp in response, reducing his protests to a whimper. 'I want her too,' Matt whispered, sinking down on to the bottom step and tucking Joshua on to his lap. 'But we've got to learn to be good without her, to look after ourselves, not to be naughty . . . What would Mummy say at such a mess, eh?' He gestured at the heaps of broken biscuit around them. 'She'd smack both our bottoms, that's what.'

Joshua managed a half smile, as if doing his best to co-operate in the business of being cheered up.

'Okay. We'll clear up together, shall we?' said Matt gently. 'You put the ones that haven't broken into the box and I'll do the rest.'

Joshua nodded solemnly before saying, 'Does Nanny – Nan – miss Mummy too?'

Matt frowned in a show of thought, hoping the tears welling in his eyes would not spill into view. 'Yes she does, in her own way. You know, Josh, if you ever want to visit them, Nan and Grandpa, you can always . . .' But he had already wriggled free of Matt's lap and was gathering up the least damaged of the biscuits, clutching them so tightly that melted chocolate oozed between his fingers.

Chapter Twelve

By Thursday, just four days before he was due to step back into the shoes of his career, Matt's postcard in Mr Patel's window had still failed to generate one single response. When he lamented the fact to Mr Patel himself, during the course of one of his many sorties to stock up on supplies, the shopkeeper's only suggestion was to highlight the advert with a fluorescent yellow pen.

'There are so many cards,' he pointed out, gesturing at the jigsaw of adverts, ranging from cottages for rent in the Dordogne to stress-relieving acupuncture. 'You must make yours stand out more. I'll do it, if you like.'

'That's very kind,' muttered Matt, seeing only the futility of such a measure and musing that one of the grocer's many and beautiful daughters, frequently to be seen manning the tills after school and at weekends, their long painted nails clicking inexpertly over the keys, would have been of far greater use. 'No one in your family looking for a bit of extra work, then?' he ventured. 'Bit of childcare after school and evenings, that sort of thing.' He peered hopefully at the back of the shop, but was rewarded only by a rare glimpse of Mrs Patel, floating down the narrow aisles like a ship in full sail.

Mr Patel shook his head regretfully. 'I would like to help, Mr Webster, but I need my girls in the shop and then they also have very many studies. Rajeet, my son, is not so busy, but he is only fourteen. I am sorry for your troubles. Women, eh?' He tutted loudly, the gleam in his eye doing little justice to Matt's sense of the scale of his own tragedy. 'Always a bother, isn't it?'

'Yes, indeed,' Matt had agreed wearily, lugging his grocery bags out into the street and wondering how to raise his search for childcare to new, more promising levels. There was a magazine called the *Lady*, which Louise had mentioned, but a glance had revealed it to be alarmingly high-powered, full of women wanting en suite bathrooms, their own cars and membership of leisure clubs. Trudging under the weight of his shopping, he reverted his thoughts instead to the dubious back-up plan of preying upon the goodwill of his father for a couple of weeks. Joshua was a handful. Four full afternoons and up to four evenings a week was a lot to ask of anyone, let alone a sixty-nine-year-old with an ex-smoker's wheeze and the inclination to spend half the day asleep. And he hadn't even mentioned New York yet, Matt reminded himself gloomily, resolving to give the Patel advert one more day, before giving up on it completely.

A night of raking over such issues proved poor preparation for the meeting with Beth Durant the following morning. Try as he might to remind himself that he was negotiating for what could prove a crucial move in his career, that to appear pushy and confident was everything, Matt was unable to shake himself into any true sense of engagement with his surroundings. The night at the Aldwych felt like a distant memory, the flicker of attraction between them nothing short of fantastical. As a married man it had been easy to indulge in such imaginings, he realised, because they were so safely improbable. Cast before her now in the role of discarded husband, he felt not merely incompetent but supremely unattractive.

Beth Durant worked from a small but plush office on a busy third floor in the heart of Covent Garden. Verdant pot plants sprawled along the windowsills and shelves, blending tastefully with the lush green carpet and framed splashes of modern art on the walls. Her desk was large, its gold-edged leather top almost completely obscured by deep but orderly piles of papers. Matt sat opposite her, twiddling the handle of his coffee cup and trying to dredge some kind of insightful remark from the blurry depths of his brain. Something that would suggest zeal and commitment. Anything to divert attention from the emotions he was really experiencing, the fearful indifference to Andrea Beauchamp and all her kind, the sudden lack of conviction not only about the importance of interviewing anybody but about his ability ever to watch a play again and say anything intelligent in response.

'More coffee?'

'Ah, yes.'

Matt watched as she crossed the room to a sleek chrome machine in the corner. She was wearing an elegant dark trouser suit, with a jacket tailored into her waist, and buttoned so as to reveal a turquoise triangle of a T-shirt and the slope of an impressive chest. Peeking beneath the hem of the trousers were soft, flat-heeled black leather shoes that looked both comfortable and very expensive. The second coffee tasted even stronger than the first; he could feel the caffeine belting round his system, pumping his heart, making his palms damp.

'So you are still keen?'

For a moment Matt wondered what she was referring to. 'About Andrea . . . very much so. Though what these creatures ever reveal in their exchanges with the media is questionable,' he gabbled, aware that he was merely echoing Oliver. 'And she's taking so long, isn't she? To make up her mind, I mean. Not that I'm saying . . .' He left the sentence hanging, seeking refuge in another glug of coffee and wondering suddenly what the point of the meeting had been. There was nothing that could not have been discussed over the telephone.

Beth Durant pressed her hands together and smiled as kindly as she dared, inwardly toying with the notion of offering some sort of commiseration. Oliver Parkin had warned her of Matthew Webster's altered circumstances. Even if he hadn't she couldn't help thinking that she would have noticed that something was amiss beyond the dreaminess evident in most people after a long break out of the office. Although he looked not so much dreamy as dazed, she decided, eyeing her visitor over the pyramid-top of her hands. There was an air of dishevelment about him that was new, a ruffled, vulnerable, unloved look, something to do with the slightly skew-whiff sprouting of his short hair and the nick of blood on his chin. 'I'm sorry. I asked you here because I really did think I—' She was interrupted by the ring of her phone. 'Ah, now this could be what I've been waiting for. Excuse me.' She picked up the receiver, turning slightly away from him to take the call.

Matt slumped a little lower into his chair, letting his facial muscles relax, feeling momentarily – absurdly – let off the hook. It had been a bad morning. Joshua, perhaps sensing an air of urgency beyond the regular challenge of getting him through the wide door of Bright Sparks by nine o'clock, chose that morning to demand matching socks and a particular sweat-shirt still buried at the bottom of the laundry basket. During the course of the tantrum provoked by this state of affairs he had imprinted small, but perfectly visible, strawberry jam stains on Matt's clean shirt, ironed specially the night before. He had been forced to wear an old grey one instead, which he did not like as much but which offered the advantages, rare in his wardrobe these days, of being clean and uncrumpled.

'March fourth? I'll see. One moment.' The chair spun round, returning Matt to the firing line. 'Tuesday, March fourth, three o'clock at the Ritz,' Beth whispered, pressing her hand over the mouthpiece. 'Shall I say yes?'

Matt nodded, black specks dancing before his eyes.

'Thank you very much,' he said when the phone was back on the hook, making a note of the date in his diary and reaching for his coat.

'It's my job,' Beth replied lightly, glancing at her watch, a fine bracelet of gold which Matt had noticed her fiddling with while she was on the phone. 'This calls for a celebration, don't you think? Not even Julia Roberts would have been so hard. On second thoughts, I take that back,' she added with a sparkling laugh, clearly thrilled with her victory. 'Twelve o'clock's not too early for lunch, I hope? And this one's on me – I'm feeling generous.'

'That's very kind, but I'm not sure I—'

'Oh, come on now, it's Friday. I know you're officially on holiday, but surely one course and a glass of wine would not be too arduous? There are about a thousand places to choose from – but then I'm sure you know that,' she added with an apologetic laugh. 'I just love the ambience of this part of town, with all those jugglers and opera singers and violinists – in Washington guys like that get moved on by the police. Back home nobody lingers over mealtimes any more, not even on a Friday. It's all fast food stuff – good fast food, you can get everything from sushi to Creole – but even so . . . Have you made up your mind yet?' she added, sliding the question in so unexpectedly that Matt, who had been steeling himself to refuse, found himself saying yes instead.

They sat in the window of a small wine bar, with tourists and shoppers streaming past on the pavement, some of them occasionally pausing to study the menu pinned to a post outside or to stare in through the glass itself, as if scrutinising exhibits in a case.

'I'd love to go for all the creamy dishes but I have to watch my cholesterol,' Beth complained, frowning at the menu and shaking her head. 'That's another thing you guys don't seem to worry about over here, cholesterol levels – in the States everybody knows where they are on that score.'

'Well, I certainly don't,' Matt confessed, laughing. 'I don't even know my weight except via which hole I'm using for the buckle on my belt.' He patted his stomach, which these days felt hollow no matter the amount or quality of food fed into it.

'How can you not know your weight?' Her eyes widened with incredulity. 'I get on the scales twice a day. I know what I weighed last week and last year, I know that I was fattest at my brother's wedding and thinnest at my mother's funeral. It's like an integral part of me, of my identity, of the way I feel okay or messed up.' She put a hand to her mouth. 'Oh God, one sip of wine and I'm shooting my mouth off. Don't listen to me. Let's just drink to Andrea Beauchamp and a great interview.'

It wasn't until after they had finished eating and were sitting with cups of coffee that Beth broached the subject of the calamities in Matt's private life, emboldened by a large glass of wine that had accompanied her pasta and a freshly lit Marlboro Light. 'I know it's none of my business, Matthew, but can I just say how sorry I was to hear of your break-up? Oliver Parkin told me, which you may think was indiscreet of him, but I'm glad that he did. Having endured some of the same stuff myself, believe me, I know what you're going through. Part of the reason I came to London was to get away from my ex. He's what they call a big player in the political scene. Though we split two years ago we kept coming across each other, getting in each other's hair. Washington is an unbelievably small city in that respect – all the same people meeting each other round dinner tables and at social functions. It was driving me crazy, hearing stuff about him all the time, knowing that he was hearing about me.' She shuddered, exhaling a long plume of smoke.

'Not a problem with which I am confronted,' confessed Matt with a short laugh. 'I don't know how much Oliver told you, but my wife has done a very thorough job of leaving me. Another man, another life. I don't even know where.' He paused. 'She used to be an actress, you know, but gave up on it completely when our son, Joshua, came along. At the time she seemed happy enough to do that, but now I can't help thinking she might have had a sort of mid-life crisis . . . I found these photos, you see, really glamorous ones, like for a portfolio or a casting or something. I keep asking myself why she had them done, who took them, whether it's the photographer who . . .' Matt broke off, embarrassed suddenly at this further evidence of his new inclination to bare his soul to half-known females, wondering if it was genuine advice that he sought or an altogether less edifying desire for attention. He still felt mildly ashamed of how his thoughts had strayed during his tea session in Laycock Road, how he had betrayed his well-intentioned audience without them even realising it.

'And your little boy, what have you told him?' Beth pressed, her eyes wide.

'That Mummy is on a long holiday,' he admitted, thinking how flimsy the explanation sounded out loud. 'And I'm not sure when she is coming back.'

Beth groaned. 'Jesus, that's so sad. At least Rob and I didn't have kids. And we both hated each other, which kept things simple,' she added cheerfully.

'Much easier all round,' Matt agreed, grateful to her for giving them the opportunity to laugh.

A few minutes later they were heading their separate ways, Matt towards the Tube and Beth to her office. After at least ten strides Matt could not resist turning to look back, finding with some surprise that she had done the same. They waved again, their hands just visible over the sea of jostling heads crowding the stretch of pavement between them.

Chapter Thirteen

Returning home with Josh later that afternoon, Matt was relieved and somewhat amazed to find two messages responding to his advert in the grocer's window. Chuckling to himself over the fact that Mr Patel's fluorescent marker should have proved so effective, he phoned back the first of the callers immediately, having to resist the urge to offer her the job on the spot.

'Mrs Rollings? My name is Matthew Webster. You called about my advertisement.'

'Oh, yes, it would suit me perfectly. Just the thing I'm looking for.' Her voice sounded faintly wheezy and rather older than it had on her message.

'And you've plenty of experience of looking after children?'

'With five of my own, I should think so.'

'Five?'

'I collect my twins at three and the others at four, so I could easily fit in another.'

'The thing is, I'm not sure that—'

'So lucky to have a boy. Mine are all girls. We were going to try again – Bert was mad for a boy – but you get past it, don't you, going back to all those broken nights and nappies? And I had a terrible time with my veins. I tell Bert, I think my poor old legs would explode if I put them through it again.'

'With five of your own, you've probably got your hands full—'

'Not at all. We're in Drake's Crescent. Is that near you?'

'I'm not sure I—'

'When did you want me to start? His nursery's not the place at the bottom of Stenning Road, is it? Because that's just round the corner from us.'

'No—'

'Shame. That would have made my life ever so easy.'

'Well, thank you for calling, Mrs Rollings. I've had quite a bit of interest expressed in the job, so I'll get back to you, if I may.'

'As you please,' she replied, sounding far less friendly, 'but I'm on hold for five hours' ironing in Bickley Road and they won't wait for ever for an answer.'

Matt dialled the second number with a rather heavier heart, chiding himself for his naïvety in ever having imagined that some magic solution to his logistical troubles was going to fall into his lap.

'Is that Josephine Davies? My name is Matt Webster. You left a message about my advertisement for childcare.'

'Yeah, I did. I want to work with kids. I'm looking for some experience.'

Matt almost groaned out loud. 'In that case . . .'

'Job-wise, that is. I mean, I spend loads of time with kids – friends' little brothers and sisters and that. And I've done proper baby-sitting too. I love it, you see. When I leave school I'm going to study to be a nursery nurse. Do it as a profession. I was going to train to work with kids in hospital, be a proper nurse – but I wouldn't like to see them sick or dying and stuff.'

'So you're still at school?' said Matt gloomily, prolonging the discussion in order to let her down lightly.

'Yeah, I'm sixteen, but I'm leaving in the summer and I'm free all Wednesday afternoons and could help most days from four until late.'

'So no homework, then?'

If the girl registered the sardonic edge in his tone she gave no sign of it. 'I do that in the mornings. I wake up really early, get it done before breakfast.'

'I see. And what are you like with an iron?' Matt asked, touched in spite of himself by her persistence.

'Oh, I love ironing,' she squealed. 'Honest, I do, I'm not just saying that because I want the work, even though I do. Your ad mentioned evening sitting – I'd be great for that 'cos I could do the ironing while your little boy was in bed.'

'And your parents, are they party to these grand plans?'

'They don't mind,' she replied quickly, the first tinge of wariness creeping into her tone.

'Look, I tell you what, perhaps you could come round so we can meet and chat a bit more about the possibilities. I was really looking for someone who could start earlier in the afternoons, but I often have to work evenings as well so we might be able to sort something out. If Joshua likes you, that is,' he added. 'I'm afraid he can be rather fussy about his friends.'

Instead of sounding intimidated, the girl laughed. 'What does he like, then? What's he into?'

'Hamsters and videos, mainly, though I try to discourage too much telly,' Matt added quickly. 'You ought to know that the pair of us are on our own, and that he . . . well, he misses his mum sometimes. He loves building things too. We've got heaps of Lego and all that kind of thing.'

'So when shall I come round?'

They settled on the following morning. Feeling faintly hopeful, Matt took a bottle of beer into the sitting room in order to contemplate a final round-up of his options. Joshua, fired up with the pizza and chocolate yoghurt that had constituted tea, was springing from chair to chair, wearing a pirate hat and eye patch that he had made at school that day.

A nanny was too expensive. An au pair was too intrusive. Mrs Rollings had sounded gruesome. Though still balking at the idea of calling upon the temporary assistance of his father, Matt was beginning to realise that taking such a step would not feel nearly so bad if he could offer a young energetic girl to help out alongside. Josephine's limited hours would dovetail perfectly with Dennis in that respect, and might even, with only a little stretch of the imagination, prove the perfect solution for when he himself finally got to the point of working from home.

Matt closed his eyes, imagining a time when the structure of his daily life had receded back to the comfortable invisibility he had once taken for granted. The main cause of these deliberations, meanwhile, was working himself into a piratical frenzy, commanding imaginary enemies with an imaginary sword. A way of escaping, Matt supposed, opening his eyes and watching fondly; a way of controlling the world, like sorting beads and counters.

'Hey, calm down there, Captain Bluebeard, or you'll fall in the sea and get eaten by the crocodiles.'

'Crocodiles,' yelled Josh, leaping off the arm of the sofa and tussling with a large teddy that had served many similar combative purposes in the last couple of years.

'You be careful now,' Matt warned over his shoulder, retreating through the open double doors into the kitchen. 'Dad's going to call Granddad and then it will be time for your bath.'

Dennis picked up the phone after just one ring, his kindly, wry tone suggesting that he had been waiting for just such a request all week.

'I'll come on Sunday, if that's all right. Give me time to sort out a few things first, shut up shop so to speak.'

'Dad, I'm so sorry to have left it to the last minute – I kept thinking something would turn up. It won't be for long – just a couple of weeks at most.'

'I know, I know. I don't mind in the least. When I said I wanted to make myself useful I meant it. Do me good to get away for a bit,' he added.

'And I'm lining up a really nice girl to help out in the evenings, so you won't have to do too long a stint on your own,' continued Matt, aware that he was leaping ahead of himself, but wanting desperately to offer something in return for the un-wavering goodness of his father's response, for there being no hint of reluctance or martyrdom. 'I'm interviewing her tomorrow morning. She sounded very promising on the phone – rough round the edges maybe, but full of heart.'

'Whatever. We'll manage just fine, don't you worry. I'll come by train. Try to be with you before dark.'

As Matt put down the receiver there was a loud thump from the sitting room. A moment or two of silence was followed by a dry alien wail that made the hairs on the back of his neck stand on end. Racing out of the kitchen, he found Joshua sprawled behind the sofa, surrounded by a small pool of blood, purplish red against the blue pile of the carpet. The eye patch, pushed back off his face, looked like a comical hair-band. There was so much blood that it took Matt a moment or two to locate the actual wound, a two-inch gash across the centre of his forehead, gaping like a pair of parted lips.

'Okay, okay, you're fine.' Seizing a crumpled pillowcase from the mountain of ironing behind the sofa, he wiped away the worst of the mess and pressed hard against the cut till the flow of blood eased. A few minutes later they were speeding down Kennington Road, Matt wishing he had a siren to stick on his roof and Joshua holding the pillowcase against his forehead with a quiet, touching obedience that was far worse than the howls.

On seeing the age and state of the patient, the receptionist's lazy look altered in an instant. Although the waiting area was almost full, they were quickly ushered down a corridor and into a small room with a bed and a desk. A nurse came in a few moments later. After a brisk inspection of Joshua's forehead, she applied a clean pad to the cut, which was still bleeding but less profusely, and got out a sheet of paper.

'So he fell off a sofa?'

'I think so, I wasn't there . . . that is, I was, but in the other room — they adjoin each other — on the telephone. I think he must have caught his head on the edge of the window ledge as he fell. He was playing pirates you see and—'

'And this other bruise — was that caused at the same time, while you were out of the room?'

'No, that was a couple of days ago at a friend's house. Some sort of contretemps in the garden — I can't claim to be a witness to that one either.' Matt smiled tightly. 'It's been a bit of a week.'

'I see. And did Joshua pass out on either of these occasions, even for a few seconds?'

Matt shook his head. 'No, I'm pretty sure he didn't.'

'And he hasn't seemed sleepy?'

Matt looked down at the dazed pale face burrowing into his jacket. 'Well, he's tired now, of course. From shock and so on. You're wondering about concussion, I suppose.'

'Yes, I am.' She frowned. 'And there was no one — your wife or partner, for instance — who was with him during either of these accidents?'

'No. We . . . it's just the two of us at the moment. Isn't it, mate?' he whispered, brushing his lips against Joshua's hair.

It wasn't until a doctor ran through many similar questions that it dawned on Matt that he was being regarded with suspicion. A single father, a bruised child, a lame story about not being around when the accident happened. The scenario spoke for itself.

'I know it looks awful,' he gabbled, as the doctor, a short, squat man with pouches under his eyes, scrubbed his hands in the sink next to the desk. 'Two head wounds in one week, but he's just at that age. Spends most of the day being a pirate —a dangerous occupation at the best of times.' He could hear the desperation in his voice.

'Well, he's going to look even more like a pirate when we've finished with him,' quipped the doctor, his expression softening, whether for Joshua's sake or his own Matt found it hard to be sure. Pulling out a surgical glove from a packet on the desk, he blew it into a comical cockerel head of a balloon and placed it in Joshua's hands. 'There you are, young man, You take charge of that while I put a bit of glue on this face of yours and then some special plasters to keep it nice and tightly closed.'

'Glue?' said Matt, momentarily distracted from fears of arrest. 'Not stitches?'

'Not these days. Now hold him tight a minute as I need to squeeze the sides together while I just—' He performed the deed while he talked, so deftly that Joshua barely flinched. 'That's it. All done. Good boy. I'll prescribe an analgesic – to be taken every four hours for two days – and no jumping around for at least a week. Take this down to X-ray and when you've got the results bring them back up to the nurse on the front desk. I don't think there's any cause for alarm but it's better to be safe, as I'm sure you'll agree,' he added, his round face darkening for a moment. 'A bit of a queue down there, I'm afraid – it could take some time.'

When they were eventually discharged, with a prescription for some painkilling medicine and a clean bill on the X-ray front, it was already quite dark. As they crossed the hospital forecourt, a grey cuticle of a moon slipped into view from behind a mist of cloud. While it was not quite raining, the air felt moist and chilled. Shivering with cold, Matt pulled the panels of his coat more securely round Joshua, who was latched on to his chest like some kind of infant marsupial, his small fingers looped tightly round clumps of his jumper, his legs hooked over his hips. Having got out into the main street, Matt stopped on the edge of the pavement, suddenly bereft of any sense as to where he should go, aware only of the dankness of the night, the blurry yellow stream of passing cars and the pulse of unhappiness deep inside. He had thought he was over the worst, that he had been beginning to wrest some order out of the chaos. It was dispiriting beyond belief to realise that the process of recovery and readjustment had barely begun, that what he had imagined to be rock bottom was merely a halfway house, that if he looked down there were many dizzying depths still to go. The consolation of love for the child in his arms, instead of easing the pain, made it worse; because of the weight of the love, the guilt, the responsibility for moulding hope and happiness in a life that still had so far to go.

It was several minutes before Matt realised he was walking in the wrong direction. He had left the car down a narrow street on the other side of the hospital, with two wheels on the pavement, on a red line, or a double yellow — he hadn't known or cared. Slowly he turned and retraced his steps. Joshua, now thoroughly asleep, was heavier and harder to hold. It was several days since he had asked about Kath, a sign perhaps that he was beginning to accept the status quo in the way that only children could, the way that made them so exploitable. He hadn't even called for her when he fell, Matt realised, marvelling at the fact, thinking what massive adjustments they had both made already, so soon into this new version of their lives.

Rain seeped from the cloud at last, mingling with a few obstinate tears that had slipped on to Matt's cheeks. He walked slowly, trying to cast his mind back to the illness and death of his mother, wanting to recall what emotional pain had felt like as a teenager. But all he could remember clearly was the anger, the sense of outrage not only at being deprived of something all of his friends took for granted, but at being set apart, tarnished with the brush of misfortune. The carrying on had not been bravery, as most observers assumed, but a deep desire to have the embarrassment of difference overlooked, to merge back into inconspicuousness. He looked down at the crown of Joshua's head, shining wet in the darkness, wishing he could protect him from experiencing such complications, wishing even that Kath had died instead of scarring them both with the stigma of desertion.

He reached the car at last, surprised in his fatalistic frame of mind not to find it shackled with wheel clamps or cellophane-packaged parking tickets. By the time they got home, stopping at a chemist *en route*, Joshua was so tired that it took several attempts to get him to swallow the prescribed spoonful of pink liquid. Afterwards, Matt, his fingers and shirt front sticky from mismanaged efforts with the medicine, staggered downstairs, empty-headed with fatigue and hunger. Seeing the large dark patch on the carpet, he fetched a half-pound bag of salt and tipped the entire contents over it, swirling it round and round in a rippling pattern a good half-inch deep. His bottle of beer, barely touched, was still on the table. Picking it up, he noticed there were still smudges of blood on his hands.

When the telephone rang half an hour later, he was stretched out on the sofa with half an eye on a celebrity quiz show, so nearly asleep that he almost did not bother to answer it.

'Matt? It's Louise. Just wondered how you were, how the week had gone.'

'Oh, fairly hellish, thank you.'

'I didn't wake you, did I? You sound sleepy.'

'No, no. Just recovering from a bad day. Well, no,' he corrected himself, 'the morning was tolerable – almost good, in fact. I appear, at last, to have secured an interview with *the* Andrea Beauchamp. But the afternoon took a nosedive, literally, when Josh cracked his head open doing a kamikaze act off the sofa. A hospital emergency department is not a place I would recommend either for relaxation or entertainment on a Friday night. They kept asking me to explain what happened. It took a while to twig that I was being eyed up as at best negligent and at worst the cause of the wound.'

'You mean . . . ?'

'Yes, I do.'

'But that's ridiculous.'

Matt shrugged. 'Not really. Just doing their job. I expect they'll be asking me about Kath's disappearance next, checking the airing cupboard for hidden weapons.'

'Oh, Matt, don't be silly.'

He sighed. 'Don't listen to me. Feeling sorry for myself. It was good of you to think of calling.'

'And is Josh all right?'

'Seems to be. They took X-rays and so on, did the job properly – we were there for hours.'

'Look, Matt, I was wondering if you wanted to get together over the weekend? Anthony's going to Europe—'

'But he's only just got back, hasn't he?'

'From Boston, yes. That was Tuesday. He's frightfully in demand at the moment. The children see him so rarely I think they think he's some sort of lodger.' She laughed sharply. 'So anyway, I thought it might be fun if we got together.'

'Thanks, Louise, but I'm interviewing a prospective baby-sitter tomorrow and I've got my dad coming on Sunday, so I'm going to spend some time getting the house straight.'

'I could have Josh if you like, or come round and help out or—'

'Thanks again, but he's pretty beaten up and the doctor said to take it very easy. Lots of TV and food. No extra excitement of any kind – especially not King Arthur games,' he added wryly.

There was a pause. 'Okay. Not to worry. When Josh is feeling better, maybe. Let me know if you'd like me to have him after school again, or if you want Gloria, or if there's anything that I—'

'Louise, I'm okay,' Matt cut in, suddenly fed up with all her sympathetic browbeating, wanting only to crawl upstairs to bed.

That night he dreamt of Kath for the first time since she had left. She was beautiful and laughing, her fringe sweeping along the tops of her eyelashes, her mouth wide and red, teasing and needy. She beckoned and he followed, many times, round twists and turns in his head, chasing the image which kept dissolving like a silver mirage on a hot road.

Chapter Fourteen

It would have been hard to say who was more surprised, Matt on seeing the carrot-headed girl from the playground or Josephine herself, who let out a small shriek of dismay before turning to scurry back down the steps.

For an instant Matt hesitated, half inclined to let her go, marvelling at life's capacity to shock with its grisly little coincidences. When at last he called after her she paid no attention, except to glance over her shoulder like a frightened rabbit. Just as he expected her to round the corner out of sight, she stopped by a grey car and tapped on the window. 'I said, hang on,' he called again. Leaving the front door open, he hurried down the steps after her. 'Of course, I had no idea that—'

'I'm sorry to have bothered you,' she muttered, giving up on the car door, which was evidently locked, and turning to face him. Most of her hair seemed to be in her eyes, a fluffy cloud of orange. 'I didn't know it was you.'

'Well, that makes two of us.'

They were interrupted by a sharp female voice from across the road. The dark curly-haired woman whom Matt had seen on the occasion of their last meeting was striding towards them, heavy-soled black boots pushing out from under the panels of her long brown coat. As well as the satchel of a handbag she carried a large black umbrella which she pointed at Matt, causing it to blow open and shut like a large flapping bird. 'Josie, is everything okay?'

'Excuse me,' began Matt.

'He's the guy who wrote that advert,' interrupted Josie wearily. 'It's him, his little boy.'

'Is it really?' The woman gave the umbrella one last shake, aiming its point at the ground this time as opposed to Matt's head. 'In that case . . .'

A plaintive cry cut her off in mid-sentence. It came from Joshua, standing a few yards away in the open front door, barefoot and still in his pyjamas. The piece of hospital gauze protecting his forehead had come loose and was hanging somewhat ghoulishly over one eyebrow.

'Nasty fall yesterday,' Matt mumbled, feeling that such an appearance called for some explanation. Remembering in the same instant that he did not have his house keys and that a sudden gust of wind could leave them both marooned in the street at the mercy of unfriendly strangers, he turned back towards the house. Joshua called out again, this time with greater volume and clarity. 'He's gone, Dad. Spotty's got outside.'

'Who's Spotty?' enquired the girl, pushing her hair out of her eyes and peering towards Joshua with new interest.

'Hamster,' muttered Matt, breaking into a run. Back at the top of his steps he hustled his protesting son inside, bundled him into his coat and wellingtons and grabbed the house keys from the hall table. 'Okay, where did you see him go, Josh? Which way exactly? Down the steps? By the dustbins? Try and tell Daddy exactly because then we have a better—'

'Is this it?' Josephine was standing at the gate, holding up the truant rodent with a look of cheeky triumph on her face. 'He was going for a walk, I think. Trying to see the world.' She stroked the hamster's smooth chestnut head tenderly with her index finger, badly bitten, Matt noticed, and dabbed with the remains of pink nail varnish. 'What a goer, what a bold, brave little thing.'

'Spotty is brave,' echoed Joshua, grinning proudly.

So it was that the interview, which had looked destined not to be, took place after all, amidst some considerable celebration, and involving not only the girl but also her mentor of a friend, who turned out to be a drama and English teacher at her school, a comprehensive near the Old Kent Road. After making coffees and endeavouring to start proceedings with the correct measure of detached businesslike interest in Josie's potential as a child-minder, Matt gave up and let the conversation find its own flow. Josie, after making a comparable effort, was soon splayed out on the floor alongside his son, sketching faces on her fingertips with a Biro and waggling them to make him laugh.

The teacher, meanwhile, who had introduced herself as Sophie Contini, looked considerably less at ease. She sat on the edge of an armchair, holding her coffee in two hands, answering Matt's questions stiffly, her face only softening when she glanced at the pair on the floor. Having declined to surrender her coat, she had eased it off behind her on the seat, as if wanting to be ready to slip her arms back into it at a moment's notice. Her hair was scraped tightly back off her face, stretching the curls out flat except for some wisps at her temples. After limping through a few pleasantries, she seemed relieved at the chance to help Matt clear away the empty mugs.

'So does your partner work full time?' she asked, following him into the kitchen.

'No . . . that is, we've recently separated.' He made a face. 'Still trying to adjust to the new circumstances. Soon, I hope to be working from home.'

'So that's why you need Josie.' The remark was a statement rather than a question, delivered without any suggestion of the compassion or curiosity Matt had lately come to expect from females. 'Could I just say . . . I don't want her getting dragged into anything.'

'I beg your pardon?'

'You know . . . domestic warfare.'

'I can assure you that—'

'Where she lives she gets quite enough of that sort of thing, not just from her own family, but on the estate as a whole . . .' She lowered her voice, casting an anxious glance back through the double doors into the sitting room. 'In the area she's from I'm afraid they all have to grow up very quickly. Don't get me wrong,' she added hurriedly, seeing the look on Matt's face. 'When it comes to little ones Josie has a truly magic touch. She just seems to be able to get on their level, knows how their minds work. A little bit of regular, secure work is just what she needs, something good for her to focus on, where she can exercise her talents. And if you're thinking about that incident in the park, she only hangs around with those girls very occasionally. She lives in a tough world, Mr Webster, where sometimes you have to be seen to be playing the game in order to survive.'

'All this is very heart-rending, but I'm not a . . .' He had been going to say charity, but she interrupted him again.

'I brought her today, but she's going to get a bike. In the meantime, if it's a late night, I've said I'm prepared to come and pick her up.'

'But what about her parents?' asked Matt, curious, in spite of himself.

She offered him a tight smile. 'Perhaps I haven't explained very well. Josie's parents are not exactly . . . functional. No doubt they were good people once – we all begin life as innocents, don't we? But in their case lack of money, misfortune, alcohol . . . let's just say they don't care for Josie in the way parents should. There's a son a couple of years older who's just as hopeless – in with a bad crowd, the usual story. That Josie has turned out to be such a sweet-natured soul is nothing short of a miracle. You really would not regret employing her to look after your little boy, I promise you.' She smiled for the first time, drawing attention to her wide mouth, and then biting her lower lip as if ashamed of it. 'She finishes school this summer, hopefully having secured enough GCSEs to qualify for an NNEB course. I've promised to help her apply – obviously a job like this would be invaluable—'

'It seems she has a lot to be thankful to you for,' commented Matt dryly.

'I do what I can. The school is full of children like her. All they need is a bit of encouragement and support . . . I have kids knocking on my door at all times of the day and night. I'd be failing if I turned any one of them away.'

'That must be good for your private life,' Matt murmured, wondering if it were possible for anyone to sound more self-righteous or take themselves more seriously.

The hazel eyes flashed defensively. 'I manage, thank you, Mr Webster. Now I think it's probably time we were going, unless you've any more questions. If you want written references I can get them from several families round me where Josie has helped out over the last year. I hope you won't hold my honesty against her. I thought it was important that you should know the whole picture.' She paused before adding, 'If that means you've already decided against employing her I think it would be far better for all of us if you just came right out and said so—'

Matt, who had been steeling himself to do exactly that, compelled to do so both by the disheartening thumbnail sketch of Josie's background and the intimidating attitude of her protector, caught a glimpse of Joshua grinning at his new friend and said instead that references would not be necessary and that he would pay her five pounds an hour. Dennis would, after all, be around to keep an eye on things, he reasoned a few minutes later, hurrying after them into the hall, his mind burning with the thousand questions he should have asked before inviting anyone to take on so important a role.

'And do you cook?' he managed, struck suddenly by the thought that the bony, speckle-faced creature, tucking her skinny arms into a scruffy leather jacket, didn't look as if she knew how to eat properly, let alone prepare meals.

'Oh, yes, I love it,' she exclaimed at once, her face lighting up. 'I can do all sorts. I'm not bad, am I, Sophie?'

'Not bad at all,' agreed her protector, giving her an affectionate push out of the door and mouthing 'Thank you' over her shoulder at Matt.

Dennis arrived the following afternoon, with one suitcase and Hoppit attached to an old chewed lead. As he opened the door, Matt's heart surged with a confusion of gratitude and despair. He was hiring a damaged teenager and a geriatric to care for his child, he thought desperately, helping ease the old tweed coat off Dennis's shoulders, and suppressing the urge to shout at the dog, who was yelping round his ankles in celebration at being released from five hours of confinement in rail carriages and taxis.

'I've hired this funny stick insect of a girl,' he said, once they were sitting with mugs of tea and a crusty fruitcake bought from Mr Patel's that morning, along with almost a hundred pounds' worth of groceries to see them through the week. The shop-keeper, watching Matt struggle up and down the aisles trying to control both his son and two of the miniature trolleys, laden with ready-made meals and cans of beer, had invited Joshua to sit up on the counter next to the till, where he was given a calculator to play with and treated to a sticky lollipop.

'Looks like you found yourself some help anyway,' he had remarked, eyeing the heaps of food as Matt's Switch card whirred through the machine. 'And one with an appetite too.'

'My father,' Matt confessed, adding quickly, 'But the advert worked very well in the end – a nice girl is going to help out with baby-sitting.'

'So I take your notice down now?'

'Yes please, for the time being anyway.'

As Matt staggered towards the exit, Mr Patel had shouted some machinegun dialect to the door marked 'Private' at the back of the shop. A moment later the boy called Rajeet, a small, wiry teenager with bright eyes and the first brush of dark hair on his upper lip, appeared and seized several of the bags from Matt's hands. He proceeded to accompany them all the way home, grinning at Joshua, who skipped alongside, waving the last remaining dot of his lolly like a baton.

'I could have coped without the girl, you know,' ventured Dennis now, managing through the slurps of his tea to sound hurt.

'Of course, I know that. The thing is, I want you to help me check her out,' Matt ventured slyly, 'decide if she's up to continuing the job once you've returned to Yorkshire and I'm based at home. She's a funny-looking thing, comes from a bit of a tough background, but is full of energy and eagerness to please. And she was great with Josh, which matters most of all. I've asked her to come for the first time at five on Wednesday, when I've got to be at the theatre and I thought you might welcome reinforcements. She's also promised to take charge of the housework, clean the kitchen floor and keep the ironing under control.'

'Ah, in that case she can come as often as she likes,' laughed Dennis, his pride salvaged as Matt had guessed it would be.

The rest of the day was spent running through Joshua's daily routine, going over the route for the walk to Bright Sparks and double-checking the whereabouts of vital phone numbers and key items of food. Joshua himself was very quiet, less pleased than Matt had expected at the sight of his grandfather and more than usually uncooperative about staying in his bed. By nine thirty that night he had come down to the sitting room so many times Matt was finding it almost impossible to conceal his impatience. Dennis, wearing an expression of determined detachment, retreated to the television, where he sat nursing a mug of tea, his slippered feet resting on Hoppit's bony back. Having dealt with the pretext for the intrusion – on this occasion a mislaid toy – Matt slung his son on to his hip and carried him back upstairs.

'I'll stay for a bit, shall I?' He pulled the duvet up to Joshua's chin and dropped his head on to his hands, wondering which one of them would fall asleep first.

'Daddy?'

'What is it?' Opening one eye, Matt reached out and stroked the pale forehead. The bruise was already a faint yellow splash, while the skin on either side of the cut – the protective gauze pad long since abandoned – was already closing over the split, knitting with wondrous neatness into a small ridge of a scar. 'How's that head?' Matt brushed his lips across the butterfly stitches.

'Is Granddad staying for ever?'

'No, just for a bit, until Daddy can do his work at home.'

'Is he staying instead of Mummy being here?'

'Sort of. To help Dad.'

'Will Mummy come back?'

'Josh, I'm not sure. Sometimes grown-ups have to do things that are hard to explain. It doesn't mean she doesn't love you, I know she does, she just—'

'Jessica said you can't go to big school without a mummy.'

'Well, Jessica is wrong,' said Matt fiercely. 'Granddad and I had to manage without my mummy when I was young and—'

'Has Mummy died as well, then?'

'No, she's just had to go away for a long time. She loves you but she doesn't love Daddy – which happens sometimes with grown-ups. As you grow older you'll meet loads of other kids whose mummies and daddies don't live together . . .'

It was a few moments before Matt realised that the target of these reassurances had fallen asleep, the eyelids dropping at last into the most perfect portrait of peaceful oblivion. He stayed kneeling by the bed for a few minutes, marvelling at how, when it came to the question of motherly love, he always sprang to Kath's defence, wondering whether it was purely for Joshua's sake or because he himself really believed such things to be true. If she had loved him how could she have left him behind? But then, thank God she had, he thought, stroking his son's pale cheek with his fingertips. In the dim glow of the nightlight he could see Joshua's eyeballs rolling restlessly beneath his eyelids, scrolling through invisible images; finding comfort, Matt hoped, wishing he could provide some comparable solace for the harsh realities of the outside world.

Chapter Fifteen

No matter how placid the weather in the rest of London, the square mile housing Matt's newspaper's headquarters in Canary Wharf seemed always to be the epicentre of a localised gale. As he stepped off the light railway, the familiar blast of wind off the river pulled the skin tight on his face. He leaned forward as he walked, as if to forge a passage with the top of his head, feeling that he could have leaned on his entire body weight without hitting the ground. As usual, the area was buzzing with bull-dozers and cranes, ten years of intense development having done little to erase the impression of a building site with aspirations beyond its means. For every finished construction, there were three more still in their infancy. Recent problems with the Jubilee Tube extension had triggered a new set of temporary signposts and a corridored maze of yellow tape. Clusters of grey-faced commuters and a few hardy tourists with cameras were emerging from a side staircase and being syphoned round a series of orange bollards towards the broad stone steps leading up to street level. Crossing to the tower block that housed his employ-ers, Matt had to dodge round three overladen skips half blocking the road. On the pavement next to them four men in yellow helmets were huddled round an open manhole, shaking their heads and rubbing their chins doubtfully.

Matt crossed the marbled foyer of the ground floor with

mixed feelings. It was good to know that his old life was still there waiting for him. Yet at the same time he experienced a tingling disquiet at the realisation that, while his personal circumstances had changed so radically, nothing at the paper would have altered at all. Where work had once embodied a world entirely and effortlessly separate from home, he had already had to make a conscious effort that morning to keep his thoughts from straying back south of the river to home; not to remember Joshua's crumpled white face pleading for him to stay, not to worry that his father's morning routine of two fried eggs and half an hour on the loo would jeopardise his ability either to be vigilant or to arrive at Bright Sparks at the appointed hour.

He entered the lift with a group of other people. Among them was a woman from a neighbouring department whom he remembered as having taken time off to have a baby the year before. He recalled the unflattering bulk of her, not just during the last few weeks but when she returned to the office three months later, still clearly exhausted and not yet adjusted to the new demands of her life. There had been many snide remarks from male colleagues, not just about her figure but about women and work in general, about the questionable nature of female career commitment. The injustice of it, only dimly felt before, hit Matt so hard that for a second or two he considered shattering the sleepy silence of morning lift etiquette and posing some companionable enquiry. He tried to catch her eye but she looked away, impatiently pressing the button for her floor and leading the way out the moment the doors parted.

Overcome with sudden shyness at the thought of running the gamut of greetings *en route* to his desk, Matt made a tactical withdrawal to the toilets. He was sick with nerves, he realised, splashing water on his face and holding out his hand to marvel at the tremor in his fingers. His freshly shaven cheeks looked faintly yellow in the glare of the basin light and there were violet shadows under his eyes. Somewhere deep inside his temples he could feel the tick of a pulse.

'Matthew, good to see you back.'

'Good to be back,' he replied quickly, spinning round to greet the tall, imposing figure of the arts editor. He held out an arm for a handshake but Phillip Legge was already crossing to the line of urinals along the opposite wall.

'Very sorry to hear of your troubles,' drawled his employer, unzipping his fly and throwing his words over one shoulder. 'I gather from Oliver you want us to rethink your contract, let you operate from behind a desk in Kennington. Not an idea that fills me with glee, I must admit. And as far as you're concerned, it would mean a cut in salary, certainly to start with. But' – he paused for a moment, rolling forward on the balls of his feet – 'it just so happens a very promising CV has been pushed my way – first in English, editor of the university magazine, active member of the Footlights, that sort of thing. Done a couple of years' hard graft on the *Manchester Post*. I've got her coming in later this morning. Meet her, see what you think. Could work out very well. Though I make no promises.' He had been standing at the urinal for the duration of this speech, while Matt hovered awkwardly in the background, wanting to appear attentive without crossing the boundaries of discretion. Even had he shared the urge to relieve himself, he was aware that some childish timidity would probably have prevented him from doing so.

'Thank you, Phillip.' It was a relief to see his boss zip himself back up and turn to the washbasins. 'I look forward to meeting her. And as for the contract, well, it's because of . . . I mean, it wasn't in my game plan, I assure you.'

'Few things are.' The sudden curtness in his tone reminded Matt both of the warning that no promises had been made, and the fact that any show of comradeship on the part of his boss was rarely to be trusted. Phillip Legge was known for his unpredictable oscillations in the treatment of his employees, being jocular one minute and lashing out with scathing acerbity the next. Having succeeded to his own elevated position through a notorious capacity for hard work and ruthlessness, his efforts at compassionate man-management were both infrequent and painfully laboured. Since his arrival on the paper two years before, the arts sector had been pared down to a rigorous and cost-effective minimum. Without the protective buffer of Oliver – who enjoyed a status beyond normal office hierarchies – Matt was sure he would not have survived so long.

Phillip shook the water drops off his hands and ran them briefly under the jet of hot air. 'I take it we're heading in the same direction?' He pushed open the door and invited Matt to accompany him back out into the corridor. 'Oliver says you've nailed Andrea Beauchamp to an interview. Well done.' He rubbed the palms of his hands together. 'Now there is a creature blessed with an extraordinary allocation of natural charms. And unattached again, according to the tabloids. Hey, you could be well in there, Matthew – the Hugh Grant of the media world, wooed by the film star for his unassuming assets.' He laughed so loudly that several heads bent at desks looked up as they passed. Matt laughed too, though inwardly the joke grated. He felt too sensitised and raw for such jibes, too close to the stammering hopelessness of real life, where there were no fairytale resolutions to ease the pain.

During the meeting, held round the circular table in Phillip Legge's office, Matt did his best to appear in touch, readily agreeing to the assignments suggested for him and assuming a look of concentrated interest as Oliver and Phillip went head to head over several issues. With the post-Christmas lull well and truly behind them, there were some hard choices to be made. Shakespeare at the York Playhouse in Leeds or Beckett at the Birmingham Rep. Tennessee Williams at the Bush in Hampstead or Lorca at the Tricycle in Kilburn. The faces of the men grew flushed as they talked. Instead of following their arguments, Matt found his thoughts drifting to Kath, to the early days. He could picture the flat in Shepherd's Bush as if it were yesterday; the bed with the folded magazine under the wobbly leg, candles flickering on the mantelpiece, something pulsing softly from the CD, Kath with her legs gripped round his waist, her eyes wide, pulling him into their stare as her hands pulled him deeper into her body. Had it been True Love or True Lust? Were the two things separate or one and the same? The pencil he had been holding snapped in two.

'You're being uncharacteristically restrained, Matthew. What do you think?'

Matt, whose daydreaming had progressed to the unhappy realisation that an ability to screw each other senseless was no guarantee either of harmony or of expertise in parenting, looked up from the broken pencil and blinked. For one mad moment he almost said as much out loud. 'I think they all sound interesting . . .'

Phillip clicked his fingers impatiently, returning his attention to Oliver. 'I'll go with you on this one. We can save the Birmingham Rep for that piece you're going to do on the North–South divide . . .'

Matt tried to imagine Kath with her casting agent, or photographer, or whoever he was; tried to imagine the extent of her emotions – the lust, love, desperation or whatever it was that had driven her away. It must have been pretty powerful. To walk out like that. To give up Joshua. He pressed the broken sections of pencil back together, pushing so hard that the join was barely visible. Unless . . . He let the pencil fall from his fingers, for the first time confronting the awful possibility that Kath would change her mind, that she might return to snatch their son from the school gates, or initiate one of those heart-rending custody battles one read about in the papers. Sunday visiting rights and access every other Christmas wouldn't do, he realised. They might have done once upon a time – before, when Kath was still around – but not now, not any more.

'Matthew?'

It was Oliver speaking. They had left Phillip's room and were walking down the corridor back towards the open-plan medley of desks that housed the lower echelons of the arts workforce.

'Went well, don't you think?' pressed Oliver, an element of forced heartiness to his tone.

'Yes . . . Oliver . . . I was just thinking . . . what exactly are a father's rights, do you know? I mean, these days does a mother still automatically get custody?'

'Why? Has Kath been in touch at last?'

'No, but now I'm worried she might . . .'

'You would work something out,' put in Oliver gently, patting Matt's arm. 'There's always a way through these muddles.'

Matt tried to look reassured. 'I guess so. Thanks.' He straightened himself, rubbing his hands together as if to dismiss the subject entirely. 'Now then, if Phillip wants me to do the grand tour with this Cambridge girl I'd better get a move on. Catch up with you later.' He raced off in the direction of his desk, leaving Oliver staring after him, a look of grim concern on his face.

The girl was very good, and very pretty, which Matt was sure would sway Phillip Legge even if he didn't admit to such things. Seeing the sparkle of ambition in her eyes, the glow of youthful self-confidence, he felt the dim stirrings of envy. Maybe he should even feel threatened, he mused, waving her off at the lifts after a guided tour of the department and returning to the mayhem of paper accumulated during the three-week neglect of his in-tray.

As he peered gingerly round the door of the canteen at lunch-time, the touch of Oliver's hands on his shoulder made him jump.

'Word is the curry's very good. If this lot leave us any, that is.' He nodded at the line of people in front of them. 'Best to get to this place by twelve or one hasn't a hope.'

'I was thinking I might go out for some air, find a sandwich instead,' ventured Matt, troubled not by lack of appetite so much as a sudden and urgent longing to be on his own.

'I wouldn't. It's pouring. And if you bugger off I won't have anyone to sit with. I come into this place so seldom these days I barely know a soul.'

That Oliver was so obviously trying to be kind only made Matt feel worse. Reluctantly he took a tray and joined the queue. The notion of Oliver not knowing anyone to sit with was laughable. The man was an institution, a minor celebrity in his own right, with a warm word for everyone, whether it was the Sri Lankan lady who cleaned the loos or one of the endless temps who circulated round departments covering for maternity leave, flu and nervous breakdowns. That Oliver managed to maintain such genuine and familiar relations when he was in the office so rarely made it all the more remarkable.

'There, look, what did I tell you,' he announced as they sat down, pointing with some triumph at the teeming grey skies framed in the window next to their table. 'Veritable cats and dogs. Not sandwich-bar weather at all.' He began unloading his tray – three courses, as well as bread and a bowlful of chutneys, currants and coconut shavings to go with his curry. 'So your father's manning the fort. That's excellent. Means there's no problem with New York, I take it? I usually book into a small hotel off Fifth Avenue, not one of the more flashy joints, but wonderfully comfortable and perfectly situated. You'll need five days to cover it all. Wonderful to see Broadway braving some real drama for a change. Quite a gruelling schedule, mind you – jet-lag, late nights and lots of writing – but great fun.' He stopped suddenly, a wedge of lurid green meat dripping off his fork. 'You are up for this, Matt, aren't you? We are into February, after all, so if not . . .'

Matt grinned, pleased to be able to show conviction about something. 'I certainly am. My father's fine about it – I broke the news last night. My friend Graham has offered to put me up for the week. To be honest, I'm looking forward to it.'

'Splendid, splendid. And Legge appears to be playing ball, doesn't he, about your contractual changes and so on?' Oliver popped a stray raisin into his mouth before turning his attentions to a bowl of sponge pudding and custard. 'Bit of luck that girl pitching her hat into the ring, Evelyn or Edwina or whatever she was. What did you make of her, by the way? Will she make subeditor of the year?'

'Erica. Erica Chastillon. I was only with her for half an hour, but yes, she seemed good. Very bright, very enthusiastic. Have me out of a job in no time, I expect.' He had aimed for a tone of wry amusement, but knew the moment the words were out that he had failed.

Oliver threw his dessert spoon with a clatter into his empty bowl. 'Bollocks.' He glared across the table, tugging at his beard, wondering how to tell his dining companion that self-doubt was a creeping infectious disease that he should ward off at all costs; that if it hung around for too long it could spread to other people's perception of those afflicted, until the worst of worse-case scenarios came true. 'You've had – you are having – a hard time, Matthew. But the fact remains, you're a fine writer, a fine critic. With or without a wife. And don't you forget that. Or others might start to forget it too.'

The warning echoed in Matt's head for the rest of the afternoon. Though the articles that needed editing for the six o'clock deadline were both unproblematic and not too numerous, he found himself labouring over every word. Urges to call home did little to help his concentration.

'If I can't find the ketchup we'll do without,' barked Dennis when Matt rang for the second time in an hour. 'Now bugger off back to work.'

Matt eyed the paragraph on his screen, wanting to delay the moment of returning to it. 'No more messages, then?'

'I told you. Louise somebody about nothing in particular and Maria somebody about looking round schools this Saturday. She's calling back tonight. Now, if you don't mind, some of us have got things to do.'

Matt put the telephone down and dropped his head into his hands.

'I'm not interrupting, am I?'

'Beth.' He leaped round his desk to clear a stack of papers off a spare chair. 'First day back, still getting to grips – you know how it is. Take a seat.'

'No thanks, I'm only passing. I've had a meeting in another part of this godforsaken island. Why dogs, that's what I want to know? Someone said it's supposed to look like a dog's leg, but it doesn't at all – I know because I got one of those A to Z maps and checked. It's just a U shape, nothing like a leg . . .'

'It was a king.'

'I beg your pardon?'

'Some king kept his dogs there. I can't remember which one. They barked a lot and so locals started calling it the Isle of Dogs.'

'Well, There you go. Another mystery solved. Thank you Matt.' She grinned 'But the real reason I came by was to invite you to a party. A week on Saturday.' She placed a white envelope on top of his computer terminal. 'If you're covering a show, come on afterwards. You won't be the last to arrive, I promise.'

'A party?' Matt picked up the envelope, shaking his head doubtfully.

'Yeah, you know, lots of people, alcohol, maybe even a good time.'

'Thanks, Beth, that's really kind, only I'm not sure I'd make the best sort of company at parties at the moment—'

'Which is precisely why you should come.' She snapped her bag shut.

'And then there's baby-sitting . . .' he began weakly.

She snorted. 'Baby-sitters – a euphemism for party-pooping if ever I heard one. Look,' she continued, her voice softening, 'you don't have to decide now. Or even until the night. Just come along if you're in the mood, okay?' She flashed him a final smile and turned on her heel with a wave. Matt watched her stride smoothly back in the direction of the lifts, aware that several of his male colleagues were doing the same.

Chapter Sixteen

The following Friday Matt arrived at the South Bank a good half an hour earlier than necessary. Louise was to join him, marking the first use in many weeks of his free companion ticket. He had made the offer during the course of one of her numerous phone calls, prompted, he decided afterwards, by a dim desire to make up for having turned down yet another string of offers to help him run his life. She had leapt on the invitation with touching enthusiasm, even when he warned her that Ibsen's *Doll House* wasn't everybody's cup of tea and that he would not be the best company because of having to make notes in the interval and rush home to file afterwards.

Two weeks of juggling his job and his home life, even with the help of his father, had sharpened Matt's impatience for the now imminent chance to give up commuting altogether. As he had predicted and hoped, Phillip Legge had offered Erica Chastillon a job on the subbing desk, releasing him to the luxury of a freelancing role from home. His relief at the news had been tempered only by the fact that, as warned, it would entail a significant drop in salary and that, because of other commitments, Erica could not start for another six weeks. Matt had broken this news to Dennis the night before, waving a copy of the *Lady*, which he had bought from Mr Patel's on the way home, and insisting that he would find some professional help in the meantime.

'Are you saying I can't manage?'

'No, I'm saying that I am preying on your kindness enough as it is. That six weeks is a lot longer than two and for that relatively short span of time I can afford to pay some highly trained female to do all the things that you are doing for free.'

'And what about Josie?'

Matt sighed. The gamble in that regard had so far paid off extremely well. In the space of barely two weeks she had not only won the hearts of both father and son but had also asserted impressive control over the laundry. Tidy piles of ironing had begun to replace the crumpled heaps behind the sofa; socks were matched and neatly tucked into their partners, underpants folded into smooth flat halves, and creaseless shirts left on coat hangers on the door handles of Matt and Dennis's bedrooms. 'Yes, well, I agree it would be a shame to let her go, but then I certainly couldn't afford to keep her on as well.'

His father had snatched the magazine away. 'And you don't have to. We're all managing perfectly well as things are.' He paused, puffing out his chest. 'Though if it's because you'd rather not have me around, then for God's sake spit it out. I'm not so senile I can't see that for a man of thirty-one to have his father hanging about the house is not an ideal situation. Though I try not to interfere or—'

'It's not that,' Matt assured him, smiling in spite of himself at the implications behind the remark. There was no question of Dennis cramping his style. There was no style to cramp. His social life was a graveyard and would continue to be so with or without the presence of his father. 'You're amazingly tolerant of me, wonderful with Joshua – I've no problem at all on that score. Even Hoppit's bad breath is something I'm coming to know and love—'

'So I'll stay,' Dennis had retorted, snapping his jaw shut, his eyes twinkling with satisfaction. 'Until this new job contract of yours kicks in anyway.'

Having bought a bottle of beer, Matt eased his way through

the gathering throng of theatre-goers and out on to the concrete walkway running parallel with the river. Leaning his elbows on the balustrade, he cast his eyes up and down the black band of water, taking in the impressively illuminated skyline and the glittering bracelets of bridges. From somewhere along the Embankment came the dim wail of an emergency siren. Matt squinted in its direction, following the sound as it joined the broken stream of yellow light flowing across Blackfriars. The scale of the scene, the sense of myriad human activity, was soothing. His domestic upset, so momentous in his own mind, was nothing, he realised, no more than the tiniest ripple in the sea of human experience.

A couple, their features impossible to make out in the evening light, had wandered to within a few yards of him.

'All I'm saying is . . .'

'That's all you ever say . . .'

Two lit cigarettes danced in the air as they argued, performing darting figures of eight and half-circles. 'You say that, but you did not . . .'

'How was I to know . . .' The woman's voice rose briefly to a pitch of audible indignation. Matt glimpsed an airy bouffant of silvery blond hair and the glint of jewel-studded earlobes. '. . . you bloody well don't . . .'

He edged along the balustrade out of earshot, fighting one of the spurts of fondness for Kath that hit him from time to time and marvelling that it could be triggered by something as unedifying as marital bickering. The air felt colder suddenly. From nowhere a breeze was picking up momentum, whirling off the water and flinging itself in his face like an icy damp cloth. Pulling up the collar of his coat, he headed back towards the light and the mounting hubbub visible through the theatre's glass doors. Louise was waiting at the entrance to the Cottesloe as they had agreed, her overcoat slung over one arm and her bag dangling from her shoulder. She wore a black velvet trouser suit, with a satin brocade trimming and a pink mohair jumper underneath. Her hair looked blonder than he remembered and as smooth as glass.

'Matt – God, I'm so hot – I always forget what this place is like. I wish to goodness I hadn't brought this.' She tossed her coat impatiently. 'With the underground carpark there's really no need, is there?'

He kissed her on both cheeks, noting the way the pink flush of her skin accentuated the glossy, baby-doll look of her appearance. 'There's a place we could leave your coat—'

'No, don't worry, it's no bother really. Look, I bought a programme. But I expect you get those free as well?'

Matt laughed. 'No, but they go on expenses. I've got boxes of the bloody things. A history of my career caged in cardboard. Takes up half the bloody attic – used to drive Kath mad . . .' Remembering a private resolution to keep the evening light-hearted, he broke off uncertainly. 'Would you like a drink? I'm already one ahead of you, I'm afraid. Got here early. Winding down in the office, rather. They've agreed I can work from home, which is good. Start in a few weeks. My father's going to manage things till then, together with that girl I told you about, the one from the playground.'

'Oh, Matt, I'm so pleased.' She linked her arm through his as they threaded their way back towards the bar. 'You said you would sort it out and you did. I think that's marvellous. I think the way you are coping is marvellous – just adapting, not looking back, being there for Josh.' When he handed her the glass of white wine she had requested she raised it to him with shining eyes. 'Here's to you. You're going to be all right, I can just feel it in my bones.'

'I wish I could share your certainty,' he laughed, touched in spite of himself by the warmth of her assurance.

A few minutes later they were seated side by side three rows from the front watching the curtain rise. As the production unfolded, Matt found his reactions hampered by the fact that he had reviewed a near-perfect interpretation of the work a few years before. In comparison, this female lead's simpering show of marital subjection seemed to him to be grossly overdone, while the husband began shouting out his words long before the climax of the story was in his sights. Louise, in contrast, sat bolt upright in her seat, clearly enthralled. During the interval she talked non-stop, even when Matt pointedly set to work with his notepad and pen.

'The worst thing is I do that with Anthony,' she chattered. 'You know, when I want something that I know he'll just hate. Like the eggshell pink we've got in our en suite – I've got all sorts of ways of pretending to agree with him but at the same time saying just enough to push him the other way. God, isn't that awful? I'd never thought of myself as calculating before,' she exclaimed, sounding thrilled.

Matt grunted absently, barely glancing up from his jottings. The set had struck him as cumbersome and self-consciously cluttered. He wanted a witty metaphor to sum it up, something to convey the almost comical way in which the actors had seemed to dodge round all the props as if fearful of tripping headlong.

'But it's so lovely to feel *stimulated*,' continued Louise, undeterred by his evident preoccupation. 'To find ideas bursting inside my head. I mean, I just don't seem to get many ideas these days. I'm afraid the old adage about motherhood annihilating brain cells is probably true – and then you get on a sort of slippery slope where the fewer you have the fewer you're likely to have. Sometimes I try and decide what I think about something – you know, something on the news or the radio – and I simply can't come to any conclusions. I just don't feel I know enough to make any definitive judgments.' She sighed. 'And the worst of it is that I don't think Anthony expects me to either. All we ever talk about is the children or what to eat for dinner.'

'That's all most cohabiting parents ever talk about,' said Matt, resignedly slotting the lid back on his pen and giving her his full attention.

'But you have ideas all the time. Look at you, scribbling away there. I always read your stuff, you know, Matt and it's so . . . *interesting*. And beautifully written. Not that I'm what you'd call a great connoisseur of the written word. Magazines and newspaper headlines – I don't seem to have the energy for anything else these days.' She swigged the last of her wine, ordered for the interval by Matt before they took their seats. 'Anthony reads all the time, of course, journals and so on. And history books.' She slapped her thighs. 'God, he loves history books, especially anything to do with war. Perhaps that's why he's just brimming with ideas about everything. When we go out or have people round I watch him sometimes in amazement. There is nothing he doesn't have a view on, no opinion which he isn't prepared to deliver with all the conviction of a gospel truth. It's really rather incredible,' she concluded with a sigh. 'And then there's silly old me, not knowing what I think about anything.'

'There are very few things on which I have a coherent view,' said Matt kindly. 'And if I need an idea on the spot I just make it up. Like this lot.' He tapped the notebook with the back of his hand. 'I try to be genuine, but sometimes a little fabrication is required, to give a piece shape, to make it *interesting*, as you so kindly remarked.'

'You're very clever, Matt,' she declared, wagging her finger at him as they returned to their seats.

'I thought he overdid it a bit in the end, didn't you?' said Louise afterwards. 'All that weeping and wailing. But I liked her very much. When will your piece come out? I can't wait to read it, having seen it together and so on. Oh, Matt, I have enjoyed myself, thank you so much.'

'Sorry we can't have dinner or anything, but I—'

'No, don't apologise, I quite understand. I ate heaps with the children. Would you like me to drop you home? That is if I can find the car – I'm such a pea-brain when it comes to remembering where I've left the bloody thing.'

'Thanks, but I drove myself.' He held the lift doors back for her as she stepped inside. Down in the carpark, their footsteps and voices echoed round the concrete. 'I'm that way.' He pointed to the far side of the concourse.

'And I think I'm that way.'

'You haven't heard from Kath again, have you?' The question burst out of him, revealing all the desperation he had sought to hide.

Louise, who had been about to tip her face for a farewell kiss, rocked back on her heels, shaking her head. 'You've got to try and forget her, Matt,' she said quietly. 'Me too. We've got to move on.'

He clenched his hands into fists. 'It's not that I want her back – I'm not sure I do any more – but I've started worrying that she will change her mind about Josh . . . that she will try to take him from me.'

'Oh, Matt, you dear thing,' she gasped, putting her arms round him. 'She won't, I'm sure she won't. I do believe she's really gone for good. And you've done so much already, coping. Any person judging the situation would see that.' She let go of him and looked into his face, her eyes glassy. 'Remember, Matt, she's the one who walked out on us. She's the one who left.'

Matt stood watching as she trotted away, peering uncertainly between the lines of cars. He wasn't the only one who had been betrayed, he reminded himself. Louise had lost her closest confidante and friend. She had almost as many adjustments to make as he did; not in practical terms maybe, but inside her own head. He turned away to search for his own car, pondering how deeply insulting desertion was for those left behind.

Chapter Seventeen

After some deliberation Matt decided that researching primary schools was an activity best conducted on his own. Joshua would get a good enough look — at St Leonard's anyway — when he went for his four-plus assessment, an ordeal scheduled for the week Matt was due in America. On being notified of the date, Matt's knee-jerk response had been to cancel the trip altogether. Further reflection, however, had led him to the conclusion that the timing was probably fortuitous. The notion of anyone attempting to cast judgment on the delightfully quirky, raw intelligence of his son made him so cross, so nerve-racked on Joshua's behalf, that it was obvious that Dennis, with all his calm down-to-earth pragmatism, would be far better placed to oversee the exercise.

Although Broadlands was within walking distance, St Leonard's, where Maria had arranged the first of their two appointments, warranted a journey in the car. Both Joshua and his father pressed their noses to the window to see him off, making grotesque distortions of their faces and leaving bleary smears on the windowpane. Matt tooted several times in response, chuckling to himself at the unlikely shape his family life had taken: three single men of three generations, and a girl of sixteen, who continued to apply herself to the smooth running of the household with an enthusiasm and diligence beyond his wildest dreams. In addition to the triumphs over their laundry, the house was beginning to shine from a more thorough attention to cleanliness; brand names of detergents and scouring creams had begun to make an appearance on the walled shopping list, written at funny angles in careful joined-up writing where *b*s often served as *d*s and most *e*s faced the wrong way. As if such vigilance were not enough, she never arrived for work without some small gift for Joshua – a button embossed with a soldier, an electric-green caterpillar in a matchbox, a sticker of a famous footballer. Dennis said that on the afternoons she was due Josh had taken to waiting for her on the bottom stair, howling with disappointment if the ring of a salesman or Jehovah's witness raised false hopes.

Although pleased by this attachment, Matt could not help worrying at its vehemence. It was one of many indications that, while his son had apparently adjusted to his new circumstances with remarkable ease, there remained much invisible healing still to be done. In the weeks since Kath's departure the volatility of his emotions had grown much more marked; euphoria meta-morphosed into abject misery in seconds, sometimes at the slightest provocation. And then there were the wet sheets – not every morning, but one out of every four or five. Bladder control had never been a problem before. Indeed, it had been one of the few causes of early parental complacency that their toddler, so awkward in many ways, had mastered the potty within a week and the even more awesome challenge of a lavatory not long afterwards.

There had been sodden sheets that morning, Matt recalled, giving a last wave to the two squashed faces as he drove off down the street. Not wanting to dent Joshua's fragile pride, he had as usual made light of the matter, whisking the affected bedding out of sight and not wiping down the plastic mattress cover – bought the week before – until he was safely downstairs. A doctor would no doubt recommend therapy, Matt reflected grimly, shuddering at the thought and clinging to the notion that the passage of time, coupled with good old-fashioned human kindness, could do the job as well. And of that there had been no shortage on any front, he reminded himself, slowing to wave at Mr Patel, whose big smile and hedgehog of lollipops had become a regular highlight of the week.

The grocer was standing on the pavement outside his shop surrounded by several members of his family. He returned Matt's greeting with an air of such obvious and uncharacteristic distraction that Matt slowed to see what was wrong. Craning his neck through the passenger window, he glimpsed several large loops of fluorescent spray graffiti along the door and main window of the shop. He could make out the words, PAKI BASTARDS, together with several crude renditions of male genitalia. On either side were two jagged holes in the pane of glass, each the size of a football. The pavement area usually designated for trestle tables of fresh fruit and vegetables was carpeted with heaps of crystal fragments.

Mr Patel approached the car, shaking his head and wringing his hands. 'Who would do this thing?' he said, as Matt wound down the window.

'God knows. Kids probably. Have you called the police?'

'Oh yes, they have been already. But what can they do? I do my best, Mr Webster, I work hard. I am with respect for everybody.' His usually beaming, vigorous face was ashen and slack with dismay. 'And the children, they are upset too. Of course, there are comments sometimes, they are used to that, but this—' He broke off, gesturing helplessly at the mess beside them.

'I'm really sorry, Mr Patel. I just wish there was something I could do but—' Matt glanced at his watch, realising that Maria would already be at St Leonard's. 'The fact is, I'm terribly late – on my way to look at a school for Josh.'

The shopkeeper managed a half-smile, revealing a brief glimpse of his handsome gold molars. 'He's a growing boy now, of course. You must go, Mr Webster. There is nothing to be done,' he added, his face grave again as he turned back to continue comforting his family.

Sobered by the episode, Matt found himself turning into the attractively landscaped crescent of a carpark, curling round the elegant red-bricked body of St Leonard's, with somewhat mixed feelings. The aura of privilege was tangible. Even the tarmac looked black and sumptuous, especially the ring-fenced, more padded version to the right of the building, which had been implanted with an elaborate construction of climbing frames and swings. Bright specks of budding winter jasmine and quince blossom jostled for space among the evergreens bordering the playground, contributing to the impression that even nature smiled on those wealthy enough to court her properly.

Matt had barely pulled up the handbrake when Maria emerged from a car the size of a cattle truck, with gleaming alloy wheels and doors that slid sideways rather than swinging open on hinges. She was wearing black leggings, black leather ankle boots and a bright red wool jacket, trimmed with fake black fur. On her head was a large black hat with a fat belt of fur round its rim. Having only ever seen her attired in jeans and a sweat-shirt, Matt felt momentarily intimidated. 'Sorry to have kept you waiting.'

'No, I just got here, honestly. It's good to see you. How are you? You look well,' she added, thinking in fact that he looked tired and unkempt. 'We've missed you at our last couple of tea sessions.'

Matt pushed open the main door of the school and stepped aside for her to enter first. 'Yes, well, I'm back at work now.'

'Of course. How's it going? When are they going to let you work from home?'

'Soon. But in the meantime my father is in charge of Joshua's social life.' He made a face, feeling a pang of disloyalty as he did so and privately thinking that Dennis would in fact be thrilled at an invitation to eat home-made cakes with Maria and her girlfriends.

A few moments later they were being guided round three floors of bright polished classrooms, centred round a handsome oak-panelled hall. Each set of rooms had its own cloakroom, lined with empty silver hooks and gleaming lavatories and basins the height of Matt's thigh.

'Of course it's not the same without the children,' trilled the headmistress, a creature moulded in a cheerful no-nonsense mode which Matt associated with females who had been to boarding school and played hockey. 'You would see then what fun we all have. We pride ourselves on being a happy school. They work half the time without even realising it. Lots of exercise too. They do games at least three times a week. We've got an absolutely splendid new gym on the far side of the playground and there are plans afoot for a pool. At the moment we take a minibus to the leisure centre, which does rather eat up the time.'

Throughout the tour, Maria took the lead, asking a string of pertinent questions ranging from details about the curriculum to the school policy on bullying. Feeling altogether less convivial, as well as disinclined to compete, Matt instead concentrated on studying compositions on the walls. He stared particularly hard at the the framed sea of white faces in school photographs, grappling as much with the notion of Josh slotting happily into so vast a crowd as the prospect of spending almost five thousand pounds a year enabling him to do so. His savings account had that week registered a balance of just over twelve thousand pounds. More than enough for a year or two but hardly very promising in the long term. If Joshua started private school that year there would be another fourteen to go. Fourteen years of three terms a year. That was forty-two terms. At an average of two thousands pounds a term, that made a total of eighty-four thousand pounds. Matt felt his mouth go dry. Unless he won the lottery or the heart of an heiress the outlook was hopeless.

'Mr Webster, any further questions?'

They were back in the main reception area, standing next to a cupboard of silver trophies. 'When are this lot given out, then?' he asked, trying to appear eager, suddenly fearful that Joshua might be prejudged on the basis of his own performance. 'Sports day?' He gave the glass cabinet a friendly tap.

The lips pursed in a momentary show of disapproval. 'At this age I think it is important to keep sport strictly non-competitive. Everyone participating, no one being disappointed. No, these awards are for excellence in work, art and music. Rather than taking the cups home, the children have their names engraved on them and then they are displayed here for all to admire.'

Maria clucked approvingly, while Matt shrank back into silence, resisting the urge to point out the futility of trying to persuade children not to outstrip each other on a sports field or anywhere else.

The sixties concrete blocks of Broadlands primary school, crammed into a small site set back from a busy road, could not have offered a more striking contrast. The playground, heaving with cracks and faded lines marking out the perimeters of various ball games, was separated from the pavement only by a waist-high wall, topped by several yards of crude metal fencing. Since the playground also constituted the main forecourt of the school, visitors arriving by car were forced to trawl for parking spaces along the road. A cluster of parents already grouped on the school steps alerted Matt to the fact that the exclusive viewing to which they had been treated at St Leonard's was not to be repeated. While they stood there, waiting to be herded inside, Maria nudged him, whispering, 'I think we might be wasting our time.'

Matt grunted, in truth feeling equally disappointed, but determined, if only for his bank balance's sake, to be more positive.

Maria bit her lip and turned away. Having fondly imagined herself to be on the brink of a new and original friendship, such a reaction — not to mention the subdued nature of Matt's behaviour throughout the morning — had left her wondering if this was in fact the case. It had been wonderfully refreshing to have a bit of testosterone floating among her small circle of friends, diluting the at times stultifying female ambience that still prevailed when it came to the rearing of young infants. All her girlfriends had agreed. When Matt hadn't got in touch after their get-together they had charged Maria with the responsibility of finding out what was going on and wooing him back into the group.

The Broadlands tour was undertaken by a slim woman, plainly dressed and with dry flyaway hair and blotchy skin. Introducing herself as a joint acting deputy head, she ushered them round the building with an edge of impatience that suggested she had many things to see to before the day was out. Though clean, the place was nothing like as spruce as its fee-paying counterpart. Ominous discolourations were visible on several walls and ceilings, while the lino floors were faded and pitted with dents and scuff marks. With an average of thirty to a class, the desks were packed so tightly together that there was barely room for an adult to move between them.

As the group approached the main hall, which served the triple purpose of assembly area, dining hall and gym, they were greeted by a muffled storm of noise. 'A drama workshop,' explained their guide, opening the door and stepping back for the parents to peer inside. They all huddled in the doorway, taking it in turns to look. Maria, who went before Matt, stepped back into the corridor with an exclamation of surprise. 'I know that woman. Sophie something . . .'

Matt just had time to glimpse Josie's dour protector, surrounded by about twenty leaping children, before the deputy head leaned across him to close the door. 'I think we'll leave them to it, don't you? Our library is the Portakabin behind the main school. If you'd like to follow me.'

'Contini — that was it,' exclaimed Maria, clapping her hands in satisfaction at having recalled the name. 'She used to teach at my eldest's nursery when we lived in Tooting. Left the place

under a terrible cloud,' she continued, pleased to see that she had
ensnared Matt's attention at last. 'An affair with a father of one
of the children in her class – if you can think of *anything* more
inappropriate. He patched it up with his wife and moved away.
Poor woman – someone told me she has since been diagnosed
with breast cancer—'

'Who, the teacher?'

'No, the wife. Brought on by stress, they say. Sophie Contini
disappeared, apparently to go back into further education . . .
though, judging by that riot, it looks as if she could do with
going back for a bit more.' She giggled. 'Hardly the best advert
for the school.'

'As a matter of fact I know her as well,' said Matt carefully.
'She teaches the girl who's helping my father look after Josh.
They're rather good friends. Josie relies on her a lot.'

'Right. Well, sorry if I've—'

'Really, there's no need to apologise. Her chequered past is of
no consequence to me. Josie is great, which is all that matters.'

'Yes, of course,' agreed Maria hastily, unable to quell the
sensation that a final chance to fan their acquaintance into
something lasting had slipped beyond her grasp.

They said goodbye a little stiffly, with hollow-sounding
promises to arrange play dates for their offspring. A few minutes
later, just as Matt reached his car, he caught sight of Sophie
herself coming out of the school gates.

'Hey,' he called, striding back down the pavement. 'I saw you
in there.'

'Yes, I saw you,' she remarked, not sounding remotely pleased
at the coincidence.

'I didn't know you taught here.'

'I don't. Just a Saturday workshop.'

'Quite a handful, by the looks of things.'

She shrugged. 'They're okay. I like to let them go a bit, use up
some energy.' She was tapping her handbag with her fingertips,
he noticed, as if eager to be released.

'I was looking with Josh in mind. I saw St Leonard's earlier—'

'No guesses for which you preferred.'

'Well, actually—'

'How's Josie getting on, anyway?'

'Fine – great in fact.'

Her face softened for the first time. 'Yes, she's a good girl. Which reminds me, I've agreed to pick her up this evening, since she's staying the night with me afterwards. She is sitting for you, isn't she?' she added, seeing the momentary blankness in Matt's eyes.

'Oh God, yes she is.' He groaned, unhappy to be reminded of the unfortunate coincidence of Beth Durant's party and his father's decision to have dinner with an old friend in Hampstead. 'But whichever one of us is back first could simply put her in a taxi, rather than cause you the bother of—'

'There's really no need,' she cut in. 'I'm a late bird anyway. I'll see you later, then.'

'Would you like a lift?' Matt called, watching her stride away down the street. 'It's on my way.'

'I like walking,' she shouted back, not even bothering to turn round.

Matt stared after her, irritated and mystified by the impression that for some reason she found his company offensive, wondering whether it was an attitude she applied to all men or reserved for him alone.

Chapter Eighteen

Later that afternoon Matt phoned Beth Durant to make a half-hearted attempt to pull out of the party altogether. He would not be out of the West End before ten thirty, he explained, and with a review to file the next day would not be able to stay beyond an hour at the very most.

'Matthew Webster, you rat. When I said you didn't have to come I was kidding. Of course you have to come. There'll be some great people here. You'll have a good time.'

'Well, can I bring something, then?' he had replied feebly.

'Just yourself will do fine.'

Matt recalled these words in a bid for reassurance as the taxi tipped him outside the front door of Beth's grey-bricked Chelsea home. Arriving alone at parties was something he had hated even as an adolescent, when shudders of social unease had been compensated for by undercurrents of sexual anticipation. Hovering on the doorstep now, he realised that, rather than being vanquished, such fears had merely been lurking in his psyche all along, hidden by the easy crutch of coupledom, the fact of having a pair of unthreatening eyes to catch across a crowded room.

The door knocker dropped from his fingers with a dull, unpromising thud. He was seriously entertaining the possibility of backing away from it when the door swung open, revealing Beth Durant, clad in a low-necked silky top with stringy shoulder straps and a short skirt. In the dim light of the hallway her bare skin glowed a honey brown. Observing that she was taller than he remembered, Matt looked down and saw that in place of the soft leather pumps were silver strappy high heels, criss-crossed around ten crimson toenails.

'I'd almost given you up,' she said, taking hold of his wrist and pulling him inside. 'We're down to the hard core. The caterers have gone but there's loads of food left. I always order too much on purpose. As for drink, we're out of red wine – just everybody drinks it these days – but there's gallons of white, not to mention all the other usual suspects – gin, whisky, Bourbon—' She shook the glass in her right hand, causing the ice cubes to chink prettily round the inch of golden brown liquid. 'My preferred tipple.' Still holding his wrist, she led him down the carpeted corridor and into a dimly lit double sitting room, where a handful of guests were sprawled round the floor and in deep beanbag-style armchairs. 'Hey, everybody, this is Matt.' There were murmurs of welcome and a few sleepily raised arms. 'We were dancing but have gotten too tired,' drawled one guest, sucking deeply on a fat joint and handing it to his neighbour. Beth squeezed his hand, whispering, 'Hope you're not offended by the presence of soft drugs.' Her lips came so close to his face that he could smell the faint bitterness of tobacco on her breath. 'Now, what are you going to drink?'

Matt asked for a gin and tonic.

'You stay right there while I get it.'

Awkward at being the only one standing, he squatted self-consciously in a space by the door.

'A smoke?' A black girl with braided hair and popping soulful eyes, curled into the armchair nearest him, held out the reefer. Matt, who hadn't dabbled in such recreational pursuits since his student days, and then only rarely, took a cautious puff, swallowing hard to bury the burning sensation in his throat and nodding in appreciation for fear that a cough might overwhelm any attempt to be more articulate.

'So, how are you doing?' enquired Beth cosily, reappearing with a fat tumbler a few minutes later and dropping gracefully to a cross-legged position at his side. 'Food?' She held out a plate heaped with tiny sandwiches and savoury pastries, taking several herself. The strappy sandals had been abandoned, Matt noticed, leaving faint dents across the arch of her feet where the straps had cut into the skin. In her cross-legged position the skirt was so short he could see the shadow of her knickers between the V of her thighs. Meaty thighs, he couldn't help thinking, seeing the swell of untoned muscle above her knees. Her lower legs were more shapely, smooth and clean shaven, apart from three small golden hairs sprouting from each big toe.

From somewhere a fresh joint appeared and other conversations restarted, rising and falling against the background thump of a disc someone had fed into the CD player. Matt, his head swimming, embarked on a brief update of his circumstances, concluding with a reference to his now imminent trip to New York.

She slapped his arm. 'Oh, I wish I'd known – I might have been able to fix things so I could tag along. I've spent ten years of my life on the East Coast. There's so much I could have shown you – places to visit and where to eat and—'

'I'll be staying with my oldest friend,' Matt explained, wondering in what capacity she would have envisaged accompanying him. 'He's been there a few months now and will look after me very well. Though . . .' He hesitated. 'The truth is, I'm not looking forward to it as much as I'd like to because it'll be my first trip away from my son. That is, my first since . . .'

'Oh, poor honey, of course – but that's so understandable.' She reached out and stroked the back of his neck with her fingernails, which were long and painted the same crimson as the toes. 'But just you wait, when you get there you'll have a ball. You'll wonder what you were worrying about. Your little boy will be fine.'

'Yes.' Matt smiled at her. He could feel himself relaxing, the tension literally seeping from his body, leaving him not only light-headed but light-limbed, as if he might float off the floor towards the ceiling roses and dado rails ranged overhead. When a cluster of guests took their leave, he slid into one of the vacant seats, sinking back into the soft leather and sipping happily at his drink, refreshed so many times he had lost count.

'It might be fun go away together somewhere, don't you think?' Beth, now lying on the carpet at his feet, lifted one foot and placed it on his knee. 'What do you say?'

'Hmm.' He studied the five dainty toes, curved in perfect gradation of size, quite unlike the Neanderthal clumsiness of his own feet. He dreamily contemplated the possibility of touching her skin, of tracing the tip of one finger from the largest red smudge to the smallest.

'A long weekend somewhere. Italy maybe.'

'Italy?'

'I've always wanted to go to Rome or Florence. St Peter's, the Ponte Vecchio, see Michelangelo's David in all his glory.' She giggled, sliding her foot between Matt's thighs, pointing her toes towards his groin.

'Sounds wonderful,' he said hoarsely, struggling to a more upright position, not averse to the movements of the foot so much as the fact that it was proceeding uninvited, not allowing him time to straighten the thoughts inside his head. Looking round the room he noticed suddenly that they were quite alone. 'Christ, what's the time?'

'Does it matter?' She blinked slowly, holding his gaze.

'My baby-sitter,' he gasped, trying to stand, only to find that his knees had been injected with jelly.

She laughed softly. 'Oh, Matt, you'll have to do better than that. Your father *lives* with you, remember? You don't need a sitter.'

'But he was going out – I had a sitter – I must call.'

She eased her leg from under him and stood up in one easy movement. 'Call, then.' She plucked a mobile phone from a bag hanging on the door handle and dropped it into his lap. 'Tell him not to wait up. Unless of course you don't want to stay.' Though there was a tremor of uncertainty in the delivery of these words, it was clear to Matt, from the slight flare in her nostrils and the unblinking gaze of her eyes, that she had every confidence in his desires. As if to remove any final trace of doubt in the matter, she peeled off her top, slinging it carelessly over one shoulder and revealing what Matt had already guessed to be an impressive pair of breasts, centred by small pointy nipples. He could feel the colour rush to his face as a confusion of arousal and terror swept over him.

'I have to go to the bathroom.' She pointed a finger at him. 'You make that call.' She turned and walked slowly from the room, exaggerating the swing in her hips. 'Just two minutes and I'll be back.'

Matt's hands slid on the telephone. Whether from shock, alcohol or drugs, his fingers were trembling so badly that he could hardly press the numbers. Somewhere deep inside he could feel the tightening of a knot of guilt. Something connected to his married self, to Joshua. Which was absurd, bloody ridiculous in fact, he scolded himself, punching in the numbers. Beth Durant was fun and affectionate. He was single. It was weeks and weeks since he had had sex.

'Hello, the Webster household.'

'Josie?'

'No, this is Sophie Contini speaking.'

'What are you . . . I mean, is everything okay?'

'Fine, thank you. I came by to pick up Josie. Your father kindly invited me in for coffee. We're just leaving. Good party?' she added, her tone somehow managing to contribute to Matt's sense that he was committing some kind of crime by enjoying himself.

'Yes, rather to my surprise . . .'

'And, let me guess, you're going to be late and Dennis is not to wait up?'

'I'd like to talk to him myself, if you don't mind.'

'Sure. I'll just get him.'

'Hi, Dad, how was your evening?'

'Grand, thank you. I'd forgotten how well we got on. Delightful wife too. They're going to come and stay when I get back home. And then I've had the pleasure of these two—' He broke off to say something that prompted a volley of merriment from his companions. 'Can't remember when I last had so much fun packed into one night.'

Matt seized his opportunity. 'That's great. Dad . . . look, I'm having something of a good time too, as it turns out. In fact I'm phoning to say that I might be a while yet, if that's okay. I'll let myself in quietly.'

'A good time, eh?'

Hearing the amusement in his father's voice, picturing the eyebrows raised for the benefit of his female audience, Matt was tempted either to get angry or to change his mind. He was prevented from doing so by the re-entrance of Beth, who had traded her few remaining items of clothing for a kimono of yellow silk, tied loosely at the waist, so as to reveal the full glorious valley of her cleavage. 'Look, Dad, I've got to go . . .'

'When a man's got to go a man's—'

'Yes, yes. I'll see you in the morning.'

Placing herself astride his lap, Beth eased the telephone from his hands and threw it across the room. Matt watched the arc of its flight as if in slow motion, spellbound by the sensation that the sequence of events was out of his hands, that it always had been, from the moment she had flipped the party invitation on to his desk. The phone landed with a clatter on the yard of parquet floor between the edge of the carpet and the skirting board. But by that time Matt had stopped watching, diverted both by a sense of his own good fortune and the thrilling but unnerving sight of hands he did not know reaching for the buckle on his trouser belt.

Chapter Nineteen

Looking out of the rain-flecked window as the airplane heaved itself off the runway, Matt felt as if he were pulling away not only from the toytown layout of southern England, but from the intricate mishmash of his own life. Regarded from so great a height, all the elements of his new existence seemed suddenly precarious and unsustainable. He felt a longing to return to the past, not so much to Kath as to the solid boundaries offered by marriage and the responsibilities of joint parenthood, the easy categorisability of Right and Wrong. He was no longer sure about anything. His work, his emotions, his future, his credentials as a father, as a man — everything was now steeped in doubt. Even when he was making love to Beth Durant the previous weekend, a core part of him had remained detached and critical, blighted by uncertainty and misgivings. Shortly after the phone call with Dennis, she had led him upstairs to bed; a water bed, as it turned out, which had rolled and bubbled beneath them, adding to Matt's sense of being tossed on currents beyond his control.

Afterwards, she was the first to speak. 'Matthew Webster, that was . . . like . . . great. It's not often a guy can hold back like that.' She lit a cigarette and tucked the sheet up round her chin, as if preparing to embark on a large messy meal.

'Er . . . good,' Matt murmured, tensing at the note of

congratulation in her tone, but relieved that his efforts had met with approval.

'Was it great for you?'

'For me too.'

'You didn't . . . you weren't . . . thinking about your wife or anything?'

'God, no. Not at all. You're so different . . . and anyway, I don't miss Kath like that – I mean, I wouldn't want to now with her even if . . .'

She put her hand over his mouth to silence him. 'You don't have to explain anything. Let's keep things as they are.'

'And how is that, exactly?' he had asked, some of his uncertainty spilling out of him.

'Simple,' she said sweetly. 'All fun and no pressure.' She kissed the tip of his nose. 'I'm really busy this coming week, and then you're in the States, so let's get in touch after that, carry on where we left off . . . if you want to, that is.'

'Oh, I do,' he had murmured, hugging her with fresh affection, pleased to accept any respite from his own confusions.

The captain's voice broke through his reverie with the information that they were flying at an unimaginable number of feet above the ground and, thanks to a strong tail wind, would make the East Coast in just under seven hours. Heavy cross-winds might cause a spot of turbulence *en route*, but the crew would do everything in their power to ensure that the passengers had a restful and pleasant journey. Matt squirmed in his seat, pushing his feet into the slot of space next to his hand luggage and wondering how being so tightly confined for so long could ever be deemed either restful or pleasant. They had now risen well above the cloud line. Through the porthole next to him there was nothing but an endless canopy of blue, so bright that his eyes ached when he stared at it. Although the in-flight entertainment programme had sounded promising, it transpired that his particular row of seats was almost parallel with the video screen. Making out even one third of the picture could only be managed at the cost of a stiff neck. The screen accommodating the next batch of rows was yards away, a moving postcard of a thing on which Matt found it impossible to concentrate. In no mood to focus on a book either, he tipped his seat back and closed his eyes, managing — despite noise, light and the inconvenience of not being horizontal — to fall into a fitful sleep.

To his surprise and delight, Graham was standing at the barrier waiting to meet him. At the sight of his old friend, something gagged in Matt's throat. He threw his arms round him with such gusto that Graham, laughing, staggered backwards, making as if to fight him off.

'Steady on.'

'It's bloody good to see you.'

'And you, you bastard.' Having re-established the distance between them, Graham gave him a friendly punch in the chest. 'I knew your flight time so it was no problem. I've even taken the day off in your honour.'

'As well as shifting your skiing holiday. What can I say? I hope you had a good time.'

'Brilliant, thanks. Powder snow and sunshine.' He picked up Matt's bag and led the way through the throng of waiting people. 'I thought about leaving you to chance it with a yellow cab, but one needs a degree in Spanish to converse with most of them — the sight of a clueless Englishman and they'd lead you a right old dance.'

'Bugger off,' retorted Matt happily, hurrying to match his companion's long stride, feeling suddenly as if he were on holiday. Among Americans he felt not so much gormless as wary; a holiday in Boston a few years before having alerted him to the fact that, while sharing many common elements of habit and language, America was in every sense a foreign country, that one was as much a tourist as on an African safari or hiking in the Andes.

Graham led him to a red Mazda, wedged into a tiny slot between a concrete wall and an estate car the length of a minibus.

Having loaded Matt's bags into the boot, he reversed deftly back towards the exit signs, his squat black wheels squeaking on the concrete floor.

'I thought you were shipping over the Porsche?'

Graham gave a regretful shrug. 'I was going to but it would have meant various costly adjustments, like having the steering wheel moved. God, I miss it though – so much more *subtle* than this thing.' He gave the dashboard a friendly slap, adding through a grin, 'Not that I'm complaining,' and accelerating so fast into the main carriageway that Matt felt the skin on his face tighten across his cheekbones.

Graham, his features poised in the expression of pleased concentration that invariably overcame him when tucked behind the wheel of a car, was looking well. Incredibly well. Life in the Wall Street fast track obviously suited him, Matt mused, taking in the new crispness to his friend's appearance, the healthy glow of his skin, which looked deeper than the evident polish of a recent suntan, and the glossiness of his strawberry-blond hair, which had been cut into a new, shorter style, exposing the enviably solid hairline along the top of his forehead. Even his clothes – leather loafers, honey-coloured chino-style cords and a hefty brown sheepskin – looked somehow different; not just smarter than he would have worn in London, but more affluent, more confident, as if he had grown into a role in which he felt completely at ease.

'About you and Kath,' Graham said, turning the noisy blast of the car's heating system down to a level that allowed conversation, 'I just want you to know it's . . . I'm really sorry about the whole business.'

Matt looked out of the window, where the cluster of tall blocks constituting the New York skyline was already coming into view, so familiar from movies and the media that it was almost hard to be impressed. While wanting badly to talk about his recent trauma, he could not resist the feeling that the time was not yet right, that they were still too tied up in the business of getting used to each other for anything approximating to their version of a heart-to-heart. 'It's bad, all right,' he said at length. 'A bolt from the blue and all that. Josh, of course, is taking it hard.'

'Of course.' They were on the bridge, Manhattan shimmering beside them, like a metal and plastic model of a city that could be plucked off a playing board and set down somewhere else. 'Though it's probably all for the best.'

'Is it?' Matt cut in, a little more sharply than he had intended.

Graham held up an arm in a mock bid to fend off an attack. 'I only meant . . . if she was unhappy and so forth. It was going nowhere good — would have fallen apart in the end. To be honest, I never thought the two of you were right for each other anyway.'

Matt, who had hunched down in his coat, sat up again in genuine surprise. 'Didn't you?'

'Nah. Kath was always . . . I don't know . . . trying to be something she wasn't. With you anyway. Take it from me, pal, you weren't suited.'

'Why did you never say so before?'

Graham let out a sharp laugh, at the same time manoeuvring the car across several lanes of traffic to one of the slip roads winding down into the heart of the city. 'Because nothing I said would have made the slightest difference, would it?'

'I suppose not.' Matt frowned, recalling with sudden clarity his early fixation with the woman he had married, the triumph of persuading so stunning a creature to share his life. There had been no question that he would marry her if he could. 'We *were* happy, you know.'

'Hey — cool it — I know you were. You've had a tough break. Shit happens and you've had more than your share of it. But it will all work out fine, just you see. In the meantime you are here and bloody well going to enjoy yourself if it kills me. Now, give me a rundown on your commitments so I can fit my schedule round you. I'll have to go into work, of course, but can be pretty flexible about the hours. Presumably you're going to be free during the day. There's a great place for brunch right on my block, and I'm within walking distance of several galleries — though if you want the Elizabeth Frink you'll need to get in a cab. There's a cinema that runs brilliant old movies round the clock and I've got a guest pass so you can use my gym whenever you want—'

'I am here to work, you know,' Matt interrupted, laughing.

'You mean going to watch three shows on Broadway?'

'Four. And I've got to write a big feature on New York theatre, why it's so much more of a closed shop than the West End, why only so few shows translate well across the Atlantic — which reminds me, can I use your computer to file my pieces?'

'You could if it was working. Sorry, pal, it crashed last week and I haven't gotten anybody round to take a look yet. The fax and phone are okay, though — you're welcome to use them.'

'My God, a few months in and you're even beginning to talk like a Yankee,' teased Matt, 'not to mention dressing like one.' He laughed, thinking with a spurt of fondness of Beth, who, in a comparable switch of environment, was still so irresistibly and irrefutably American. And the sex hadn't been bad at all, he reflected, remembering again their night together, reassured greatly just by the fact that it had happened, not caring why or where it was headed.

'This is the worst bit at the moment,' growled Graham, clicking his fingers with irritation at the traffic, which a long series of bollards and ticker tape was squeezing from three lanes to one. A few workmen, looking somehow more heroic and self-important than their British counterparts ever seemed to, were striding around in padded jackets, tight jeans and heavy-soled boots, waving the cars past and climbing in and out of construction vehicles. 'Forever digging up the fucking roads for something.' Graham revved the engine impatiently.

'Just like home,' remarked Matt dryly.

'Four more blocks of this and we're out of it. My flat's that way.' Graham carved the air next to his window with his hand. 'Third floor of a warehouse, converted by two high-powered architects a few years ago. All beams, open space and high ceilings – you'll love it.'

'Even nicer than Borough, then?' Matt twisted his neck to look out of Graham's side of the car, experiencing a shiver of unease at the towering grey blocks, so tall and packed that the patch of yellowy grey representing the sky looked like a dim unreachable light at the end of an inverted tunnel.

'I've placed it with an estate agent, didn't I tell you? The UK property market's reached such a high everyone says it's going to nosedive or plateau out at best. The agent reckons I'll get four fifty, which isn't bad when you think what I paid.'

'And what was that?' asked Matt faintly, a little perturbed at the sense that even at a distance of two thousand miles Graham was somehow more on top of things back home than he was.

'Two twenty. You ought to get your place valued, you know, I bet it's worth a fortune. With Kath gone, it might be wise to move, get somewhere smaller, put the money into the stock market—' Catching sight of the expression on Matt's face, he broke off. 'Only a thought. Obviously it's early days to be rearranging your life.'

Halfway down a narrow alley of a street, Graham fired a console at a large steel door, which slowly opened, revealing the dark mouth of a small underground carpark.

'You get rats down here sometimes,' he remarked cheerfully, seizing Matt's suitcase from the boot and leading the way to the lift. 'And cockroaches. We have this ghostbuster of a guy who comes by every few weeks, sprays stuff down the drains and plug holes – all part of the landlord's service. Hey, are you okay? You look kind of pale – you don't actually see the little bastards very often—'

'It's not that.' Matt ran a hand over his face, feeling suddenly haggard and drained. 'Jet-lag, I guess.'

Graham gave a dismissive laugh. 'Bit early for that, I'm afraid.

We've got the whole day to go yet. I thought you might want to shower and then we could find some food. A bloody Mary and some eggs Benedict will soon sort you out.'

Matt made a face. 'Coffee and scrambled eggs maybe. Graham . . . thanks for taking me in like this and for being so . . .' He laughed awkwardly, aware that, as ever when confronted with raw displays of emotion, his friend was looking stricken and impatient. 'Well . . . it's good to be here.'

'Any time.' Graham clicked his heels together and gave a mock salute. 'And now may I show you to your quarters?' The lift had deposited them outside a door on a small landing with polished wooden floorboards and lime-green walls. 'Don't worry, it gets better inside.' A moment later Matt was stepping into the largest single living space he had ever seen, the length of three London buses and just as wide. The far end was kitted out with state-of-the-art chrome kitchen units and a crescent-shaped breakfast bar, while the other side of the room was taken up by a huge leather suite and a television with a screen the size of a door. The area in between was spacious enough to house a massive medieval-style dining-room table, a desk and several man-size polished wooden artefacts. Sweeping up to split levels on either side were two symmetrical staircases, without banisters and curving in gentle spirals to what were clearly bedrooms, suspended from the ceiling like giant shelves. Looking up at each one, Matt was able to make out the ends of wide beds and sleek matching sets of bedroom furniture.

'There's a loo down there off the kitchen and each bedroom wing has its own en suite. What do you think? Fucking brilliant or what?'

'It is, it is,' murmured Matt, overwhelmed not only by the original and vast dimensions of the flat but by the realisation, hitherto only half acknowledged, that Graham was seriously wealthy. 'What did you say these people were paying you?'

Graham grinned. 'I didn't and you don't want to know.'

'No, I don't think I do,' Matt muttered, walking farther into the room and swinging his arms out as if trying to fill up some of the space. 'I love these staircases.' He touched the wood of one of the steps, thinking how hazardous they would be for a four-year-old and how lucky Graham was to be able to ignore such considerations.

'So do I, even if they're not exactly ideal for *entertaining*,' remarked Graham dryly, leading the way up the left-hand one. 'I haven't put the acoustics to the test yet – nor do I intend to during your stay,' he added hastily, 'but my guess is that noise from the guest suite to the main suite would travel rather efficiently. Definitely a one-man pad.' He dropped Matt's case on to the bed and turned back towards the stairs. 'Call if you need anything. And don't get any smart ideas about a kip.' He looked at his watch. 'I'll give you half an hour max, then we're out of here.'

'Half an hour it is.' Matt waved him off down the stairs, feeling not so much bossed about as pleasantly taken in hand. After weeks of grappling with the new mercurial state of his own life, it was sheer delight to be organised by someone else, to have a clear schedule to follow and no one's welfare to worry about but his own.

Chapter Twenty

Sitting alone on her blue chintz sofa, Louise stared disconsolately at the telephone on the table beside her. She had been on the verge of calling Matt, only to remember that he was in New York. Both children were in Wimbledon with her parents for the week, providing her with a keenly anticipated break from the humdrum routine of family life. Gloria had taken the opportunity to fly to Barcelona with the most recent male acquaintance to emerge from the frenetic fog of her social life. The plan had been for her and Anthony to take off somewhere nice as well, until a couple of last-minute work hitches had made Anthony plead the necessity of remaining within driving distance of the hospital. He had presented a very appealing case for the luxury of having some time on their own at home; of lazy lie-ins and being able to go out without the burden of negotiating the rollercoaster social life of their employee. He would keep his work commitments to the barest minimum, he assured her, so they really could have the best of all worlds — comfort, familiarity, and freedom all rolled into one.

Sitting alone on her sofa that Tuesday afternoon, with the quiet tick of the house around her, Louise could feel her faith in such a scenario slipping away. Anthony had spent most of the previous day ensconced in his study. A two-hour sortie to the hospital that afternoon had predictably stretched to three. They were supposed to be going to the cinema – Leicester Square and a curry afterwards – but she was already doubting whether even this unambitious plan would be realised. It seemed increasingly as if the simplest, most everyday things required enormous conviction before they could be made real, that each day required a huge effort of drive and reinvention of which she was growing less and less capable.

To have longed for time alone, only to feel that one was not only wasting but failing to enjoy it, was depressing. When the children were around, even with Gloria to help out, Louise had the constant feeling that there were one million things which being a mother prevented her from attending to. Yet now they were gone, she could not for the life of her conceive what such things were or why they had felt so pressing. It had taken just one day to catch up on her letter-writing, clear the laundry baskets and the ironing pile. The house was both tidy and clean. The fridge and larder were stocked with more food than either she or Anthony could eat during the course of six days, especially if they dined out as often as he promised.

In a dim bid for reassurance she dialled Anthony's direct line at the hospital.

'Hello, it's me.'

'Hello, darling, all well?'

'Yes.'

'Having a lovely relaxing day?'

'Yes.'

'Good . . . I'm almost finished here. But rather than me traipsing home first, why don't we meet outside the cinema?'

'All right.'

'It's only sensible, isn't it?'

'Oh, yes.'

'Fine. See you later, then.'

Louise carefully put the phone down and sat staring at the extravagant swirling blue designer fabric on either side of her knees, feeling grey and small and quite lost against its bold pattern. In fact all the accoutrements of her life made her feel grey and lost, she decided, casting her eyes round the expensive, tasteful furnishings of the room and recalling with some wonderment the pleasure she had taken in putting it all together. Paint, lampshades, curtain ties, scatter cushions, rugs, all painstakingly selected to merge and complement each other, like myriad pieces in a huge collage; a brilliant backdrop for any life, a palette of colour and imagination, and yet . . . Louise stood up, so quickly that she staggered a little from dizziness, seeing stars dance in the corners of her eyes. No one was perfectly happy, she comforted herself, crossing the room and switching off the lights. Standing in the dimness of the hallway she paused, arrested by the thought of Kath. Nothing had felt quite right since she'd gone. Worse still, Louise was beginning to glimpse an understanding of why she had gone, of why anyone might want to jump from the rails of her own life to something fresh and full of promise.

In the kitchen the fruitcake she had baked that morning sat on the wire cooling rack, plump with dried fruit and almonds. Without the children bullying for leftovers, Louise had wiped out the inside of the bowl herself, running her finger round the rim and licking scoops of the sweet mixture till she felt sick.

After a few moments' deliberation, Louise eased the cake off the rack, wrapped it in a large square of greaseproof paper and placed it carefully in a tin which had housed all the cheese biscuits over Christmas. Tucking it under her arm, she scooped up her handbag and coat, pulled the front door behind her and got into the car.

It was a duty call, she told herself, pulling up some ten minutes later a few yards from the front door of Matt's house. The thought of her own father managing in a comparable situation was laughable. He couldn't even find the butter dish without her mother's help, let alone see to the needs of a small child. During the course of that week the extent of his involvement with his grandchildren would, she knew, not stretch beyond story-reading and pushing swings in the park. All the vital things – cleanliness, food, sleep – would be managed by her mother.

Getting no immediate response to her ring, Louise bent down and peered through the letter flap. Encouraged by light and a sound suggesting that the house was occupied, she tried again, several times in succession.

'Bloody hell, I'm coming, I'm coming.'

A young girl whom Louise recognised at once from the brief glimpse she had had of her in the park seven weeks before opened the door. She was wearing voluminous khaki trousers, with wide, fraying hems, trailing well over the platformed soles of her trainers, and a black T-shirt which looked as if it had been shrunk several times in the wash. In her hand was a duster and a can of polish. Round her neck hung a Walkman headset, attached by black wire to a small cassette player tucked into the waistband of her trousers.

'Sorry, I had these on.' She plucked at the headset, which was still pulsing with a tinny noise. 'Can I help?'

'I've come to see Joshua – and his grandfather,' replied Louise, unable to mask the ring of disapproval in her tone. While Matt had sung the praises of his young protégée, she had not been able to help wondering at the prudence of bestowing any sort of childcare responsibility on a creature from such a background. The sight of Josie now, waving the duster as if she were mistress of the house, curling her tongue round chewing gum between sentences, did nothing to assuage such reservations. 'I promised Matt I'd drop by while he was away – just to keep an eye on things, you know.'

Josie gave her a sharp look. 'They're out at the moment – gone to the park. I'm doing a couple of hours' housework. I'd do it when they were around only Josh's got a thing about the hoover – doesn't like the noise, which is fair enough if you think about it.' She hesitated a moment before adding, 'You could come in if you wanted to wait for them.'

'Thank you. I will,' replied Louise firmly, the girl's evident lack of enthusiasm only sharpening her determination to cross the threshold.

Having so recently had nothing to do but survey the pristine interior of her own home, Louise felt a curious mixture of envy and dismay at the cheerful chaos prevailing in the Webster household. Kath would have had a fit, she thought sadly, pressing herself against the wall to get past a large cardboard box trailing with Sellotape and bits of string.

'A time capsule,' explained Josie, giving the box a tap as she slid her own wiry frame past it in order to follow Louise into the living room. 'I'm having a grand sort-out in here.' She waved her duster at the piles of toys and books scattered across the carpet. 'Cup of tea?'

'Yes, thank you – but I can make it,' said Louise hastily, 'I know my way quite well round the kitchen. And I'll take this through, while I'm at it. A little something for tea,' she added, tapping her nails on the lid of her tin, driven to make the observation by the blank look on the girl's face. 'Don't let me stop you getting on with your work.'

'Right . . . no. I'll just carry on out here.'

The lack of animation in Josie's expression became rather more understandable at the sight of the kitchen, where a sweet smell and a sink full of unwashed patty-tins bore testimony to some considerable baking efforts on her own part. Tutting loudly at the mess, Louise set her tin down and rolled up her sleeves in preparation to do battle with the washing up.

'There's no need. I was going to do that next.'

'You've clearly got more than enough on your plate next door,' she replied, her voice brisk. 'It won't take a minute.'

'I don't want you to do it,' said Josie doggedly, not understanding her own reactions beyond an intuition that Louise was hostile, that she wasn't offering help so much as disapproval and criticism. She remembered her from the incident in the playground. She hadn't liked the look of her then either, with her smart, expensive clothes and disapproving rich-lady smirk. 'I said I'll bloody do it,' she repeated, snatching the rubber gloves from Louise's hands.

'How dare you . . . I . . .'

'Look, just sit down and have some tea, won't you?' pleaded Josie, conscious suddenly that she might be addressing a creature valued by her employer for some reason. Maybe even his girlfriend, she reflected, inwardly cringing at the thought. 'It's very kind of you and everything, but if you clear up it makes me feel guilty and Mr Webster pays me to clear up so it wouldn't be right.'

This unhappy exchange was brought to a merciful conclusion by the sound of a key in the lock and Joshua bursting into the kitchen, his elfin face streaked with mud and two lines of dribble streaming freely from his nostrils. Ignoring Louise, he grabbed hold of Josie's left leg.

'Hello, I'm Louise,' she said, holding out her hand to Dennis, noting as she did so the echo of Matt among the craggy features, and the same firm set of the jaw. 'I think we've spoken on the phone.' Even the hairline was similar, Dennis's receded but firm head of silky grey suggesting Matt had little further to worry about on that score. 'Just dropped by to see how you were getting on.'

'Well, how kind. Josie, is the kettle on?'

Josie and Louise exchanged a brief glance, as Josie seized the kettle and wedged it under the tap. 'It is now. And there's loads to eat 'cos this . . . Louise brought a cake.' She dropped three tea bags into three mugs and folded her arms. 'Tea coming right up.'

Unable to ignore the sight of Joshua's streaming nose a moment longer, Louise took a tissue from her sleeve and swiped it deftly across his upper lip. 'Aren't you going to even say hello?' she asked, bending down to get his attention.

'Hello,' he shouted, before skidding out of the room and diving into the cardboard box in the hall.

Louise was relieved that, instead of joining her and Dennis,

Josie continued with her household chores, occasionally breaking off to have a noisy swig of tea or to exchange a few squeals through the flap in Joshua's box. Matthew's father was a gentle, kindly man, she could see at once, and even older than she had expected. Despite the strong lines of his features and the brightness of his eyes, he had that edge of physical frailty which she associated with men approaching seventy; a subtle slowness in even the mildest movement, evident in every turn of his head and the way he got up from his chair. He coughed a lot too, trumpeting into a handkerchief with a violence that made her jump.

'Look, do feel free to call me about absolutely anything, won't you?' she urged, feeling after twenty minutes of polite, if rather strained, chitchat that it was time for her to go. 'I've got loads of time this week. It would be a pleasure to help out, it really would.'

'That's kind, but I'm sure there'll be no need.'

'And any problems with . . .' Louise lowered her voice, gesturing with her thumb at the doorway through to the kitchen, where Josie was working up a lather of froth and bubbles at the sink, jigging her skinny hips in time to whatever was pulsing through her headset.

'Josie? Unlikely to be any trouble there. The girl's a treasure.'

'Is she? Oh, good,' murmured Louise, marvelling at such blanket loyalty for so spiky a teenager and privately attributing it to the fact that desperate situations called for desperate remedies. Matt, in his present circumstances, had to make do with what he could get, she reminded herself. 'There's my number anyway,' she added sweetly, tearing off a piece of paper from the handy pad she kept in her bag, 'just in case.'

It wasn't until trying to buy a choc-ice at the cinema that Louise realised that her purse was not in her handbag. Since the tickets were prepaid and she had her credit cards, it was not a major crisis. Anthony, as usual, had wadges of cash in his wallet, which he used not only for confectionery but for dinner and paying the NCP carpark afterwards. It was bound to be at home, he assured her, even after she had gone into some detail about her visit to the Websters, focusing particularly on the mess the place had been in and the sly unpleasantness of the girl.

'But it wouldn't make any sense for her to steal it, now, would it? She'd lose her job.'

'Only if she was found out.'

'Really, darling, it seems very unlikely all the same. I bet you it's on the kitchen table, or in your other bag, the brown one you used last night.'

'Maybe.' Louise closed her mouth round the word, disappointed that Anthony did not share her suspicions, that he should choose to side with a surly teenager whom he had never met, rather than with his own wife.

Chapter Twenty-One

It was well past three o'clock in the morning when they finally
tumbled out into the street, the heat from their breath and skin
steaming at the touch of the cold air. It was snowing. Not the
wet, uncertain flakes which Matt associated with England, but
huge, tufty, substantial things that held their shape as they fell,
and packed together after they had landed, converting the drab
dirt of the pavement to a soft carpet that squeaked underfoot.
Looking up, Matt saw that the patch of yellowy sky which had
left him feeling so buried that afternoon had been converted into
a star-prinked tableau, an opening rather than a closing, a
telescope to the universe. With the snow swirling about them,
even the dullest of the skyscrapers had taken on a fairytale
prettiness, contributing, as much as alcohol already had, to
Matt's sense of wellbeing and bonhomie. With Graham accompanying him to the theatre, it had felt like old times, only better
for being so exceptional, so needed. Afterwards, Graham had
insisted not only on a three-course dinner, but a visit to a
cramped, seedy nightclub, where they drank quantities of bottled
beer, served by semi-naked women on rollerblades. Matt hadn't
been anywhere like it since his stag night, when Graham and a
couple of other friends of the time had rounded off celebrations
by bundling him into a Soho bar where women in stilettos and
thongs simulated sex with metal poles. Kath, out the same night

with some girlfriends for a markedly unriotous meal in a Thai restaurant, had sulked for days afterwards, muttering about sexual stereotypes and the inability of men to develop controlled relationships either with pints of beer or their penises. Sincere protestations from Matt that what little he could recall of the evening had involved no erotic pleasure at all fell on deaf ears.

On this occasion Matt enjoyed himself enormously, not because of the waitresses, whom he found over-made-up and generally unalluring, but because of being able to lose himself in the deafening anonymity of it all. The mesmeric pulse of the music, so powerful that it made the tables shake, and the intermittent sweep of the disjointing strobe lights, facilitated the sense – growing ever since his arrival – that he was being taken out of himself, that the burdens of everyday life were no longer his. As the evening wore on he gave up the effort of trying to say anything intelligible to anybody and instead enjoyed the spectacle of Graham horsing around on the dance-floor, partnering chairs and imaginary companions, oblivious to any irritation or amusement he was causing in the process.

Apart from a low spot during the latter stages of their meal, all traces of jet-lag had magically disappeared. Striding along the pavement now, with Graham playing some sort of hopscotch game beside him, and the taste of the snow on his tongue, Matt felt widely, vividly awake, as if he could never be tired again.

'Taxi!' Graham hopped to the edge of the pavement, waving both hands. The driver slowed before getting a better look at his prospective clients and accelerating away again. 'Arsehole—'

'But it's nice to walk – let's walk.'

'I'm hopping.'

'Okay, you hop, then.'

'Ministry of silly walks, remember?' Graham flapped his arms and bounced on up the pavement, echoing choreographical feats which had caused a near-riot on the dance-floor.

'You drove that girl away,' remarked Matt, prompted by a sudden vivid snapshot of a woman with freckled skin and big breasts who had sat at their table for a while, taking long, suggestive swigs from Graham's bottle of beer. 'She liked you,' he added, hurrying to catch Graham up, the smooth soles of his shoes slipping hopelessly on the snowy ground.

'She liked *you*, only you were too dumb to notice it, as per bloody usual.'

'Crap.'

'Yeah, yeah.' Graham had abandoned his hopping and was now walking backwards in front of Matt, taking huge strides and sticking his arms out for balance. 'Has there been anyone, then – since Kath?' Seeing the flicker of hesitation in Matt's expression, he punched the air with his fist. 'Yes – I knew it.'

'You don't know anything,' exclaimed Matt, annoyed, even through the fug of inebriation, at his friend's exuberance. 'It's not that simple . . . I mean, I don't know what – or if—'

'How many times?'

'What?'

'Bed. The new woman. How many times?'

'Just once.' Even though it was cold and they were drunk, Matt could feel himself flushing. Years of banter and camaraderie had not often led down such acutely personal avenues, not even during the days before Kath, when drunken girlfriend talk had been more frequent and less restrained.

Graham stopped walking backwards and waited until Matt drew level. 'The question is, was it good?' he whispered, slurring the words and clumsily swinging one arm across Matt's shoulder.

Aware that without the buffer of alcohol he might have felt inclined to tell Graham to fuck off and mind his own business, Matt instead found himself trying to answer the question honestly. 'Yes. But weird too . . . like I wasn't given much choice in the matter.'

Graham giggled, tightening his grip on Matt's shoulder. 'All the better. Go for it, that's what I say. You are single, pal – might as well get used to it. Women these days hold the reins more – know what they want and so on.'

They had at last reached the door of his block, and Graham was involved in a fumbling hunt for his keys, rocking between the balls of his feet and his heels from the strain of concentration. Matt, in contrast, felt greatly sobered and suddenly very cold. It was still snowing hard. His feet were wet, he realised, curling his toes inside his socks, and staring morosely at the worn leather of his shoes, caked white on every side.

'What about your love life?' he countered, feeling that in terms of intimate revelations a certain redressing of the balance was called for. 'Who am I depriving tonight?'

Having successfully extracted his keys from a tangle with his handkerchief, Graham stared at them, looking suddenly rather solemn. 'No one. The fact is, I've changed, old boy . . . bit of a new leaf.'

On getting through the door, he staggered so badly that Matt hooked an arm round his elbow to steady him for the walk across the polished floor of the main hall. In the unforgiving light of the lift he saw that his friend was in a worse state than he had realised: his handsome honey-coloured face had a definite tinge of grey, dew-drops of sweat had burst out along his forehead and upper lip, and his eyelids were so heavy that only half the brilliant blue of his pupils was visible. Outside the door to the flat, Matt had to prop him against the wall in order to prise the keys from his fingers and negotiate the door lock. Since there was no question of tackling the spiral stairs, he made for the sofa instead, staggering and swaying from the effort of preventing Graham sinking to the floor.

'Shoes . . . there we go.' Matt slipped off the smart leather loafers, unable to resist a grimace at the decorative tassel, and wedged a cushion under Graham's neck. Nudged by some dim and distant segment of his sober self, Graham murmured profuse thanks before turning on his side and collapsing into sleep. By the time Matt laid his jacket over him he was the picture of peaceful innocence, smiling to himself in his dreams, his hair golden and unkempt, his knees curled protectively to his chest.

Knowing from the thickness between his temples and the raw feeling at the back of his throat that the countdown to his own hangover had already begun, Matt fetched a can of Coke from the vast and surprisingly well-stocked fridge before going back for a final check on the sofa. Joshua would already be waking up, he mused with some disbelief, squinting at his watch as he sank back into one of the wide chairs, still feeling not sleepy so much as heavy-limbed. He imagined his father going through the ritually resisted trials of the morning – tracking down clothes, teeth-cleaning, hair-brushing, shoelace-tying. While a part of him missed it terribly, another part felt a flood of fresh gratitude at being so distant. Not just because it was a break, but because it was helping him to see things clearly, to make out some order among the muddle. Three more weeks would see both the arrival of Erica and the departure of his father. His new life as a non-commuting parent could then start in earnest – Josie as his part-time home help, Beth as his girlfriend . . . There was a future after all, a way through.

Waves of fatigue engulfed him at last, so fiercely and thoroughly that it took all his remaining strength to get up from the chair and cross the floor to the staircase. Sinking to his hands and knees, he climbed the entire way like an amateur on a rock face, not looking down for fear of the drop on either side.

Chapter Twenty-Two

The next morning Graham was astonishingly – infuriatingly – bright-eyed and energised. Streaming with chat and plans for the day, he woke Matt with a cup of tea and a glass of pink grapefruit juice. Graham had never suffered from bad hangovers, Matt recalled gloomily, eyeing his friend through narrowed eyes as he hauled himself upright among the pillows, his own head feeling as if someone had spent the night tying all the cranial blood vessels in knots.

'Slept well?'

'You clearly did.'

'My sofa's a very comfortable piece of furniture,' replied Graham smugly. 'There's half a box of fresh bagels left if you fancy breakfast, and some coffee in the pot – it's a thermal job so should keep hot for an hour or so. I've got to go into the office for a while – then I thought we could meet at my gym this afternoon, work up a bit of a sweat before tackling this evening's entertainment. Good fun last night, by the way. Rather you than me having to write about that play, though. It was crap, wasn't it? Or have I remembered wrong?'

'Refined crap, and I don't want to go to a gym.'

'Yes you do. You'll love it. Lots of Lycra and bulging flesh – more entertainment than in a multiplex cinema.' He pulled on a long grey cashmere coat and flexed his hands into black leather gloves. 'Help yourself to anything you want, won't you. The fax is on the desk next to the computer. See you around three. If you leave the phone for six rings the machine will take it.'

The walls shuddered from the force with which he slammed the door. In the unforgiving light of morning the flat felt more of a big empty space than a structural marvel. Taking a bagel, some coffee and his laptop, Matt returned to the spacious comfort of his bed and launched into a concentrated effort to compose his review. The play had been based on a bestselling book released the year before, a simple tale of betrayal which had taken the reading population of the world by storm and left publishers marvelling and scratching their heads. The paucity of plot, camouflaged in the original by patches of fine writing, had been ruthlessly exposed on stage, leaving the actors to ham up the dialogue for nuance and hidden meanings. Matt worked slowly, his progress hampered not only by his headache but by a vivid image of Kath reading the book on which the play was based. Eighteen months and a lifetime before, during an early September break to a whitewashed fisherman's cottage across a road from a pebbled beach in Brittany. After the pressure and general disruption of the Edinburgh Festival Matt had been longing to get away, to be able to enjoy rather than curse the heat wave which had gripped Europe for the previous five weeks. As things turned out, the weather broke almost the moment they rolled off the ferry, bringing not only dense cloud cover but northerly winds which whipped the sea into a frenzy.

Aged just three and suffering from a bad head cold, Joshua had not responded favourably either to the journey or to the sudden change in his environment. His sleeping patterns deteriorated to such a degree that Kath pulled him into bed between them every night. The beach, to which they tramped determinedly each day in spite of the inclemency of the weather, offered little consolation. Unnerved by the unseasonal wildness of the water, their son had screamed at every suggestion of venturing near it, eventually forcing them to decamp with their belongings back up to the ugly high tideline of dried seaweed and bleached items of rubbish. The book had constituted his wife's chief line of defence against such trials, Matt remembered, leaving him the task of entertaining Joshua, a challenge managed largely through a steady supply of ice creams and expensive plastic toys from the beach shop. The image of Kath, huddled under beach towels, her expression inscrutable behind the sunglasses which she insisted on wearing in spite of – or maybe to spite – the bubbled grey sky, burned in his mind. Had she loved him then, he wondered? He remained motionless for a few moments, his fingers poised over the keyboard of his laptop, which was half submerged among the padded folds of the duvet. At the time he had been aware only of the obvious obstacles to their happiness – the weather, Josh's cold, broken nights – never imagining, not wanting to imagine, bigger issues seething underneath. Matt pressed his knuckles into his eyes, wearied by the hold such memories still had over him, wishing he could airbrush them from his mind with the same ease with which Kath had walked out of his life.

By ten o'clock icy pockets of air seeping across the rafters and up the staircase alerted Matt to the fact that Graham had forgotten to reprogramme the flat's heating system for daytime occupancy. Pulling on the clothes strewn on the floor next to his bed, his fingers stiff with cold, he set off in search of a dial or control panel by which to remedy the situation. The feature wasn't due to go to press until the weekend but, because of the time difference, he had only two hours in which to prepare the review. After a failed, cursory search for something resembling an airing cupboard or an under-stair cubby-hole, he gave up and dialled Graham's office.

'You have reached the voice mail of Graham Hyde. Please leave your message after the tone.'

'It's me and this place is like the North Pole,' Matt hissed, pulling his hands deeper into the sleeves of his jumper and staring morosely at the wedges of snow framing the string of windows running along the wall above his head. Too high for a view of anything but the upper levels of other buildings, they looked like a series of framed black-and-white photographs of urban living; no people, only concrete and blanched sky. 'If you can spare the time I'd be grateful for some directions as to the whereabouts of the bloody thermostat responsible for heating this place.'

A few minutes later, while dropping a soggy tea bag into the swing-bin next to the fridge, Matt's eye was caught by a rectangular inset in the wall, clearly the outline of a small door of perhaps five foot in height. There was no handle and the tiny hinges had been painted the same egg yolk yellow as the walls, but its outline and keyhole were unmistakable. After trying to prise it open with his fingertips, Matt, spurred both by the mounting cold and the approach of his deadline, embarked on a methodical search for the key, finding it at last on top of the fridge, slid between a juice extractor and an espresso machine. A few moments later he was stepping into an enclosed dark space that smelt faintly of gas and paint. A light switch to his left revealed a concrete room of no more than seven feet square, its walls lined with pipes and thick wires. In the near corner were propped a pair of skis, poles and boots. Opposite them, next to a cylindrical water tank, sat what was obviously a boiler. After a few minutes' study of his options, Matt pressed a red switch to its *on* position and was immediately rewarded by a promising whir of ignition. He was already stepping back towards the doorway when his eye was caught by a silvery shimmer in the shadow along the far wall. Closer inspection revealed a portable rail of clothing, covered by a dark blanket. The shimmer of silver turned out to belong to a silky cocktail dress, with a sequinned neckline and shoulder straps. Alongside it hung several other expensive-looking items of female evening wear and a selection of skirts and dresses. Slung across the lower section of the rail were three or four pairs of evening shoes, dangling rather forlornly by their heels, their shiny straps glinting in the dim light. Puzzled, feeling for some reason that he had trespassed, Matt hastily let the blanket fall back into place and retreated to the kitchen. After locking the door, he carefully returned the key to its niche on top of the fridge.

His tea, left to its own devices, had formed a thin film of creamy scum on the surface. He was stabbing thoughtfully at it with a teaspoon when the phone rang.

'Don't worry, I found it—' he began, breaking off in surprise at the sound of Beth Durant's bemused response.

'Found what?'

'Sorry, I thought you were Graham. This place is like an icebox – I've spent the last half-hour looking for a heating switch.'

'And you've found it.'

'Yes. How are you?'

'I'm good, thank you.'

'I thought you weren't going to ring.'

'I wasn't, but then I wanted to talk to you. So I called up your father, who was sweet, and got this number and here I am. So how's it going over there?'

Matt swigged his warm tea. It was good to hear her voice, good to feel that beneath that self-contained exterior she was missing him. 'Fine, it's going fine. Not a great play last night and too much alcohol afterwards – but it's fun. This friend I'm staying with has got the most amazing flat – one huge room with split levels.'

'So that's why your voice sounds kind of echoey.'

'Does it?'

'Matt, do you miss me?'

'I do. Quite a lot in fact,' he ventured, his confidence blossoming at the breathy eagerness in her tone. 'It will be good to get together again.'

'I've booked Italy.'

'You've what?'

'You know, like I said and you agreed?'

'Did I?' he murmured, struggling to recall anything so concrete but pleased none the less. 'When for exactly? I mean, I'd love to, but there is the business of getting time off – and Josh of course—'

'It's only a weekend – Florence. Friday to Monday. May bank-holiday. The busiest weekend of the year – that's why I had to book. I thought you'd be pleased.'

'And I am . . . I really am,' he assured her, performing rapid mental aerobics with regard to work and childcare. His father would be back in Yorkshire by then. Josie was still too young to be left in sole charge for so long. He would have to call upon the services of Louise. 'Nice to have something to look forward to.'

'Me too.' There was a meaningful pause, while each pondered the implications of these admissions, aware that they were edging beyond the breezy friendliness with which they had parted ten days before. 'So how's your friend treating you?'

'Great – apart from freezing me to death.' Matt went on to recount his adventure in the boiler room.

Beth hooted with laughter. 'Maybe this guy you've known for two decades is a closet transsexual . . . oh, I love it, that's really good.'

'I couldn't think of anything less likely,' said Matt, managing to laugh himself, unequal to the task of explaining that the rack of clothes had for some reason unnerved him, that since Kath's betrayal he was beginning to doubt his ability to really know anyone, even himself.

'Mind you, being a transsexual is no big deal these days,' she continued, 'not as far as weirdness goes. I had a friend once who knew someone who wished he could have both legs amputated – it's this real disease called apotemnophilia. The poor guy spent his life looking for a surgeon prepared to put him out of his misery. I mean, can you imagine anything more gross than *wanting* to be a cripple?'

'You are a mine of interesting information.'

'Does that mean I can call again?'

He laughed again, more genuinely this time. 'Any time.'

Revitalised by the phone call and several slices of toast, Matt returned to his laptop and spent a largely trouble-free couple of hours finishing off his piece. He had just successfully fed it through the fax machine when Graham himself came in, looking somewhat wearier than he had first thing that morning.

'I turned the heating back on. It was fucking freezing.'

'Did you? Sorry about that.'

'Took me a while to find the boiler room.'

'Ah, you went in there, did you? There's a dial in the corner above the sofa you could have used instead. If you turn it up high enough it automatically triggers the whole system into action.'

'I saw those clothes — on the rail. Quite a collection.'

Graham groaned, dropping his face into his hands. 'Don't remind me. I'm doing my best to forget their owner.'

'A girlfriend? You didn't say.'

Graham scowled. 'That's because it was not worth mentioning. Whirlwind job. She moved in lock, stock and barrel — I thought it was the Real Thing.' He made quotation marks with his fingers, laughing bitterly. 'She moved out just as fast — found some other guy prepared to buy her anything she wanted. I threw a lot of her stuff away — and the rest I just wanted out of sight. Thought I'd give it to charity or something.'

'And there was me thinking you'd developed a secret cross-dressing habit.'

Graham clapped his hand to his mouth in mock horror. 'God, you're on to me — how will I cope with the shame?'

'If you let me off this afternoon's exercise regime I won't tell a soul.'

Graham pretended to consider the proposition seriously for a moment before shaking his head. 'Sorry, no can do. Last night has really caught up with me — I need a serious sweat. So I can do it all again tonight with a clear conscience.' He grinned impishly, looking more himself. 'And anyway, you look like you could do with a bit of toning.'

'I do not.' Matt looked down at his stomach, the edge of real indignation in his voice. One of the few benefits of Kath's departure was that the weight had fallen off him. The faint swell once threatening round his belt-line had completely dissolved, returning his waist to its natural slimness and giving greater prominence to the broadness of his chest. Long since accepting the fact that he would never attain the lithe athleticism of his friend, Matt had lately dared to believe that in the general scheme of thirtysomething decay – physical at least – he wasn't doing too badly.

A couple of hours later, clad in a pair of baggy Bermudas and an old T-shirt of Graham's, he nonetheless found himself entering a roomful of imposing exercise machines. As Graham had promised, the place offered an irresistibly interesting variety of spectacles, ranging from muscle-bound creatures pumping the heaviest weights to less shapely specimens mournfully pitting their strength against pedals and pulleys. One mountain of a woman in particular caught Matt's eye, gripping the crossbar of her bike as if her life depended on it, her generous rear end swamping the seat like bulging saddlebags. Leaving Graham to show off his prowess on the more technically taxing equipment, Matt confined himself to modest spurts of rowing and jogging, trying to avoid both his own sweating face in the wall mirrors and those of his fellow exercisers. Since this ruled out practically everything in the room, he spent most of the time watching the panel of blinking numbers recording his progress, pondering the profoundly dispiriting experience of running with all his might and getting nowhere. When at last he stepped off the conveyor belt, the ground continued to heave beneath his feet. Sinking down on a bench with a towel to recover, he watched Graham rounding off his own work-out with a series of professional looking stretches. He had taken off his T-shirt and slung it round his neck, revealing his impressive keyboard of abdominals and trim waist. The mountainous lady was watching too, Matt observed, feeling sorry for the pink pudding face, so obviously transfixed by envious longing. And Graham knew the woman was watching, Matt suddenly realised, glancing from one to the other. He was doing it for her, showing off to her, letting her get an eyeful. It occurred to him in the same instant that if he did not already know Graham he might think he was a bit of a jerk. He pulled the towel farther over his head, screening the view from sight. To even think such a thing felt cruelly disloyal. Graham was his oldest friend, one of the few constants in an otherwise rambling and not entirely satisfactory life. Behind his narcissism lay a genuine struggle – to be admired, to be successful, to be kind.

'So this woman, the one who walked out – did you like her a lot?' he ventured, suspecting suddenly that Graham was doing a more than usually effective job of burying his feelings on the subject. They were alone by the lockers in the changing rooms, towelling themselves dry from a shower.

'The woman who—? Oh, God, yes, like hell. I was mad for her.' He scowled briefly before relaxing his handsome face into a broad smile. 'But life carries on, doesn't it? You've just got to watch out for the opportunities and grab them with both hands.'

Matt opened his mouth to offer some wry response, but was drowned by the buzz of Graham's electric razor, which he had whipped out of his bag and begun sliding across his cheeks, twisting his mouth to accommodate the cut of the blades.

Chapter Twenty-Three

Strolling across the concourse of JFK three days later, Matt could still feel an uncomfortable tightness in his limbs, particularly his thigh muscles, which the exertions on the running belt seemed to have shrunk by several inches. It had been so bad the day before that Graham, much amused, had given him a tube of white cream to rub into the most afflicted areas, a pungent-smelling substance which created an icy burning sensation and left his skin so sticky that he could feel it clinging to the inside of his trousers.

Now that his trip was coming to an end it seemed to have passed in a flash. Somehow he had met his deadlines. Even the big piece was all but finished, requiring just one more edit to pare it down to size. As a host Graham had continued to exceed all expectations, taking great swathes of time out of his working day and putting himself entirely at Matt's disposal. Without jeopardising Matt's work commitments, they had managed to tour several key landmarks of the city, including Central Park, the World Trade Center and the Statue of Liberty. In the evenings Graham attended the remaining three productions without the slightest sign of weariness, taking Matt out afterwards to a string of excellent restaurants, each one offering a different national cuisine from the last.

As a finishing touch to these generous attentions he had

insisted on chauffeuring Matt to the airport for his early morning flight home. Instead of tipping him out under the sign for departures, as Matt had expected, he parked and came into the main building to accompany him through the rigmarole of checking in. Even when Matt announced that he had to purchase gifts for Dennis and Joshua, Graham remained undaunted, cheerfully leading the way through the mall of retailers, throwing out suggestions as they went.

'Does he like dinosaurs?' He picked up a huge wind-up toy and waggled it at Matt, who was staring hopelessly at the array of Disney figures and monogrammed items of clothing.

'He'd love it, but it's too big and too much.'

'What about this, then?' Graham plucked a monster mask off a shelf and put it over his face, growling.

'Too scary. He's . . . easily scared.'

'Oh, yeah . . . of course.' Graham hurriedly replaced the mask. 'Is that since . . . because of everything that's happened at home?'

Matt was grateful. The scarcity of such enquiries had cast the only faint shadow over an otherwise splendid few days. 'Partly. Though he was always a timid little chap anyway, as you might remember. Tends to regard the world as more of a threat than an adventure.'

'Does he miss Kath?'

'Of course,' said Matt quietly, 'though you see it more in the way he behaves than what he actually says. But things are getting better. My father has been fantastic and that girl I mentioned – Josh really likes her a lot.'

'So you think he – that both of you – will be all right?' He had picked up a small gingery lion with long droopy whiskers which he was winding round and round his fingers. 'Because you of all people, Matt . . . you deserve to be happy because you are a *good* person. Bloody sight better than the rest of us . . .' He dropped the lion back among a trayful of its peers. 'This new woman you've met, I really hope it works out.'

There was a concern in his voice that Matt had never heard before. 'Thank you for that and for being so—'

'I know, I know. I'm a complete saint. Now can we get on with this before you miss your flight?'

Smiling to himself, Matt picked up one of the lions, which were floppy and friendly and under ten dollars, and a baseball cap advertising the New York Giants. 'I'll get a good malt from duty-free for Dad – he'll appreciate that far more than a paperweight or a pair of socks.'

Watching Graham stride ahead of him out of the shop, Matt sensed that his friend was at last eager to be rid of him. Jostling for space among the throng of people amassing in front of the security barrier, they hurriedly shook hands and patted each other's arms.

'You take care now.'

'I hope everything works out for you.'

'You make it sound like I'm leaving the planet,' Matt joked, giving a final wave as the crowd closed in around him, herding him towards the departure lounge.

Seven hours later Matt found himself staring out over the tidy grid of England with considerably more confidence than when he had waved it goodbye five days before. It was spring, he realised, spotting even from the height of several thousand feet the new verdure of the land, the glinting hints of colour sewn into the landscape. Although the week had flown by, the sense of progress inside his own head and heart made it feel suddenly as if his absence had lasted an age. Bugger Kath, he thought cheerfully, bracing himself as the ground rushed up to meet the airplane wheels and the brake force tightened his belt across his stomach. He had a son whom he adored, a near-perfect contract of self-employment, a house worth twice what he had paid for it, a saintly father, a clutch of friendly females. Even a girlfriend, he reminded himself, smiling at the thought of Beth. During the course of the week they had enjoyed several more transatlantic phone calls, each one a little more intimate than the last. Matt had forgotten the pleasure of being wanted, the feeling that there was someone awaiting his return.

On reaching baggage reclaim, he called home to confirm his safe arrival. Greeted with his own voice on the answer machine, and seeing from a glance at his watch that it was five o'clock, Matt guessed that Dennis and Joshua would be on their way back from a sortie to the park.

'Dad, just to say I'm at Heathrow. Hope all's well. See you soon.'

He was standing leaning on his trolley, torn between signs to the taxi rank and the more arduous option of a train, when two cool hands were placed over his eyes.

'Surprise.'

'Beth? What on earth?'

'Aren't you pleased?'

'Of course I am. And amazed.'

'Amazed I can cope with,' she murmured, putting her arms round his neck and pulling his face close to hers.

Matt eagerly returned the embrace, inwardly marvelling at being unexpectedly chaperoned from two airports in the space of one week. She was looking more glamorous than he had ever seen her, attired in a pale blue wool skirt suit, sheer tights and high-heeled tanned leather shoes.

'I was going to drive you straight home, but now that I've got hold of you I don't want to let you go. Nor do you, by the feel of it,' she added in a whisper, pressing her pelvis more firmly against him and tipping up her chin so that her hair fell prettily off the back of her shoulders. 'God, it's good to see you.'

'And you,' Matt murmured, not minding that they were provoking glances of interest and curiosity from the crowds milling about them. Just as he would stare were he in their shoes, he mused, smiling down at the attractive woman in his arms and thinking what a perfect picture of reunion they created.

'Now then, I've got to be somewhere at six thirty.' Beth

grabbed his carry-on bag, suddenly all bustle and businesslike. 'If we hurry we've got time.'

Picking up his suitcase, Matt began trotting after her. 'Time?'

She swung round to look at him, her eyes flashing. 'For sex,' she said, so loudly that Matt feared he was not the only one to hear. 'Don't you want to?'

'Of course. I mean—' He nearly said he always wanted sex, but realised it might not be the most endearing of remarks and instead performed a quick mental appraisal of the time implications of such an indulgence. 'The thing is,' he explained, once they were both settled inside her car, 'they'll be waiting for me at home – I've left a message saying I'm on my way. Josh will be expecting me—'

'That is so sweet.' She slapped both sides of the steering wheel, shaking her head, her voice ringing with admiration. 'Of course you want to see your little boy, of course you do. That is so right.' When she turned to him there were tears in her eyes. 'I'm sorry, Matt, I wasn't thinking straight.' She started the engine, still shaking her head. 'I'll drop you home.'

'That's very kind, but really, any Tube or railway line will do. I was expecting to make my own way—'

'Nonsense,' she cut in, her American accent giving equal emphasis to each syllable. 'I was thinking of myself as usual, a habit I've perfected since my divorce. I used to spend my entire life thinking of my dear husband, second-guessing his every whim, subsuming every desire of my own – God, Matt, I sometimes feel I wasted the first thirty years of my life. I was this sheltered little girl who kind of went along with the sexual revolution but secretly believed men were superior – because of my mom, I guess, who looked up to my dad like he was some kind of god. When I met Robert I tried to do the same, combining my career with rushing home to have his dinner ready, making myself especially beautiful on Friday nights when he generally like to have sex. Is that pathetic or what? Now I'm like, I'll have sex when the hell I want to – and if guys think I'm too pushy then that's their problem. Oh God, I'm talking too much as usual, aren't I? And you probably do think I'm too forward – like back there, saying I wanted sex. Did that bother you, Matt?'

'No,' he said, even though, if he were honest, it had a little bit. He took her hand off the steering wheel and pressed her fingers to his lips. 'You just said it a bit loudly – I was worried half the airport would want to join us.'

She giggled, slipping her hand back on to the wheel.

'No news on your wife, I suppose?' she asked a little later.

'No, and I don't care any more either,' said Matt firmly. 'And I've decided I'm not even worried she'll come back for Josh. So much time has gone by and after what she did she'd have no hope of winning custody.'

'I should think not.' Beth sighed. 'You know what, Matt?' I would really like to meet the little guy – he sounds so cute. And if you and I are going to be seeing a bit of each other . . .'

Matt was genuinely touched. 'I would really like that too, though maybe not today,' he added hastily, picturing both Joshua's and Dennis's faces if he sailed through the door with Beth hanging on his arm. 'If you don't mind.'

'Of course not.' She reached across and squeezed his thigh, just above the knee where it tickled. 'What about Sunday, then? The three of us could do some kind of excursion together – the Dome, or the zoo.'

'Okay.' He laughed, in truth somewhat nervous at the prospect. 'Not the Dome maybe, but the zoo – Josh would love that.'

She pressed her lips together in satisfaction. 'It's a date, then. So long as we make it a late start – I need at least half the day in bed on a Sunday before I can be nice to anyone. Even you,' she whispered, seizing the opportunity of a red light to lean over and press her lips to his.

Chapter Twenty-Four

'Bad traffic?' enquired Dennis, a trace of testiness in his voice.

The initial exuberance of the reunion having subsided, they had all moved into the kitchen. Unequal to admitting to the shameful truth that he had, after all, returned from Heathrow via Beth Durant's water bed, Matt busied himself with the kettle, muttering something about a mess-up in baggage reclaim and the difficulty of getting a taxi. That his father was in a bad mood had been clear to him from the moment he opened the door, even through the exchange of affectionate pleasantries and the heart-jumping thrill of having Joshua in his arms. Attributing it to the understandable strain of having been in sole charge for a week, Matt made as big a deal as he could of presenting the malt whisky, and insisting that Dennis was to do nothing but put his feet up for the entire weekend.

They took their tea into the sitting room, where Joshua, thrilled with his lion and his baseball cap, which was much too large, even on the tightest notch, trampolined round the furniture emitting squeaky roars of celebration. It took the biscuit tin to secure a bit of peace and quiet, whereupon Matt launched into a fresh effort to appease his father. 'Not long now and you'll be safely back in your own home.'

'No hurry, it's . . .' A wheezy cough prevented him from continuing.

'That's quite a noise — have you had time to see a doctor?'

Dennis shook his head fiercely. 'The cough's no bother,' he rasped, banging his chest in an apparently successful effort to force it into co-operation. 'Though there has been some kind of trouble that you should know about . . . woman trouble, to be exact.'

'Woman trouble?' Matt began to laugh but stopped, guessing from the expression on his father's face that he was about to learn the origins of his ill-humour.

'Granddad is cross with Louise,' put in Joshua, managing even through a mouthful of biscuit to convey a certain awe at being privy to so adult a piece of information.

'Louise? Whatever for?'

'Sticking her bloody nose in, that's what for — coming round here at all times, getting Josie so upset—'

'Josie?' Matt felt a wave of panic. 'How?'

'Accused her of taking her purse — of all things.' Dennis rolled his eyes at the ceiling.

'When, for God's sake?'

'The first time she came — Tuesday afternoon. Had a cup of tea. Next thing I know she's on the phone ranting about her wallet being taken from her bag. Comes by in person to confront poor Josie. And then goes and gets Sophie involved.'

Matt dropped his face into his hands with a groan. 'Dad, why didn't you call me about all this? I thought we agreed that if there was any sort of real problem—'

Dennis dismissed the suggestion with an angry wave of his hand. 'It wasn't a real problem. At least not at first. It's just sort of . . . gathered pace.'

'But of course Josie wouldn't take a purse — or anything else for that matter.'

'You try telling your friend Louise that. Josie's so upset she's threatening never to set foot in this house again.'

'I'm not surprised.' Matt let out a low whistle of disbelief. 'And this purse of Louise's — where exactly was it found?'

Dennis threw up his arms in exasperation. 'That's the point. It never has been found. Louise swears it was in her handbag when she visited, but we've turned this place upside down—' He broke off for another bout of coughing. 'I must confess to being sick to death of the whole subject. I just hope you're up to sorting it out.'

Matt shot him a weary smile. 'I expect I'll manage. I'm just sorry you got caught up in the middle of it. Louise seems to have appointed herself my guardian. She feels sorry for me, I guess. Wants to help.' He made a face.

'Good intentions can mask terrible deeds.'

'No need to be melodramatic, Dad,' replied Matt tightly. 'I'll talk to Louise first and then clear things with Josie and Sophie.' Noticing that Joshua, bored of adult conversation, was attempting to cram his lion into the video machine, he reached over and pulled him on to his lap. 'What a palaver, eh?'

'Palaver,' repeated Joshua, liking the word.

'Have you been a good boy for Granddad?'

Dennis answered for him, his face creasing into the first full smile since Matt's return. 'He's been as good as gold. We've had a grand time, haven't we?'

Joshua nodded, dancing his lion on his knees. 'We went to McDonald's 'cos I didn't wet my bed.'

'Did you now?' Matt raised his eyebrows at his father, who grinned sheepishly, murmuring, 'A bit of bribery never hurt anyone.' He levered himself up from his chair and began reaching for the empty tea mugs.

'Leave it, Dad. I've told you, I'm in charge for the weekend. Have a lie-down or something.'

Dennis looked indignant. 'I don't want a lie-down.'

'Well, go and see your mate in Islington, then, or treat yourself to a pint at the Pheasant—'

'Now that is not a bad idea,' Dennis conceded, rubbing his palms together.

'So I can have you all to myself,' said Matt, hugging Joshua more tightly.

'Sorry, Granddad, but Daddy wants me now,' said Joshua, clearly concerned as to whether his grandfather would be able to manage without him.

'We'll ask Louise and the girls to meet us in the park tomorrow morning, shall we? And on Sunday I thought we'd go to the zoo.'

'Zoo, zoooo.' The child erupted from the sofa and began a charge of celebration round the ground floor, piloting the lion above his head as if it were a toy plane.

'So he has been all right, then?' pressed Matt, lowering his voice.

'Oh, yes.' Dennis chuckled. '*He's* all right.'

'Oh God, and the assessment at St Leonard's — how did that go?' Matt clapped his hand to his mouth, appalled that he had forgotten.

'Oh, that was fine. He got a bit upset afterwards because he had drawn this picture of a fire truck and they wouldn't let him take it home — needed it for further analysis, I suppose.' Dennis chuckled, shaking his head despairingly. 'Utterly daft, the whole process.'

'Yes, isn't it,' murmured Matt, his mind slipping back to the more immediate problem of the purse, inwardly quailing at the prospect of playing peacemaker between the three women.

Louise's initial wail of protest when he broached the subject in the park the following day did little to allay such fears.

'Why does nobody believe me? I *know* I had it when I went to your house and then it wasn't there at the theatre. I've searched the car a hundred times.'

'Maybe it fell on to the pavement and someone picked it up—'

'That's what Anthony says.' She gave a cross tug at the big furry lapels of her sheepskin, making no effort to hide her irritation with her husband. Their week, as far as she was concerned, had gone from bad to worse. They had eaten out twice only, both pleasant enough meals, but with the conversation dominated either by disputes about her purse or the piece of research Anthony was working on, which was reaching the usual fever pitch of near-completion. They had made love once, on the Wednesday, but Louise's heart hadn't really been in it. That Anthony seemed not to notice this fact, or, worse still in Louise's eyes, not to care about it if he had, had not made matters any better. While Anthony had made the most of a less punishing schedule to sleep long and deeply in ten-hour stretches, Louise had found herself tossing for hours every night, her mind knotted with niggling worries and a suffocating sense of injustice about her husband and life in general. Instead of feeling refreshed at the sight of the children spilling out of her parents' car on Friday afternoon, she was aware only of a deep, angry weariness that the whole painstakingly organised separation had been a waste of time.

'I know you've been trying to help,' said Matt gently, 'but really, I do not believe that Josie would ever be so dishonest.'

'Why you trust that girl is beyond me. She's sullen and rude, with so many chips on her shoulder it's a wonder she can stand up. And as for that woman friend of hers' . . . Louise whistled. 'God, she's something else altogether.'

Matt chuckled. 'Now on that score I would have to agree with you. Sophie Contini is quite a case. If it's any consolation she's horrible to me too.'

Louise hooked her hand round Matt's elbow and smiled for the first time. 'It is, Matt. Thank you. An enormous consolation.'

'Apparently she tried to run off with a married man a couple of years ago and it all fell through,' he continued, using a tone of confidentiality he knew Louise would appreciate, and giving her hand a companionable pat. They were nearing the playground. Up ahead the tallest of the slides was just visible through the trees, its yellow paint catching the afternoon sun.

'Really? So she's bitter and twisted,' remarked Louise,

sounding satisfied. After a few moments' silence she added, 'And I'm wrong.'

'I'm afraid you are. Wonderfully intentioned, but wrong.'

'And I've got everyone's backs up unnecessarily.'

'I'm afraid you might have.'

'Bloody hell.'

'Never mind. I'll explain to Josie and the dreaded Sophie. It will all be fine. Though I'm sorry about the purse. Was there much in it?'

Louise shrugged. 'Forty odd pounds, library cards, passport snaps of the children – nothing too serious.'

Taking the opportunity of their arrival at the playground to disengage his arm, Matt held open the little gate for her to pass through.

'How gallant,' said Louise teasingly, letting the children charge through first and then tipping her head towards him with exaggerated gratitude.

And that's her sorted, thought Matt, turning away to hide a smile of satisfaction. A little grovelling to Josie and her friend and the whole situation would be resolved. He took his time pulling the gate closed, for the first time feeling relaxed enough to appreciate the expanse of verdant grass and prettily landscaped pathways spread out around them. Bursts of colour bubbled in every flower-bed, while the trees' spiky winter haircuts were being transformed by bud clusters and patches of green fuzz. Surveying the scene, Matt felt a lift of conviction similar to the one he had experienced on looking out of the airplane window. He was on a roll, and no bickering about mislaid purses or anything else was going to stop it. Seeing Louise wave for assistance over two free swings and three eager children, he pulled the gate behind him and set off across the playground at a trot, extending his stride in the happy realisation that the pain in his leg muscles seemed at last to have melted away.

Chapter Twenty-Five

Feeling the stitch tighten under her ribs, hurting like the twist of a knife, Sophie slowed her pace and concentrated on her breathing. It always came at around the same time, half an hour or so into the run, when the first reserves of her energy had been worn down and the back-up, developed over two years of hard work, had yet to kick in. Sunday morning was by far her favourite slot for exercise. She loved the thick quietness of the curtained windows and empty roads, the sense of suspension, as if the city were holding its breath against all the noise and friction on which it habitually thrived. Usually she headed south, taking a route through Camberwell towards Herne Hill and Brixton, where a few dog-walkers would already be strolling round Brockwell Park and sleepy paper-boys crouching over their bikes. Instead, wanting a change, she had set off in the opposite direction, steering a course down Borough High Street towards London Bridge. Running over the bridge itself, the wind tugging at her hair and the gleaming domes and towers ranged before her like mountain peaks, Sophie felt a rush of pure happiness. Seeing another lone jogger across the road, heading back the way she had come, she almost shouted out a greeting, so strong was the warmth inside her, the sense, so rare these days, of being wholly at peace with the world.

Once across the bridge, however, the mood began to slip from her grasp. The City itself was like a ghost town, its silence containing the unmistakable aura not so much of inactivity as absence. With her clothes now thoroughly damp from sweat, she found herself shivering in the shadows of the buildings towering above her, their polished windows blinking like watchful eyes. Scampering along the foot of the high wall of the Bank of England running down Prince's Street, she felt suddenly like an insect in a tunnel, and glanced several times over her shoulder to be sure she was alone. It was a relief to reach the relative openness of Moorgate, with its traffic lights and Marks and Spencer, and to realise from a glance at her watch that it was time to be turning back for home.

As she retraced her steps, there were signs everywhere that the metropolis was stirring from its slumbers; more cars had filtered on to the roads and here and there Sunday traders were pulling their shutters up. Just past the Elephant and Castle roundabout her path was blocked by a large family crowd, clad in brilliant tribal colours, the hems of their gowns trailing on the dirty pavement, their hats as tall as wedding cakes. Small children were hanging on the arms of the adults, their slack, sleepy faces suggesting recent and reluctant eviction from their beds. Sophie, her breath now coming in short, tight spurts, her legs leaden, had to run along the road for several yards to get past them. As she did so someone from the group shouted, 'Run, lady, run.' She half turned, wanting to offer a smile, but stumbled and almost lost her balance. Someone in the crowd laughed. Leaping back on to the pavement, she accelerated away, her heart bursting, her contact lenses, irritated by sweat, sliding uncomfortably across her eyes. Turning into her own road at last, she slowed to a staggering walk for the final few yards.

Though her body ached, her mind felt sharpened and re-freshed. The prospect, once so crushing, of another busy Sunday, marking books, catching up on laundry, fielding demands from the clutch of pupils who made regular use of her 'open house' policy, now glowed in her mind as something not only manageable but full of potential satisfaction. The headache, pulsing between her temples as it always did after a bad night's sleep, had vanished. Banging her front door shut behind her, she took several long deep breaths, dropping her head to her feet, letting her hair and fingernails trail on the floorboards. When at last she raised herself upright, she felt so dizzy from the blood pumping behind her eye sockets that she had to steady herself against the wall.

It was only as she was tugging off her trainers that Sophie remembered she faced an added burden that morning in the form of Matt Webster. Kicking her shoes in the direction of the coatstand, which was far too broad-branched for the hall but didn't fit anywhere else, she headed for the stairs. She took each step slowly, pulling herself by the banister and frowning in a bid to recollect quite how the man's telephoned apologies about the vile behaviour of his girlfriend had resulted in an agreement to flog the matter still further over a cup of coffee. She had drunk two glasses of wine, Sophie recalled gloomily, a tactic to which she quite often resorted on a Saturday night when trying to feel like one of the independent single women so frequently profiled in the media instead of an overworked schoolteacher with a crap social life; with the result that she had felt gracious and amenable, only too willing to convey the impression that she had nothing better to do on Sunday mornings than offer guidance as to how to handle sixteen-year-old girls with hurt feelings and fragile egos.

Under the needling heat of the shower, Sophie felt her body revive. Twisting her hair up into a towel, she paused before pulling on her bathrobe, looking over her shoulder at her reflection in the large oval mirror on her bedroom wall with a shrug of indifference. That her exercise regime had offered various improvements to what had always been a more than passable figure struck her as a matter of some irony. She ran for her brain rather than for her body, for the sense of empowerment afterwards, the fleeting feeling that she was on top of things. The fact that two years had passed since anything more animate than a pane of glass had seen her naked gave her perverse satisfaction. Not because she enjoyed being celibate, but because a part of her could not help believing that such deprivation was the least she deserved.

Grim-faced at the memory of her shame, still so fresh after so much time, Sophie crossed the landing back to her bedroom and dropped to a cross-legged position on the floor. It had been a bad couple of weeks. The sight of Maria Schofield, smug and sly in her big fur hat during one of Miss Brannock's tours, had brought it all back to her: the whispering behind hands, the looks of pity and contempt, the utter humiliation when the man whom she had loved to distraction had returned to his wife and left her to face the vilification alone.

Closing her eyes and resting her hands palm upwards on her knees, Sophie tried to empty her mind of everything but light. To let everyday preoccupations float away. To breathe steadily and evenly. The manual suggested many other things as well, but she couldn't remember them and didn't want to interrupt the session by crawling to her bedside table to look them up. Palettes of colour swam before her eyes. Instead of relaxing she could feel herself tensing up. After a while she became aware of a tickle on the tip of her nose. Unignorable, irresistibly intense. She would try again later, she told herself, rubbing at it with a groan of relief and pulling on some jeans and a voluminous Sloppy Jo sweat-shirt. Seeing the time, she set off downstairs at a jog, the long strands of her wet hair streaming over her shoulders.

Matt pulled up the handbrake and succumbed to one of the many eye-watering yawns which had punctured the morning. The body clock that had so efficiently adapted to New York time was showing considerable reluctance to perform the same process in reverse. After a marathon performance the day before, he had sunk into a deep coma of a sleep around midnight, only to find himself fully awake again at four. As he twisted under the covers in the small hours, some of the old fears and uncertainties had returned. At each squeak of rubber wheels and every slam of a car door his heart had clenched, not hopeful as he had been during the early days, but terrorised by the thought of Kath's return. He had nothing for her now, not forgiveness and certainly not his son. By the time he felt sleepy again, Joshua was cartwheeling into the bedroom to herald the start of a new day.

As they approached Sophie Contini's doorstep, the sun popped out from behind a mountainous cloud, lending a cheerful sheen to the chipped window frames and row of patched slate roofs. She took a while to answer the door, time enough for Matt to register serious misgivings about this last-ditch attempt of his to broker something more amicable than a frosty truce with the person so clearly – so maddeningly – crucial to the success of his childcare arrangements. Josie had responded positively enough to his reassurances on the phone, brushing aside the purse fiasco with cheery brusqueness, but not without several references to the opinions of her mentor along the way. It had taken all Matt's patience not to burst out that he cared only for Josie's feelings in the matter, and that if she were ever to have a hope of making her own way in the world she would have to learn to break free from the clutches of her English teacher.

'Mr Webster—'

'For goodness' sake, call me Matt – please.'

'Come in.' Sophie opened the door wider, offering him a brief smile before crouching down to talk to Joshua. 'I'm glad you decided to come too. I haven't got many toys but I do need some help in the kitchen. I hope you're good at mixing.'

'Can Lion help?' he enquired, waggling his new companion in her face.

'He certainly can, though we'll have to be careful not to get his lovely fur dirty. Come along and I'll show you what needs doing.'

Matt followed, almost tripping over the legs of a large mahogany coatstand and feeling somewhat superfluous. She led the way to the back of the house, where two rooms had clearly been knocked into one, creating a large, airy kitchen-cum-living room. A worn pine table, on which sat a full fruit bowl and several stacks of school books, occupied centre-stage. To one side was a deep, comfortably battered looking sofa, covered in bright cloths and huge scatter cushions. Although the overall impression of the room was orderly, every available surface – the mantelpiece, shelves and windowsills – was crammed with objects – pots of pencils, ornaments, candlesticks, tins and postcards. The walls were just as busy, covered from skirting board to ceiling with framed prints and huge collages of photographs. Behind the door next to a radiator was a rail of drying laundry displaying a pair of jogging bottoms, a pink T-shirt, a sweat-shirt, and several pairs of white pants, hung in perfect triangles between three equally white bras.

'Coffee?'

Matt spun round, hoping that she hadn't suspected him of scrutinising her underwear, but judging from the crease of disapproval on her face that she probably had. 'That would be very nice.' He smiled, wanting to set the conversation on the right track, wondering who had taken the place of the adulterous father Maria had mentioned.

'How do you take it?'

'White no sugar. Thanks.'

'I expect you would prefer juice,' Sophie said, her voice softening as she turned to Joshua, who was already standing on a chair beside her wielding a wooden spoon, a large drying-up cloth fastened round his neck by way of an apron. 'Now, let's put Lion safely up there where he can watch' – she gently propped the animal on top of a spaghetti jar – 'while you set to work on this. Over here on the floor would be a good place, I think – lots of elbow room.' Taking hold of a solid brown mixing bowl with one hand and scooping Joshua up with her free arm, she set him down on the ground. 'See, it's sludgy when it should be smooth,' she explained, helping him jab at the mixture with his spoon. 'It's home-made play-dough. We can make it any colour you like. Well, almost.' She began pulling little bottles off a herb shelf. 'Green, blue, black, pink, yellow or orange. Like magic.'

Although pleased to see his son so beautifully entertained,

Matt himself was feeling more awkward by the minute. She was behaving almost as if he weren't there, as if she had no clue as to the purpose of his visit. Which was to make her into an ally instead of an enemy, he reminded himself, trying out another generous smile as she handed him his coffee, and being rewarded only by the faintest twitch of the broad mouth, of the kind bestowed upon a tiresome child.

'About the purse.'

'There's really no need to go over it all again.' She gestured at the sofa for him to sit down, before seating herself astride a chair at the far end of the kitchen table. 'So long as Josie knows that she has your trust, that's all that matters.'

'Yes. And I think I've reassured her on that score. But . . . well, I wanted also to offer a proper apology to you. Being subjected to Louise on her high horse' – he made a comic face – 'is an alarming experience at the best of times—'

'It didn't alarm me.' She gave a defensive toss of her hair, revealing a large grey stain of damp across the back of her sweat-shirt. The surface curls of her hair had dried first, but underneath the heavier tresses were still dark and black from the shower. 'I just thought it was out of order.'

'Yes, it was,' agreed Matt wearily, beginning to despair at the persistence of her hostility. 'She meant to help me, I think . . .' He frowned. 'My wife, Kath, is – was – a good friend of hers. Since she left Louise has been wading to my assistance on a regular basis. In some ways I feel rather sorry for her – she's got a stuffy husband, too much money and nothing to do except supervise the au pair.'

'God, do you talk about all your friends like that?'

'No, I was only . . . what exactly is your problem?' Matt set his mug of coffee down with such force that some of it slopped on to the table.

'What is *my* problem?' Sophie let out a sharp laugh. 'I like that.' She kept her voice sharp too, wanting to disguise the extent of her shock at his outburst.

'I have tried,' Matt hissed, glancing anxiously at Joshua, 'to be friendly.'

'I'm sorry it's been such an effort.' Her brown eyes flashed at him. Pulling a tissue from her sleeve, she leaned across and swiped away the pool of coffee round his mug. 'Thank you, but I do not need befriending. And from what I have seen of your life you have little need for . . .' She stopped suddenly, catching her breath as if literally to swallow the remains of the sentence.

'Oh yes?' Matt folded his arms. 'And what have you seen of my life?'

'Nothing. I shouldn't have—'

'No, I insist. What have you seen of my life exactly?'

She pushed her hair out of her face and blinked at him. 'Look, I'm sure you're a perfectly wonderful person and everything and I'm thrilled that you've taken on Josie, but it's just that it really . . . annoys me' — she clenched her jaw round the words — 'that a man left alone with a child is seen as this *endearing* object of pity, that women, in particular, seem to relish the opportunity to come flocking to your aid. Whereas mothers, far more frequently abandoned by their men, left often with no job and several mouths to feed, are not given the time of day. I mean, look at you — you've got a good job, do-gooding busybodies like Louise and Maria Schofield queuing up to help you. You've got a great house, Joshua can go to any school you choose—'

'That's not true,' interjected Matt, latching on to the easiest way to staunch this flow of vitriol. Wary of being overheard by their young audience, they were both talking in fierce whispers. 'To afford a place like St Leonard's for more than a few terms I'd have to sell the house. We don't know if he's got in yet, and even if he does I'm not at all sure I want to send him there because it struck me as stuck-up and élitist and I thought the headmistress was a pompous witch. But I'm afraid to say I wasn't entirely inspired by the wonderful Broadlands either. Though I'm sure that you, and many like you, strive to do excellent work there, as a doting father of a somewhat troubled child I feel I have every right to want to entrust his care to an institution which I can be sure will nurture his every tentative step down the bumpy road towards attempting to become a well-adjusted unfucked-up human being.' As Matt paused for breath the doorbell rang. For a moment neither of them moved. 'How timely,' he remarked, getting to his feet.

'You don't have to go,' she said in a tight voice. The doorbell rang again, longer and louder this time.

Matt gave an unfriendly laugh. 'But I think it wise, don't you? Since I have failed spectacularly in my mission to improve community relations and the next in no doubt a long line of visitors sounds rather impatient. If you could prevent your own animosity from colouring Josie's opinion of me, I would be grateful. She's the best thing that's happened to Josh since his mother left.' He strode over to his son, still seated on the floor with the mixing bowl between his legs, surrounded by messy blue sausages.

'We have to go home, Josh.'

'Why?'

'It's lunch-time.'

'Josh has made lunch. Look.' He gestured proudly as his doughy creations.

'Ah, yes, well . . .'

'You could take them home and cook them,' interjected Sophie, reappearing in the doorway followed by a tousled teenager with swarms of pink spots on his cheeks and a clutch of books under his arm. 'This is Sean – he's come for some help over his course work.'

There were mumbled greetings all round.

'You could put them in this, Joshua,' she continued with forced brightness, tugging open a drawer and yanking out a see-through polythene bag. 'Then they'll be safe. Fifteen to twenty minutes at no more than a hundred and ten,' she muttered, clearly aiming the directions at Matt but not looking at him. 'And remember, they're for pretend eating only,' she reminded

Josh, deftly slipping the rolls into the bag and hoicking him to his feet.

It wasn't until they were safely in the car that Matt remembered the lion, still perched on the spaghetti jar in the kitchen. He sat with the engine running, torn between the unappealing prospect of his son's misery on realising he had mislaid his new toy and the equally unappealing notion of having to re-present himself on Sophie Contini's doorstep. He had never met anyone who embodied so baffling a mixture of warmth and coiled resentment. Used to being regarded as a mild, affable person – too mild and affable, apparently, to sustain Kath's interest – to be the focus of such impenetrable dislike was a new and unsettling experience. Even beyond the question of how it affected Josie, there was an unfairness to it that Matt could not help minding very deeply.

Lost in such thoughts, with Josh intently squeezing the bag to convert his blue sausages into more interesting shapes, Matt was caught off guard by the sight of Sophie herself, springing from her house in her socks, waving the missing toy.

He slowly wound the window down. 'Thank you.'

'Just caught you, then. I was worried you might have gone.'

'No. We were plucking up our courage to come in,' he said dryly, passing the lion to the back seat.

'Look, I—' She was dancing on her toes with cold and the wind was blowing her hair madly about her face.

'Oh-oh, more visitors,' cut in Matt, revving the engine and indicating a pair of girls hovering by the open front door.

She glanced round. 'Oh, yes, they're from my drama group. Look . . .' She bit her lip, pulling the sleeves of her pink sweatshirt over her hands, 'What I said . . . I just speak my mind sometimes, that's all.'

Not even an apology, marvelled Matt, giving her a final terse nod before accelerating away down the street and silently vowing to make no effort to cross her path again.

Chapter Twenty-Six

After such an inauspicious start to the day the thought of seeing Beth for the grand excursion to the zoo gave a considerable boost to Matt's spirits. Their hasty lovemaking on Friday afternoon had been wonderfully intense and animalistic. Beth's crescendo of groans during the course of it had been so uninhibited that he had even found a moment or two in the midst of his own, less articulated sexual ecstasy to wonder about the thickness of the walls separating them from her neighbours. In the shower that evening it had given him some satisfaction to note the faint circular bruises where her fingers had gripped his arms, and a bluish patch on his shoulder where she had sucked at his skin. He had an enormous amount to thank her for, he reflected fondly, not just for giving new hope to his emotions, but also for stepping into the breach on the physical side of things. For no matter how much his grown-up intellectual self might whisper that not having sex was the very least of his worries, Matt was well enough acquainted with the vagaries of his own psyche to acknowledge that romping on water beds with libidinous women was a crucial and effective method of charging depleted levels of self-esteem. It gave a spring to one's step, a tingle of confidence quite unlike any other.

Lost in such thoughts, Matt barely noticed the heaviness of the Sunday traffic, nor the grey clouds, closing ranks overhead.

Behind him, Joshua, replete from an early lunch, not of blue sausages, as he had originally desired, but of more conventional brown pork ones, slept soundly, his lion gripped to his chest.

Beth herself, stirring reluctantly from her bed just a few miles away, peered out at the grey sky through the chink in her curtains with less equanimity. Although curious to meet her lover's child, she was also rather daunted by the prospect, and wished now that the pair of them were meeting alone, to sip cappuccinos in a café maybe, or share a bag of popcorn in a cinema. The fact that she had instigated the outing herself was, she knew, one of the more drastic signs that the bold take-it-or-leave-it attitude with which she had entered into the relationship with Matt was already in tatters; that, as usual, her hard post-marital armour was melting under the glare of a new love interest. Try as she might, the tactic recommended by her therapist, of letting a relationship idle, of seeing where it drifted of its own accord, just did not come naturally. She could not help wanting to fan every flame to its fullest potential, to push at the boundaries, to see if the intimacy would – if it could – lead anywhere other than between the silk linen weave of her sheets.

Beth sighed, letting the curtain fall back into place. Going into her en suite bathroom, she checked her roots in the mirror before setting about preparing her face for the day. She had never liked zoos very much anyway, even as a child. All the most interesting animals seemed to be buried out of sight or caged at too great a distance for proper scrutiny. And it was going to rain, she observed, pulling back the bedroom curtains properly and exclaiming in surprise at the sight of Matt's car reversing into a tight space in the street below.

'The traffic was solid through to Vauxhall and over the bridge and then suddenly melted to nothing,' he explained, standing somewhat sheepishly on her doorstep a few minutes later, one hand thrust into his pocket, the other running back through his hair in a hopeless attempt to keep the sweep of his fringe – long due for another cut – from flopping into his

eyebrows. 'We've done the last few miles in two minutes flat.' As
if suddenly remembering himself, he sprang forward and kissed
her on both cheeks. 'We didn't catch you in bed or anything, I
hope . . .'

'Don't be silly,' she replied, tugging at the hem of her polo
neck, hastily pulled on over a pair of chocolate-brown corduroys.
'And where is . . . ?' She peered up and down the empty
pavement, wondering with a spurt of empathy if the child felt
as nervous about the introduction as she did.

'Josh? He's in the car, asleep . . . we've had quite a busy
morning. Thought I'd leave him for a few minutes, say hello
properly, maybe grab a quick coffee.' He slipped his arm round
her waist and kissed her on the lips.

'Is that safe?' she murmured, speaking through the kiss. 'In
the States people who leave their children in cars get arrested.'

'Really?' Matt pulled a face. 'Well, I've locked the doors and
if we sit in your living room I can keep an eye on him through the
window.'

'If you're happy, so am I,' she declared, hurrying into her
kitchen to activate her espresso machine and thaw two frozen
Danish in the microwave. Remembering Joshua, she rummaged
in the bottom of a cupboard and found a large bag of liquorice
allsorts, which she placed on the tray ready to take through into
the sitting room.

'A little present for when he wakes,' she explained, pointing
at the sweets as she handed Matt his coffee and pastry.

'How kind, Beth – thank you.' Matt beamed at her, secretly
hoping that his own abhorrence of liquorice had not been
genetically infused into his son, whose knowledge of confectionery had not progressed beyond lollipops and chocolate
buttons. 'When it comes to childcare all ammunition is most
gratefully received. Just joking,' he added hurriedly, seeing the
look on her face. 'He's really not much trouble these days. Early
on, babyhood and so on, was extremely tough at times, but the
more he grows up, the more he realises he can do things for

himself, that he can command some control over situations, the easier he has become. It's made me appreciate that a lot of toddlers' tantrums are probably just sheer frustration at not having the ability to articulate anything, at being so bloody powerless . . .'

Beth nodded, while her thoughts drifted to a dreamy appraisal of Matt himself, of the mild-mannered, distinct Englishness that she found so irresistible, the innate modesty, and the dark-browed, soulful eyes which told more of his sensitivity than words ever could. The way his wife had treated him was so unbelievably cruel that it made her heart ache just to think of it.

They had ten minutes to themselves before Matt hurried out to the car, returning with a pink-cheeked, pixie-faced urchin of a boy with the same floppy hair as his father and big brown eyes. Seeing how he nestled into Matt's chest, one small hand slipped under the V-edge of his jumper, the other clutching a small, floppy orange lion, Beth found all her apprehensions subsumed by tenderness.

'Oh, Matt, he's so cute, and so like you. Those eyes, my goodness, and the hair . . . it's extraordinary. Hey, little guy, I brought you some sweeties.' She seized the packet of allsorts and dangled them near Joshua's face. 'And who is this?' she exclaimed, tweaking the lion. 'What is his name?'

Joshua, who had been sucking his index finger, slowly removed it from his mouth and whispered, 'Lion.'

'I know, sweetie, but doesn't he have a name?'

'He's called *Lion*,' interjected Matt quickly, sensing Joshua's bafflement at the line of questioning.

'Oh, I get it. Well, that's a cool name too. And we're going to see lots of big cats where we're going, that's for sure. And we'll take your sweeties too, okay?'

By the time they got to Regent's Park the weather had settled into a breezy drizzle, too mild to justify the use of a brolly but sufficient to convert Beth's carefully styled curtain of hair into a messy frizz. Catching sight of herself during one of several toilet breaks, she felt sufficiently downcast to wrap her scarf over her hair to limit any further damage. The floppy-brimmed hat she usually wore as protection in such circumstances had somehow got left in the hall, along with the bag of liquorice allsorts, to which she had been rather looking forward. Aware that it would be wholly inappropriate to sulk, she did her best to match the cheerfulness of her companions, remarking on all sorts of things to which she would not normally have given a second glance. Thankfully, with the limited concentration span of a four-year-old dictating their movements, there was no question of taking too long over anything. Not even the monkey cages, where the various apes, as if themselves subdued by the dismal weather, sat huddled among their playground of tree branches and rope swings, staring at each other and picking their noses like bored children. After an early spurt of energy, Joshua was hoisted on to his father's shoulders, where he remained, more or less, for the rest of the afternoon. Having first found this endearing, Beth began, after a while, to feel somewhat left out. While aware that Matt might well have resisted any attempt to hold her hand, she would at least have liked to have been able to brush arms, or bend near his face from time to time. Waiting at the railing round the penguin pool, she felt sufficiently in need of reassurance on the matter to slip her hand down inside the back of his jeans, reaching so far that her fingers slid under the band of his underpants.

'Hey,' he exclaimed, seizing her wrist in protest, 'your hands are cold.'

'Yeah, they could do with warming up,' she replied wryly, pleased at least to have reminded him of her existence.

'Let's just watch this lot get their tea and then head back. Okay? Apart from anything else my shoulders are killing me.'

'Could he perhaps walk for a little bit?'

'Josh, do you want to walk?' Matt shouted, cocking his head to look up at his burden. Joshua gave an emphatic shake of the head. 'See?' Matt grinned ruefully. 'The trials of parenthood.'

The zoo shop, where they stopped *en route* to the exit, was crowded with visitors, most of them children, accompanied by fraught-looking adults wielding smaller, bundled siblings and bag-laden pushchairs. Seeing the sizable length of the queue for the check-out, and beginning to sense some of Beth's frustration, Matt suggested that she take a place in the line while he helped Joshua choose a souvenir.

'No, why don't you go to the line and I'll help him select the gift,' she insisted. 'I would love it to be from me, something to remember the day by. Would you like me to buy you a present, Josh?' Joshua, now back on his own two sturdy short legs, performed a little jump, nodding his head vigorously at the same time.

'Say yes please,' scolded Matt, laughing.

'Come on, Josh, look at these models over here.' Beaming at Matt, Beth led the little boy by the hand to the far side of the shop and began pointing out things on some of the higher shelves. All that was within his immediate reach were trays of rubbers and key-rings and pencils.

'Look, a wooden model of a dinosaur, maybe, or there are some fluorescent ones – that means they glow in the dark, really bright even when all the lights are off. Spooky, huh?'

Joshua frowned. 'I want this,' he said at length, squatting down and picking out a key-ring attached to a small furry seal. 'I like this.'

'Are you sure, honey? You could have something else too if you want.'

He shook his head, looking suddenly a little nervous and glancing round for Matt. Beth straightened, smiling down at him. 'How about I buy you something else anyway?' She turned and began examining the prices on the boxes of models, tempted to select a big one, but worrying that so generous a gift might embarrass Matt. 'Okay, well I like this guy. He's called a pterodactyl, which is a kind of dinosaur bird. Looks like he not only glows in the dark but dangles from a string—' She looked down to find that Joshua's brown ruffled head had been replaced by an unfamiliar blond curly one. 'Joshua?' She scanned the crowded aisle, tutting to herself in irritation. Replacing the toy on the shelf, she elbowed and excuse-me'd herself across the shop to the queue for the till, expecting to find that Joshua had scuttled back to his father. But Matt was standing alone, arms folded, lost in contemplation of his neighbour's coat collar.

'Hey, Matt, Josh has wandered off somewhere. You might have more luck finding him than me – it's so crowded and you're taller—'

'He's what?'

'I just turned my back for one second and—'

He didn't wait for her to finish the sentence but rushed into the throng of people, shouting Joshua's name. Hearing the crack of terror in his voice, Beth could feel her own adrenalin levels surge, not just with alarm but with anger at the whole situation. Having checked the aisles nearest to her, and seeing that Matt was covering the far end of the shop, she pushed open the door and stepped outside. With the best of the afternoon behind them the path was filled with people heading back towards the exists and carpark. At the thought of Joshua being swept along by such a tide, Beth's heart lurched. And she would be to blame, she realised, looking round wildly, her eyes blurring with tears. And he was a beautiful child – chocolate eyes, long dark lashes, a cherubic mouth – just the kind to catch the eye of a pervert. She began to run in one direction and then the other, having no idea where to start, what to do, trying to peer round people and over the tops of their heads. With the drizzle now the last thing on her mind, she tugged her scarf from her neck and wound it round and round her hands, so tightly that the blood pumped in her wrists. They had to call the police. She turned and rushed back towards the shop entrance only to see Matt coming out of it, Joshua cradled in his arms.

'Oh, thank god, thank god . . . oh, you naughty boy, Daddy and I were so worried—' she exclaimed, rushing up to them.

'Not naughty,' Matt corrected her tightly, the smile drying on his face. 'He was looking for me. You can't take your eyes off them for a moment, not at this age—'

'It wasn't my fault, he just took off and with it being so damn crowded in there . . . Oh, heck, at least he's okay, that's all that matters, isn't it?'

'Yes, yes it is . . . I'm sorry if I . . . it's just that . . .' Matt pulled Joshua more closely into him, struggling to articulate how the brief panic inside the shop had tapped into his darkest fears. 'It's just that if anything happened, I couldn't bear it . . . he's all I have.'

'You have me,' Beth whispered, not looking at him, knotting the scarf round her neck with trembling fingers, 'if that means anything to you.'

'Of course it does, but—'

She clapped her hand to her mouth. 'Oh God, Matt, we're arguing. Oh, I'm sorry. Of course he means the world to you – of course. I'm so sorry, losing him like that. What can I say?' Silent tears, suppressed for so long, spilled down her cheeks. Standing there in the rain, her hair feeling like a lumpen helmet, her damp scarf chilling her neck, with Matt glowering at her, she felt utterly dejected. It seemed that every hope, not just for the day but for Matt, was in tatters.

Shifting Joshua's weight to one arm, Matt reached out and took hold of her hand. 'No, I'm the one who should be sorry. Of course it wasn't your fault. I overreacted. You've been wonderful, you are wonderful.'

They walked hand in hand for several yards, casting smiles of apology and affection at each other, united by the knowledge that they had weathered the crisis and were all the more closely bonded for having done so.

Later that night, nuzzling Joshua as he tucked him into bed, Matt could smell the faint but distinct aroma of Beth's flowery perfume on his skin. From when she had insisted on kissing him, no doubt, he mused, chuckling at the memory of how Joshua had puckered his face in resistance, grimacing like a rude old man.

As he put his head on his own pillow a couple of hours later, the phone rang.

'Hey, it's me.'

'Hello, you.'

'You sound sleepy . . . and sexy. Wish you were here.'

'Me too.'

'Sorry to call so late, only I forgot to tell you that Andrea Beauchamp faxed me to say she can't make this week after all and wants to push the interview back to Monday, April ten. Same venue but at five thirty not three. Will that be okay?'

Matt wrested his brain from its sleepy state in order to think ahead. That was two weeks away, his very first day working from home, in fact. With Dennis back in Yorkshire he would be at the mercy of Josie and his own dubious organisational skills. 'It'll take some sorting, but I should think so. Tell her yes.'

'After that it's only a couple of weeks till Florence. I can't wait.'

'Me neither. Waking up together . . . me not scrambling home like a guilty adolescent . . .' He sighed, wishing he could fast-forward to the point where it would feel all right to behave more like a normal adult couple. 'I'd love to be able to invite you back for the night, you know that, don't you, Beth? But with my father around – and Joshua still so—'

'I know, it's okay, you don't have to explain. Your little guy has been through so much. Whenever you're ready is good enough for me.'

Matt put the phone down and pulled both of the pillows from Kath's side of the bed into his arms. Burying his nose in them, he breathed deeply, trying to imagine the smell of soft warm skin instead of washing powder and cold linen.

Chapter Twenty-Seven

By the end of the next two weeks Matt was counting the hours until his father's departure. During the last few days everything grated – the dog smells, the endless cups of tea, the daily mountain of soggy tea bags blocking the old waste-disposal unit next to the sink. Even the fits of coughing, unvanquished by an assortment of sticky linctuses and large pink pastilles left lying in half-used packets around the house, made him want to cry out in irritation. Dennis, he knew, had put his life on hold on his behalf and had done the job marvellously. Yet Matt felt increasingly that his own life had been on hold as well, that he desperately needed some of his own space back to be able to move on.

Dennis fussed so much about missing the train that they arrived at King's Cross with almost forty-five minutes to spare. Wanting to atone for his unseemly eagerness to be rid of him, Matt insisted that they stay to the last minute to see him off. It was early on Sunday morning and few of the shops were open. There was little to do except drink foul tea and discourage Hoppit and Joshua from chasing pigeons. It was hard to mask his relief when the time finally came to get on to the platform.

'Dad, thank you for everything – you've been unbelievable.'

'Just glad to help. And I'm going to miss this little fellow more than I can say.' Handing Hoppit's lead to Matt, Dennis bent down and picked Joshua up for a final hug. 'You look after your dad, you hear me? And that Josie friend of ours. You keep them in order.' His eyes looked pink and rheumy with tears, Matt noticed, guilty tenderness exploding in his heart. He was nearly seventy, he reminded himself, no longer just his father, but a shrunken, wiry old man with weak lungs.

'You'll be fine, the pair of you,' Dennis called, placing his mouth with some difficulty near the open upper section of the carriage window. 'Come up and visit any time. And Matt, this Italy jaunt of yours – if Louise changes her mind I could always come down to help out.'

'That's kind, Dad,' Matt shouted back, wondering if the frissons of tension that had shadowed every mention of his weekend away arose from some sort of knee-jerk disapproval at the notion of his having a new girlfriend or simply because Dennis didn't like Louise. 'But Louise insists she'll be able to manage. She's got all sorts of things planned already – the new Disney movie, Chessington, you know what she's like.'

Dennis made a face. 'Wanting to make up for you know what, I expect.'

'Probably.' Matt frowned, thinking not about the purse but about how Louise too had been odd about Italy, gushing with such enthusiasm about helping out that Matt knew at once that a good portion of it was forced. It was as if deep down the pair of them didn't want him to get a new life, as if they had enjoyed their part in the drama of the last few months so much that they didn't want to let go. 'I've got to put Kath behind me some time,' he had ventured to Louise. 'I know it seems weird for everybody, me included, but I can't just keep my life on hold—'

'Oh, of course. It'll be marvellous, I'm glad for you – you so deserve it, Matt, really you do. And I'm so glad you asked me to help out because . . . since Kath . . . Our friendship – well, it means a lot to me, Matt, it really does.'

Unable to reciprocate with any truth, ashamed that he was, as ever, courting her assistance out of convenience rather than affection, Matt had blushed and changed the subject, inwardly vowing to make Italy the last favour he ever asked of her.

He drove home from the station via a cluster of superstores in the Old Kent Road where he purchased two flat packs containing a filing cabinet and a set of shelves, and a box of plastic tools for Joshua. Progress in terms of actually constructing his purchases was somewhat harder; rapidly tiring of the limited capacity of his own implements, Joshua kept interrupting his father with tearful entreaties to be allowed to use the grown-up versions instead. After several such tantrums Matt gave up and set about making paper airplanes out of the instructions sheets, reminding himself that it didn't matter how long it took to construct a set of shelves. Months of the luxury of working in his own home stretched ahead. The strain of charging between office and home, the guilt of relying so heavily on his father, were over. The previous week had seen a very satisfactory handover of his office duties to the formidable Erica. From now on a weekly meeting to discuss the allocation of performances to be covered was the only official act required of him. Oliver, after years of resistance, was at last hooked up to the Internet and so taken with the whole business that every time Matt logged on he was greeted by a fresh clutch of rambling e-mails. Apart from evenings at the theatre, all of which were covered by Josie, Matt's sole extracurricular commitment for the coming week was the rescheduled interview with Andrea Beauchamp, due to take place the following afternoon.

'It's going to be great, isn't it?'

'What is, Daddy?' replied Joshua, who had been momentarily distracted from airplanes and arguments about hammers by the discovery of a woodlouse crawling along the skirting board.

'You and me. Dad working at home. Being able to take you to school and pick you up. It's going to be great. Though we'll miss Granddad, of course, won't we?'

'And Mummy.' He spoke slowly, tapping the insect with his finger until it curled up into a small armoured ball.

'And Mummy,' Matt echoed hoarsely. 'Of course, Josh, you'll always miss Mummy.' He reached out and stroked his son's head. Ignoring him, Joshua bent his face near the woodlouse and blew hard, watching with apparent fascination as the tiny creature, still in its spherical form, rolled for several inches before disappearing down a crack in the floorboards.

Chapter Twenty-Eight

Andrea Beauchamp seemed much smaller than the screen version of herself. Even having seen her on the stage, Matt was unprepared for the petiteness of her frame, the tiny, flighty hands – the nails bitten raw, he noticed – and the bony schoolgirl legs, shown off by a miniature leather miniskirt and dark tights with artful ladders up the ankle and thigh. Her eyes, the upper lid accentuated by a thick brush stroke of blue, looked huge for her face, as did her mouth, highlighted by scarlet lipstick and a full set of large, even white teeth. Her hair, which had been hidden by a twenties bob of a wig for the part of Amanda, was streaked blond and brushed into messy peaks, contributing to the impression of a gamine child playing the part of a woman.

She shook his hand quickly – dismissively – blowing a cloud of cigarette smoke over his shoulder. 'I've ordered you tea.' She kicked off two gold slipper-style pumps and arranged her legs into a yogic cross-legged position on the sofa. 'I prefer water.' She looked at her watch, a huge yellow plastic child's toy of a contraption covering several inches of her wrist. 'I have thirty minutes.'

Matt could feel his carefully rehearsed list of questions slipping from his mind, intimidated not by any sort of suppressed sexual enthralment, but by her sheer brusqueness, the way she couldn't even be bothered to look at him. In fact, much to his surprise, seeing her close to he could muster no physical attraction for her at all;

there was something at once starved and rapacious about the big red mouth which put him off, while her boyish body looked too angular and fidgety to encourage thoughts of grabbing hold of it.

'Thank you for agreeing to——'

'And I'd like the tape running from the start.'

'The tape. Of course.' Matt fumbled in his briefcase for his small cassette player and set it up on the table between them. 'In fact I'm not a journalist as such, I'm a theatre——'

'Yeah, yeah.' She waved her skinny arms. 'Same difference. You all want to know the same things.'

'Probably,' he conceded, offering her a nervous smile.

'You're familiar with the no-go areas, I take it?'

'Oh, yes. Basically, you are only happy to be questioned about your work.'

'Got a problem with that?' she snapped.

'Not at all. In your shoes I would say exactly the same,' he replied dryly. He paused, distracted by the sudden realisation that the last time he had seen this woman had been the very day Kath left. He looked at the date on his watch. Almost fifteen weeks to the day. It was ten past five. At home Josie would be getting Joshua's tea ready; something with pasta and sweetcorn, she had said; he had been flying out of the door, not concentrating.

'Excuse me? You were saying?'

Matt blinked at her. 'I'm sorry. I . . .'

'You were saying?' she prompted again, her eyes flickering with a sort of amused impatience.

Matt struggled to compose his thoughts, appalled at his sense of disconnection but unable to fight it either. 'I was thinking . . . you've got a career and two children. I'm on my own with just one little boy to worry about, but still I——'

'Oh, I get it.' She folded her arms, grinning for the first time. 'It's called get the girl to talk by confessing details of your own life, is that it?'

Matt blushed. 'No, I——' He leaned forward from the plush silky armchair and pressed the rewind button on the tape recorder.

Rubbing his palms together, he made a fresh attempt to appear businesslike. 'It really was nothing of the sort, I assure you. I'm not that clever.' The machine clicked back into life. 'Could we start again, do you think?' He glanced at his watch. 'Still fifteen minutes to go. Let's begin with Amanda. How have you enjoyed the part?'

After fifteen minutes, almost to the second, of questions about her West End run and future projects, Andrea rocked forward over her crossed legs and pressed a chewed finger on to the Off button on his cassette recorder. 'So you're a single parent too, are you?'

'Er, yes, not by choice . . . that is, my wife left us a few months ago. The night I saw your play, actually.' He gave an apologetic laugh and began packing his things into his briefcase.

'My bastard left me too,' she said slowly. 'You can print that if you want.'

Matt stopped rummaging with his things, looking over the top of his briefcase in astonishment. 'I thought that—'

'I kicked him out? Yeah, well, that's what I wanted everyone to believe. But now I don't care. Sometimes I read about myself and I think about how I feel inside and the two are so totally disconnected that I want to freak out. You can print that too.' She smiled. There was a faint sprinkling of gingerly freckles across the bridge of her nose and cheeks. 'You're the first journalist I've liked in a long while, Mr Webster. I hope I've given you enough for an interesting article.' She uncoiled her legs and stood up, slipping her feet back into her tiny gold shoes. 'Ever written anything other than newspaper stuff?'

'No. It's my boss, Oliver Parkin, who's the big literary giant. He wrote a biography of—'

'That's what I want. Someone to write my biography, you know, authorised. Someone I can trust. You got a card?' She took a fresh cigarette from a packet in her shoulder bag and lit it with a flame the size of a blowtorch.

'A card? I think so . . . somewhere . . .'

'Will you send me my quotes before you print?'

'Yes, by all means. Here we are.' Having found three

somewhat weather-beaten cards in one of the back compart-
ments of his briefcase, Matt handed one to her. 'And thank you.
I'll be in touch – with the quotes and so on . . .'

'I hope I like the piece.' She gave him a warning smile, smoke
billowing from her lips.

'So do I,' he agreed with a laugh. 'I've always fancied a chance
to write a life story, especially one as interesting as yours.'

'Keep it up, Mr Webster, flattery gets you everywhere,' she
quipped, slinging her bag over her shoulder and leaving him with
a nonchalant wave.

Some forty-five minutes later, still marvelling to himself at
the unexpected turn the interview had taken, Matt raced up the
steps to his front door. Not wanting the bother of digging for his
keys, and knowing how Josh loved to answer the door, he rang
the bell, resting his forehead against the cold wood while he
collected his breath. He had phoned Beth on his mobile in the
cab. She had been as excited as he was, teasing him about the
necessity of making the article as eulogistic as possible and
warning him that Andrea Beauchamp was known both for
seizing her own initiatives and getting her own way.

It took a few moments to register that his ring had prompted
no response. Lifting the letter flap and peering inside while he
groped in his various pockets for his keys, Matt experienced the
first prickle of foreboding. He had left Josie, saucepan on the
hob and wooden spoon in hand, overseeing Joshua's ten-minute
reading duty. *Sammy's Dirty Shoes*, or had it been *Tammy's*?
Slamming the door behind him, he strode into the hall, calling
Joshua's name even though he knew, from the echo of his voice
in the silence, that nobody was home.

In the kitchen the tea things were crammed into the washing-
up bowl, soaking but not washed up. Bits of sweetcorn and
squiggles of soggy pasta floated in the water submerging the
plates. Matt, his heart thumping, rushed out through the sitting
room to the bottom of the stairs, where he paused, arrested by a
vivid flashback of the night Kath had left, hearing again the eerie

chime of the empty coat hangers. As his surroundings swam back into focus he saw, with some terror and incredulity, that a note had been propped against the pot on the hall table.

Felt one of my headaches coming on, real bad, so have gone to Sophie's. Took the old pushchair 'cos Josh was tired. Sorry. Josie.

Matt sank back on to the bottom stair, trembling at the revelation of how fragile he still was. It was the not knowing, he realised miserably, burying his eyes in the palms of his hands; where Kath was, who she was with, what she really thought. Lifting his head, he peered through the slits in his fingers at the familiar hallway – the picture that always hung crooked, the three cracks above the front door, the wooden floorboards, which they had always meant to get sanded. Perhaps Graham was right, he thought wretchedly; perhaps he should sell up and move on. He could pay off the mortgage and buy somewhere smaller, or move to the country, or move out of the country. Somewhere without memories. Somewhere with schools for traumatised four-year-olds. Somewhere without unanswered questions and guilt.

Badly shaken, aware that no such place existed, except perhaps, many years down the line, within the confines of his own head, it was a while before Matt could steel himself to leave the house.

Having got as far as Sophie Contini's doorstep, he took several deep breaths to compose himself, inwardly cursing Josie for having made the encounter necessary. And for having made gratitude necessary, he reminded himself, fixing his face into a smile in preparation for the sight of the teacher's stony face.

'Shh,' Sophie whispered, not looking particularly stony and raising her finger to her lips the moment she had opened the door. 'He's asleep. Come in.'

'If you don't mind I think I'll just—'

'He only dropped off a minute ago. Look.' She pointed through the half-open door into her small front room, where Joshua was curled in an armchair among a heap of cushions. 'Shame to wake him so soon.'

'Maybe but . . . and where is Josie?' Matt blurted, all his tension and irritation coming out in a rush. 'My bathroom cupboard is loaded with analgesics. I really can't see why she had to come scurrying round here. It's not fair on you – or me for that matter—'

'Josie gets migraines. When one starts she knows she has about half an hour before she's so nauseous she can't stand up. Her vision goes too. They usually last a few hours. She's upstairs in my spare room. I assure you, coming here was the best thing she could have done. Cup of tea? How did your interview go? Josie said it was with someone very famous, but she couldn't remember the name.'

Reluctantly Matt followed her into the kitchen. The clothes stand was in its usual place, decked this time with three sets of brightly patterned socks and a couple of T-shirts. Stepping past it, he made a show of studying some of the photographic collages on the walls. 'Your family?' he asked, putting his hands behind his back and staring politely at the pictures, most of which seemed to be of blond, honey-skinned children posing with pets and paddling pools.

'My sister's. She's always taking photos. Sends me the best ones every year.'

'And they don't live in south London by the look of things.'

'Italy. We're quarter-Italian. I'll let you help yourself to sugar and milk.'

'Really? I'm about to go to Italy,' he ventured stiffly. 'Florence for a long weekend.'

'Yes, Josie mentioned it. A romantic break.'

'Something like that,' he muttered, the recollection of her outburst about pitying females making him little inclined to discuss the matter further. Crossing the room to the table where she was setting down their mugs of tea, he managed to trip over a pair of trainers. 'Sorry, I . . .'

'No, my fault.' She leaped across the room and seized the shoes. 'Florence, you lucky thing. My sister's not far from there – a place called Orvieto. I go there every summer.'

Still wanting to change the subject, he indicated the trainers, which were splattered with fresh mud and looked scuffed and creased from use. 'Do you take a lot of exercise?'

'I run,' she said, tapping the soles of the shoes together, making it sound, so Matt couldn't help thinking, more like a permanent state of being than a hobby.

He grimaced. 'My friend in America made me run, on a machine. Couldn't walk for days afterwards.'

'It's different if you do it a lot.' She dropped the trainers next to the sofa and gestured at him to take his tea. A few moments of silence followed. Matt watched over the rim of his mug as she fiddled with one long twirly strand of dark hair, winding it round and round her finger and letting it drop. He blew hard on his tea, wishing that he had had the sense to scoop Joshua off the sofa and go straight home.

'I suppose you know all about me.'

'No. Why?' He looked up sharply, all his wariness of her returning.

'Because I saw you with Maria Schofield at Broadlands that day. And if you're friends with her then—'

'We're not really friends,' he began. 'In fact I haven't seen her for weeks . . .'

'I just hate that,' she continued, ignoring him, 'when you know people are talking about you, saying stuff when they know nothing – *nothing*.'

'Look, I assure you—'

'What do you think of me?' She rounded on him, her dark corkscrew curls swinging over her shoulders, her eyes flashing.

Caught off guard, wondering at the woman's capacity for confrontation, Matt could only stammer a response. 'What do I . . . ? What does it matter what I . . . I mean, I only know you because of Josie.'

'Oh, come on, you can do better than that.' She slapped both palms down on the table.

Matt put his half-drunk tea down and stood up. 'I really do not see the point of this.'

'Oh, go on, I bet there's loads of stuff you're bursting to say. I was rude to you the other day, wasn't I? Why not get your own back? Come on.' She beckoned at him, like a boxer inviting someone to spar.

'Let me see.' He took a deep breath. 'I really don't—'

'For God's sake.' Her voice was scornful. 'Be honest. No one ever is these days. No one says what they think. It's all politeness and crap and thinking things you don't say. It drives me mad.'

Matt eyed her levelly, taking a deep breath. 'All right, then. I think you fill your life with other people's problems as a way of avoiding your own.'

The wide hazel eyes held his gaze, only for an instant, but sufficient for Matt to register dismay before she blinked and looked away. He was about to speak again, to qualify, apologise, retract the admission she had forced out of him, when he saw that she was pointing over his shoulder. Joshua was standing in the doorway, sleepily rubbing his eyes. His T-shirt was hitched up, revealing the small swell of his belly, and his hair was all flat on one side from being pressed against the sofa cushions. As Matt bent down, holding out his arms to him, he noticed a dark circular stain of damp round the baggy crotch of his trousers.

'Oh, no, Josh you've . . .'

'It doesn't matter,' whispered Sophie quickly. 'Please don't say anything to him. It doesn't matter at all. Take him home. He's exhausted, poor love.'

'Thank you,' Matt mumbled, not looking at her as they made their way into the hall. She opened the door and stood back for them to pass through.

'Don't forget the pushchair.' She looped it over his arm.

'Tell Josie I hope she gets better soon,' he muttered, tightening his hold on Joshua, feeling the dampness of the sodden dungarees pressing through his shirt.

Chapter Twenty-Nine

Letting his sunglasses slide down his nose, Matt peered lazily about him. Tall trees, nudging limbs and heads like gossiping adults, swayed overhead, breaking up the glare of the sunlight and casting dappled shadows on the turquoise blue of the pool. Though scrubby and tough underfoot, the grass surrounding the mosaic poolside glimmered like velvet, each blade as pruned and perfect as the huge oval flower-beds inlaid into it, brilliant palettes of pink and purple and crimson. A zigzag path of white stone led up the gentle incline of the hillside towards the hotel, a sweeping whitewashed villa of a place, with sloping roofs of rust-red tiles and huge wooden shutters on its windows. Inside, the rooms were high-ceilinged and cool, furnished with huge antique pieces of furniture and tulip-bulbed wall lights.

Turning on his side, relishing the feel of the sun on a new part of his body, Matt watched as a tall dark-haired youth, dressed in an impeccable starched white uniform, trawled a long-handled net through the pool water for perhaps the twentieth time in an hour, catching the few stray specks marring its pristine surface. From his new position he had a better view of the valley rolling below them, its curves lined with mile upon mile of olive trees, ordered like marching armies, and filled with so many different shades of green that he found himself trying to count them. Somewhere in the distance, beyond the farthest band of colour, lay Florence itself. They had circled it on the drive from the airport, glimpsed its famous domes through the trees as the taxi climbed northwards, glinting in the morning sun with a perfection quite unmatched by any of the numerous photographic reproductions Matt had seen of the place. Remembering the moment, Matt reached out across the inches separating their sunbeds and took Beth's hand.

'I was expecting a cheap pension,' he murmured, sliding his fingers, oily from suncream, between hers. 'Somewhere poky with a view of a carpark.'

'I wanted it to be a surprise. Besides, there aren't any carparks in Florence, they're all on the outskirts. All the pensions have views of is streets and people and churches.' She was lying on her back, her head tilted up to the sun, her sunglasses pressed firmly against her eyes. She wore a pink-and-green bathing costume, cut up to her hip bones on either side and with two large ovals stencilled out of its front and back.

'I'm going to pay my share.'

'Don't start that again,' she groaned. 'You're a poor single father. This is my treat, I told you.'

Matt squeezed her fingers again. 'Last time I came to Italy it rained, every day.'

'Yeah, you said.'

'I mean, I still thought it was lovely,' he continued dreamily. 'Who wouldn't think Venice was lovely, for God's sake, but to see this' – he gestured at their surroundings – 'to be here, and with this weather . . .' His voice cracked with exultation. He looked at Beth, yearning as he had all day for a response that showed that the level of her pleasure matched his. 'Hey, you, let's swim.'

'No way. It's too cold.'

'Cold? Don't be daft. It's wonderful. Look.' He reached over and plucked off her sunglasses.

'Believe me,' she said, squinting at him, one hand at her eyebrows to ward off the sunlight, 'after summers in Washington, DC, this is chicken-feed. I swim to cool off, which means I need to be hot. Looks like I'm not the only one either,' she added, nodding at their fellow guests, all stretched on sunbeds with books and magazines.

'Silly, isn't it,' murmured Matt, staring longingly at the pool, thinking of how Joshua would have loved it, how he would have been squealing with impatience to get his armbands on and do one of his flying leaps from the side. 'It's like grown-ups don't know how to have fun any more.'

'I assure you I'm having fun,' she retorted with a laugh, sliding back into a horizontal position, her glasses safely back over her eyes.

After hesitating for a few more minutes, Matt approached the poolside on his own, a little self-conscious in the trunks the hotel had lent him, which were of the nylon stretch variety as opposed to the baggy Bermuda style he preferred. Aware that several sun-bathers were watching him, he dived straight in, working off the shock of the water with a couple of lengths of crawl before turning over for some more leisurely backstoke. When he got out the air felt much more chilly on his wet skin. Hugging himself, he scampered back to his sunbed. As he picked up his towel he deliberately flung an arm in the direction of Beth, who had turned on to her stomach, scattering a few drops of water on to her bare back.

'Oh, you brute. Cold, horrible water. Get off – Oh, you are *so* cruel.'

Detecting genuine irritation in her tone, Matt backed off and pulled his towel round his shoulders. She rolled on to her back, lit a cigarette and picked up her novel, a thriller by an American author he had never heard of.

'Can we go into Florence now?'

'Oh, Matt, it's far too late – everything closes round lunch-time. We've got all tomorrow – and half the next day.'

'A walk, then.'

'Oh, honey, in a little while, okay? I'm just so comfortable right now.'

'I'm not very good at doing nothing,' he confessed, noting with some dismay a few minutes later that she had finished her chapter and still not put her book down.

'That's because you haven't had enough practice, poor sweetheart.' She puckered her lips and blew him a kiss. 'You go on a walkabout if you want to. I don't mind.'

Matt pulled on his loafers as protection against the coarse grass and strolled round the hotel grounds, drinking in the magnificent setting but wondering if a seedy pension might in fact have made him feel rather more absorbed, more of a participant than a spectator.

Later that evening they took their seats in the marble-floored dining room. Matt would have preferred to have sat at one of the tables outside, but Beth, dressed for the evening in a small silk black dress, said she would be too cold. When Matt offered to fetch her a jumper from the room she insisted that she preferred eating inside anyway, so vehemently that he suspected that she was in fact enjoying wearing the dress and didn't want it covered up with anything that might undermine its elegance. And it was a hell of an elegant place, he reasoned, surveying the dressy costumes of their fellow diners, feeling suddenly rather shabby in his chinos and loafers. The meal was elegant too, comprising small, intricately constructed portions, each one a work of art in its own right. Beth chose slivers of veal while Matt opted for pasta, a soft, melting version that made him wonder if he could ever manage the English packeted replica again. He talked about Joshua, while she listened, a little politely he felt; and then she talked about her ex-husband, delivering a string of hilarious anecdotes about the worst incidents in their marriage. During the course of these exchanges they drank not only an entire bottle of red wine but also two glasses of nectary sweet white to accompany their desserts, with the result that Matt left the dining room feeling not only repelete but also rather sleepy. Which wouldn't do at all, he scolded himself, turning aside to hide a yawn as Beth took his hand for the walk back towards their bedroom.

'You undress me,' she whispered, the moment they were inside. Taking hold of his hands, she steered them towards the zipper on her dress. Beneath the dress there was nothing but a silky black thong. Matt knew because she had paraded round the room in it before settling at the dressing table to do her face. Lying on the bed, taking in the image, he had felt not so much aroused as curious as to the discomforts of such a garment.

'Those pants. Don't they . . . I mean, don't you want to . . . just yank that thing out?'

Beth had thrown back her head in laughter. 'This?' She casually flicked the flimsy strip of material. 'Oh, you soon get used to it – better than an ugly panty line. Besides, *everybody's* wearing them now.'

Not everybody, he had thought, an image of Sophie's laundry flickering across his mind; three triangles, white as new hankies.

The zipper caught on a wedge of material and took a few moments to ease free. Watching the dress fall to a pool of black silk round her ankles, all Matt's post-prandial sleepiness dissolved. 'Take me,' she whispered, before grasping him with a force that suggested she had no intention of the invitation being interpreted literally.

It was fine, of course. Sex was always fine, reflected Matt, frowning to himself as he lay in the dark afterwards, wondering when, if ever, he would feel close enough to his new girlfriend to confess that some of her embraces felt uncomfortably close to manhandling. It was nice to be mauled by a female occasionally – bloody nice – but not every time.

'What are you thinking?' She nestled closer to him, all gentle tenderness now.

'About us,' he replied quickly. 'About how brilliant it is to get away, to spend an entire night together. No distractions, no Joshua.'

'He's with your wife's friend, right?'

'Louise. That's right.'

'Do you miss him?' she continued softly, beginning to stroke Matt's forearm with her fingertips.

'Oh, no, not at all. He knows Louise really well, and she's good with him. She'd even hired this indoor tent as a treat for the weekend – they'd put it up in this big games room they've got on the top floor. You should have seen Joshua's face . . .' Matt stopped, feeling the usual pang of guilt that Louise's relentless kindness did nothing to increase his inclination to like her.

'It's just that . . . there is something I've been meaning to ask you,' Beth continued.

'Go on,' said Matt carefully, aware suddenly that she had not been listening to him. He watched the varnished red fingernails still stroking his forearm, feeling a sudden, inexplicable frisson of distrust.

'Do you – would you ever, do you think, want more kids?'

'Christ, I don't know – I haven't really thought. I shouldn't think so. One is quite enough. And why do you ask that?' He tried to sound teasing, while inside his heart exploded in sudden terror that she was about to announce she was pregnant.

'Because I've had my tubes tied.'

'Your what?'

'Fallopian tubes. Those little freeways that carry eggs to the womb. I had them tied, years ago now. Robert didn't want kids either, thank God. My own folks were such crap parents it kind of put me off. And – before you ask – no, I don't regret it.'

Matt, who had assumed from various allusions made during the course of the previous few weeks that she was on the pill, could not for a moment think how to respond. 'Did it hurt?'

'No, silly.' She punched him lightly in the chest, before snuggling back down into the crook of his arm. A few minutes later she was asleep. Though Matt closed his eyes and tried to follow suit, it was hopeless. Her hair, bunched up under his chin, felt ticklish, and his shoulder was stiffening from the weight of her head. Looking round the darkened room, he saw that a pool of silver was falling like a ghostly stage light on to the floor, granted access by a chink in the curtains and three broken slats on one window shutter. Easing himself free, he slid out of bed and crossed the room, clenching his feet as they made contact with the icy stone floor. The slice of night sky was like a piece of a magician's cape, decorated with winking stars and a silvery moon. Matt stared at it for several seconds, crossing his arms and shivering against the cold. He couldn't imagine wanting to have another child, with Beth or anyone else. Yet neither could he muster any empathy for the notion of a young woman inviting a doctor to tie her reproductive organs in knots. Which was unreasonable in the extreme, Matt told himself, turning to look at the figure submerged among the bedclothes, groping in his heart for a trigger of something beyond mild affection, for some sense of excitement or anticipation about their future together. Instead, an ugly thought, one which which had been pushing for recognition all day, burst into his conscious mind: that they were unmatched and always had been; both on the rebound from things they hadn't begun to resolve, absorbed by their own needs rather than each other's.

By the time Matt crept back to bed he was frozen. Easing himself between the sheets, silently entreating the creaks of the mattress to fall silent, he clenched his body into a ball while the warmth seeped back to his toes.

Chapter Thirty

When Matt woke at nine, Beth was still asleep, curled away from him with one arm thrust up under the pillow and the other tucked against her chest. Grateful for a reprieve, he tiptoed into the bathroom and stepped under the shower in order to contemplate his options. While certain that — for his own part at least — the pleasures of the Uffizi would be all the easier to enjoy if he came clean about the inconvenient sea change in his feelings, he remained less sure that Beth would be able to react so positively. There had been no grand talk of love or lifelong commitments, but neither had she made any reference to the early provisos about no pressure and having fun. And she was paying for the bloody hotel, Matt reminded himself gloomily, ducking his head back under the jet of water and closing his eyes.

He opened them a couple of seconds later to find Beth herself peering round the shower curtain, her faced lined and heavy with sleep.

'Telephone,' she shouted, gesturing at him to turn the taps off. 'From England. Louise, I think.'

Skidding on his wet feet, Matt seized a towel and ran to the bedroom telephone.

'Joshua's fine,' Louise said at once, her voice rising and falling amidst the crackles of a bad line. Relaxing, Matt balanced the phone between his ear and shoulder and knotted the towel round his waist. 'Thank goodness for that. But you're breaking up badly, Louise – I can hardly hear you.'

'I said . . . some bad news, I'm afraid . . . father . . . massive heart failure . . . very upset.'

Matt felt his mouth go dry. 'Jesus – Dad – when, for Christ's sake?' He dropped to his knees on the hard floor, remembering the frailty he had observed at King's Cross, the irrepressible, hateful cough. There followed an adrenalin rush of guilt at the realisation that the strain of looking after Joshua had taken its inevitable toll.

'Not your father, Matt, no,' said Louise, her voice and the line suddenly going clear. 'Kath's. Lionel has died. Gillian phoned to tell me last night. Found him herself, apparently, all blue in the face and slumped among the rose bushes. An ambulance was there in minutes but it was already too late. She's distraught about him and about Kath too. Because obviously she wants her at the funeral.'

Riding a rollercoaster of relief and fresh shock, Matt slumped on the floor with his legs stretched out in front of him and his back against the side of the bed.

Beth, emerging from the bathroom in a towelling robe, hurried to his side. 'Matt, honey? What's happened?' She cupped his head in her hands, steering his gaze to meet hers.

Matt made a face, putting his hand over the receiver. 'Kath's father has died.'

'Oh, God.' She kissed his nose. 'Poor baby.' She retreated to the dressing table, tutting sympathetically.

'I'm really sorry to disturb you over there,' continued Louise. 'I just thought you ought to know.'

'Of course – of course I had to know. Jesus.' Matt ran his free hand through his wet hair, thinking not of Lionel but of Kath. 'But how's Kath going to hear what's happened when no one knows where the hell she is?' The situation was so absurd he almost laughed out loud.

'Exactly. Gillian is desperate about it, slagging her off as an outcast one minute and coming up with international advertising campaigns to get hold of her the next. I think they really believed — as we all did — that after so many months Kath would have let us know where she is . . . they've been so hurt . . .'

'Yeah, well, they're not the only ones,' muttered Matt darkly. 'Bloody hell, what a mess.'

'I think she's going to put notices in all the main newspapers and hope for the best . . . Matt, are you still there?'

'Yes — sorry — I was just thinking . . . I suppose I ought to go to the funeral.'

'Will you take Josh?'

'I don't think so.'

'And of course I must go. Poor Gillian, I know she's awful, but I do feel sorry for her.'

Matt sighed. 'If you give me her number I'll call now, offer my halfpence worth of condolence. They were horrible to each other most of the time, but I suppose that won't stop her missing him like hell. The mysteries of human attachment, eh? Thanks for telling me, Louise. Sorry you're caught up in it all.'

'I've known them longer than you, don't forget.'

'Yes, of course you have. Let's talk when I get back to London tomorrow. If the flight's on time I'll be with you by five-ish.'

With such a start to the day it was nearly lunch-time before a taxi deposited Beth and Matt in a lay-by next to a coachpark on the outskirts of Florence. Consulting the clutch of tourist leaflets given to them by the hotel, Beth led the way, exclaiming at everything in a manner that Matt could not help finding immensely grating. The quieter he became the more she seemed to feel the need to make up for it. Nothing, not even the most humdrum architectural feature, escaped exuberant comment. Trailing after her along the wide corridors of the Uffizi, which they tackled first, he felt increasingly as if her words were getting in the way of the spread of beauty around him, blocking the avenues down which his own mind would have chosen to travel if given the space and quiet to do so. As the day progressed, so did his sense of wonderment at how their relationship had staggered so far. It was as if, having dislodged one conviction the night before, everything else had come tumbling down on top of it. All he could feel between them was distance and disconnection. It seemed nothing short of incredible that he had ever imagined anything else.

Beth, he knew, assumed his air of distraction to be related to Louise's phone call. Thus shielded from the immediate necessity of confessing the true nature of his feelings, Matt tried to close his mind to the idea of disillusioning her. It would, he knew, be both sensible and infinitely easier to wait until the weekend had run its course, to play along until they were safely back in England. But as they climbed the stone steps of Giotto's campanile, with Beth for once not only lagging behind but pulling on the tails of his shirt, puffing and squealing for physical assistance to get her to the top, Matt felt everything building to a crescendo that could no longer delay expression. A few moments later, as they leaned their elbows on the balustrade, taking in the panoramic acres of domes and spires and tiled roofs, the truth tumbled out of him.

'Beth, I'm sorry, but I've realised that things are not going to work out between us.' The sentence, rehearsed inside his head scores of times during the course of the morning, sounded not nearly as gentle or articulate when voiced out loud. Instead it hung between them for a few long seconds, while Matt thought wildly of how to nudge it towards the reasoned, adult discussion he had anticipated, the weighing up of the pros and cons, admitting to their differences, nothing ventured nothing gained, no harm done, a flutter of fond regret maybe.

'You're dumping me,' she wailed, shattering every last dreg of such hopes. 'You bastard, you're dumping me.'

'Beth, I . . . for goodness' sake . . . I thought . . .'

'Thought what?' She turned on him, putting the view behind her, her voice shrill. 'That I would invite someone for whom I felt nothing very much on a long weekend to one of the most romantic cities in the world?'

'I suppose I thought that because it hadn't been feeling right for me it wouldn't for you either . . . I'm sorry, I . . .'

'Sorry?' She spat the word so ferociously that Matt could actually make out three or four flecks of saliva flying from the corners of her mouth.

He was aware of a cluster of students to their right staring with unabashed interest, their curiosity clearly more captivated by a domestic row than by the glories of the Italian Renaissance. To their left several Asian businessmen in dark suits and with cameras dangling from their wrists were posing for a photograph, jostling for position along the balustrade. Spread out round the immediate perimeter of the tower was a rather unattractive mesh of safety wire, clearly designed to preserve the lives of reckless tourists or would-be suicides. Which was probably just as well, reflected Matt grimly, returning his attention to his companion's crumpled face with a fresh sense of desperation.

'Sorry?' she repeated. 'Oh my, what for? For using me, maybe? For picking me up and wringing me out like a dishcloth and then throwing me away when . . .' Rather to Matt's relief, she was too overcome to complete the sentence. Casting a scowl over his shoulder at the ogling students, he tentatively reached out and touched her arm. 'Let's go back down,' he said gently. 'This isn't the place . . .'

'No, Matthew Webster,' she said through sobs, 'this is not the place. Shame on you. Shame on you.' Somehow, he steered her towards the entrance to the stairwell. The air inside felt so damp and chilly that he shivered inside his shirt. Though her hand remained limp and unforgiving he managed to keep a firm hold of it for the journey down the twisting stone steps, driven by a fear that the day's dramas would be rounded off by physical injury. It was a relief to emerge back into the May sunshine in the piazza below. Beth, still sobbing quietly, shook herself free of his hand.

'We need a coffee,' he said, injecting the words with as much compassion as he could, wanting her to know that he too felt bad.

Watching Beth press her trembling lips to the rim of a large espresso a few minutes later, he was half tempted to be kinder still, to retract everything he had said and resort to the easier, sweeter road of reconciliation. That she had calmed down made him like her a bit more too.

'I guess it was that call this morning, huh? Got you thinking about . . . you know, Kath . . .'

'Something like that,' he whispered, for the first time play-acting his part a little, deciding that to attempt a rundown on the infinitely more complicated reasons behind his change of heart would cause unnecessary pain. There was just so much truth a being could endure in one day, he reflected dryly, thinking not just of the woman opposite him but of his marriage, how he had filtered out the truth as it suited him, not reading the signs, till they were too entrenched to be discernible and there was nothing to save but their son.

Chapter Thirty-One

The funeral and cremation of Matt's father-in-law took place on the Saturday following his return from Umbria. All resolutions to resist any more of Louise's kindness crumpled at her sensible offer to drive them both to Berkshire for the ordeal. In spite of numerous notices in all the main papers, and even a couple of radio announcements – the inspiration of Lionel's brother who had connections with the BBC – there had been no word from Kath; a result which Matt could have predicted from the outset, but which nonetheless increased his sense of responsibility and compassion towards his mother-in-law. Every time he rang, in a bid to offer at least telephonic support during the course of the week, she seemed to be in a state of near-hysteria.

It's like a badly scripted soap opera, he confided to Graham, neglecting his Friday night review in order to pen one of several e-mails inspired by the subject. Beside him the first rays of the sun were firing up the green dome of the War Museum. Next door Joshua lay gooey-eyed with sleep in front of the small bedroom telly.

Hysterical mother, mourning the man whom she seemed to do a bloody good job of hating for thirty-five years and clamouring suddenly for the only daughter in whom she used to stick pins for recreation. And, oh yes, not forgetting, of course, the daughter has meanwhile repeated the cycle of familial bliss by running out on her own husband and son. Not only unbelievable but HILARIOUS!! I mean, Jesus, who needs entertainment when life throws up such baskets of goodies? Makes the all-female version of Richard III — to which I must shortly return my attention — seem positively tame. (Not a feminist statement at all, the press blurb said, but simply because the parts were too good for men to keep all to themselves. All Shakespeare's ladies were played by men, of course, a fact which many people forget and which I'm sure could lead to some enormously profound observation on my part if only I could be bothered.) Must check out. Think of me today. Cheers.

Checking his electronic mailbox as he was closing down the computer an hour later, Matt was pleased to find that Graham's response had already made its way back through cyberspace.

The funeral of the in-law of an ex-wife is a tall order. Good luck. Sorry not to have been a great correspondent recently but things have been gathering pace on the work front — looks like I'm going to be moving capital cities again, opening an office in Sydney. Leaving any moment. Too good a package to refuse. Glad you made that trip here when you did, as Aussie will be rather harder to visit. Bye. Graham.

Louise arrived so far in advance of their agreed time that Matt invited her in for coffee. She was looking drawn but glamorous in a close-fitting knee-length black dress and matching coat. She had been getting thinner recently, he realised, noting the faint hollows in her naturally round cheeks and the new angular prominence to her jaw. As he put the kettle on Josie arrived, looking contrastingly dishevelled, but cheerful and full of chatter about plans as to how she and Joshua would fill the day. At the sight of Louise in the kitchen, she tensed visibly, adopting an expression of such sullen hostility that Matt found himself wondering suddenly about the missing purse. For the first time since the incident a flicker of suspicion entered his mind. As if reading his thoughts, Josie caught his gaze and held it defiantly for a few seconds, before making some excuse to leave the room. Telling himself that he was imagining things, Matt went to say farewell to his son, searching the little face as he had done all week for any signs of perturbation at the notion of having lost a grandparent to an eternity of good times in Heaven. When he had first broken the news it had been the connection with

Kath that had interested him most. 'So is Mummy with her daddy, then?' he enquired, frowning from the effort of picturing the scene.

Matt had been tempted to say yes, to give a version of events that would put the seal on their private tragedy once and for all. It took some courage to stick to the truth. 'No, Josh, Mummy hasn't died. She's had to go and live somewhere else where we can't see her,' he said, repeating the old explanation with some weariness. 'Not because she stopped loving you, but because she stopped loving me. It's hard to understand, I know. When you're older I hope it will be easier.' Kneeling before him in the hall that Saturday morning, however, Matt was relieved to see that his son appeared to be in no need of a recap of such harsh truths. The five months since Kath's departure were a lifetime for a four-year-old, he realised, giving a parting ruffle to the tousled hair and wishing that adult rhythms could adjust so deftly.

'Shit, I haven't got any flowers,' he exclaimed, on seeing a wreath of pink and white roses laid out on the back seat of Louise's car.

'It doesn't matter, we'll say they're from both of us.'

'No, I must get something. Stop at the shop on the corner, would you? Mr Patel always has a bunch or two.' Sure enough, next to the trestle tables of vegetables spread before the now repaired front window, was a black plastic bucket containing several clusters of red and yellow carnations, their colours prettily offset by wiry-stemmed sprigs of tiny white flowers. Seeing Matt approach, Mr Patel himself came scurrying outside, grinning warmly and waving his hands at the sky.

'Such very fine weather we are having now. This is why we love England so. Sunshine and not too hot.'

'Reckon these would do for a funeral?' asked Matt, brandishing two bunches of the carnations.

The grocer's face fell. 'Oh, no, Mr Webster, you are having to go to a funeral on such a day as this. Was it – is it – someone in your family?'

'Not my immediate family, no.' Matt made a face, touched by

the concern in the older man's tone, but not wanting to be drawn into any involved explanations.

'And your lady friend is driving you.' Mr Patel gestured approvingly at Louise, double-parked alongside with her hazard lights flashing. 'That is good.' He beamed, nodding his head. 'And I have my new window and new bolts on my door. We are all surviving, Mr Webster, with God's help.'

'I guess we are.' Matt smiled back. 'Twelve pounds I owe you.' He fished in his wallet for a note. 'There's the ten and if you hang on a minute I . . .' He began searching the pockets of his suit jacket, momentarily forgetting that as an outfit that had required the dust brushing off its shoulders from lack of use it would be unlikely to yield much in the way of small change.

'Oh, but ten will be fine, Mr Webster.'

'I've got a twenty.'

'No, no, ten is good. Your lady is looking impatient.' He winked and then, as if suddenly recalling the solemn business of the day, gave a grave shake of his head and hurried back inside the shop.

'Best I could do,' said Matt, waving the carnations at Louise with a rueful grin. He placed his humble offering next to the wreath and then strapped himself into the front seat, managing to complete both manoeuvres without any obvious glances in the direction of Louise's hem-line, which seemed to have retreated several inches up her thighs. Although slim, she had wide ankles and dimples in her knees. An almost pretty face was marred by too much make-up and hair so tampered with that it had assumed the shiny straw look of a Barbie doll. Guilty at so uncharitable an appraisal, Matt kept his head turned firmly towards the window, where parades of scruffy shops were receiving dramatic illumination from the May sunshine. 'It's going to be hot,' he said, loosening his tie and laying his jacket across his knees.

'I thought South Circular, M3.'

'Sounds fine. I'm in your hands.' He tipped his head back against the rest and closed his eyes.

'Busy week?'

'Mad. Five nights out on the trot. Making up to my boss for being away.' Matt kept his eyes closed, seeing not images from that week's clutch of theatres but the shadowed lighting of the Umbrian hotel bedroom in which Beth and he had played out the last unimpressive gasps of their relationship. The showdown in the Florence café had been followed by the frustrating and somewhat anticlimactic discovery that it was impossible to change their tickets for an earlier flight home. In no mood for the dining room, they ordered their evening meal from the room service menu and ate sitting at separate ends of the small sofa, staring at the incomprehensible antics of a local TV station as an excuse not to talk. Since it was considerably warmer than it had been the previous night, Matt had opened the shutters and latches of both windows as far as they would go. He chewed his way through the food mechanically, not tasting anything, aware only of a light breeze on the back of his neck and a mounting sadness at being in so spectacular a place with entirely the wrong person. No amount of wanting to be in love again could make it happen, he realised bleakly, no matter how hard one shut one's eyes.

They had retreated to the big double bed early, huddling on to their respective sides in tacit respect of the oceans of new emotional distance between them. None the less, in the small hours, long after Matt had imagined his companion to be asleep, he had felt a warm palm reaching across the icy linen waste, massaging its way up his thigh, in a bid, he supposed, for some sort of passionate reconciliation. Matt, who felt passionate only about his ineptitude in getting himself into such an impossible situation, had to use considerable physical strength to keep the hand at bay.

'Just sex, Matt,' she pleaded, flailing to release his grip on her arms, 'to make us both feel better. Like a way of saying goodbye.'

'I don't . . . I'm sorry, I can't — it wouldn't feel right.'

Beth had thrown herself back on to the pillows with a snort of a laugh. 'Jesus — of all the guys in the world, I have to pick the one who needs his brain engaged to have sex.'

Matt opened his mouth to deny the accusation, only to falter at the realisation that, although not quite true, it was probably a compliment. In truth, he felt perfectly capable of having sex; indeed, he would almost have welcomed the diversion. Yet at the same time he could not face the deeper emotional tangle that would no doubt follow on from such indulgence, the hopes it might arouse in the cold light of morning. Instead, grim-faced and clutching two pillows and the counterpane, he decamped to the sofa, contemplating how a combination of wishful thinking and physical attraction had masked the now obvious fact that the pair of them were, and always had been, hopelessly ill suited.

The sofa was very narrow and fitted with cushions that sagged uncomfortably under his body weight. Telling himself that a sleepless night was the least he deserved, for blind stupidity if nothing else, made the minutes pass no more quickly. It was not until the eruption of a rather charming Italian version of the dawn chorus that he finally lost consciousness, only to wake a couple of hours later with a stiff neck that lingered for days afterwards.

'Tired?' ventured Louise now, speaking a little too loudly out of the fear that her companion was falling asleep.

Matt, tearing his concentration back to the present, rubbed the back of his neck and yawned.

'Sorry your trip to Florence didn't work out,' she continued carefully, having spent several minutes privately rehearsing how to broach the subject. Although Matt had made the state of play between him and his press agent girlfriend quite clear on his return, the combined diversion of Joshua and the crisis of Kath's father had made it hard to satisfy her curiosity as to the details.

'Yeah, well.' Matt stretched. 'Just confirms that I'm crap at relationships, I guess.'

'It does nothing of the kind,' she replied stoutly. 'You've just been unlucky. And you are marvellous with Joshua, which is the most important relationship of the lot.'

'Thank you.' He opened his eyes properly and turned to smile at her. 'You are always very kind.'

Louise flushed. 'And I've been meaning to say, I just loved your article on Andrea Beauchamp. She really seemed to open up to you.'

Matt chuckled, flattered in spite of himself. 'She did a bit. Can't think why. Took pity on me, I think. Single parents of the world unite. And she even hinted I might be a contender to write her life story, all twenty-eight years of it.'

'Wow, that's amazing – would you like to?'

Matt frowned, shaking his head and returning his gaze to the window. The clogged grime of Wandsworth had been replaced by the ordered world of the rural suburbs, shining and civilised under the hot sun. 'If the money was right, maybe. She'd hardly be an easy employer, but then . . .' He hesitated. 'It's beginning to dawn on me that when Josh starts at full-time school – wherever the hell it is—'

'I thought he'd been accepted by St Leonard's.'

'He has, but I'm just not sure either that it's the right place or that I could keep pace with the fees.'

'I see.' She looked surprised. 'Sorry – you were going to say something and I interrupted.'

'Just that if I carry on like this I'm hardly going to get to see him at all. Being out four or five times a week doesn't matter so much now because he's around for the afternoons and heading for bed by the time I leave. But as he gets older the evenings are going to be when he needs me most. Even if it's only for help with French vocab and how to construct an equilateral triangle without a compass.'

'God, I wouldn't have a clue on that,' burst out Louise with a laugh, before adding in a different, smaller voice, 'Anthony's never around in the evenings.'

'No, but at least one of you is there.'

'True.' She smiled tightly. 'When the time comes I'll just have to swat up on geometry.'

'But of course it's not just the homework,' persisted Matt, 'it's more *being* there, to have arguments with, to grate against, to have a laugh and a . . .' He shrugged his shoulders helplessly. 'The truth is I love what I do, but it's so dreadfully antisocial and selfish. The thought of abandoning it fills me with terror. But then I can't help thinking that if I got commissioned to write one book it might lead to another – Oliver has had all sorts of offers since his name got into print. Or maybe I could simply broaden my base,' he continued, thinking out loud, 'become a freelancer, more of an arts generalist. Money could be a problem, but with property so high, if I got short of cash I could easily sell up and move somewhere else . . .'

'Oh, Matt, you wouldn't want to move,' she exclaimed, adding quickly, 'But you are so right, about change – it is scary, it takes courage, but sometimes it is the only thing to do.'

'Sentiments which Kath would no doubt share,' he remarked darkly. 'You know, I still can't help wondering where the hell she is. I've tried not minding, but I can't help it.'

'Neither can I . . . neither can Gillian.'

Reminded thus of the sombre business of the day, they continued the rest of the journey in silence, sealing their windows tightly so as to enjoy the full benefits of the air-conditioning.

The pews of the small Saxon church were so packed that Matt found himself wondering what hidden charms had lain buried in the bristling grey-lipped exterior of his father-in-law. Or maybe death did trigger a genuine volte-face in emotions, he mused, remembering Gillian's outbursts of despair on the telephone that week, the peculiar display of longing for someone towards whom she had shown so much criticism and hostility. Seeing only half a pew's worth of space at the front of the church, left obviously for Gillian and the bevy of supporters who had helped her cope with the trials of the week, Matt and Louise turned towards the back, where several small wooden chairs had been set out in front of the vestry door. While the organ wound its way through an introductory, Matt cast his eyes up to the gnarled beams criss-crossing the ceiling, recalling with some wonderment that this was where he and Kath were originally to have sworn undying love; until Gillian's manipulative tantrums over organising the event had propelled them towards a registry office instead. Outside, the mid-morning sun was pulsing life into the stained-glass windows. Each segment of glass shimmered like liquid, projecting faint rainbow images on to the worn stone floor. Motes of golden dust danced in the sunbeams, angled from the windows like heavenly wands. Taking it all in, the celebratory beauty of it, somehow ironic against the dark clothes and taut faces of the congregation, Matt felt his eyes fill with tears; not for Lionel, he realised quickly, so much as for himself, for the rubble of his personal life, and because of one of those sporadic stabs of loss – invariably triggered by a funeral service – for his mother.

When Louise tugged on his arm, he let a second or two pass before daring to look at her, the knowledge that she would applaud a display of manly emotion making him less rather than more inclined to exhibit it. She was pointing across to the open side entrance to the church, where six pall-bearers had appeared, staggering a little under the weight of the coffin balanced on their shoulders, the tails of their black coats flapping like raven wings against the arch of indigo sky. Ahead of them walked the priest, a rotund female with steely cropped hair and spectacles that twinkled in the light. She walked with an air of studied reverence, her head bowed towards the floor, her hands crossed over the swell of her robe. Gillian was in the cluster of mourners following behind, one arm supported by a balding, less robust version of Lionel and the other looped through the elbow of an elegant female with a silky French bun of white-blond hair. Both women were wearing hats, Gillian's wide-brimmed, while her companion's was a more chic, saucer-shaped creation, tipped at a somewhat roguish angle towards the front of her head. Clouds of dotted veil hung from the front brim of each, masking their features and expressions, though there was a sufficient view of the younger woman's neck, a swan-like Audrey Hepburn-style attribute, to reveal that she was in possession of an impressive suntan.

'Bloody hell,' gasped Louise, so loudly that several heads tilted round in offended surprise. 'It's her. It's Kath.'

Matt stared again at the procession, craning his neck to see over and round the body of the congregation, catching only glimpses at a time. He knew at once, without needing to check the line of Louise's gaze, to whom she was referring. In his heart he too had known, from the moment the woman stepped inside the church, poised on her high heels, the small square black handbag hanging from one hand, the smart, expensive cut of her dress clinging flatteringly to the slim curves of her body. Then there was the familiar swan elegance of the neck, the slight roll of the hips as she walked. Kath, but not Kath. The same but coloured differently, more sharply outlined, like a catwalk version of the woman he had known.

The priest spoke but he heard no words. The organ started but he could not sing.

Abide with me, fast falls the eventide,
The darkness deepens, Lord with me abide.

Matt opened and closed his mouth, staring through the bobbing hats and heads towards his wife, standing next to her mother in the front row, her profile a black cloud of speckled gauze, her shoulders rising and falling slightly as she pitted her voice against the reedy swell of music.

Chapter Thirty-Two

There was a chilling, split-second vacuum of a moment when Matt thought he wanted her, before shock and anger rushed in, filling his face with blood and his body with so much adrenalin that he could feel his limbs shaking from the pressure of it. He swayed forward, at such an angle that he had to press all ten toes into the soles of his shoes to keep himself upright. An arm slid across his back and he heard Louise whispering, her voice dislocated, as if belonging to no part of the world to which he had any physical connection or relevance.

'Matt, are you all right?'

He nodded, steadying the service sheet in front of his face, while his eyes sought out the black-veiled profile and stayed there, drilling into it, willing it to turn round.

'Do you want to go?'

He shook his head. The trembling in his legs was easing. He could make out the words of the hymn. For the last verse he even managed to produce a noise from his vocal cords, more of a rumble than a tune, but somehow calming none the less. As they sat down Louise nudged him. 'She must know we're here. Gillian will have told her.'

'What? Oh yes, she must.' Matt looked back towards Kath, knowing suddenly that she felt his eyes on her neck, that she was resisting turning round.

As the service progressed, Matt felt at an increasing distance from it. The brother, his voice cracking, read a short poem about the deceased slipping into another room. After they had stood for 'The Lord Is My Shepherd' there was another reading, something from the Bible this time. Then the lady vicar, in a low, surprisingly attractive sonorous voice, delivered the customary eulogy on the deceased, referring to many things Matt had never known: a love of ornithology, an early passion for ballroom dancing, prize-winning capabilities in the garden, with roses in particular. Throughout it all Matt only had eyes for the half-profile in the front pew, while the hurt and curiosity, suppressed and sidelined for so many months, raged like a furnace in his heart.

The procession trooped out of the church, and still she looked neither to right nor left. By the time Matt and Louise got outside, screwing up their eyes in the glare of the sun, the convoy of hearses and limousines had already started on the short journey to the crematorium, shown on a small map printed on the back of the service sheet. Louise, as if anxious Matt might charge down the road after them, squeezed her hand round his arm and kept it there while they found their way back to her car.

'How did she find out, that's what I want to know,' she muttered, pulling out of her parking space and joining the line of cars edging down the narrow lane from the church. 'And why the hell didn't Gillian warn us?'

'Perhaps she didn't know. Perhaps she only turned up at the last minute.' Matt wound down his window, seeking real air as opposed to the icy blast hissing out of the vents in the dashboard. He was breathing heavily, he noticed, as if he had been running. He could feel cold tickles of sweat snaking down from his armpits.

'Let's just go back to London, Matt, we don't need to do this.' She had come to a halt at a T-junction where a large blue sign was giving them the option of returning to the motorway.

'I do,' he interrupted quietly. 'I need to do this very badly. I need to hear what she has to say, what she plans to do. Who the fuck she's with.' He almost choked over the words. 'And if she thinks she's getting Joshua . . .'

'Oh, Matt, I'm sure she . . . that it's just the funeral that's brought her back. I mean . . . oh God, I'm not sure I can bear this . . . for you, I mean . . .'

Glancing at her face, Matt was touched to see that she was on the verge of tears, literally chewing her bottom lip in a bid to maintain self-control.

'Ignore me . . . sorry . . .'

'Don't cry.' He squeezed her arm. 'You've been fantastic, about everything, right from the start. And I am very grateful even if I haven't been very good at communicating it.'

'You've been fantastic too,' she said in a small voice, dabbing at the corners of her eyes with a tissue.

A moment later they were pulling into the carpark of the crematorium, a large concrete box of a building that made Matt vow silently to have his own corpse consigned to a hole in the ground. Leaving their floral tributes in a hallway already lined with wreaths, their group was ushered into a large square room decorated in various shades of green. Several rows of chairs had been set out, facing the coffin and the small curtained stage from which it was to be whisked away for incineration. Gillian, Kath and their cohorts were already seated in the front row, their heads averted, their veils still protecting their expressions. From two speakers set on either side of the stage, 'Jesu Joy of Man's Desiring' was seeping into the room, sounding so tinny that instead of elevating the occasion it reminded Matt of mood music in cheap hotels.

Although the service only lasted for ten minutes, it seemed an interminable length of time before the curtains at last swished the coffin from view. Seeing both women lift their veils after the final prayer, Matt braced himself, fearful yet eager to meet Kath's gaze at last. This was the moment he had been waiting for, he realised, the chance, after five long months, for a proper showdown; the chance for truth. Instead of turning round, however, his wife pitched forward, sinking dramatically first to her knees and then to her stomach, with her arms flung out like those of a diver. The next instant Gillian was crouching at her side, tugging, for some reason Matt could not quite fathom, at the saucer hat, scattering hatpins across the thin green carpet.

'She's fainted,' she shrieked. 'Oh God, she's fainted.'

Louise, along with almost every other member of the congregation, rushed forward to offer assistance. A few minutes later a sturdy young man, sweating visibly but looking somehow triumphant, emerged from the mêlée with Kath in his arms and Gillian trotting alongside, waving a handkerchief and calling for water and air. Matt, taking in the scene, found himself entertaining the uncharitable suspicion that the display had somehow been deliberate, out of a subconscious bid for the limelight maybe, or – more likely – as a way to avoid him. Though she was limp in the arms of her rescuer, he had a strong impression that the mascara-lashed eyelids opened fractionally as she was carried past, that she too was watching him and had been all along.

'The strain, I suppose,' commented Louise, as they trooped back to the car for the short drive to Gillian's home. Waitresses sporting frilly aprons and solemn faces were waiting to greet them in the hallway with trays of canapés and drinks.

It was a good half-hour before Kath appeared downstairs, looking drawn but immaculate, her ruby-red lips twitching in strained appreciation of all the well-wishing meted out by the waiting guests. She had removed her jacket, revealing more both of her tanned skin and the elegance of her dress, which had narrow shoulder straps and a low-cut back, showing off to excellent effect her trim waistline and long legs. And the hair was remarkable, mused Matt, eyeing her from the farthest corner of the room – not one hint of a dark root, and swept so becomingly back off her face that it was hard to conjure up any image of the trim dark fringe that had gone before. After so long a wait, he was aware suddenly of a wonderful feeling of calm. She could

come to him, he decided, returning his attention to an elderly
gentleman who was saying something about leylandii bushes and
heavy rain.

'Six foot in as many months.'

Even feeling the tap of her hand on his shoulder, he did not
turn at once, but lingered, smiling at the old man, before
excusing himself from their conversation.

'It was good of you to come.'

Her voice sounded different, lower and more controlled.

'And you,' he replied dryly, eyeing her over the rim of his
glass. 'And I'm sorry about your dad, obviously.'

'Obviously,' she echoed, blinking slowly.

'How did you hear?'

She felt for her bun with her fingers, pressing invisible pins
back into place. 'Newspapers. It was a shock. I felt I had to come,
even though . . .'

'Don't think this protects you,' Matt burst out, the anger
suddenly a hard ball in his throat, impossible to contain,
'from what you did. Jesus.' He squeezed the glass in his hand.
'Jesus, Kath, you . . . . Is he here?' He gestured at the room. 'Your
new—'

'Of course not,' she interjected coolly, adding, 'Shall we go
outside?' She turned and led the way through the throng of
guests to the French windows on the far side of the room. 'I can't
think why everybody is in here anyway. It's so bloody hot.'

Matt glanced back to see Louise staring after them. She was
standing twiddling an empty wineglass between her fingers,
looking pink-faced and uncomfortable, wedged between Kath's
mother and the young man who had come to the rescue after the
fainting fit.

They walked in silence across the lawn towards some curvy
metal garden chairs set on a circle of flagstones next to an
ornamental pond.

'Let's make this as easy as possible on each other—' she said,
performing a little self-conscious flutter with her hands as she sat

down. She turned to him, looking up from under the curl of her lashes, as if they were no more than a pair of acquaintances at a cocktail party. As if they had nothing more contentious to discuss than the weather.

'Easy? For fuck's—'

She held up her hand. Matt gripped the cold metal arms of the chair, silenced not so much by the gesture of command as the hand itself. Not the hand he had known, but a new, smooth, manicured one, with long varnished nails and perfect moon-crescent cuticles. 'Who is he?' he said, the question snapping out of him in precisely the tortured, unguarded way he had privately vowed to avoid.

'You don't know him,' she replied evenly, turning to look across the lawn to where some other guests had ventured out of the house.

'Oh, well that's all right, then,' he sneered. 'That makes it all absolutely bloody fine.'

'Don't shout.'

'I am not shouting,' he retorted, raising his voice still further, 'although I think perhaps a little shouting might be called for, don't you? In the circumstances. Being abandoned with my four-year-old son was not exactly how I had envisaged spending the dawn of the new millennium—'

'How is he?'

Matt opened his mouth to shout about what Joshua – what both of them – had been through, to berate her for her selfishness, to crack the veneer of her composure with details of the slow, difficult fight back to normality. But something clenched inside, something which he recognised at once as fear. The last thing he wanted was to arouse her compassion, to make her feel for one single instant that they – that Joshua – needed her back. 'He's doing fine.'

'Not a day goes by when I don't think of him.'

Matt stared at the pond. A bulbous-nosed gnome, complete with red spotted hat and fishing rod and basket, was perched on a jutting stone at the near edge, surrounded by tumescent lily buds and a floating carpet of fat green pads. 'Happily, he does not return the compliment.'

She sat back in her chair, pressing her hand to her mouth as if to stifle a cry; but when she spoke her voice was tight and firm. 'I loved – love – him, but he ate me up, sucked me dry till I felt there was nothing left. Nothing of the real me.' She tapped her chest. 'Inside, I was empty. I couldn't carry on.'

Matt, marvelling at this audacity in seeking his understanding, said nothing.

She clipped open her handbag and pulled out a slim white envelope. 'The least I can do is this. Here is money for him. My . . . I have money now. I want you to take this for Joshua.' She placed the envelope on Matt's knee.

'I don't want your fucking money,' he growled, jiggling his leg until the envelope fell on to the grass.

She bent down and picked it up with a heavy sigh. 'Oh, Matt, what do you want?'

'An explanation,' he said darkly, folding his arms and glowering at his elderly gentleman friend, who had dared to stray to the far side of the pond.

Kath ran one finger round the edge of the envelope. 'If you insist.' She spoke slowly, pausing for breath between each word. 'We should never have got married. I didn't have the heart, or the guts, to pull out. And I kept thinking, as one does, that things would change, get better, or that you would see that whatever we had at the beginning was well and truly over. Then' – her voice tightened – 'I got pregnant, which was like this rollercoaster thing, strapped into this terrifying process, hurtling towards something for which I knew I wasn't ready, but all the time having to be brave and then, Christ, as if that wasn't bad enough, we get a baby who doesn't sleep, who appears to take no pleasure in life at all. And you're just getting on with your life all the time while mine is turned upside down, inside out, bled empty until . . .' She looked at him, her eyes glittering. 'And suddenly there I was, living an existence I had never envisaged or wanted. Housewife. Mother. And no good at either because I resented every day, every hour, every . . . And then . . .' She tapped the envelope against one palm of her hand. 'Well, I think you know the rest.'

'A knight in shining armour carries you away,' he jeered.

'Something like that,' she murmured.

'Might I perhaps know how you met? Was it across the vegetable counter in Tesco's, eyes engaging over a mountain of carrots? Or a pick-up in the park, maybe, holding hands behind trees, snatched teas in seedy cafés while the baby sleeps? Or was he a photographer, a snapping shark with a phallic lens—'

'For God's sake—'

'I found the photos, under your drawer lining.'

She let out a scornful laugh. 'Those? They were nothing – I had them done on a whim, on a day when I thought getting back into acting might make life more bearable—'

Matt slapped his thighs with both hands. 'Then it's the milkman. It has to be. We've had a new one since you left, much older, with a chipped front tooth and acne scars. Which can only mean—'

'Matt, cut it out – this won't do any good—'

'Well, when, then? At least tell me that. How long did Sir Galahad sit on his prancing charger, waiting to whisk you away? A few months? Years?'

She mumbled something, for the first time looking ill at ease.

'Speak up, I can't hear you.'

'Years,' she said steadily, meeting his gaze. 'Two years, to be exact.' She got up from the seat, brushing out the tiny creases that had appeared in the lap of her dress. 'I'm sorry, but you did ask. And now I must talk to Louise. It's probably going to be a very long time before I see her again.' She dropped the envelope back into his lap. 'You'd be a fool not to take this. It's fifty thousand pounds.'

'So you fell in love with money, did you?' he pressed, his voice reedy from shock, not at the sum she was offering but the fact that in a few sentences she had rewritten six years of his life. 'Jesus . . . you lying bitch. Who is he? Tell me his name. I have a right to know that at least.'

'No you don't.' She tossed her head at him. 'You have no rights over me at all. I have a new life, one that I really want. You have . . . our son.' She made as if to walk away, before half turning back to him, her fists clenched. 'And don't you ever dare think this has been easy for me. Don't you dare. At least I've faced up to our failure — to my failure. At least I had the courage—' She broke off, tight-lipped from the effort of regaining her composure. 'I have lawyers drawing up divorce papers. It'll just be paperwork. I don't want anything.'

'You can't just reinvent yourself, Kath. Nobody can.'

She smiled suddenly, her face lighting up in a way that reminded him of the creature he had fallen in love with six years before: 'Oh, but that's where you are wrong, Matt, really wrong. I can. I have.'

She strode away across the lawn towards the house, swinging her hips so vigorously that the old man sneaked an admiring stare. Matt remained on the cold metal seat, swallowing the hollow realisation that while Kath might have given up the stage soon after they met, she had never stopped playing a part. He signalled to the old man, gesturing at the empty seat. The man did a mock salute in response and came tottering over, conjuring from his jacket pocket a small silver hip flask.

'Get some of that down yer,' he growled, unscrewing the lid and handing it across to Matt. 'And if you don't mind my saying so, I think you're well shot of that one.' He nodded in the direction of Kath, who had linked arms with Louise and was leading her back through the French doors.

Matt managed a bitter laugh. 'So do I, as it happens, so do I.' He tipped the narrow mouth of the flask to his lips, relishing the burn of the whisky across his tongue and down the back of his throat.

'Left you a farewell, has she?' he remarked, nodding at the envelope.

'Yes, and do you know what?' replied Matt. 'I think I'll leave it with this little fellow over here.' Picking up the envelope, he tore it into tiny strips which he stuffed, several at a time, into the gnome's fishing basket, alongside a miniature plastic trout and a box of worms.

Chapter Thirty-Three

It was with some trepidation that Matt asked for the car keys. Whereas his state of inebriation still felt distant and manageable, held in suspension through shock perhaps, Louise looked as stupefied as a boxer struggling to come round from a hard blow. She was slumped in a hall chair, her hair flopped over one half of her face and her legs stuck out stiffly in front of her, like a puppet with no knee joints.

'Keys please, Louise,' she sang, dangling the keys at him and then trying to swipe them from his reach. 'Kath's gone,' she said next, pointing at the front door. 'Taxi. Airport. We had a chat.' She put her finger to her lips. 'Big chat. Girl talk. Mum's the word. Poor Matt, poor, poor Matt.' She shook her head mournfully.

'Come on, then.' Matt tapped his feet in a show of impatience, thankful that he had resisted following up the old man's whisky with any more wine. Before embarking on a search for Louise he had even managed a half-decent conversation with his mother-in-law, expressing both condolences and – more of a challenge – an open invitation for her to see Joshua whenever she chose. Aware that the subject of Kath was then only a breath away, he had hastily excused himself with talk of traffic and baby-sitting deadlines.

'What I need,' said Louise, 'is a drink.' She pulled herself upright and looked about her, as if a full glass might be within reach. 'Oh, I say, steady on,' she exclaimed with a giggle, as Matt, ignoring the request, slung one of her arms across his shoulders and heaved her to her feet. 'Where are we going?'

'Home,' he replied grimly, steering her through the front door and across the road to the muddy field that had served as a carpark. Although the day was hot, the ground, soaked by a recent bout of heavy rain, still oozed moisture underfoot. As they entered the field, Louise broke free, staggered for a moment, and then embarked on a skipping dance along one of several squelchy ridges left by the tyre tracks of manoeuvring cars. Specks of mud spurted up her ankles. 'I want my keys back,' she declared, charging the last few yards to her car and flinging herself at the bonnet as if greeting a long-lost friend. 'Please let me drive, Matt – it's my car – please.'

'You can drive tomorrow,' he replied dryly. 'Now stop quibbling and get in.'

'Ooh,' she crooned, sliding into the seat beside him, 'a man who takes control. I just love that.'

Ignoring her, Matt started the engine. After a bad couple of moments when the back wheels spun against air and Louise shrieked with excitement, they lurched out of their muddy slot and across the field. Once on the open road, Matt wound his window right down, partly to counteract the heat and partly to keep his senses clear, a challenge made no easier by his passenger, who had embarked on a stream-of-consciousness-style evaluation of the events of the afternoon and life in general.

'Kath said happiness is everything, that we've only got one chance and to make the most of it and that a life of sacrifice only makes you bitter and resentful and miserable and unlovable. I know she's hurt you, but I really think she might be right. And you've got to admit, she looked *fabulous* – like some kind of film star or something, which is funny if you think about it because that's probably what she always wanted to be, deep down. And she does want you to be happy, you and Josh, and me, she wants me to be happy too. But to move right away – I wouldn't like that. You're not going to move really, are you?'

'Pardon?' Matt jumped at the question. He had been driving automatically, seeing nothing beyond the racing tarmac of the road, only half connected to consciousness. Keen as he was to get home, he realised that he had to sober up if they were to complete their journey safely. Seeing a large roadside pub a few minutes later, he swung into the forecourt, coming to a stop next to a sandwich board promising cheap meals and a friendly welcome to coaches.

'Oh, goody, I need the loo,' declared Louise happily, tottering to the bar after him. 'And a large glass of red wine. And lots and lots of sandwiches. I'm starving.'

Inside, the air was heavy with smoke and the heat of bodies. Matt ordered Louise's wine with some reluctance, together with a round of cheese-and-tomato sandwiches and a pint of iced orange juice for himself. By the time Louise returned from the toilets his drink was half gone and he felt almost ready to return to the car. The sandwiches, on thin, floppy brown bread, with swirls of margarine curled along the edges, looked unappealing.

'There's a lovely garden out the back—'

'Let's just drink up and go.' He eyed her wine, hoping suddenly that it might induce sleepiness instead of loquacity for the final leg of their journey home. He wanted more than anything to be alone, to be allowed the space and silence to absorb what Kath had told him. A sort of creeping relief had begun to seep through him. All the uncertainty was over. Josh was truly his. Kath could bugger off back to her new lover and be damned.

But Louise had other plans. 'This way,' she trilled, seizing her glass and the plate and nodding at him to follow. 'It's lovely, see?' She gestured through the open back door of the pub at a half-acre of fruit trees and white metal trellises, crawling with pink and white roses. Although a handful of rustic picnic tables were dotted about the place, most people were sitting on the grass. In the far corner a wooden climbing frame swarmed with small children. Matt swung his legs over the first empty seat they came to, taking a sandwich even though he wasn't hungry. Deliberately ignoring Louise, he sipped the last inch of his orange juice and watched the antics in the playground through half-closed eyes. After a few moments his thoughts began to drift, back to that first afternoon in the park after Kath had gone; Louise all horrified sympathy and Joshua having his head stamped on. The tide of relief swelled again. Hurt as he was by Kath's ugly revelations, he felt released. He knew the bulk of the truth at last; enough to close the chapter and move on.

A lazy wasp hovered round the rim of his orange juice before settling on a blob of pickle left by the previous occupiers of the table. Aware suddenly that Louise had not spoken for a while, he glanced up. She was staring at him intently, looking so blanched and serious that he feared she might be about to throw up.

'Okay?' He smiled at her.

'Matt, tell me how you feel.'

Disinclined to rake over the intimate details of his conversation with Kath, Matt shook his head. 'It's over, that's all that matters. She's gone, really gone this time, and she's not coming back for Josh. Ever. And to be honest' – he stretched, raising the palms of his hands to the sky – 'I feel nothing. Except contempt. And even, deep down, a certain amount of pity. At some stage whoever she's with will start not to be enough and she'll have to repeat the whole business again, reinvent herself for someone new.'

'No, I mean, about us. How do you feel about us, Matt?'

'Us?'

She gave a nervous laugh. 'I'm not stupid, Matt, I've read the signs. I know that you've been going through the same hell I have – it would be too corny, wouldn't it, too pat, too dreadful, one break-up leading to another . . .'

'Louise, what are you talking about?'

She broke off, shaking her head in a show of affectionate

despair. Both hands were cupped round her now empty wineglass and two flecks of wholemeal bread were stuck to her chin. 'I know I'm pissed, which is why . . . oh, Matt, I care for you so much. And I know you care for me. I've seen all the signs, all the signals that you . . .'

'Signals?' he whispered, as yet too incredulous of the direction the conversation was taking to think how to stop it.

'You can't hide chemistry, can you, Matt? And God, it's not as if we haven't fought it.' She took hold of his hands, leaning forward, her hair falling into her eyes. The morning's smooth sweep of blue eyeshadow had receded to a thin greasy line across the middle of her lids, visible only when she blinked. 'I've tried with Anthony, God how I've tried. And you – making a go of it with that dreadful American woman, when you knew all along it was hopeless, fighting the truth, growing between us all the—'

'Stop.' Matt spoke so loudly that not only the people at the neighbouring table but a fat black Labrador, sprawled on the grass next to them, looked up in alarm. 'Louise, you do not know what you are saying,' he scolded gently, lowering his voice. 'You have drunk too much. I don't mind – let's just forget it ever happened.'

She ran her hands up over her face and through her hair, clearing it from her eyes, which he saw now were faintly bloodshot, the inner rims red against the sticky tangle of her mascara. 'You mean you don't care for me at all?' Not only her bottom lip but her entire lower jaw was trembling.

'Oh, Louise, how could you have . . . ? I mean, I like you, of course, and I'm incredibly grateful for all the ways you've helped me, but it never crossed my mind that—'

'But you started it,' she gasped, 'with that kiss . . .'

'What kiss?' He snorted in disbelief, truly amazed.

'That afternoon at my house . . . and then the theatre, that doll's-house play with that woman stuck in that hateful marriage – like you knew that's how it was for me, which it is, so trapped and alone, Anthony never there. You were so understanding and kind . . . oh God.' She was crying properly now, wrenching out each word between sobs.

'Louise, please,' pleaded Matt, 'you don't mean any of this. I know you don't.' Finding a grubby but presentable hanky in his trouser pocket, he pressed it into her clenched hands. 'You're just overwrought. We both are – it's been a hell of a day. You love Anthony, of course you do. He is perfect for you, clever and rich and handsome, which I will never be. Kath doing her disappearing act screwed both of us up for a while, made us lose perspective . . .' He spoke softly and urgently, saying anything that came into his head, wanting only to move on from so terrible, so absurd a misunderstanding. And it seemed to work, because she stopped crying and buried her nose in his handkerchief, trumpeting away the residue of her tears. Shaking his head in wonder, Matt reverted his attention to the wasp, which had returned to his now empty glass, accompanied by two fatter looking peers. Picking up the beer-mat, he slipped it deftly over the top, trapping the three insects inside.

'Better?' he asked, injecting as much normality into his tone as he could; as if bringing her round from a fainting fit instead of from a declaration of love. Louise stared back at him. Her eyes were puffy and smeared. Strands of damp hair stuck to her cheeks and forehead.

'Bollocks to you, Matt Webster.'

'Look, Louise, I only—'

'You're right, you are crap at relationships. Totally crap. And do you know something else? Kath thinks so too. And Graham.'

'Graham?' He laughed. 'What the hell has Graham got to do with this?'

For a moment she looked uncertain, as if conscious of having taken a step farther than she had intended. 'Because that's who Kath is with, that's why. She told me this afternoon. It was Graham all along. Behind your back, all that time.'

'That's not possible.' He laughed again. 'Kath never liked Graham.'

'After his marriage bust up, that's when it started. She told me everything this afternoon, swore me to secrecy. For your sake,' she sneered, 'not to hurt you any more than she has already. And if you're wondering when, there were plenty of opportunities, with you always shooting off somewhere – Chichester, Stratford, Edinburgh – and then when Joshua started nursery.' She giggled. 'I think your friend had regular morning meetings south of the river.'

'Not true,' whispered Matt. 'Graham would never do that. Besides . . . in New York he said there was nobody.'

Louise interrupted him with a clap of her hands. 'New York – now that's the best bit. Kath was there all the time, camping out in a hotel round the corner. She said you found her clothes, all new ones bought by Graham, hidden in a basement or something because of your visit. She said it was like being in a Raymond Chandler novel, trilbies and dark glasses, spying round lampposts, sneaking sex at lunch-times. They sent messages on their mobile phones, those written kind that you have to sign up for specially. And e-mails in the middle of the night . . . told you the computer wasn't working, didn't he? And where do you think she got that suntan anyway? A week in Sydney, that's where. They've been house-hunting.' She paused, saving the best till last. 'Kath was only there today because of you, because you told Graham about Lionel. That's how she found out.'

Matt stood up so quickly that black specks danced in the corners of his eyes. He held out his hand. 'My handkerchief, please, if you've finished with it.'

Louise stared disconsolately at the damp crumpled square of cotton for a few moments before handing it over. Then she traipsed after him back to the car, not speaking now because there was nothing left to say.

Chapter Thirty-Four

It was getting dark by the time they got back to London. The lights were on in Louise's front room. Though the curtains were drawn, the central bay window had been left open. Strains of something classical were drifting out of it – Mozart perhaps, or Puccini. Beneath the window the electric blue of a ceanothus bush glowed in the half-light, as if radiating all the sunlight absorbed during the day. Matt got out of the car first and handed Louise the keys. Her face looked ghostly, her hair bedraggled. Though he hated her, he was grateful too. At least he knew it all now, the ugly extent of it.

She walked slowly across the drive to the front door, her shoes crunching on the gravel, her head hung in what looked like shame. Matt watched from the gate, feeling an ache of something akin to envy as the door swung open, revealing a mouth of welcoming light and the solid figure of Anthony there to greet her. He caught a glimpse of them reaching for each other before the door closed, slamming the image from view.

He had told Louise he would find a taxi but now it seemed a better idea to walk. The air was heavy; he could feel the heat of the day pulsing through the soles of his shoes. Segments of fresher tarmac were still soft underfoot, melted from subjection to the sun. On the radio in the car there had been talk about the onset of a heat wave that could last into July and beyond;

premature worries about low reservoirs and hosepipe bans. Matt, his jacket slung over his shoulder and his sleeves rolled up to the elbow, walked fast, zigzagging his way through the leafy toast rack of roads. On either side of him sleek convertibles gleamed in driveways, their bonnets dusted with the confetti of fallen blossom.

He felt too hollow even to cry. Nothing had changed, yet everything had. It was like going back to the beginning – to January – only far, far worse. The depth of the deception took his breath away. So sustained, so absolute. Not only a lost marriage but a lost friendship too. Except worse, because loss suggested there was something to mourn, something once possessed and cherished, instead of mere delusion. No memory felt safe any more, not even of the earliest times, before Graham and Kath had met. The woman whom he had married had not loved him. The man whom he'd imagined to be a friend had merely been seeking a foil for his own brighter light. Being clever had counted for nothing in the end. His life had been a fiction, a bad play . . . *a living death*. Matt alighted on the memory of the phrase with a bitter laugh of recognition, thinking that it wasn't Kath's life it had described so much as his own.

By the time he reached Camberwell High Street, his smart, infrequently worn black shoes had rubbed a raw spot on the back of his left heel. Several bars and pubs were still open. Clusters of drinkers, spilling out on to pavements in search of cooler temperatures, were joshing and chatting like guests at a street party. Matt slowed by a particularly rowdy group, scanning their expressions, seeking something – a friendly face, some key to their jollity. Wanting to delay the return to his own life, so dark and uninviting, he elbowed his way through the group to the pub door. Propped next to it was a young man on a sleeping bag, with a scrawny dog and a cap full of change. Matt handed him a five-pound note before going inside, resisting the urge to squat down and confess that in spite of his suit and shaven face he knew only too well how it felt to be alone and unlucky.

He didn't join the drinkers outside but stayed at the bar talking to a stringy Scotsman with a wispy moustache and watery eyes. After two pints and three whisky chasers he was pouring out the entire sorry tale, including the absurd role of the misguided Louise, whom he painted in such a viciously witty light that the Scotsman cackled in appreciation.

'That's women for you,' he hissed, before proceeding to deliver an infinitely more heart-rending life story of his own, so full of tragic twists and turns that Matt felt quite humbled and then somewhat disbelieving. 'But I've got six kids and I love them all,' he concluded, his red eyes misty with sentiment, making a big show of waggling an empty glass which Matt had filled several times already. Reminded thus of his own responsibilities, he took his leave, almost tripping over the legs of the homeless man as he hurried into the street.

It took so long to steer the key into the lock that Matt seriously began to wonder if he had picked up the Scotsman's keys by mistake. When the lock finally gave way he fell rather than walked through the door, managing only to stay upright with the aid of the hall table. 'Oh, bloody hell, it's you,' he said, as not Josie but Sophie emerged from the sitting room.

'You're very late.'

He pushed past her into the kitchen and ran himself a glass of water, pressing it so hastily to his lips that at least half dribbled down his chin and on to his shirt front.

'You should have called.'

'I should have done a lot of things,' he retorted, aware that his voice was badly slurred but unable to make the necessary adjustments to it. 'But life does not always turn out the way one expects, does it, now? There are all those unexpected little things that bugger everything up—'

'You're drunk.' There was distaste in her voice and some surprise.

He blinked at her, grinning. 'Yes. And you, as usual, are in a bad mood.' He poured himself some more water, tried to drink it all, but gave up halfway through, messily tipping the remainder down the sink. 'So what happened to my dear employee this time? A migraine, was it? Is she tucked up at your place with a hot-water bottle?'

'A boyfriend, a really nice boy. They had arranged to go out together. She was expecting you back hours ago. Your mobile's been switched off. She called me in desperation. I'm doing as much as I can to encourage the relationship, to help her towards some sort of real independence from me. I thought you would approve,' she added, before shaking her head and muttering, 'Although I can see that now is probably not the best time to talk about such things.' She unhooked her handbag from the back of a kitchen chair. 'Don't worry, I'll let myself out.'

'You're going? So soon? Oh, no, no, I won't hear of it. All that tea and sympathy you dish out to everybody – I want some. I need some. And if Josie's off your hands surely there's room in the queue for me?'

'Matt, don't be—'

'Hey, come on, you're the Marjorie Proops of south-east London, aren't you? And I think you'll agree I've been patient, waiting my turn all these months . . . Now, let's see, where to start?' He rubbed the palms of his hands together. 'Well, you know about my matrimonial difficulties, of course.' He chuckled. 'Who the fuck doesn't? Less well known is that my dear wife, who incidentally made it to her father's funeral this afternoon – rather touching of her to bother – has embarked on her new life not with a photographer, or a casting agent, or an old flame, but with my best friend. *My* best friend. And not only that – wait and listen to this – turns out they were screwing each other before that for *two years*. Amazing or what? I mean, you've got to take your hat off to them – such stealth, such perfectly accomplished deception for so long. And then to cap it all, Louise – *Louise* – chooses this afternoon to tell me that she thinks I've been leading her on, that just because I once kissed her cheek and invited her to a play about an unhappy housewife I want to get inside her knickers. I mean, for fuck's sake . . . Now if I were to kiss you, that would be different, because you, as far as I know, are unattached and . . . well, to be frank, much prettier than Louise who's got this terrible *preserved* look to her, like she's been pickled in cosmetics. Where are you going? Wait here, I haven't finished . . .' He staggered after Sophie, who had backed into the hall during the course of this diatribe and was standing with one hand on the door latch.

'Well, what do you think?' pressed Matt, wishing he could make her understand that he really did want her help, that he was drowning in unhappiness. He walked to the door and put his hand on hers. 'Say something, for God's sake.'

'I think you've had a bad time . . .'

'Ah. Very good. Very insightful. Although I think, even in my sodden state, I might have been able to draw a similar—'

'Look, Matt, you don't have the monopoly on human suffering, you know.' She glared up at him without any trace of intimidation. 'Others of us have mucked up too and picked up the pieces. I might also add that as someone who was once so sure she'd found True Love she was prepared to break up a marriage for it, I'm hardly the person from whom you should be seeking advice.'

'But you didn't, did you . . . break up the marriage?' He squinted down at her, noting suddenly that her pupils, seen close to, were not dark brown at all but flecked with intriguing dots of black and green.

'No. He changed his mind. Decided I wasn't his True Love after all, but a bit on the side. Can I go now?'

'No.' He could feel her fingers under his, trying to push the latch down.

'Why?'

'Fair question.' He could feel himself swaying, looking down at her as if from an enormous height. 'I think . . . probably . . . because I want to kiss you.'

'I'll slap your face if you do.' The hazel eyes held his, still unafraid and even, so it seemed to Matt's befuddled senses, a little amused.

'Maybe that's a risk I'm prepared to take.'

'I wouldn't advise it. I'm strong. I work out. And I want to go home.' She reached out with her free hand and lifted his fingers off hers. Matt did not resist. He felt suddenly drained, weak-kneed and exhausted.

'Sorry, I don't know what—'

'It doesn't matter. Go to bed. If you've got any analgesics I should take them. Oh, and I left a note for you on the hall table, about a new primary school. Though you might digest it rather more effectively in the morning,' she added wryly, tossing the words over her shoulder as she closed the door.

Disinclined to test his powers of balance across the now heaving expanse of floorboard at his feet, Matt sank to his knees and crawled back towards the hall table. Between the telephone and a stack of mail was a small white card. Though tidily composed, the words kept jumping out of line, as if intent upon escaping the page.

The Garden Primary School, opens September at 106 Doben Road. Two small reception classes for five year-olds. Excellent head teacher, Mrs Cherry, tel: 020 7483 2099.

Unclenching his eyes from the effort of focusing, Matt curled up in a foetal position on the hall rug, the card clasped to his chest. Seeing Joshua's *Lion King* slippers at the bottom of the stairs, he pulled them under his face by way of a pillow. An inner voice ranted for a while about hall floors being no substitute for beds, before the last threads of his consciousness succumbed and he slipped into a heavy sleep.

Chapter Thirty-Five

Matt did not stir until the early hours, when the combination of a noise in the street and a sandpaper throat propelled him up the stairs, via the bathroom, to his own bed. There, perhaps because his brain was already steeling itself for consciousness, or perhaps because of the monumental headache pulsing in his cranium, he dreamed vividly and unhappily until roused by his son and an assortment of furry animals.

'I'm afraid Daddy's not very well this morning, Josh, he needs to sleep a bit more,' he croaked, removing the lion, now made grubby by love, from his face.

'Have you got a bug?'

'A bug, yes, most definitely a bug. A big bad bug.'

'Will it fly into me?' Josha looked concerned.

'No, it only likes daddies.' Matt smiled, for a moment forgetting both the pain in his head and the tatters of his life. 'But it will be gone soon. Do you mind watching telly downstairs, old fellow, just till it's breakfast time?'

Alone again, Matt pulled a pillow over his head, wishing he could smother both the pain of his hangover and the myriad images of his many failures. Kath, Graham, Louise, Sophie. He had cocked up on every front. And then there was Beth, perhaps the saddest indicator of all that instead of metamorphosing into a latter-day superman of a single father, complete with career and personal life, his entire existence had broken down irretrievably.

Driven out of the house a little later in search of newspapers and fresh supplies of analgesics, Matt was almost unsurprised to find a policewoman and several yards of yellow ticker tape cordoning off the entrance to Mr Patel's shop. It confirmed the indisputable fact that life was crap, a question of grim survival and little else. More unsettling was the news, gleaned from a neighbour, that Mr Patel, preparing for opening during the early hours, as was his wont, had been attacked and was in intensive care in Guy's hospital. Recalling how he had awakened from his drunken stupor on the hall floor, with the dim sense of there having been a commotion in the street outside, Matt felt a twinge of guilt. Maybe, on another night, in another less fucked-up life, he could have done something; scared the thugs away, called an ambulance.

'Ow, Daddy, you're hugging too tight. I want to see the policeman — and I want my lolly.'

After explaining, with some difficulty, the absence of both Mr Patel and the customary Sunday morning lollipop, Matt took Josha's hand and walked on to the newsagent's in the high street. There he made his purchases, including a shamefully vast ice cream for Joshua and a can of Coca-Cola for himself. He took several swigs before they left the shop, relishing the cold sweetness in his dry throat and the rush of sugar in his veins. Emerging into the sunshine a few minutes later, he caught sight of the unmistakable figure of Sophie Contini in running shorts and a tight vest of a T-shirt jogging along the pavement on the opposite side of the road, her dark hair flying loose. Matt stared, his stomach tightening at the hazy recollections of his dissolute behaviour the previous night. The sports gear suited her well, revealing neat, tight muscles and strong shoulders — features hitherto concealed by her wardrobe of baggy clothes. As Matt watched she turned, checking both ways for traffic before sprinting across the road just a few yards ahead of them. His heart raced in preparation for the inevitable moment of recognition. As she glanced his way, he prepared a sheepish smile, only to find her gaze drift unseeingly across his face. There was no acknowledgment at all, not even disapproval. A moment later all that was visible were the heels of her trainers, kicking with each step as she flew up the road.

On getting home he phoned Josie to apologise. 'I realise I've not been the greatest . . . well, not the most reliable of people, mucking you around and so on, but all that is going to change. I mean I really am going to get my act together, for Josh anyway.'

'Are you all right? You don't sound great.'

'Me? I'm fine. Just a little tired . . .'

'You mean hungover, more like.'

'I suppose Sophie has spoken to you,' said Matt gloomily.

'Sophie? No. But you'd been to a funeral, hadn't you? And anyone late back from a funeral is bound to be getting pissed. Hope you didn't mind her taking over. She's great like that, always helping out . . . and by the way I'm sorry if I seemed rude to your friend yesterday – it's just that me and her, we don't . . .'

'It's quite all right, it doesn't matter,' Matt assured her wearily, Louise being the last subject he wanted to talk about. If Josie stole ten purses a week he couldn't imagine minding so long as she was nice to Joshua.

'Look, do you want me to come over?'

He hesitated. The headache had eased, leaving a great lassitude which he knew reached far beyond the effects of the previous evening's overindulgence.

'You could go back to bed. Sleep it off,' she added shyly.

He gave a tired laugh. 'If you could spare me a couple of hours or so that would be very helpful. Much as I would like to return to bed, there are other things I've got to do instead.'

Enquiries about Mr Patel revealed the happy news that he had been moved from intensive care to a regular ward. In spite of having prepared himself for the worst, Matt was still deeply shocked to see the state of the old man's face, puffed with crimson and yellow, so bad on one side that his entire eye was obscured from view. Evidently undeterred by this handicap, he was sitting up in bed reading a newspaper when Matt approached.

'Oh, Mr Webster, is it? How kind, how kind of you to come. Very kind indeed.'

'I hope you don't mind. I just wanted to say how sorry I was . . .' Matt set his bag of grapes down on the bedside table, wondering now he was there quite what to say. His presence in the hospital stemmed, he knew, not just from human compassion, but from a desire to be near someone else who had suffered a rain of blows; to seek comfort and solidarity among the ranks of the world's defeated. 'After that business with your window and now this – it's just too bad.'

'It's a bloody outrage, isn't it?' Mr Patel's one visible eye flashed with indignation. 'The same youths, I'm sure of it, only I saw them this time, got a good look. And I've told the police inspector.' He thumped the bedcovers, so lustily that Matt feared the tube coming out of his wrist might be wrenched from the vein. He leaned towards Matt, lowering his voice. 'This time those buggers are going to jail and no mistake about it.' He gently eased himself back against the pillows. 'Four broken ribs and a knife in my back. I ask you, Mr Webster, what is this world of ours coming to?'

'What will you do now? I mean, with the shop and so on . . . will you carry on?'

'Oh, by Jove I will. With God's will. My brother is coming from Birmingham to help for a few weeks. I have good insurance. We will all be right as rain in no time.'

'You are very brave, Mr Patel,' said Matt quietly, getting up to go.

The bruised features twisted into a smile. 'No, Mr Webster, I think I am just very cross, very cross indeed. And the police are good people, they are trying to help me. But how are you, Mr Webster? How was your funeral?'

'Pretty bad.'

'I thought so.' Mr Patel nodded thoughtfully. 'You are looking bad.'

'Which is saying something coming from you,' rejoined Matt, too weary either to consider the diplomacy of the remark or to check the involuntary burst of laughter which accompanied it. He was pleased to see the old man start to laugh as well, until he clutched his ribcage in agony.

'Oh, God, Mr Patel, sorry. I . . . I didn't mean to . . . Look, I'd better go.'

'Oh yes, you go . . . back to your little boy,' spluttered Mr Patel, managing, even through the effort of composing himself, to express enormous warmth. 'A fine boy. And you a fine father.'

Matt snorted dismissively. 'Oh yes. Very fine. A diet of confectionery, frozen food and videos.'

'You love him,' said the shopkeeper quietly, 'you care for him, you do what you can. In the end, that is all that matters.'

Matt returned home feeling both humbled and fractionally less defeated. Josie had not only performed one of her miraculous whirlwind tidy-ups, but had also baked a huge carrot cake, dripping with white icing and drifts of shredded coconut. On the back of an envelope next to the cake was an arrow and the words *Help yourself. Have taken Josh to meet Mick (boyfriend) in park. Back for tea.*

Taking a cup of coffee and a wedge of cake upstairs, Matt switched on his computer. There were two e-mails. One from Oliver about their weekly meeting the following day and one from Graham. Matt braced himself, his mind for a moment racing with wild hopes of explanations and apologies, of some reasoned, understandable narrative that he could forgive. Then he remembered that Louise's indiscretion had been without Kath's blessing and that unless Graham's conscience had performed a miraculous volte-face, he would still be playing the role of loyal friend.

Leave for Sydney tomorrow. Will get in touch in due course, when I get sorted. All the best, Graham.

Staring at the message, Matt knew instinctively that he was looking at a cowardly farewell note. There would be no getting in touch on any level. Graham was tunnelling away to Australia with Kath, to be as far away from him as they could possibly manage. His finger hovered over the delete button, before sliding the cursor to the reply box instead. Silence might have been nobler, more dignified certainly. But he was too angry for that. He took his time composing his reply. Since words were the only weapons at his disposal he wanted to be sure they were as sharp as he could make them, to give them at least a chance of reverberating beyond the instant it took Graham's eye to skim down the screen.

This will be my last e-mail too, Graham. I know about you and Kath, you see. I know the whole sordid story. Truth, like poison, always surfaces in the end. And if you're wondering how I'm feeling then I can tell you it's not good, not the sort of feelings I'd wish on my worst enemy. But there we go. Crap happens. I may have been dim, but at least I am honest. You and Kath will tire of each other, and when you do you will lie about it, as you have lied to me. Next time the pain will be yours. Meanwhile, I have my integrity (sounds pious, I know, but I've every fucking right) and my son, whom I value more than life itself.

Next, he e-mailed Oliver, explaining that he would be resigning from his recently negotiated contract, just as soon as a suitable replacement could be found. Moments after he had sent the message the telephone exploded into life.

'Over my dead body. What has got into you, Matthew? Really, just when I thought everything had been sorted out so beautifully. Has Phillip . . . has somebody said something?'

'No—'

'Well, what the hell is all this about?'

'It's about Joshua,' said Matt simply. 'I've made a mess of everything else . . .'

'But you've got that marvellous girl . . .'

'Yes, for the time being. But Josie is not going to be around for ever. There'll be a string of replacements, most of them not nearly so marvellous. And meanwhile, more and more of the time Joshua is at home will be when I'm out at work. It has at last dawned on me, Oliver, that I'm not going to just bump into somebody else, that some sort of long-term female substitute for Kath is not waiting round the corner, and that it is up to me to reorganise my life to accommodate—'

'But you have reorganised your life, for God's sake, you couldn't have done more.'

'Oliver, I appreciate your support, but . . .'

'If this is about that half-baked idea of writing about Andrea Beauchamp for a living, then you can forget it. Not only because the whole project is highly unlikely to materialise, but also because biographers – ghost writers – even of famous people, get paid peanuts. Take it from me—'

'It's not that,' Matt cut in, all the more fiercely for the fact that Oliver had touched a nerve. Secretly, he had pinned a few hopes on the actress and was disappointed she had done nothing to get in touch. 'There are other jobs . . . I was thinking of going to see one of those consultants who help you change career.'

'And get charged thousands to be told what you know already. Matthew, you are so good at what you do.'

'That's not a good enough reason to do it, Oliver, not now I'm a single father. I've got to stop thinking of myself, of my own happiness. Being out four nights a week, charging all over the country, it just won't do. Joshua needs me. And I need him,' he added quietly. 'It's a two-way thing. I thought working from home would be the answer, but it's not. Obviously I'll work out my contract if necessary, but ideally I would like to stop in two months. That way I'll be free for Joshua's summer holidays. He's due to start full-time school in September, that is if I ever sort out where the hell he's going – I've got the name of another place I'm going to try this week. Whatever happens he's going to need all the support he can get.'

'Well, that's admirable, Matthew, I take my hat off to you.' Oliver sounded weary. 'May I ask what you will do for money?'

'We'll be fine for a while. If necessary I'll sell the house — prices keep going up. Oliver, I'm sorry to let you down and so on — if I thought there was any other way I—'

'Don't apologise to me, dear boy.'

'And I'll talk to Phillip tomorrow. Obviously he's going to be pissed off and I don't see why you should take the flak.'

After Matt had put the phone down he went and stood at the window. He thought about calling his father but decided to save it for later, knowing he might need some of his no-frills wisdom to see him through the week. He was due to come and stay at the end of the month anyway; partly by way of a celebration for his seventieth birthday and partly to fulfil his own suggestion of taking Joshua back up to Yorkshire for half-term. Remembering Dennis's barely concealed excitement at the prospect, Matt smiled, for the first time raising his gaze from the chipped paint of the windowsill. With early summer in full swing, the uglier urban elements of his view were less visible, shrouded from sight by the bursting green of trees in their prime. Three gardens away laundry hung from a line, bobbing on the light breeze; pillowcases, seven socks, three T-shirts, five pairs of pants, two handkerchiefs. Thinking with tiresome predictability of Sophie, wondering glumly what she would make of his obsession with her underclothes, Matt blinked and looked away. In the midst of all his other woes the way she had ignored him that morning still rankled. Cutting him dead like that, looking through him as if he didn't exist. When all he had wanted, all along, was to be friends.

Opening the window wider, he leaned his elbows on the sill and took a deep calming breath. In the distance the dome of the War Museum roof glinted like a jewel on a cushion of green. The worst was known, he reminded himself, turning in towards the room and silently vowing that whatever muddles followed would be of his own making.

Chapter Thirty-Six

The days that followed felt different, easier, as if he had stopped pushing against an invisible weight. Phillip Legge, while not attempting to disguise his impatience, promised to release Matt just as soon as he could find someone suitable to take his place. Since Erica Chastillon's performance on the subbing desk had proved somewhat less spectacular than anticipated, it was generally acknowledged that a solution would have to be sought in other quarters. The mere fact of having laid his cards on the table made Matt feel better. He set off on his evening assignments with a lighter heart and rediscovered some of his old fluidity in writing about them afterwards.

With the approach of her exams, Josie took to turning up for her baby-sitting duties with a sackful of books under her arm. Knowing Joshua's capacity for disruption, and fearing for her grades, Matt tentatively suggested he should seek alternative help. Mr Patel, back behind his till with a strapped ribcage and shadows where the bruises had been, had volunteered his son, Rajeet, for evening childminding. He was saving up to buy a computer, he explained, and needed to supplement his pocket money. Josie, looking hurt, had asked whether her friend Mick could come with her instead, free of charge. Unsure of how to respond, Matt consulted Joshua, whose eyes had at once widened with pleasure.

'Mick teaches me football. He can do thirty-four kick-ups without stopping.'

'He's got lots of little brothers,' explained Josie. 'And he'd be able to test me on stuff when Josh is in bed. We're saving too,' she added, a little defensively, 'for a car. Mick's got his test.'

Matt had relented, agreeing to a compromise whereby Rajeet Patel came on Fridays and Josie, with Mick if she chose, could continue to manage everything else.

'But Josie, I just want to say that your priority, even when Mick is here, must be Joshua. I don't want to find . . .'

'Him and me snogging on the sofa?' she finished cheekily.

'Exactly.'

'Don't worry . . . I mean, you don't want to do it in someone else's house, do you?'

Feeling like an old-age pensioner, aware that it would be a long time before he did anything in his own or anybody else's house, Matt had accepted these assurances with a wry smile. A new domestic pattern emerged as a result; one that worked very well. Of particular satisfaction to Matt was how the altered arrangements were encouraging Joshua to spread his affections more freely, to cling with less desperation either to Josie or himself. Even after a couple of weeks the difference was noticeable. His new minders complemented each other beautifully, with Rajeet particularly strong on the indoor books and board games department, while Mick, a lanky teenager with a fiercesome haircut and a gentle smile, showed endless patience in the garden, diving after Joshua's little kicks with all the panache of a goalie having a bad Wembley final. So worn out was Joshua by these new attentions that sometimes he was in his pyjamas before Matt left for the theatre, waving sleepily from the bottom stair, soft toy under one arm and a book under the other, so like the perfect, textbook version of the happy child that it gave Matt a lump in the throat just to look at him.

With this new, simpler version of his life, the only immediate hurdle remained the question of Joshua's new school. Even though Matt had seized upon the information in Sophie's note and contacted Mrs Cherry as soon as he could, she had sounded sufficiently preoccupied to leave him with lingering doubts as to whether The Garden would in fact provide the solution after all. To add to his anxieties, the only appointment she could offer him had been the distant date of the first Friday in June, the day Joshua broke up for half-term. All the other parents he knew had sorted out their infants' futures weeks before, some opting for St Leonard's, some for Broadlands, a few for schools in ridiculously distant places like Dulwich and Blackheath. No one was going to The Garden. No one even seemed to have heard of it. A brand-new school was a dreadful risk, Maria Schofield had warned him, wagging her finger in a way which had made Matt glad that Joshua had slipped from the mainstream tea circuit into occasional play dates with quieter children of whom Maria and her gang had probably never heard. A mild temptation to consult Louise on the matter was easily quelled. She had not been in touch since their showdown in the beer garden, and Matt could see the sense of in leaving things that way.

On the morning of his appointment with Mrs Cherry he awoke early with a stomachful of nerves, aware that, in terms of Joshua's personal happiness at least, this was the next vital link in the chain. As he was leaving the house the postman, arriving at the bottom of the steps, pushed a single envelope into his hands, of bright yellow, handsomely addressed in sloping black ink. Matt, thinking with a surge of quite illogical hope of Andrea Beauchamp, tore at the flap, only to find that Lousie had mustered the courage to make contact after all.

Dear Matt

You are probably wondering why you have not heard from me. The truth is I have longed to get in touch many times, but have managed to resist. Anthony is trying very hard. He guessed there was someone else, though I haven't — and never will — tell him who. More importantly, he has realised that part of why it happened was because he had been neglecting me. We have decided to move to the country, Dorset probably, though Gloucestershire is lovely too. Looking at houses is helping to keep me busy, and happy, as I have always been a country girl at heart. I know you do not want to admit to what there was between us, Matt, but that makes it no less real for me. The number of times I thought of you, the dreams I had of how things could be between us, so real it was sometimes like they had actually happened. But enough. Looking back won't help us to move on. In case you're wondering, I won't be in touch with Kath either. I could never be her friend after what she has done to you. I hope you have forgiven me for telling you about Graham. No one loves the bearer of bad news, do they? Hugs to Joshua. Take care of yourself. You are very special and deserve to be happy.

Louise.

Everyone had their own version of their life, mused Matt, shaking his head in wonder as he screwed up the letter and dropped it into his wheelie bin. Everyone was at the centre of their own drama, casting acquaintances and lovers in subsidiary roles, the extent of which was often beyond the participants' wildest imaginings. He thought of Kath and what her story of their marriage would have been, how vastly different to his; being trapped with a hateful husband, an intoxicating illicit romance, the tragedy of leaving her son. To an impartial listener it would seem like a rich narrative indeed, with Kath glittering in the role of heroine, the wronged wife, sacrificing motherhood on the altar of her new love. Everyone read from their own scripts, he realised, encouraged rather than depressed by the thought, contemplating how good he was at judging such things from a theatre seat and how hopeless in real life.

After checking the *A–Z*, he locked up the car and set off down the street, whistling softly. It was going to be another hot day, but he was ready for it, having at the last minute traded his sensible grey suit for a pair of clean shorts and a smartish T-shirt. He wanted to present himself to Mrs Cherry as he was, to be frank about his situation, what he wanted from a primary school, what Joshua wanted.

The Garden turned out to be a twelve-minute walk away, in a handsome Victorian house at one end of a maze of streets Matt wouldn't have known existed unless he had consulted the map. A man in dirty white overalls was up a ladder painting the G of Garden as Matt approached, reminding him, though he barely needed it, that this was a brand-new establishment with no track record and no recommendation beyond that of a woman who seemed to hold him in the lowest regard.

'I thought we'd sit in the garden,' said Mrs Cherry, slipping her fingers free of his hand almost before he had got hold of it and turning to lead the way down a long central hallway to a glass door. 'The place is still swarming with workmen, but they break for lunch any minute and I'll show you round then. I've made a pot of tea, or would you prefer something cold? All I've got is orange juice, I'm afraid.'

Matt followed her through to the back of the house, their footsteps echoing on the bare boards. She was tall and slim, with gingery brown hair swept into a loose French bun and startled blue eyes that looked both alert and perpetually amused. Although she was probably in her mid-forties, her demeanour was of a woman much younger, an impression heightened by the simple blue cotton dress she was wearing and her girlish flat-heeled sandals.

'I can see where you got the name for the school from,' said Matt, admiring the huge space stretching before them, most of it laid to lawn, apart from the nearest third which was taken up by new, soft-looking tarmac and several sets of climbing frames. At the far end of the grassed area were two small, robust-looking goals, still covered in polythene.

'The curriculum will include all sorts of sports,' said Mrs Cherry with a laugh, noting the direction of his gaze.

'Good,' said Matt, smiling. 'Football is Joshua's new passion – Peter Pan doesn't get a look in these days.'

'Ah, Joshua, yes, he sounds a lovely child. I've heard all about him,' Mrs Cherry explained, seeing his look of puzzlement, 'from Sophie Contini.'

'Oh yes, Sophie, of course.'

'We met on a course about eighteen months ago and have kept in touch,' she explained. 'The idea of starting the school was only just beginning to take off – I was still waiting to hear if I'd got the grant. I don't know how much Sophie has told you,' she continued, 'but I've run a small nursery for many years now, just a couple of roads away – started it when my own lot were small and I couldn't find anywhere I liked. Anyway, for years parents have been begging me to extend on up to primary level. Not having the space there I kept putting it off, and of course finding the right site was hard . . .' She clapped her hands. 'But you haven't come here for a history of the bureaucratic and logistical nightmare of getting a new school off the ground. Would you like to look round now? Still ladders and paint pots, I'm afraid, but we're nearly there. Half the ground floor has been converted for the hall and kitchens, which leaves room for two small classrooms and one cloakroom, and of course the staffroom and my study – a cubby-hole, but I'm sure I'll manage. On the first floor we've got two further classrooms, each with cloakrooms, which leaves the top floor for art and craft – one huge room full of light. Oh yes, and there's the library, which is in the basement. Sounds dreary but I think the conversion has worked particularly well down there – it's spacious but really snug and with lines of ceiling lights everywhere to make up for the—'

'Mrs Cherry, I . . . it all sounds wonderful. But presumably Joshua isn't the only one wanting to be considered . . . and I can't help being surprised you've got any spaces left. Most schools seem to have closed their lists months ago.'

They had got as far as the doorway into what was obviously the main hall. In the far corner, across a considerable yardage of freshly varnished floorboards, a young man in splattered jeans was leaning on an upright piano sipping from a mug and smoking a cigarette.

She laughed. 'Yes, well, in an ideal world my lists would have closed months ago as well — I shall be more organised next year. And yes, Joshua is among several children hoping to be accepted. I shall meet all of them for a short interview — quite different from the grilling he got at St Leonard's, I assure you . . .' She hesitated. 'Obviously, Mr Webster, it would be unprofessional of me to make any guarantees, but I cannot envisage any enormous problems. I'll give you the forms before you leave. We need a small deposit, I'm afraid, of fifty pounds, but happily the fees themselves are well below your usual private institutions — for the time being anyway,' she added, making a face. 'In fact,' she confided, lowering her voice, 'I *had* been hoping to lure Sophie herself over here, but then who can blame her for choosing Italy instead. She's been talking of making such a move ever since I met her . . .'

'Italy?'

'Her sister and brother-in-law run a language school there. Near Orvieto. Sophie's going to join them. She's bilingual . . . I assumed you knew . . .' She broke off, looking momentarily puzzled, before pushing open another door, revealing a room with windows fronting on to the garden at one end and a huge white board at the other. 'Not very big, but then that's what I believe in — small classes, individual attention. We're going to have no more than ten in each room, with a maximum of twenty in each of the three years. The reception class is the one that's now almost full. The other two will obviously take a little more time . . .'

For the remainder of the tour Matt said very little, distracted not by the obvious and happy fact that he had found a place and a person to whom he could entrust the next three years of his son's education, but by the notion of Sophie going to Italy. Deserting the sunny grime of south-east London for olive groves. Deserting him.

Chapter Thirty-Seven

He wasn't an impetuous man, Matt reminded himself, striding with what felt like enormous impetuosity in the rough direction of Sophie Contini's home, his head raging with uncertainty as to what he would say when he got there. That he didn't want her to go to one of the most attractive countries in Europe? That he had always treasured the sight of her damp underwear? That she was the most intriguingly hostile female he had ever known? He had no argument to offer, he realised gloomily, slowing his pace, in danger of coming to his senses. Just a perverse and indefensible sense of loss at the prospect of her not being around, like the loss of something unvalued but taken for granted being suddenly snatched away.

Matt altered his pace so often and took so many wrong turns that by time he arrived at the correct doorstep he was uncomfortably hot. His hair, which had been swept neatly back from his face for the interview with Mrs Cherry, was flopping round his eyes and ears. If she wasn't there it was a sign he shouldn't have come, he told himself, ringing the bell and nervously checking his watch. Seeing that it was still only half past two all his apprehensions were momentarily overtaken by gloom. Of course she wouldn't be there. It was a Friday. She was a teacher. Joshua himself would only just be coming out of school, to be greeted by Dennis, whom Matt had collected from

King's Cross that morning, full of dry quips about edging into his eighth decade.

When the door opened Matt was so surprised he took a step backwards. Instead of picking on one of the more cogent expressions of the feelings that had propelled him to her door, his terror got the better of him. 'I didn't think you'd be in,' he muttered, clasping his hands behind his back in a bid to disguise the fact that they were trembling. The pose, coupled with the look of wariness in her eyes, made him feel suddenly like a doorstepping salesman with a suitcase full of products no one wanted to buy. Intrigued by his silence, she opened the door a fraction wider, revealing the fact that she was clad only in what looked like a man's shirt and small white ankle socks. 'I'm not very well. I took the day off.'

'Well, in that case, I'm sorry, I . . .' he muttered, beginning to back away.

'No, come in, I'm feeling much better now.' She opened the door wider, frowning over his shoulder. 'Where's your car?'

'Er . . . I walked. From The Garden. I wanted to say thank you.' He grinned, confidence flowering under the discovery of a legitimate pretext for his visit. 'Mrs Cherry, she's great, the whole place looks great. And so willing to consider Joshua. I can't thank you enough . . . I . . .'

'Unless you don't want to catch my germs,' she added, ignoring this torrent of gratitude and starting to close the door.

Matt shook his head, made mute by the realisation that he would love to catch whatever she had and more besides.

Inside, the hall felt pleasantly cool and dark. She poured him some fresh lemonade, which she said she had made herself, and then sat quietly watching him while he drank it. So quietly that he felt bound to speak.

'And I also wanted to apologise for that night – after the funeral I—'

'No need.' She crossed her legs, revealing a smooth triangular portion of thigh.

'If there's no need,' he burst out, trying not to look at her legs, images of them attractively packaged in running shorts flashing unhelpfully across his brain, 'why the hell did you cut me dead in the street the next day?'

'What are you talking about?' She rolled her eyes, looking impatient.

'The next morning – I saw you running – in the high street round the corner from me. I was with Josh. You just completely ignored me.'

'I didn't see you.'

'You did. You looked right at me.'

She burst out laughing, bringing spots of colour to her cheeks, which were otherwise very pale. 'I probably wasn't wearing my lenses – I often don't when I run in the morning. The sweat gets in my eyes and irritates them.' She began to laugh again, but then seemed to check herself, getting up and running herself a glass of water at the sink instead. 'So that's cleared that up, then.'

'Yup, I guess it has.' Matt pushed away his empty glass, reading the note of dismissal in her tone and feeling utterly helpless in the face of it. He stood up, pushing his hands into his shorts pockets. 'I'd better go.'

'Okay, then.' She put her empty glass down on the draining board.

'Fine.' He pushed his chair out of the way, anger at his ineptitude getting the better of him. 'I just can't seem to accept that you don't like me, can I? If it wasn't so sad it would be extremely amusing.'

'I do like you,' she muttered.

'Do you? Oh, good. In that case perhaps you would indulge me with a little of that honesty you're so keen on. I'll start, shall I? Because, dumb as it sounds, I actually came here to tell you . . . to tell you that I don't want you to go to Italy or any other part of the globe, because for some mystifying and utterly infuriating reason I can't get you out of my mind – just the thought of you

. . .' He broke off, diverted by the memory of Louise's delusions and how he must appear to this poor bemused, half-dressed woman who had been trying to sleep off an illness. 'I'm sorry. I really am going now. God, what you must think of me. I—'

'I think,' said Sophie quietly, folding her arms, not moving from her position in front of the sink, 'that it's fucking typical that—'

'It's all right, I'm out of here, out of your life.' He raised his hands as if surrendering under attack and began backing towards the door.

'I haven't finished.'

'I don't think I want you to.'

'I think it's fucking typical,' she repeated, eyeing him steadily, so steadily that he stopped moving and dropped his hands to his sides, 'that the moment I decide to get my act together, to change my life, do something to jump-start me back towards at least a hope of personal happiness, you come along and decide to say all this.' She flung her arms out and slapped her thighs.

'Look, I've said I'm—'

'I'm going to fucking Italy *because* of you, you great dope. I'm going because you were right – I have spent two years blocking out my own problems with everybody else's. And because ever since Josie got me to talk you into employing her I've been looking for excuses to be near you. Because, even in your objectionable state the other night, I could think only that a kiss from you, even a drunken, beery kiss, would be absolutely bloody wonderful. And when that happened, when I had sunk so low, I decided the only thing to do was to accept this offer that my sister's been pushing at me for months and go somewhere where I might have a chance of forgetting you altogether.'

Matt folded his arms, feeling his heart thumping in his chest.

'And please stop grinning because I've signed the contracts and I *am* going, I bloody well am. I risked everything for a man once before and it didn't pay off. I tell you, Matt, it didn't pay off at all . . .'

It was a moment or two before he realised she was crying. Which made it easier to cross the room and put his arms round her. Instead of melting at his touch, she began pummelling his chest with her fists, sobbing profanities. Matt held on tight, not minding the fists or the language, just absurdly happy at the feel of her tears through his T-shirt, wetting his skin.

'Shit, shit, shit.'

'So you've liked me all along,' he murmured, kissing the top of her head. 'You were horrible because you liked me.'

'You didn't need me,' she retorted, pushing the words out through a hiccoughing sob, 'you had so many others . . . bees round a bloody honeypot. Just because you're good-looking, with an angelic child . . . you were revelling in it.'

'Now there you are wrong, I never revelled in it . . . well, all right then, maybe fractionally, right at the beginning, when frankly I would have seized on anything that didn't make me feel like a total reject . . . I didn't have a clue to what to do, I was just thrashing around, grabbing at anything for comfort . . .'

'You talked about being in the queue for me . . . well, that's how I've felt about you . . . people, women especially, tripping over themselves to help you . . . Maria Schofield and her cronies, that hateful Louise woman, not to mention your agent—'

'You mean Beth—'

'When Dan left me no one came flocking to my aid – I was ostracised, the scarlet woman who had got her comeuppance.'

'I didn't want any of them. I want you.'

'Why?' She looked up at him, her cheeks smeary, her nose pink from crying. 'I've been horrible to you for months and months.'

He grinned. 'I know. Perhaps that's why; because you were the only one who didn't seem to want something from me, who recognised that I had to sort myself, that there weren't any miraculous short cuts . . . This Dan – are you sure you don't still love him?'

'God, no.' She reached across the sink for a square of kitchen paper and blew her nose dismissively. Matt kept his arm across her shoulders, fearful that if he let go she might slip from his grasp.

'Does this mean you'll come to lunch on Sunday?'

'Matt, have you been listening to anything I've said? I'm about to leave London and start a new life. To prove to myself that . . .' ,

'You don't need to prove anything, Sophie, not to me.' He put his finger under her chin and tilted her mouth to meet his. He kissed her gently, barely brushing his lips against hers, not wanting either to hurry the pleasure or scare her away.

'Twelve o'clock would be fine,' he continued, as if the matter were settled. 'It's my dad's birthday. I'm sure you remember him – he liked you a lot from the start. And Josie is coming, with Mick of course. And also my boss, Oliver Parkin, who's marooned in London because of work while his family decamp to the Isle of Wight – they've got a big house there, go every chance they get. The plan is to eat in the garden – I'm borrowing some extra chairs from Mr Patel. I've bought a barbecue and bagfuls of meat and some ready-made marinades. But I *am* making dessert – Josie's given me two recipes, a sort of strawberry sludge which sounds easy and a chocolate thing which sounds bloody hard—'

'Matt, Matt, stop.' She tried to put her hands to her ears but he caught hold of her wrists. 'It would be mad, utterly mad, to start anything. I need to go away, I need to . . .'

'Come to lunch on Sunday. Please.'

'Oh God, maybe . . . I don't know. I'm ill, remember?'

'Oh yes,' he said, kissing her again, properly this time.

Chapter Thirty-Eight

By Sunday morning there was a new heaviness to the heat. The panoply of blue sky which had dominated the week bore a greyish tinge, thickening to the colour of slate as the morning progressed. Undeterred, Matt dragged the kitchen table into the garden, together with an assortment of chairs, a packet of paper napkins and most of the contents of his cutlery drawer. They would be seven in all, counting Sophie. She could sit in the middle down one side, he decided, smiling to himself as he laid out the knives and forks, between Dennis and Mick and opposite him so he could look at her. Telling himself that such excitement was premature had done little to staunch its advance. Ever since Friday afternoon there had been a sort of tightness across his chest and the back of his throat, as if his vocal cords were in a perpetual state of readiness to shout for joy. Nothing was sorted, of course, nothing certain, he hadn't breathed a word to anyone; but the world once again seemed full of possibilities, full of hope, not just for Joshua now, but for himself as well.

Back inside the kitchen Matt returned his attention to the squares of chocolate he had left to melt in a saucepan on the stove. They looked lumpen and unpromising, quite unfit for mixing into the smooth egg white and sugar concoction that Josie had instructed him to prepare first. On the floor behind him, in the space vacated by the table, Joshua was playing contentedly with his pets, which either by a process of immaculate conception or a misdiagnosis of gender had recently multiplied in number to four. Going to the pet shop earlier that week in a bid to put the new arrivals up for adoption had resulted only in the purchasing of a larger cage. A much larger cage, divided rather like the rooms of a small house, complete with a gym for entertainment and burrows where they could all curl up to sleep during the day. Seeing the look of wry amusement on the shopkeeper's face as he handed over the cheque, Matt had had to restrain himself from explaining that it was not just his son's pleadings which had won him round, but the poignant realisation that four rodents could provide a better image of conventional family unity than any he himself had achieved.

Stabbing at the bubbling chunks of chocolate with a wooden spoon that Sunday morning, however, it seemed to Matt that their own version of family life wasn't so bad. Mr Patel's kind words on his hospital visit still burned in his heart. Joshua knew he was loved, all right, not just by himself and Dennis, but by the small group of friends and helpers now so integral to his life. Nor did they lack for the occasional female touch, he mused, thinking of Josie, who appeared unannounced at his elbow a moment later, squealing at the sight of the mess in the saucepan.

'Oh my gawd – you have to melt it *over* heat, I said.'

'This is over the heat,' he retorted, stirring the glutinous lumps, now sticking with treacle-like obstinacy to the bottom of the pan, furiously.

'No, like in a bowl over a saucepan of boiling water, otherwise it . . . well, it goes like that.' She pointed with some disgust at the chocolate before bending down to greet Joshua and rummaging in a cupboard for a pudding basin. 'I thought you were going to make it yesterday – it's supposed to set in the fridge overnight. Like this strawberry thing—' She dipped her finger into the bowl of pink liquid Matt had put through the blender a couple of hours before. 'Did you make that this morning too?'

He nodded, pretending to look meek, but unable to disguise

the fact that his culinary shortcomings were low on his list of priorities for the day. 'The weather was so great we spent most of yesterday at this adventure park place in Kent, then I had to be at a theatre in Hampstead for the evening and it didn't seem fair to ask Dad to put on an apron for his own birthday lunch. Anyway, what the hell? We'll call it choco-strawberry sludge, mix the two together and serve it up with straws instead of spoons . . .'

'You're in a good mood,' she remarked, giving him a funny look as she began salvage operations on the melting chocolate.

'Yes, I am, aren't I? He grinned. 'And I've been meaning to ask, where did you learn to be such a marvellous cook?' He stepped to one side and watched in admiration as Josie added a teaspoon of brandy to the chocolate lumps and deftly converted then to the texture of liquid silk.

'My dad, he used to be a chef in the army . . . though he doesn't cook much now, prefers to be out with his mates, down the betting shop mostly, blowing his benefit. I could put more brandy in if you like, make it really tasty.'

'Go on, then,' said Matt, watching her fondly, seeing afresh the marvel of a child emerging with her heart so intact from such unpromising circumstances and feeling a stab of admiration for the part Sophie had played in the process. 'I trust you completely,' he added, trying to catch her eye, wanting her to know that he was talking about something deeper than the ups and downs of everyday life.

If Josie noticed his efforts there was no indication of it. 'There we are,' was all she said, splashing in another spoonful of brandy and tipping the mixture in with the egg whites. 'You can do the rest, otherwise it won't be yours, will it? Would you like me to lay the table?' She stepped over to the back door to peer into the garden.

'No, it's already done, thanks.'

'Oh, I thought we were six. Who's the extra?'

'I bumped into Sophie on Friday – she said she might be able to drop by.'

'Did she? That's nice.'

Matt thought he saw a twitch of a smile, but in the same instant she dropped to her knees to talk to Joshua, so it was hard to be sure. The next minute she was all smiles anyway, cooing over the baby hamsters, joining in the still-raging debate as to how they should be christened.

Oliver arrived dead on twelve o'clock, brandishing two bottles of red wine and a signed copy of his book by way of a birthday present for Matt's father. Dennis, by then deep in consultation with both Mick and an instruction manual for the mobile phone Matt had given him for his birthday gift, looked genuinely touched.

'I've been wanting to meet you,' he said, leaping up from the sofa and giving him a vigorous shake of the hand.

'And I you,' boomed Oliver, 'and I'm a marvel with these things.' He seized the phone from Mick and began asking what it was they all needed to know.

One more guest and they would be complete, calculated Matt happily, slipping back out to attend to the barbecue, which was in danger of setting fire to the overhanging branches of his neighbour's tree.

Forty-five minutes later, however, with the chicken drumsticks and steaks looking not so much charred as blackened, and with clouds ranging in dark and menacing shapes overhead, Matt saw no option but to summon those that had arrived to the table.

'There was only a chance she'd come,' he explained, trying to look cheerful as his guests cast quizzical looks at the empty place setting. 'She didn't promise. All the more food for us. Hope no one likes their meat rare.' He carved his steak energetically, forcing his disappointment aside, telling himself there would be other lunches, hordes of them, and evenings too. Nonetheless, when the phone rang some twenty minutes later he knocked over his chair in his haste to reach it.

'Matt, it's me, Beth. How are you?'

He exhaled slowly, closing his eyes. 'Beth, what a surprise.'

'I won't keep you long,' she went on, as if sensing some element of his disappointment. 'Just a courtesy call really, to see that you were okay and to tell you that I'm seeing someone that you know. I just didn't want you to hear it from other sources, Matt. It's Phillip Legge. One of those silly coincidences – I just didn't want you to mind—'

'Of course I don't mind.' He almost laughed out loud, partly in surprise, but mostly at the absurd notion that he should mind with whom Beth Durant chose to share her bed.

'And I couldn't help being curious about the Andrea Beauchamp thing, whether you'd heard—'

'No, not a word. Which is of course what I expected. I mean, life isn't like that, is it?' he said bitterly. 'I mean, things don't happen just because you want them to.'

'I also thought you'd like to know that Phillip rates you very highly.'

'Thanks, Beth. I appreciate it.'

Matt put the phone down and took a deep breath, determined to cling on to the remnants of his good mood and make the most of the party. In a couple of hours he would be waving goodbye to Joshua, booked with his grandfather on the 4.35 from King's Cross. Thanks to a lengthy altercation concerning the imprudence of introducing hamster families to the delights of rail travel, they hadn't even made a start on the packing.

'I've got some news for you,' declared Oliver, once Matt had resumed his seat at the table. 'Some rather exciting news.' He paused, looking round to check then he had the attention of his audience, revelling in the moment like a conjuror with a deep hat. 'The fact is that, contrary to your own opinions on the matter, your contributions to the arts pages of our fine publication are greatly prized. So much so that a plot has been hatched to retain your services. In other words, you are to be offered another post. One that you will be able to perform working entirely from home.'

'I do that already,' said Matt, smiling but puzzled.

'Ah.' Oliver tapped the side of his nose, tinged scarlet from a lifetime's devotion to red wine, 'But I mean *entirely* from home. The big box in the living room – terrestrial, satellite, previews—'

'You mean the telly?' said Mick, frowning.

'I do indeed. Matthew here is to be offered the chance to turn his critical eye upon a smaller but infinitely varied stage. The perfect job for a man in your position – tapes sent in advance of every programme, all work to be conducted from the comfort of your own living room – filed electronically, of course, but you've been doing that for years.' Oliver grinned, making no secret of his satisfaction at the proposal. 'Of course I'll be sorry to lose you, but at least you'll remain within reach, so to speak. The rather tidy aspect of it all is that our current TV critic, Luke Holmes, whose writing I've always rather liked, has agreed to have a go at your slot. A straight swap.'

'You mean his job is going to be watching telly?' gasped Josie, incredulous.

'I like the telly,' piped Joshua, gathering from the expressions on the faces about him that something significant was being discussed.

'And I'm sure your assistance will prove invaluable,' said Oliver, turning to his small dining companion with twinkling eyes. 'And now we're all going to say well done to Daddy,' he added, topping up Joshua's plastic glass with juice and his own with wine.

'Hang on, I haven't said yes yet,' put in Matt, laughing at the line of raised glasses round the table. 'I mean, I need to think it over, consider the pros and cons, the long-term implications . . . oh, hell, of course I'll give it a go – thank you, Oliver, thank you indeed. But look,' he protested, 'this toast should be to you, for doing whatever the hell you did to make this possible . . . and to Dad because it's his birthday and because I would not have survived the last six months without him. And Josie too for the same reason, and Mick, of course, and . . . oh God, I give up – you're all marvellous and I can't find the words.'

With such unexpected good news, Oliver's fine wine and the infectious merriment of his guests, Matt was able to shift his disappointment about Sophie to the back of his mind. Although served with a soup ladle, the desserts were warmly received, with not only Joshua but Mick and Oliver opting to consume them through a straw. The place set for Sophie, at first carefully guarded, slowly began to submerge under the general clutter of the meal, until it was hard to imagine how they would have fitted anyone else round the table.

The rain didn't start until Matt had fetched a cheeseboard and a tin of assorted crackers. Within minutes it was sheeting down and they were all scampering back into the kitchen clutching glasses and bottles and plates of half-eaten food. All except Oliver, who remained at the table like some latter-day King Canute, bellowing that no amount of water should come between a man and his cheese.

Chapter Thirty-Nine

By the time Matt had completed a hasty round-up of Joshua's clothes and possessions, Dennis was casting anxious and pointed looks at his watch. Seeing how the lunch was going, he had suggested calling a taxi, worried not so much by his son's sobriety as the lateness of the hour.

'And I must give you some money,' said Matt, making a show of patting his pockets, in truth feeling suddenly bereft at the imminent prospect of returning to an empty house alone.

'Whatever for?' growled Dennis, his impatience now so out of control that he had put on his coat and was standing by the front door.

'I don't know – treats, ice creams, stuff like that . . .' Matt examined the contents of his wallet, scowling at the discovery of nothing more promising than a wad of unfiled receipts. 'Damn. I'll stop at a cashpoint on the way – or I suppose there'll be one at the station—'

'But I've got some money, Daddy,' said Joshua, tugging at his father's trousers. 'You can have my money.'

'That's very generous,' said Matt, ruffling his hair, 'but your piggy-bank is meant for you and Daddy can easily get some more from his own bank.'

'But I've got lots,' Joshua shrieked, racing upstairs, oblivious to his grandfather's groan of frustration at the prospect of further delay.

Matt shrugged helplessly. 'I've got to pretend to borrow some or he'll be hurt.'

A moment later Joshua reappeared at the top of the stairs. 'See, Daddy, told you, I got lots,' he chirped, waving not the small piggy-bank Matt had expected to see but a fat brown purse. 'Lots and lots,' he repeated, clipping it open and extracting a fistful of banknotes, which he threw down the stairs.

'By God, he has too,' exclaimed Dennis, momentarily distracted from his anxieties. 'Where did you get that lot, then, Josh?'

It was Matt's turn to groan. 'Where do you think? Oh, Josh, I don't believe this, I really don't.' He knelt down and pulled his son on to his lap. 'I can't use this money, can I? Because it's not mine. And it's not yours either. It's Louise's. Where did you find it, Josh? And why didn't you tell Dad about it before – remember when we were all looking so hard?'

'Hey, go easy on him,' muttered Dennis.

'I just want to know why you didn't tell me, Josh.'

'Forgot,' Joshua said, in a tiny, barely audible voice, his gaze fixed on the floor. 'Forgot. Till Daddy needed some money.' He looked up, his face brighter from having worked out the logic of his position.

'Can you remember where you found it?'

'There.' He pointed at once under the hall table.

'Next time you find something important like this, you tell me straight away, okay? Now, we're going to put this money back inside, like this.' He gathered up the notes and slipped them into the purse. 'And we're going to give it back to Louise. Because it's hers and she was very sad to lose it. And when we next see Louise you're going to say a big sorry. Okay?'

An hour later, having seen Dennis and Joshua on to the train, Matt dropped a Jiffy bag containing the purse and an explanatory note of apology through Louise's letterbox. It felt like the last loose end, the final unravelling of the mess in which the year had begun. The letter flap was metal and on such a tight spring that it clamped over his hand, as if bent upon stapling him to the front door. In his haste to snatch his fingers free, Matt scraped a layer of skin off his knuckles. Though he had only dared to approach the house because it looked safely shuttered and quiet, he sprinted back to his car, casting nervous glances over his shoulder, his stomach in knots at the notion of renewing his entanglement with Louise.

It was still raining, but with less ferocity. Having licked the blood from his knuckles, Matt turned the key in the ignition and set off for home. He drove slowly, thinking with affection of his father and son speeding away from London, and – with rather more complicated emotions – of Sophie Contini. Several attempts to reach her on his mobile had met with no success, not even the dim consolation of her voice on the answer machine.

Finding no space anywhere near his own house, he parked outside Mr Patel's, which had recently acquired a metal grid of a shutter for the front window and door. Glimpsing a shadow of movement inside, he stooped to peer through the metal bars, but could make out nothing beyond the blink of the freezer lights. He turned with a sigh and set off down the street, taking small steps, absently counting the cracks in the pavement. Though the news of his job change was tremendous, he could not focus on it. The rest of the evening, the week, stretched uninvitingly before him. There wouldn't even be the distraction of clearing up, since Josie and Mick, much against his insistence, had done everything, not only washing the crockery but returning it to cupboards and drawers as well. The kitchen table was safely back in its allotted space, Mr Patel's three chairs stacked in the hall. Order had been restored on every front, leaving nothing but the prospect of brooding over Sophie and the disheartening fact that he appeared to have scared her away after all.

Thus engrossed, he did not look up until he was level with

his front door; and even then it took a split second or two to associate the woman preoccupying his thoughts with the figure on his doorstep. She was drenched, her hair black and heavy, her face streaming with rain. Although apparently dressed for exercise, her legs were bare apart from socks and trainers; she had on a thin grey mackintosh which looked as sodden as the rest of her.

'Funny day for a run.'

'I haven't been running. I was going to.' Her voice trembled, whether from perturbation at the sight of him or the chilling effect of her wet clothes it was hard to tell. 'And then I didn't know where to run to but here. And then I thought I didn't need to run, I could walk. So I put this on.' She hugged her arms round her mackintosh.

'Why didn't you come to lunch? Why didn't you call? I thought—' He remained with one foot on the bottom step, feeling suddenly that in spite of rain and uncertainty and a desperate longing to grab hold of her, there was no need to hurry. None at all.

'I couldn't face it . . . with us so . . . with everybody looking and wondering.'

'Just stage fright, then?'

'And other frights too. Like what hope is there for us and whether Joshua likes me enough—'

'You have absolutely no fears on that score – the blue sausages won him round completely.' He paused, relieved to see her smile. 'I'm the one who should be worried, competing with you two, charming the pants off each other—'

'Stop.' She shot out a hand, halting his progress up the steps. 'Before you come any closer I have to tell you that I am still going abroad in July, and that I want – I need – you to help me be strong about it, because I know what I'm like, that I'll cave in and back out because it's easier to stick with what I've always done and because it would mean I could stay near you—'

'Sounds reasonable enough—'

'No, Matt, I mean it. It would be good for me to go and work abroad, even if it's only for a year. It's just Sod's law that you've chosen this moment to bulldoze your way into my life.'

'Bulldoze? I like that. Crawl on bended knee, more like. Can I move now?'

'Not till you've promised – not to let me give up on the idea of Italy just because of you.'

'Oh, bollocks, of course I promise. I'd promise if it was Ulaan-bloody-baatar – or the moon. Just so long as frequent visits are allowed and you in turn promise to take me to Florence where I've got a bit of catching up to do . . . Can I come closer now? If we've only got a month in which to get to know each other properly I'd appreciate being allowed to make the most of every second.' He took the last four steps two at a time, fearful that she might change her mind and take off down the street. 'Got you,' he murmured, pulling her to him and pressing his lips to her wet face.

'For now anyway,' she whispered, smiling so broadly that for a few moments it was hard to kiss him back.

The rain thickened, but they stayed where they were, clasping both each other and the prized, irrepressible hope that accompanies new love. On the pavement below, Mr Patel, who had come by to explain that he would need his chairs that evening, hurried on unseen, his black umbrella tipped against the slant of the rain.